IRANICA
UNIVERSAL LIBRARY

RUBÁIYÁT
OF
OMAR KHAYYÁM

菲兹杰拉德《鲁拜集》
译本五版汇刊

［波斯］奥马尔·海亚姆 著
［英］菲兹杰拉德 英译
钟　锦 中译

上海三联书店

图书在版编目(CIP)数据

菲兹杰拉德《鲁拜集》译本五版汇刊：英、汉/(波斯)奥马尔·海亚姆著；
(英)菲兹杰拉德英译；钟锦汉译.–上海：上海三联书店，2020.4
（寰宇文献）

ISBN 978-7-5426-6879-0

Ⅰ.①菲… Ⅱ.①奥… ②菲… ③钟… Ⅲ.①诗集–伊朗–中世纪–英、汉
Ⅳ.①I373.23

中国版本图书馆CIP数据核字(2020)第050851号

菲兹杰拉德《鲁拜集》译本五版汇刊

著　　者：[波斯]奥马尔·海亚姆
英 译 者：[英]菲兹杰拉德
中 译 者：钟　锦
特约策划：黄曙辉
责任编辑：吴　慧
题　　签：童衍方　王蛰堪　王思斯　朱银富　李天飞
装帧设计：崔　明
监　　制：姚　军
责任校对：张大伟
出版发行：上海三联书店
　　　　　(200030)上海市漕溪北路331号A座6楼
印　　刷：北京虎彩文化传播有限公司
开　　本：700毫米×1000毫米　16开
印　　张：28.75
字　　数：360千字
版　　次：2020年4月第1版
印　　次：2020年4月第1次印刷
书　　号：ISBN 978-7-5426-6879-0/I·1574
定　　价：198元（精装）

总　目

前言

菲兹杰拉德《鲁拜集》译本第一版
菲兹杰拉德《鲁拜集》译本第二版
菲兹杰拉德《鲁拜集》译本第三版
菲兹杰拉德《鲁拜集》译本第四版
菲兹杰拉德《鲁拜集》译本第五版

醹醅雅
波斯短歌行
莪默绝句拗唐集
莪默绝句捣宋集
菲译第五版鲁拜集

海亚姆的《鲁拜集》和菲兹杰拉德译本

波斯是诗的国度。不仅诗人众多,似乎个个还才思泉涌,下笔动辄上万行。菲兹杰拉德就把波斯诗人和希腊诗人相比拟,说他们像饶舌的孩子,奇情异彩散发起来仿佛有无限精力。海亚姆短短的四行诗——就是后来风靡世界的《鲁拜集》,势必湮没其中,我们也就无须惊讶他的诗名一直隐而不彰。波斯文学史向有"诗坛四柱石",指的是:菲尔多西、鲁米、萨迪、哈菲兹。爱默生讲过"波斯七大诗人",还要再加上安瓦里、内扎米、贾米。无疑,这些才是波斯的一流诗人。如果有人想把海亚姆排上去,那真是件不可思议的事情。

虽然海亚姆生前不以诗名,直到死后五十多年才有人提及他的四行诗,但这件不可思议的事情居然成了真。随着《鲁拜集》的风靡,海亚姆成了一个响亮的名字。他不仅跻身一流诗人之列,甚至成为波斯诗人的代表。这个转变发生在1859年,英国诗人爱德华·菲兹杰拉德翻译出版了《奥马尔·海亚姆的鲁拜集》。这是诗坛的奇迹,也是翻译界独一无二的事件。160年后,仍然留给我们无尽的反思。

奥马尔·海亚姆全名阿甫尔法塔赫·奥马尔·本·易卜拉欣·海亚姆·内沙浦里,生于呼罗珊的内沙普尔,塞尔柱王朝最著名的天文学家、数学家、医学家、哲学家,自然,后来也是最著名的诗人。他一生事迹不多,大概著述就是他的生平。现存著作,《鲁拜集》之外,还有命名为马立克·沙希星算表的天文图表,以及一些论文,其中的《代数论》比较知名。

菲兹杰拉德译本的序文《奥马尔·海亚姆:波斯的天文学家诗

人》,对他的介绍足够满足我们知人论世的要求。需要提及的是,序文中最动人的尼查木和哈桑的故事,其实并不可靠。伊朗学者们考证,即使奥马尔和哈桑可能同学,那时尼查木已经四十开外,早已做了首相。但是,由于菲兹杰拉德的讲述,已经广为流传,似乎只要提到海亚姆,就一定会讲这个故事。

"鲁拜"的波斯文意思就是"四行诗",是波斯的一种诗体,每首四行,每行十一音节,多为一、二、三句押韵,也有四句全押的,形式上很像我们的绝句。由于唐代和西域的密切关系,杨宪益等很多学者认为鲁拜和绝句有着共同的渊源,不过这很难得到确切的证明,所以更多的人还是持怀疑态度。也有学者如王蒙认为,新疆维吾尔乃至塔吉克、乌兹别克、哈萨克等广大地区流行的"柔巴依"(波斯文"Roba'i",英文"Ruba'i"),和鲁拜更为接近。黄杲炘大概认为它们其实就是一回事,而且柔巴依的译音更准,他的译本坚持叫《柔巴依集》。张晖从波斯文直接翻译的译本,也叫《柔巴依诗集》。不过,郭沫若的《鲁拜集》译名已经约定俗成,不论事实真相如何,大家广泛采用的还是鲁拜。

海亚姆《鲁拜集》的特色,菲兹杰拉德序文里作了天才式的评论。让人疑惑不解的是,虽然《鲁拜集》中译本众多,这篇序文却很少译出,评论也就常常被忽视了。我对菲兹杰拉德的评论有点补充。他的观点,和一些学者,比如著名的法文本译者尼古拉斯等,还是有较大差异的。他更倾向于认为海亚姆是无神论者,另外的学者则认为是神秘主义者,是个苏菲派诗人。双方各执一辞,各有道理。其实这跟如何认定海亚姆的作品有很大的关系。归于海亚姆名下的鲁拜多达上千首,但可以确认出自海亚姆之手的不会超过150首,伊朗文学家伏鲁基进行了严格的考订,认为只有66首。多达上千首的鲁拜既然思想各异,如何认定又颇具争议,必然导致学者们对海亚姆的不同认识。不过,一致的观点是,海亚姆语言质朴、理趣浓厚,在波斯诗人里独树一帜。

现存《鲁拜集》最早的写本曾经认为是收藏在剑桥大学图书馆

的公元1207年抄本，共收录鲁拜252首。自从1957年苏联科学院根据这个抄本出版波斯文俄文对照本后，引起学者们的广泛研究，最终认定它只是一个早期古写本，抄写年代肯定比1207年晚很多。尽管如此，这个版本还是在我国产生了很大的影响。著名波斯语学者张鸿年根据这个版本翻译的《鲁拜集》，在1991年（文津出版社）、2001年（湖南文艺出版社）、2017年（商务印书馆）三次出版。另外一个重要的早期写本就是"乐园"本。按照波斯人根据阿拉伯字母计数的方法，"乐园"一词的七个波斯字母所代表的数字之和是867，正好是写本抄成的希吉来历867年，即公元1462年。抄写者的名字也留了下来，叫亚尔·阿合玛德·本·胡赛因·拉希迪·大不里士。这个抄本年代可靠，数量又多，共554首，影响也很大。四川人民出版社2017年出版了张鸿年、宋丕方的中译本。菲兹杰拉德似乎并未看到这两个抄本，根据他的序文，他看到的是另外两个抄本。"我们知道只有一本在英国，就是牛津包德勒图书馆编号乌斯利第140号的写本，公元1460年写于设拉子。这里包括158首鲁拜。有一本在加尔各答亚洲协会图书馆，我们得到一个副本，包括仍不完备的516首，还被各样的重出和劣制品种充斥。"他的译本自第二版起，还参考了法国学者尼古拉斯的版本。

　　菲兹杰拉德在他的译本的第一版序文里，谈到了海亚姆的诗歌在波斯和东方并不流行的原因，不知道为什么，从第二版开始，这段文字被删除了。无论如何，菲兹杰拉德在写这段文字时，或许根本想不到，正是他自己的译文让海亚姆在全世界流行。

　　爱德华·菲兹杰拉德，英国萨福克郡布莱德菲尔德镇人，生于1809年3月31日。1826年就读于剑桥大学三一学院，同学中后来的名流甚多，比如著名桂冠诗人丁尼生和小说家萨克雷。1851年他出版《幼发拉诺尔》，勾画这段生活，假托古人，笑谈当时。连续印过三次，却都是匿名的。大概剑桥生涯对他后来最大的影响就是结识了爱德华·B.考威尔。考威尔的东方学造诣甚深，他敏锐地发现了海亚姆和他的诗,菲兹杰拉德的翻译正是受他引导。

菲兹杰拉德家境优裕,但为人温良,生活简淡,在伍德布里奇附近过着隐居式的生活。友人伯纳德·巴顿,是位贵格会教徒诗人,菲兹杰拉德娶了他的女儿。不久,因为孤僻不偶的性格不适合婚姻生活,就离婚了,以后也没有再娶。巴顿身后,他帮助印了他的诗集,附有他所写的巴顿传略。他独居生活不过读书写作,偶尔和两个水手放舟海上,一去一两天,有时也会跟考威尔一起,所带不过一块大饼,几瓶红酒,当然也少不了书。

1852年他出版《珀洛尼厄斯》,近于书话,可从中窥见其读书之一斑。1853年出版翻译的《卡尔德隆戏剧六种》,这大概是他在友人的勉强下唯一的署名作品。1856年出版翻译贾米的《萨拉曼和阿布萨尔》。1859年出版的《鲁拜集》为他赢得了全部的声誉。1876年出版修订译本《阿伽门农王》(初版为自印,时间不详)。他还翻译过《俄狄浦斯王》和另外两种卡尔德隆戏剧,生前仅有未定稿。

菲兹杰拉德和诗人乔治·克雷布的孙子克雷布教士是朋友,他去莫顿教区看望克雷布时,想着手写一本《克雷布读本》。未能完成,于1883年在克雷布家中辞世。1889年,友人威廉·奥迪斯·赖特编辑出版了他的三卷本文集,1903年又出了七卷本的文集和书信集。

1858年,菲兹杰拉德把《鲁拜集》75首的译稿交给出版商夸里奇,次年出版。销售状况很不好,从五先令贱卖到一便士。名诗人罗塞蒂和斯文伯恩等人买到后,大加赞誉,二百本于是一下卖空,但仍然没有太流行。过了快十年,才因为读者的需要于1868年出了第二版,增加到110首。查尔斯·艾略特·诺顿在1869年10月号的《北美评论》上写了一篇评论,《鲁拜集》才真正得到广泛关注,其诗句开始被频繁引用了。1872年,菲兹杰拉德出版了第三版,确定为101首,编次看起来也很有讲究。1879年,《鲁拜集》跟《萨拉曼和阿布萨尔》合刊,这就是第四版,也是菲兹杰拉德的生前定本。

1889年，赖特根据菲兹杰拉德自己的个别修改，将《鲁拜集》收入三卷本文集中，是为第五版。这时《鲁拜集》已经声名远振，各个国家都在争相翻译、出版。据说，迄今为止，《鲁拜集》的版本之多，仅次于《圣经》和莎士比亚的作品。

  这五个版本，尤其前三版，都有繁复的修改，可以看出菲兹杰拉德的精心。为了便于对照，从赖特编辑的第五版开始，一般都会附有各版译诗的异文和编次对照表。其实不仅原诗，连序文和注释都有修改。第一版序文，到第二版时进行了不少增删，尤其是增加了一段针对尼古拉斯版本的评论。第三版对那段针对尼古拉斯版本的评论进行了删改。第四版又把这段删掉了。第五版按照第三版重新恢复，由于这是赖特编辑的，不知是否菲兹杰拉德的本意了。第一版注释最少，但第十七首的注释中有一段详细介绍波斯波利斯城，后来各版都删略了。第二版续有增添。第三版基本确定。到第四版，只在第三版的基础上增加了一小段，见于第八十七首。第五版没有改动。

  菲兹杰拉德译本的风行，至少有两个原因应该注意。其一有关原作，在波斯诗人们巨大篇幅的诗作中，《鲁拜集》的短小精悍占了便宜。如同爱德华·伯朗所说："正像财产越多越无暇顾及一样，如果每位诗人少写些作品，人们反而会多读一些他们的诗，会更好地了解这些作品的价值。"其二有关译作。菲兹杰拉德大胆地将原作重新剪裁，加以天才的再创造。这使得译文和原诗情调颇有差异，它变得既颓废，又乐观。世纪末的颓废，和古波斯的黄金幻景，一种神奇的交织，居然倾倒了现代无数的读者。它最先在美国得以流行，不是没有缘故的。关于海亚姆的原文和菲兹杰拉德的译文之间优劣的争论，关于菲兹杰拉德的翻译是否算得合格的争论，至今一直存在。但是不能否认的是，是菲兹杰拉德给了海亚姆在最伟大的诗人中间一席永久的地位。这是很值得我们反思的。

  菲兹杰拉德译本出版的年代和"九"有太多的因缘，第一版在

1859年,第四版在1879年是二十周年,第五版在1889年是三十周年。今年2019年,五个版本影印本的彙刊得到黄韬、黄曙辉先生的支持,列入《寰宇文献》在上海三联书店出版,是一百六十周年。

感谢两位黄先生对我的信任,允许配上我的翻译。根据菲兹杰拉德译文翻译的《鲁拜集》中译本繁多,至今已有胡适、徐志摩、郭沫若、闻一多、成仿吾、林语堂、吴宓、朱湘、梁实秋、屠岸、李霁野、黄克孙、黄杲炘、孟祥森、陈次云、柏丽、木心、眭谦等上百人相继全译或选译过,使用新体和旧体的都有。我自己三年前也曾出版过一个旧体诗译本。这次根据五版原样,用了八个月的时间重新翻译,译文改了百分之七十以上,还增加了新体翻译。有关翻译的具体情况,都写在译序里了。

我的翻译得到两位老师的支持。叶嘉莹先生尽管认为我应该把精力放在更重要的事情上,但在三年前我的旧体译本出版时,她还是给我写了推荐语。赵馥洁先生一直跟我说,这个尝试的意义未见得逊于学术论文,希望我认真做好,还跟我一起琢磨译文的遣词造句。那个旧体译本出版后,他亲自给我写了书评。我还想提及的是,我曾将译稿用电子邮件发给黄克孙先生,他很快回复了我两封邮件,一封写道:"钟锦先生:谢谢您寄下的七言绝句译诗。现在有这种文学修养的人恐怕已不多了。您的工作对于发扬固有文化有一定的意义。克孙。"另一封传给我他自己译本1952年的钢版本书影。我知道,黄先生的话客套成分居多,但让我心里觉得很温暖。遗憾的是,他忽然驾鹤而去,没能看到我译本的出版。

我的英文、中文能力都很有限,幸运的是,得到了很多的帮助。在翻译中参考了郭沫若、梁实秋、黄克孙、黄杲炘、柏丽、眭谦诸位先生的译本。最初的文言译稿由眭谦兄校阅,白话译稿由蒋益博士校阅,在最后,我最没有把握的地方由黄福海兄一一审订重译,这给了我极大的信心。周兮吟、田争争帮我翻译了涉及的法文,汪莹、王逸群、程羽黑、宋政滢、黄真等都随时解答过我的疑问。顾家华先生提供了菲兹杰拉德译本的相关版本信息,远在澳大利亚的艾博先生指出了我的前言里的一些硬伤。译文从一版到五版,由童衍方、王蛰堪、王思斯、朱银富、李天飞五位先生赐予题签,让这个版本大为增色。大家的帮助都让我铭感在心,在此一并致谢。但是,我相信,错误和不如人意之处必有很多,都应该由我自己负责。同时,真诚地希望得到读者朋友的指正和赐教。

钟锦 2019 年 8 月 29 日

RUBÁIYÁT

OF

OMAR KHAYYÁM,

THE ASTRONOMER-POET OF PERSIA.

Translated into English Verse.

LONDON:
BERNARD QUARITCH,
CASTLE STREET, LEICESTER SQUARE.
1859.

RUBÁIYÁT

OF

OMAR KHAYYÁM,

THE ASTRONOMER-POET OF PERSIA.

𝔗ranslated into 𝔈nglish 𝔙erse.

———

LONDON:
BERNARD QUARITCH,
CASTLE STREET, LEICESTER SQUARE.
1859.

G. NORMAN, PRINTER, MAIDEN LANE, COVENT GARDEN, LONDON.

OMAR KHAYYÁM,

THE

ASTRONOMER-POET OF PERSIA.

OMAR KHAYYÁM was born at Naishápúr in Khorassán in the latter half of our Eleventh, and died within the First Quarter of our Twelfth, Century. The slender Story of his Life is curiously twined about that of two others very considerable Figures in their Time and Country: one of them, Hasan al Sabbáh, whose very Name has lengthen'd down to us as a terrible Synonym for Murder: and the other (who also tells the Story of all Three) Nizám al Mulk, Vizyr to Alp the Lion and Malik Shah, Son and Grandson of Toghrul Beg the Tartar, who had wrested Persia from the feeble Successor of Mahmúd the Great, and founded that Seljukian Dynasty which finally roused Europe into the Crusades. This Nizám al Mulk, in his *Wasýat*—or *Testament*—which he wrote and left as a Memorial for future Statesmen—relates the following, as quoted in the Calcutta Review, No. 59, from Mirkhond's History of the Assassins.

"'One of the greatest of the wise men of Khorassan was
'the Imám Mowaffak of Naishápur, a man highly honoured
'and reverenced,—may God rejoice his soul; his illustrious
'years exceeded eighty-five, and it was the universal belief
'that every boy who read the Koran or studied the tradi-
'tions in his presence, would assuredly attain to honour and
'happiness. For this cause did my father send me from
'Tús to Naishápur with Abd-u-samad, the doctor of law,
'that I might employ myself in study and learning under
'the guidance of that illustrious teacher. Towards me he
'ever turned an eye of favour and kindness, and as his pupil
'I felt for him extreme affection and devotion, so that I
'passed four years in his service. When I first came there,
'I found two other pupils of mine own age newly arrived,
'Hakim Omar Khayyám, and the ill-fated Ben Sabbáh.
'Both were endowed with sharpness of wit and the highest
'natural powers; and we three formed a close friendship
'together. When the Imám rose from his lectures, they
'used to join me, and we repeated to each other the lessons
'we had heard. Now Omar was a native of Naishápur,
'while Hasan Ben Sabbah's father was one Ali, a man of
'austere life and practice, but heretical in his creed and
'doctrine. One day Hasan said to me and to Khayyám, 'It
'is a universal belief that the pupils of the Imám Mowaffak
'will attain to fortune. Now, even if we *all* do not attain
'thereto, without doubt one of us will; what then shall be
'our mutual pledge and bond?' We answered 'Be it
'what you please.' 'Well,' he said, 'let us make a vow,
'that to whomsoever this fortune falls, he shall share it
'equally with the rest, and reserve no pre-eminence for him-

'self.' 'Be it so,' we both replied, and on these terms we
' mutually pledged our words. Years rolled on, and I went
' from Khorassan to Transoxiana, and wandered to Ghazni
' and Cabul; and when I returned, I was invested with
' office, and rose to be administrator of affairs during the
' Sultanate of Sultan Alp Arslán.' "

"He goes on to state, that years passed by, and both his old school-friends found him out, and came and claimed a share in his good fortune, according to the school-day vow. The Vizier was generous and kept his word. Hasan demanded a place in the government, which the Sultan granted at the Vizier's request; but discontented with a gradual rise, he plunged into the maze of intrigue of an oriental court, and, failing in a base attempt to supplant his benefactor, he was disgraced and fell. After many mishaps and wanderings, Hasan became the head of the Persian sect of the *Ismailians*,—a party of fanatics who had long murmured in obscurity, but rose to an evil eminence under the guidance of his strong and evil will. In A. B. 1090, he seized the castle of Alamút, in the province of Rúdbar, which lies in the mountainous tract, south of the Caspian sea; and it was from this mountain home he obtained that evil celebrity among the Crusaders as the OLD MAN OF THE MOUNTAINS, and spread terror through the Mohammedan world; and it is yet disputed whether the word *Assassin*, which they have left in the language of modern Europe as their dark memorial, is derived from the *hashish,* or opiate of hemp-leaves (the Indian *bhang,*) with which they maddened themselves to the sullen pitch of oriental desperation, or from the name of the founder of the dynasty, whom we have seen in his quiet collegiate days, at Naishápur. One of the countless victims of the Assassin's dagger was Nizám-ul-Mulk himself, the old school-boy friend."

"Omar Khayyám also came to the Vizier to claim his share; but not to ask for title or office. 'The greatest boon 'you can confer on me,' he said, 'is to let me live in a 'corner under the shadow of your fortune, to spread wide 'the advantages of Science, and pray for your long life and 'prosperity.' The Vizier tells us, that, when he found Omar was really sincere in his refusal, he pressed him no further, but granted him a yearly pension of 1,200 *mithkáls* of gold, from the treasury of Naishápur."

"At Naishápur thus lived and died Omar Khayyám, 'busied,' adds the Vizier, 'in winning knowledge of every 'kind, and especially in Astronomy, wherein he attained to a 'very high pre-eminence. Under the Sultanate of Malik 'Shah, he came to Merv, and obtained great praise for his 'proficiency in science, and the Sultan showered favours 'upon him.'"

"When Malik Shah determined to reform the calendar, Omar was one of the eight learned men employed to do it; the result was the *Jaláli* era, (so called from *Jalal-ul-din*, one of the king's names,)—'a computation of time,' says Gibbon, 'which surpasses the Julian, and approaches the 'accuracy of the Gregorian style.' He is also the author of some astronomical tables, entitled Zíji-Malikshāhí," and the French have lately republished and translated an Arabic Treatise of his on Algebra.

These severer Studies, and his Verses, which, though happily fewer than any Persian Poet's, and, though perhaps fugitively composed, the Result of no fugitive Emotion or Thought, are probably the Work and Event of his Life, leaving little else to record. Perhaps he liked a little Farming too, so often as he speaks of the "Edge of the Tilth" on which he loved to rest with his Diwán of Verse, his Loaf —and his Wine.

"His Takhallus or poetical name (Khayyám) signifies a Tent-maker, and he is said to have at one time exercised that trade, perhaps before Nizám-ul-Mulk's generosity raised him to independence. Many Persian poets similarly derive their names from their occupations; thus we have Attár, "a druggist," Assar, "an oil presser," &c. (Though all these, like our Smiths, Archers, Millers, Fletchers, &c. may simply retain the Sirname of an hereditary calling.) "Omar himself alludes to his name in the following whimsical lines:—

> 'Khayyám, who stitched the tents of science,
> Has fallen in grief's furnace and been suddenly burned;
> The shears of Fate have cut the tent ropes of his life,
> And the broker of Hope has sold him for nothing!'

"We have only one more anecdote to give of his Life, and that relates to the close; related in the anonymous preface which is sometimes prefixed to his poems; it has been printed in the Persian in the appendix to Hyde's *Veterum Persarum Religio*, p. 499; and D'Herbelot alludes to it in his Bibliothéque, under *Khiam* :—*

---

* Though *he* attributes the story to a Khiam, "Philosophe Musulman qui a vécu en Odeur de Sainteté dans la Fin du premier et le Commencement du second Siècle," no part of which, except the "Philosophe," can apply to *our* Khayyám, who, however, may claim the Story as *his*, on the

'It is written in the chronicles of the ancients that this 'King of the Wise, Omar Khayyám, died at Naishápur in 'the year of the Hegira, 517 (A.D. 1123); in science he was 'unrivalled,—the very paragon of his age. Khwájah Nizámi 'of Samarcand, who was one of his pupils, relates the follow-'ing story: 'I often used to hold conversations with my 'teacher, Omar Khayyám, in a garden; and one day he said 'to me, 'my tomb shall be in a spot, where the north wind 'may scatter roses over it.' I wondered at the words he 'spake, but I knew that his were no idle words. Years after, 'when I chanced to revisit Naishápur, I went to his final 'resting place, and lo! it was just outside a garden, and trees 'laden with fruit stretched their boughs over the garden 'wall, and dropped their flowers upon his tomb, so as the 'stone was hidden under them.'"

Thus far—without fear of Trespass—from the Calcutta Review.

Though the Sultan " shower'd Favours upon him," Omar's Epicurean Audacity of Thought and Speech caused him to be regarded askance in his own Time and Country. He is said to have been especially hated and dreaded by the Súfis, whose Practice he ridiculed, and whose Faith amounts to little more than his own when stript of the Mysticism and formal Compliment to Islamism which Omar would not hide under. Their Poets, including Háfiz, who are (with

---

Score of Rubáiyát, 77 and 78 of the present Version. The Rashness of the Words, according to D'Herbelot, consisted in being so opposed to those in the Korán: "No Man knows where he shall die."

the exception of Firdúsi) the most considerable in Persia, borrowed largely, indeed, of Omar's material, but turning it to a mystical Use more convenient to Themselves and the People they address'd; a People quite as quick of Doubt as of Belief; quite as keen of the Bodily Senses as of the Intellectual; and delighting in a cloudy Element compounded of all, in which they could float luxuriously between Heaven and Earth, and this World and the Next, on the wings of a poetical expression, that could be recited indifferently whether at the Mosque or the Tavern. Omar was too honest of Heart as well as of Head for this. Having failed (however mistakenly) of finding any Providence but Destiny, and any World but This, he set about making the most of it; preferring rather to soothe the Soul through the Senses into Acquiescence with Things as they were, than to perplex it with vain mortifications after what they *might be*. It has been seen that his Worldly Desires, however, were not exorbitant; and he very likely takes a humourous pleasure in exaggerating them above that Intellect in whose exercise he must have found great pleasure, though not in a Theological direction. However this may be, his Worldly Pleasures are what they profess to be without any Pretence at divine Allegory: his Wine is the veritable Juice of the Grape: his Tavern, where it was to be had: his Sáki, the Flesh and Blood that poured it out for him: all which, and where the Roses were in Bloom, was all he profess'd to want of this World or to expect of Paradise.

The Mathematic Faculty, too, which regulated his Fansy, and condensed his Verse to a Quality and Quantity unknown in Persian, perhaps in Oriental, Poetry, help'd by its very virtue perhaps to render him less popular with his countrymen. If the Greeks were Children in Gossip, what does Persian Literature imply but a *Second Childishness* of Garrulity? And certainly if no *ungeometric* Greek was to enter Plato's School of Philosophy, no so unchastised a Persian should enter on the Race of Persian Verse, with its "fatal Facility" of running on long after Thought is winded! But Omar was not only the single Mathematician of his Country's Poets; he was also of that older Time and stouter Temper, before the native Soul of Persia was quite broke by a foreign Creed as well as foreign Conquest. Like his great Predecessor Firdúsi, who was as little of a *Mystic;* who scorned to use even a *Word* of the very language in which the New Faith came clothed; and who was suspected, not of Omar's Irreligion indeed, but of secretly clinging to the ancient Fire-Religion of Zerdusht, of which so many of the Kings he sang were Worshippers.

For whatever Reason, however, Omar, as before said, has never been popular in his own Country, and therefore has been but charily transmitted abroad. The MSS. of his Poems, mutilated beyond the average Casualties of Oriental Transcription, are so rare in the East as scarce to have reacht Westward at all, in spite of all that Arms and Science have brought us. There is none at the India House, none at the Bibliothêque Imperiále of Paris. We know but of one in England; No. 140 of the Ouseley MSS. at the Bodleian, written at Shiraz, A.D. 1460. This contains but 158 Rabáiyát. One in the Asiatic Society's Library of Calcutta, (of which we have a Copy) contains (and yet incomplete) 516, though swelled to that by all kinds of Repetition and

Corruption. So Von Hammer speaks of *his* Copy as containing about 200, while Dr. Sprenger catalogues the Lucknow MS. at double that Number. The Scribes, too, of the Oxford and Calcutta MSS. seem to do their Work under a sort of Protest; each beginning with a Tetrastich (whether genuine or not) taken out of its alphabetic order; the Oxford with one of Apology; the Calcutta with one of Execration too stupid for Omar's, even had Omar been stupid enough to execrate himself.*

The Reviewer, who translates the foregoing Particulars of Omar's Life, and some of his Verse into Prose, concludes by comparing him with Lucretius, both in natural Temper and Genius, and as acted upon by the Circumstances in which he lived. Both indeed men of subtle Intellect and high Imagination, instructed in Learning beyond their day, and of Hearts passionate for Truth and Justice; who justly revolted from their Country's false Religion, and false, or foolish, Devotion to it; but who yet fell short of replacing what they subverted by any such better *Hope* as others, upon whom no better *Faith* had dawned, had yet made a Law to themselves. Lucretius, indeed, with such material as Epicurus furnished, consoled himself with the construction of a Machine that needed no Constructor, and acting by a Law that implied no Lawgiver; and so composing himself into a Stoical rather than Epicurean severity of Attitude, sat down to contemplate the mechanical Drama of the Universe of which he was part Actor;

* " Since this Paper was written" (adds the Reviewer in a note) "we have met with a Copy of a very rare Edition, printed at Calcutta in 1836. This contains 438 Tetrastichs, with an Appendix containing 54 others not found in some MSS."

himself and all about him, (as in his own sublime Description of the Roman Theatre,) coloured with the lurid reflex of the Curtain that was suspended between them and the outer Sun. Omar, more desperate, or more careless, of any such laborious System as resulted in nothing more than hopeless Necessity, flung his own Genius and Learning with a bitter jest into the general Ruin which their insufficient glimpses only served to reveal; and, yielding his Senses to the actual Rose and Vine, only *diverted* his thoughts by balancing ideal possibilities of Fate, Freewill, Existence and ˙Annihilation ; with an oscillation that so generally inclined to the negative and lower side, as to make such Stanzas as the following exceptions to his general Philosophy—

> Oh, if my Soul can fling his Dust aside,
> And naked on the Air of Heaven ride,
>   Is't not a Shame, is't not a Shame for Him
> So long in this Clay Suburb to abide!
>
> Or is *that* but a Tent, where rests anon
> A Sultán to his Kingdom passing on,
>   And which the swarthy Chamberlain shall strike
> Then when the Sultán rises to be gone?

With regard to the present Translation. The original Rubáiyát (as, missing an Arabic Guttural, these *Tetrastichs* are more musically called), are independent Stanzas, consisting each of four Lines of equal, though varied, Prosody, sometimes *all* rhyming, but oftener (as here attempted) the third line suspending the Cadence by which the last atones with the former Two. Something as in the Greek Alcaic, where the third line seems to lift and suspend the

Wave that falls over in the last. As usual with such kind of Oriental Verse, the Rubáiyát follow one another according to Alphabetic Rhyme—a strange Farrago of Grave and Gay. Those here selected are strung into something of an Eclogue, with perhaps a less than equal proportion of the "Drink and make-merry," which (genuine or not) recurs over-frequently in the Original. For Lucretian as Omar's Genius might be, he cross'd that darker Mood with much of Oliver de Basselin Humour. Any way, the Result is sad enough: saddest perhaps when most ostentatiously merry: any way, fitter to move Sorrow than Anger toward the old Tentmaker, who, after vainly endeavouring to unshackle his Steps from Destiny, and to catch some authentic Glimpse of TOMORROW, fell back upon TODAY (which has out-lasted so many Tomorrows!) as the only Ground he got to stand upon, however momentarily slipping from under his Feet.

RUBÁIYÁT

OF

OMAR KHAYYÁM OF NAISHÁPÚR.

I.

Awake! for Morning in the Bowl of Night
Has flung the Stone that puts the Stars to Flight:[1]
   And Lo! the Hunter of the East has caught
The Sultán's Turret in a Noose of Light.

II.

Dreaming when Dawn's Left Hand was in the Sky[2]
I heard a Voice within the Tavern cry,
   "Awake, my Little ones, and fill the Cup
"Before Life's Liquor in its Cup be dry."

III.

And, as the Cock crew, those who stood before
The Tavern shouted—"Open then the Door!
   "You know how little while we have to stay,
"And, once departed, may return no more."

IV.

Now the New Year[3] reviving old Desires,
The thoughtful Soul to Solitude retires,
　　Where the WHITE HAND OF MOSES on the Bough
Puts out,[4] and Jesus from the Ground suspires.

V.

Irám indeed is gone with all its Rose,[5]
And Jamshýd's Sev'n-ring'd Cup where no one knows;
　　But still the Vine her ancient Ruby yields,
And still a Garden by the Water blows.

VI.

And David's Lips are lock't; but in divine
High piping Péhlevi,[6] with "Wine! Wine! Wine!
　　"*Red* Wine!"—the Nightingale cries to the Rose
That yellow Cheek[7] of her's to'incarnadine.

VII.

Come, fill the Cup, and in the Fire of Spring
The Winter Garment of Repentance fling:
　　The Bird of Time has but a little way
To fly—and Lo! the Bird is on the Wing.

VIII.

And look—a thousand Blossoms with the Day
Woke—and a thousand scatter'd into Clay:
　　And this first Summer Month that brings the Rose
Shall take Jamshýd and Kaikobád away.

IX.

But come with old Khayyám, and leave the Lot
Of Kaikobád and Kaikhosrú forgot:
   Let Rustum lay about him as he will,[8]
Or Hátim Tai cry Supper—heed them not.

X.

With me along some Strip of Herbage strown
That just divides the desert from the sown,
   Where name of Slave and Sultán scarce is known,
And pity Sultán Máhmúd on his Throne.

XI.

Here with a Loaf of Bread beneath the Bough,
A Flask of Wine, a Book of Verse—and Thou
   Beside me singing in the Wilderness—
And Wilderness is Paradise enow.

XII.

" How sweet is mortal Sovranty!"—think some:
Others—" How blest the Paradise to come!"
   Ah, take the Cash in hand and wave the Rest;
Oh, the brave Music of a *distant* Drum![9]

XIII.

Look to the Rose that blows about us—" Lo,
" Laughing," she says, " into the World I blow:
   " At once the silken Tassel of my Purse
" Tear, and its Treasure [10] on the Garden throw."

XIV.

The Worldly Hope men set their Hearts upon
Turns Ashes—or it prospers; and anon,
   Like Snow upon the Desert's dusty Face
Lightning a little Hour or two—is gone.

XV.

And those who husbanded the Golden Grain,
And those who flung it to the Winds like Rain,
   Alike to no such aureate Earth are turn'd
As, buried once, Men want dug up again.

XVI.

Think, in this batter'd Caravanserai
Whose Doorways are alternate Night and Day,
   How Sultán after Sultán with his Pomp
Abode his Hour or two, and went his way.

XVII.

They say the Lion and the Lizard keep
The Courts where Jamshýd gloried and drank deep:[11]
   And Bahrám, that great Hunter—the Wild Ass
Stamps o'er his Head, and he lies fast asleep.

XVIII.

I sometimes think that never blows so red
The Rose as where some buried Cæsar bled;
   That every Hyacinth the Garden wears
Dropt in its Lap from some once lovely Head.

XIX.

And this delightful Herb whose tender Green
Fledges the River's Lip on which we lean—
  Ah, lean upon it lightly! for who knows
From what once lovely Lip it springs unseen!

XX.

Ah, my Belovéd, fill the Cup that clears
To-day of past Regrets and future Fears—
  To-morrow?—Why, To-morrow I may be
Myself with Yesterday's Sev'n Thousand Years.[12]

XXI.

Lo! some we loved, the loveliest and best
That Time and Fate of all their Vintage prest,
  Have drunk their Cup a Round or two before,
And one by one crept silently to Rest.

XXII.

And we, that now make merry in the Room
They left, and Summer dresses in new Bloom,
  Ourselves must we beneath the Couch of Earth
Descend, ourselves to make a Couch—for whom?

XXIII.

Ah, make the most of what we yet may spend,
Before we too into the Dust descend;
  Dust into Dust, and under Dust, to lie,
Sans Wine, sans Song, sans Singer, and—sans End!

XXIV.

Alike for those who for To-DAY prepare,
And those that after a To-MORROW stare,
   A Muezzín from the Tower of Darkness cries
"Fools! your Reward is neither Here nor There!"

XXV.

Why, all the Saints and Sages who discuss'd
Of the Two Worlds so learnedly, are thrust
   Like foolish Prophets forth; their Words to Scorn
Are scatter'd, and their Mouths are stopt with Dust.

XXVI.

Oh, come with old Khayyám, and leave the Wise
To talk; one thing is certain, that Life flies;
   One thing is certain, and the Rest is Lies;
The Flower that once has blown for ever dies.

XXVII.

Myself when young did eagerly frequent
Doctor and Saint, and heard great Argument
   About it and about: but evermore
Came out by the same Door as in I went.

XXVIII.

With them the Seed of Wisdom did I sow,
And with my own hand labour'd it to grow:
   And this was all the Harvest that I reap'd—
"I came like Water, and like Wind I go."

XXIX.

Into this Universe, and *why* not knowing,
Nor *whence*, like Water willy-nilly flowing:
   And out of it, as Wind along the Waste,
I know not *whither*, willy-nilly blowing.

XXX.

What, without asking, hither hurried *whence?*
And, without asking, *whither* hurried hence!
   Another and another Cup to drown
The Memory of this Impertinence!

XXXI.

Up from Earth's Centre through the Seventh Gate
I rose, and on the Throne of Saturn sate,[13]
   And many Knots unravel'd by the Road;
But not the Knot of Human Death and Fate.

XXXII.

There was a Door to which I found no Key:
There was a Veil past which I could not see:
   Some little Talk awhile of ME and THEE
There seemed—and then no more of THEE and ME.[15]

XXXIII.

Then to the rolling Heav'n itself I cried,
Asking, "What Lamp had Destiny to guide
   "Her little Children stumbling in the Dark?"
And—"A blind Understanding!" Heav'n replied.

XXXIV.

Then to this earthen Bowl did I adjourn
My Lip the secret Well of Life to learn:
  And Lip to Lip it murmur'd—"While you live
"Drink!—for once dead you never shall return."

XXXV.

I think the Vessel, that with fugitive
Articulation answer'd, once did live,
  And merry-make; and the cold Lip I kiss'd
How many Kisses might it take—and give!

XXXVI.

For in the Market-place, one Dusk of Day,
I watch'd the Potter thumping his wet Clay:
  And with its all obliterated Tongue
It murmur'd—"Gently, Brother, gently, pray!"

XXXVII.

Ah, fill the Cup:—what boots it to repeat
How Time is slipping underneath our Feet:
  Unborn TO-MORROW, and dead YESTERDAY,
Why fret about them if TO-DAY be sweet!

XXXVIII.

One Moment in Annihilation's Waste,
One Moment, of the Well of Life to taste—
  The Stars are setting and the Caravan
Starts for the Dawn of Nothing[16]—Oh, make haste!

XXXIX.

How long, how long, in infinite Pursuit
Of This and That endeavour and dispute?
   Better be merry with the fruitful Grape
Than sadden after none, or bitter, Fruit.

XL.

You know, my Friends, how long since in my House
For a new Marriage I did make Carouse:
   Divorced old barren Reason from my Bed,
And took the Daughter of the Vine to Spouse.

XLI.

For "Is" and "Is-not" though *with* Rule and Line,
And "Up-and-down" *without*, I could define,[14]
   I yet in all I only cared to know,
Was never deep in anything but—Wine.

XLII.

And lately, by the Tavern Door agape,
Came stealing through the Dusk an Angel Shape
   Bearing a Vessel on his Shoulder; and
He bid me taste of it; and 'twas—the Grape!

XLIII.

The Grape that can with Logic absolute
The Two-and-Seventy jarring Sects[17] confute:
   The subtle Alchemist that in a Trice
Life's leaden Metal into Gold transmute.

XLIV.

The mighty Mahmúd, the victorious Lord,
That all the misbelieving and black Horde [18]
  Of Fears and Sorrows that infest the Soul
Scatters and slays with his enchanted Sword.

XLV.

But leave the Wise to wrangle, and with me
The Quarrel of the Universe let be:
  And, in some corner of the Hubbub coucht,
Make Game of that which makes as much of Thee.

XLVI.

For in and out, above, about, below,
'Tis nothing but a Magic Shadow-show,
  Play'd in a Box whose Candle is the Sun,
Round which we Phantom Figures come and go. [19]

XLVII.

And if the Wine you drink, the Lip you press,
End in the Nothing all Things end in—Yes—
  Then fancy while Thou art, Thou art but what
Thou shalt be—Nothing—Thou shalt not be less.

XLVIII.

While the Rose blows along the River Brink,
With old Khayyám the Ruby Vintage drink:
  And when the Angel with his darker Draught
Draws up to Thee—take that, and do not shrink.

XLIX.

'Tis all a Chequer-board of Nights and Days
Where Destiny with Men for Pieces plays:
  Hither and thither moves, and mates, and slays,
And one by one back in the Closet lays.

L.

The Ball no Question makes of Ayes and Noes,
But Right or Left as strikes the Player goes;
  And He that toss'd Thee down into the Field,
He knows about it all—HE knows—HE knows! [20]

LI.

The Moving Finger writes; and, having writ,
Moves on: nor all thy Piety nor Wit
  Shall lure it back to cancel half a Line,
Nor all thy Tears wash out a Word of it.

LII.

And that inverted Bowl we call The Sky,
Whereunder crawling coop't we live and die,
  Lift not thy hands to *It* for help—for It
Rolls impotently on as Thou or I.

LIII.

With Earth's first Clay They did the Last Man's knead,
And then of the Last Harvest sow'd the Seed:
  Yea, the first Morning of Creation wrote
What the Last Dawn of Reckoning shall read.

LIV.

I tell Thee this—When, starting from the Goal,
Over the shoulders of the flaming Foal
   Of Heav'n Parwín and Mushtara they flung, [21]
In my predestin'd Plot of Dust and Soul

LV.

The Vine had struck a Fibre; which about
If clings my Being—let the Súfi flout;
   Of my Base Metal may be filed a Key,
That shall unlock the Door he howls without.

LVI.

And this I know: whether the one True Light,
Kindle to Love, or Wrathconsume me quite,
   One Glimpse of It within the Tavern caught
Better than in the Temple lost outright.

LVII.

Oh Thou, who didst with Pitfall and with Gin
Beset the Road I was to wander in,
   Thou wilt not with Predestination round
Enmesh me, and impute my Fall to Sin?

LVIII.

Oh, Thou, who Man of baser Earth didst make,
And who with Eden didst devise the Snake;
   For all the Sin wherewith the Face of Man
Is blacken'd, Man's Forgiveness give—and take!

* * * * * * * *

KÚZA-NÁMA.

LIX.

Listen again. One Evening at the Close
Of Ramazán, ere the better Moon arose,
   In that old Potter's Shop I stood alone
With the clay Population round in Rows.

LX.

And, strange to tell, among that Earthen Lot
Some could articulate, while others not:
   And suddenly one more impatient cried—
"Who *is* the Potter, pray, and who the Pot?"

LXI.

Then said another—"Surely not in vain
"My Substance from the common Earth was ta'en,
   "That He who subtly wrought me into Shape
"Should stamp me back to common Earth again."

LXII.

Another said—"Why, ne'er a peevish Boy,
"Would break the Bowl from which he drank in Joy;
   "Shall He that *made* the Vessel in pure Love
"And Fansy, in an after Rage destroy!"

LXIII.

None answer'd this; but after Silence spake
A Vessel of a more ungainly Make:
 "They sneer at me for leaning all awry;
"What! did the Hand then of the Potter shake?"

LXIV.

Said one—" Folks of a surly Tapster tell,
" And daub his Visage with the Smoke of Hell;
 " They talk of some strict Testing of us—Pish!
" He's a Good Fellow, and 'twill all be well."

LXV.

Then said another with a long-drawn Sigh,
" My Clay with long oblivion is gone dry:
 " But, fill me with the old familiar Juice,
" Methinks I might recover by-and-bye!"

LXVI.

So while the Vessels one by one were speaking,
One spied the little Crescent all were seeking:
 And then they jogg'd each other, " Brother! Brother!
" Hark to the Porter's Shoulder-knot a-creaking!"

* * * * * * * *

LXVII.

Ah, with the Grape my fading Life provide,
And wash my Body whence the Life has died,
   And in a Windingsheet of Vine-leaf wrapt,
So bury me by some sweet Garden-side.

LXVIII.

That ev'n my buried Ashes such a Snare
Of Perfume shall fling up into the Air,
   As not a True Believer passing by
But shall be overtaken unaware.

LXIX.

Indeed the Idols I have loved so long
Have done my Credit in Men's Eye much wrong:
   Have drown'd my Honour in a shallow Cup,
And sold my Reputation for a Song.

LXX.

Indeed, indeed, Repentance oft before
I swore—but was I sober when I swore?
   And then and then came Spring, and Rose-in-hand
My thread-bare Penitence apieces tore.

LXXI.

And much as Wine has play'd the Infidel,
And robb'd me of my Robe of Honour—well,
   I often wonder what the Vintners buy
One half so precious as the Goods they sell.

LXXII.

Alas, that Spring should vanish with the Rose!
That Youth's sweet-scented Manuscript should close!
   The Nightingale that in the Branches sang,
Ah, whence, and whither flown again, who knows!

LXXIII.

Ah Love! could thou and I with Fate conspire
To grasp this sorry Scheme of Things entire,
   Would not we shatter it to bits—and then
Re-mould it nearer to the Heart's Desire!

LXXIV.

Ah, Moon of my Delight who know'st no wane,
The Moon of Heav'n is rising once again:
   How oft hereafter rising shall she look
Through this same Garden after me—in vain!

LXXV.

And when Thyself with shining Foot shall pass
Among the Guests Star-scatter'd on the Grass,
   And in thy joyous Errand reach the Spot
Where I made one—turn down an empty Glass!

TAMÁM SHUD.

NOTES.

[1] Flinging a Stone into the Cup was the Signal for "To Horse!" in the Desert.

[2] The "*False Dawn;*" Subhi Kházib, a transient Light on the Horizon about an hour before the Subhi sádhik, or True Dawn; a well known Phenomenon in the East. The Persians call the Morning Gray, or Dusk, "*Wolf-and-Sheep-While.*" "Almost at odds with, which is which."

[3] New Year. Beginning with the Vernal Equinox, it must be remembered; and (howsoever the old Solar Year is practically superseded by the clumsy *Lunar* Year that dates from the Mohammedan Hijra) still commemorated by a Festival that is said to have been appointed by the very Jamshyd whom Omar so often talks of, and whose yearly Calendar he helped to rectify.

"The sudden approach and rapid advance of the Spring," (says a late Traveller in Persia) "are very striking. Before the Snow is well off the Ground, the Trees burst into Blossom, and the Flowers start from the Soil. At *Now Rooz* (*their* New Year's Day) the Snow was lying in patches on the Hills and in the shaded Vallies, while the Fruit-trees in the Garden were budding beautifully, and green Plants and Flowers springing upon the Plains on every side—

'And on old Hyem's Chin and icy Crown
'An odorous Chaplet of sweet Summer buds
'Is, as in mockery, set—'—

Among the Plants newly appear'd I recognized some old Acquaintances I had not seen for many a Year: among these, two varieties of the Thistle; a coarse species of the Daisy, like the Horse-gowan; red and white Clover; the Dock; the blue Corn-flower; and that vulgar Herb the Dandelion rearing its yellow crest on the Banks of the Watercourses." The Nightingale was not yet heard, for the Rose was not yet blown: but an almost identical Blackbird and Woodpecker helped to make up something of a North-country Spring.

⁴ Exodus iv. 6; where Moses draws forth his Hand—not, according to the Persians, "*leprous as Snow*,"—but *white* as our May-Blossom in Spring perhaps! According to them also the Healing Power of Jesus resided in his Breath.

⁵ Irám, planted by King Schedad, and now sunk somewhere in the Sands of Arabia. Jamshyd's Seven-ring'd Cup was typical of the Seven Heavens, 7 Planets, 7 Seas, &c. and was a *Divining Cup*.

⁶ *Péhlevi*, the old Heroic *Sanskit* of Persia. Háfiz also speaks of the Nightingale's *Péhlevi*, which did not change with the People's.

⁷ I am not sure if this refers to the Red Rose looking sickly, or the Yellow Rose that ought to be Red; Red, White, and Yellow Roses all common in Persia.

⁸ Rustum, the "Hercules" of Persia, whose exploits are among the most celebrated in the Shah-náma. Hátim Tai, a well-known Type of Oriental Generosity.

⁹ A Drum—beaten outside a Palace.

¹⁰ That is, the Rose's Golden Centre.

NOTES.

¹¹ Persepolis : call'd also *Takht'i Jamshyd*—THE THRONE OF JAMSHYD, "*King-Splendid*," of the mythical *Peeshdádian* Dynasty, and supposed (with Shah-náma Authority) to have been founded and built by him, though others refer it to the Work of the Genie King, Ján Ibn Jann, who also built the Pyramids before the time of Adam. It is also called *Chehl-minar—Forty-column;* which is Persian, probably, for *Column-countless;* the Hall they adorned or supported with their Lotus Base and taurine Capital indicating double that Number, though now counted down to less than half by Earthquake and other Inroad. By whomsoever built, unquestionably the Monument of a long extinguished Dynasty and Mythology; its Halls, Chambers and Galleries, inscribed with Arrow-head Characters, and sculptured with colossal, wing'd, half human Figures like those of Nimroud; Processions of Priests and Warriors —(doubtful if any where a Woman)—and Kings sitting on Thrones or in Chariots, Staff or Lotus-flower in hand, and the *Ferooher*—Symbol of Existence—with his wing'd Globe, common also to Assyria and Ægypt—over their heads. All this, together with Aqueduct and Cistern, and other Appurtenance of a Royal Palace, upon a Terrace-platform, ascended by a double Flight of Stairs that may be gallop'd up, and cut out of and into the Rock-side of the *Koh'i Ráhmet*, *Mountain of Mercy*, where the old Fire-worshiping Sovereigns are buried, and overlooking the Plain of Merdasht.

Persians, like some other People, it seems, love to write their own Names, with sometimes a Verse or two, on their Country's Monuments. Mr. Binning (from whose sensible Travels the foregoing Account is mainly condens't) found several such in Persepolis; in one Place a fine Line of Háfiz: in another "an original, no doubt," he says, "by no great Poet," however "right in his Sentiment." The Words somehow looked to us, and the "halting metre" sounded, familiar; and on looking back at last among the 500 Rubáyiát of the Calcutta Omar MS.—*there* it is: old Omar quoted by *one* of his Countrymen, and here turned into hasty Rhyme, at any rate—

> "This Palace that its Top to Heaven threw,
> And Kings their Forehead on its Threshold drew—
> I saw a Ring-dove sitting there alone,
> And 'Coo, Coo, Coo,' she cried, and 'Coo, Coo, Coo.'"

So as it seems the Persian speaks the English Ring-dove's *Péhlevi*, which is also articulate Persian for "Where?"

BAHRÁM GÚR—*Bahrám of the Wild Ass*, from his Fame in hunting it—a Sassanian Sovereign, had also his Seven Castles (like the King of Bohemia!) each of a different Colour; each with a Royal Mistress within side; each of whom recounts to Bahrám a Romance, according to one of the most famous Poems of Persia, written by Amír Khusraw: these Sevens also figuring (according to Eastern Mysticism) the Seven Heavens, and perhaps the Book itself that Eighth, into which the mystical Seven transcend, and within which they revolve. The Ruins of Three of these Towers are yet shown by the Peasantry; as also the Swamp in which Bahrám sunk, like the Master of Ravenswood, while pursuing his *Gúr*.

[12] A Thousand Years to each Planet.
[13] Saturn, Lord of the Seventh Heaven.
[14] A Laugh at his Mathematics perhaps.

NOTES.

[15] ME AND THEE; that is, some Dividual Existence or Personality apart from the Whole.

[16] The Caravan travelling by Night (after their New Year's Day of the Vernal Equinox) by command of Mohammed, I believe.

[17] The 72 Sects into which Islamism so soon split.

[18] This alludes to Mahmúd's Conquest of India and its swarthy Idolaters.

[19] *Fanúsi khiyál*, a Magic-lanthorn still used in India; the cylindrical Interior being painted with various Figures, and so lightly poised and ventilated as to revolve round the Candle lighted within.

[20] A very mysterious Line in the original;

U dánad u dánad u dánad u ——

breaking off something like our Wood-pigeon's Note, which she is said to take up just where she left off.

[21] Parwín and Mushtara—The Pleiads and Jupiter.

[22] At the Close of the Fasting Month, Ramazán (which makes the Musulman unhealthy and unamiable), the first Glimpse of the New Moon (who rules their Division of the Year) is looked for with the utmost Anxiety, and hailed with all Acclamation. Then it is that the Porter's Knot may be heard toward the *Cellar*, perhaps. Old Omar has elsewhere a pretty Quatrain about this same Moon—

> " Be of Good Cheer—the sullen Month will die,
> " And a young Moon requite us by and bye:
>   " Look how the Old one meagre, bent, and wan
> " With Age and Fast, is fainting from the Sky!"

FINIS.

RUBÁIYÁT

OF

OMAR KHAYYÁM,

THE ASTRONOMER-POET OF PERSIA.

Rendered into English Verse.

SECOND EDITION.

LONDON:
BERNARD QUARITCH,
PICCADILLY.
1868.

JOHN CHILDS AND SON, PRINTERS.

OMAR KHAYYÁM,

THE

ASTRONOMER-POET OF PERSIA.

OMAR KHAYYÁM was born at Naishápúr in Khorassan in the latter half of our Eleventh, and died within the First Quarter of our Twelfth, Century. The slender Story of his Life is curiously twined about that of two other very considerable Figures in their Time and Country: one of whom tells the Story of all Three. This was Nizám ul Mulk, Vizyr to Alp Arslan the Son, and Malik Shah the Grandson, of Toghrul Beg the Tartar, who had wrested Persia from the feeble Successor of Mahmúd the Great, and founded that Seljukian Dynasty which finally roused Europe into the Crusades. This Nizám ul Mulk, in his *Wasiyat*—or *Testament*—which he wrote and left as a Memorial for future Statesmen—relates the following, as quoted in the Calcutta Review No. 59, from Mirkhond's History of the Assassins.

"'One of the greatest of the wise men of Khorassan was
'the Imám Mowaffak of Naishápúr, a man highly honoured
'and reverenced,—may God rejoice his soul; his illustrious
'years exceeded eighty-five, and it was the universal belief
'that every boy who read the Koran or studied the tradi-
'tions in his presence, would assuredly attain to honour and
'happiness. For this cause did my father send me from
'Tús to Naishápúr with Abd-us-samad, the doctor of law,
'that I might employ myself in study and learning under
'the guidance of that illustrious teacher. Towards me he
'ever turned an eye of favour and kindness, and as his pupil
'I felt for him extreme affection and devotion, so that I
'passed four years in his service. When I first came there,
'I found two other pupils of mine own age newly arrived,
'Hakim Omar Khayyám, and the ill-fated Ben Sabbáh.
'Both were endowed with sharpness of wit and the highest
'natural powers; and we three formed a close friendship
'together. When the Imám rose from his lectures, they
'used to join me, and we repeated to each other the lessons
'we had heard. Now Omar was a native of Naishápúr,
'while Hasan Ben Sabbáh's father was one Ali, a man of
'austere life and practice, but heretical in his creed and
'doctrine. One day Hasan said to me and to Khayyám, 'It
'is a universal belief that the pupils of the Imám Mowaffak
'will attain to fortune. Now, even if we *all* do not attain
'thereto, without doubt one of us will; what then shall be
'our mutual pledge and bond?' We answered, 'Be it
'what you please.' 'Well,' he said, 'let us make a vow,
'that to whomsoever this fortune falls, he shall share it
'equally with the rest, and reserve no pre-eminence for him-

'self.' 'Be it so,' we both replied, and on those terms we 'mutually pledged our words. Years rolled on, and I went 'from Khorassan to Transoxiana, and wandered to Ghazni 'and Cabul; and when I returned, I was invested with 'office, and rose to be administrator of affairs during the 'Sultanate of Sultan Alp Arslán.'

"He goes on to state, that years passed by, and both his old school-friends found him out, and came and claimed a share in his good fortune, according to the school-day vow. The Vizier was generous and kept his word. Hasan demanded a place in the government, which the Sultan granted at the Vizier's request; but discontented with a gradual rise, he plunged into the maze of intrigue of an oriental court, and, failing in a base attempt to supplant his benefactor, he was disgraced and fell. After many mishaps and wanderings, Hasan became the head of the Persian sect of the *Ismailians*,—a party of fanatics who had long murmured in obscurity, but rose to an evil eminence under the guidance of his strong and evil will. In A. D. 1090, he seized the castle of Alamút, in the province of Rúdbar, which lies in the mountainous tract, south of the Caspian Sea; and it was from this mountain home he obtained that evil celebrity among the Crusaders as the OLD MAN OF THE MOUNTAINS, and spread terror through the Mohammedan world; and it is yet disputed whether the word *Assassin*, which they have left in the language of modern Europe as their dark memorial, is derived from the *hashish*, or opiate of hemp-leaves (the Indian *bhang*), with which they maddened themselves to the sullen pitch of oriental desperation, or from the name of the founder of the dynasty, whom we have seen in his quiet collegiate days, at Naishápúr. One of the countless victims of the Assassin's dagger was Nizám-ul-Mulk himself, the old school-boy friend.[1]

"Omar Khayyám also came to the Vizier to claim the share; but not to ask for title or office. 'The greatest boon 'you can confer on me,' he said, 'is to let me live in a 'corner under the shadow of your fortune, to spread wide 'the advantages of Science, and pray for your long life and 'prosperity.' The Vizier tells us, that, when he found Omar was really sincere in his refusal, he pressed him no further, but granted him a yearly pension of 1200 *mithkáls* of gold, from the treasury of Naishápúr.

"At Naishápúr thus lived and died Omar Khayyám, 'busied,' adds the Vizier, 'in winning knowledge of every 'kind, and especially in Astronomy, wherein he attained to a 'very high pre-eminence. Under the Sultanate of Malik 'Shah, he came to Merv, and obtained great praise for his 'proficiency in science, and the Sultan showered favours 'upon him.'

"When Malik Shah determined to reform the calendar, Omar was one of the eight learned men employed to do it; the result was the *Jaláli* era (so called from *Jalal-u-din*, one of the king's names),—'a computation of time,' says Gibbon, 'which surpasses the Julian, and approaches the

---

[1] Some of Omar's Rubáiyát warn us of the danger of Greatness, the instability of Fortune, and while advocating Charity to all Men, recommending us to be too intimate with none. Attár makes Nizám-ul-Mulk use the very words of his friend Omar [Rub. xxxi.], "When Nizám-ul-Mulk was in the Agony (of Death) he said, 'Oh God! I am 'passing away in the hand of the Wind.'"

'accuracy of the Gregorian style.' He is also the author of some astronomical tables, entitled Zíji-Malikshahí," and the French have lately republished and translated an Arabic Treatise of his on Algebra.

"His Takhallus or poetical name (Khayyám) signifies a Tent-maker, and he is said to have at one time exercised that trade, perhaps before Nizám-ul-Mulk's generosity raised him to independence. Many Persian poets similarly derive their names from their occupations; thus we have Attár, 'a druggist,' Assár, 'an oil presser,' &c.[1] Omar himself alludes to his name in the following whimsical lines:—

> 'Khayyám, who stitched the tents of science,
> Has fallen in grief's furnace and been suddenly burned;
> The shears of Fate have cut the tent ropes of his life,
> And the broker of Hope has sold him for nothing!'

"We have only one more anecdote to give of his Life, and that relates to the close; it is told in the anonymous preface which is sometimes prefixed to his poems; it has been printed in the Persian in the appendix to Hyde's *Veterum Persarum Religio*, p. 499; and D'Herbelot alludes to it in his Bibliothéque, under *Khiam*:—[2]

"'It is written in the chronicles of the ancients that this 'King of the Wise, Omar Khayyám, died at Naishápúr in 'the year of the Hegira, 517 (A.D. 1123); in science he was

---

[1] Though all these, like our Smiths, Archers, Millers, Fletchers, &c., may simply retain the Surname of an hereditary calling.

[2] "Philosophe Musulman qui a vécu en Odeur de Sainteté dans la Fin du premier et le Commencement du second Siècle," no part of which, except the "Philosophe," can apply to *our* Khayyám.

'unrivalled,—the very paragon of his age. Khwájah Nizámi 'of Samarcand, who was one of his pupils, relates the follow- 'ing story: 'I often used to hold conversations with my 'teacher, Omar Khayyám, in a garden; and one day he said 'to me, 'My tomb shall be in a spot, where the north wind 'may scatter roses over it.' I wondered at the words he 'spake, but I knew that his were no idle words.[1] Years after, 'when I chanced to revisit Naishápúr, I went to his final 'resting-place, and lo! it was just outside a garden, and trees 'laden with fruit stretched their boughs over the garden 'wall, and dropped their flowers upon his tomb, so as the 'stone was hidden under them.'"

Thus far—without fear of Trespass—from the Calcutta Review. The writer of it, on reading in India this story of

[1] The Rashness of the Words, according to D'Herbelot, consisted in being so opposed to those in the Korán: "No Man knows where he shall die."—This Story of Omar recalls a very different one so naturally—and, when one remembers how wide of his humble mark the noble sailor aimed—so pathetically told by Captain Cook—not by Doctor Hawkesworth—in his Second Voyage. When leaving Ulietea, "Oreo's last request was for me to return. When he saw he could not obtain that promise, he asked the name of my *Marai*—Burying-place. As strange a question as this was, I hesitated not a moment to tell him 'Stepney,' the parish in which I live when in London. I was made to repeat it several times over till they could pronounce it; and then 'Stepney Marai no Tootee' was echoed through a hundred mouths at once. I afterwards found the same question had been put to Mr Forster by a man on shore; but he gave a different, and indeed more proper answer, by saying, 'No man who used the sea could say where he should be buried.'"

Omar's Grave, was reminded, he says, of Cicero's Account of finding Archimedes' Tomb at Syracuse, buried in grass and weeds. I think Thorwaldsen desired to have roses grow over him; a wish religiously fulfilled for him to the present day, I believe. However, to return to Omar.

Though the Sultan "shower'd Favours upon him," Omar's Epicurean Audacity of Thought and Speech caused him to be regarded askance in his own Time and Country. He is said to have been especially hated and dreaded by the Súfis, whose Practice he ridiculed, and whose Faith amounts to little more than his own when stript of the Mysticism and formal recognition of Islamism under which Omar would not hide. Their Poets, including Háfiz, who are (with the exception of Firdausi) the most considerable in Persia, borrowed largely, indeed, of Omar's material, but turning it to a mystical Use more convenient to Themselves and the People they addressed; a People quite as quick of Doubt as of Belief; as keen of Bodily Sense as of Intellectual; and delighting in a cloudy compound of both, in which they could float luxuriously between Heaven and Earth, and this World and the Next, on the wings of a poetical expression, that might serve indifferently for either. Omar was too honest of Heart as well as of Head for this. Having failed (however mistakenly) of finding any Providence but Destiny, and any World but This, he set about making the most of it; preferring rather to soothe the Soul through the Senses into Acquiescence with Things as he saw them, than to perplex it with vain disquietude after what they *might be*. It has been seen, however, that his Worldly Ambition was not exorbitant; and he very likely takes a humorous or perverse pleasure in exalting the gratification of Sense above that of the Intellect, in which he must have taken great delight, although it failed to answer the Questions in which he, in common with all men, was most vitally interested.

For whatever Reason, however, Omar, as before said, has never been popular in his own Country, and therefore has been but scantily transmitted abroad. The MSS. of his Poems, mutilated beyond the average Casualties of Oriental Transcription, are so rare in the East as scarce to have reacht Westward at all, in spite of all the acquisitions of Arms and Science. There is no copy at the India House, none at the Bibliothèque Imperiále of Paris. We know but of one in England: No. 140 of the Ouseley MSS. at the Bodleian, written at Shiraz, A.D. 1460. This contains but 158 Rabáiyát. One in the Asiatic Society's Library at Calcutta (of which we have a Copy), contains (and yet incomplete) 516, though swelled to that by all kinds of Repetition and Corruption. So Von Hammer speaks of *his* Copy as containing about 200, while Dr Sprenger catalogues the Lucknow MS. at double that Number.[1] The Scribes, too, of the Oxford and Calcutta MSS. seem to do their Work under a sort of Protest; each beginning with a Tetrastich (whether genuine or not), taken out of its alphabetic order; the Oxford with one of Apology; the Calcutta with one of Expostulation, supposed (says a Notice prefixed to the MS.) to have

---

[1] "Since this Paper was written" (adds the Reviewer in a note), "we have met with a Copy of a very rare Edition, printed at Calcutta in 1836. This contains 438 Tetrastichs, with an Appendix containing 54 others not found in some MSS."

risen from a Dream, in which Omar's mother asked about his future fate. It may be rendered thus :—

"Oh Thou who burn'st in Heart for those who burn
"In Hell, whose fires thyself shall feed in turn;
"How long be crying, 'Mercy on them, God!'
"Why, who art Thou to teach, and He to learn?"

The Bodleian Quatrain pleads Pantheism by way of Justification.

"If I myself upon a looser Creed
"Have loosely strung the Jewel of Good deed,
"Let this one thing for my Atonement plead :
"That One for Two I never did mis-read."

The Reviewer, to whom I owe the Particulars of Omar's Life, concludes his Review by comparing him with Lucretius, both as to natural Temper and Genius, and as acted upon by the Circumstances in which he lived. Both indeed were men of subtle, strong, and cultivated Intellect, fine Imagination, and Hearts passionate for Truth and Justice; who justly revolted from their Country's false Religion, and false, or foolish, Devotion to it; but who yet fell short of replacing what they subverted by such better *Hope* as others, with no better Revelation to guide them, had yet made a Law to themselves. Lucretius, indeed, with such material as Epicurus furnished, satisfied himself with the theory of so vast a machine fortuitously constructed, and acting by a Law that implied no Legislator; and so composing himself into a Stoical rather than Epicurean severity of Attitude, sat down to contemplate the mechanical Drama of the Universe which he was part Actor in;

himself and all about him (as in his own sublime description of the Roman Theatre) discoloured with the lurid reflex of the Curtain suspended between the Spectator and the Sun. Omar, more desperate, or more careless of any so complicated System as resulted in nothing but hopeless Necessity, flung his own Genius and Learning with a bitter or humorous jest into the general Ruin which their insuficient glimpses only served to reveal; and, pretending sensual pleasure as the serious purpose of Life, only *diverted* himself with speculative problems of Deity, Destiny, Matter and Spirit, Good and Evil, and other such questions, easier to start than to run down, and the pursuit of which becomes a very weary sport at last!

With regard to the present Translation. The original Rubáiyát (as, missing an Arabic Guttural, these *Tetrastichs* are more musically called) are independent Stanzas, consisting each of four Lines of equal, though varied, Prosody; sometimes *all* rhyming, but oftener (as here imitated) the third line a blank. Something as in the Greek Alcaic, where the penultimate line seems to lift and suspend the Wave that falls over in the last. As usual with such kind of Oriental Verse, the Rubáiyát follow one another according to Alphabetic Rhyme—a strange succession of Grave and Gay. Those here selected are strung into something of an Eclogue, with perhaps a less than equal proportion of the "Drink and make-merry," which (genuine or not) recurs over-frequently in the Original. Either way, the Result is sad enough: saddest perhaps when most ostentatiously merry: more apt to move Sorrow than Anger toward the old Tentmaker, who, after vainly endeavouring to unshackle his Steps from Destiny, and to catch some authentic Glimpse of TOMORROW, fell back upon TODAY (which has out-lasted so many Tomorrows!) as the only Ground he got to stand upon, however momentarily slipping from under his Feet.

While the present Edition of Omar was preparing, Monsieur Nicolas, French Consul at Rescht, published a very careful and very good Edition of the Text, from a lithograph copy at Teheran, comprising 464 Rubáiyát, with translation and notes of his own.

Mons. Nicolas, whose Edition has reminded me of several things, and instructed me in others, does not consider Omar to be the material Epicurean that I have literally taken him for, but a Mystic, shadowing the Deity under the figure of Wine, Wine-bearer, &c., as Háfiz is supposed to do; in short, a Súfi Poet like Háfiz and the rest.

I cannot see reason to alter my opinion, formed as it was a dozen years ago when Omar was first shown me by one to whom I am indebted for all I know of Oriental, and very much of other, literature. He admired Omar's Genius so much, that he would gladly have adopted any such Interpretation of his meaning as Mons. Nicolas' if he could.[1] That he could not appears by his Paper in the Calcutta Review already so largely quoted; in which he argues from the

[1] Perhaps would have edited the Poems himself some years ago. He may now as little approve of my Version on one side, as of Mons. Nicolas' on the other.

Poems themselves, as well as from what records remain of the Poet's Life.

And if more were needed to disprove Mons. Nicolas' Theory, there is the Biographical Notice which he himself has drawn up in direct contradiction to the Interpretation of the Poems given in his Notes. Here is one of the Anecdotes he produces. " Mais revenons à Khéyam, qui, resté étranger à toutes ces alternatives de guerres, d'intrigues, et de révoltes, dont cette époque fut si remplie, vivait tranquille dans son village natal, se livrant avec passion à l'étude de la philosophie des Soufis. Entouré de nombreux amis il cherchait avec eux dans le vin cette contemplation extatique que d'autres croient trouver dans des cris et des hurlemens," &c. " Les chroniqueurs persans racontent que Khéyam aimait surtout à s'entretenir et à boire avec ses amis, le soir au clair de la lune sur la terrasse de sa maison, entouré de chanteurs et musiciens, avec un échanson qui, la coupe à la main, la présentait à tour de rôle aux joyeux convives réunis.—Pendant une de ces soirées dont nous venons de parler, survient à l'improviste un coup de vent qui éteint les chandelles et renverse à terre la cruche de vin, placée imprudemment sur le bord de la terrasse. La cruche fut brisée et le vin repandu. Aussitôt Khéyam, irrité, improvisa ce quatrain impie à l'addresse du Tout-Puissant: 'Tu as brisé ma cruche de vin, mon Dieu! tu as ainsi fermé sur moi la porte de la joie, mon Dieu! c'est moi qui bois, et c'est toi qui commets les désordres de l'ivresse! oh! (puisse ma bouche se remplir de la terre!) serais tu ivre, mon Dieu?'

" Le poète, après avoir prononcé ce blasphème, jetant les yeux sur une glace, se serait aperçu que son visage était noir comme du charbon. C'était une punition du ciel. Alors il fit cet autre quatrain non moins audacieux que le premier. 'Quel est l'homme ici-bas qui n'a point commis de péché, dis ? Celui qui n'en aurait point commis, comment aurait-il vécu, dis ? Si, parce que je fais du mal, tu me punis par le mal, quelle est donc la différence qui existe entre toi et moi, dis ? ' "

I really hardly knew poor Omar was so far gone till his Apologist informed me. Here we see then that, whatever were the Wine that Háfiz drank and sang, the veritable Juice of the Grape it was which Omar used not only when carousing with his friends, but (says Mons. Nicolas) in order to excite himself to that pitch of Devotion which others reached by cries and "hurlemens." And yet, whenever Wine, Wine-bearer, &c., occur in the Text—which is often enough—Mons. Nicolas carefully annotates "Dieu" "La Divinité," &c.: so carefully indeed that one is tempted to think he was indoctrinated by the Súfi with whom he read the Poems. (Note to Rub. ii. p. 8.) A Persian would naturally wish to vindicate a distinguished Countryman; and a Súfi to enrol him in his own sect, which already comprises all the chief Poets of Persia.

What historical Authority has Mons. Nicolas to show that Omar gave himself up " avec passion à l'étude de la philosophie des Soufis " ? (Preface, p. xiii.) The Doctrines of Pantheism, Materialism, Necessity, &c., were not peculiar to the Súfi; nor to Lucretius before them; nor to Epicurus before him; probably the very original Irreligion of thinking men from the first; and very likely to be the spontaneous growth of a Philosopher living in an Age of social and political barbarism, under sanction of one of the Two and Seventy Religions supposed to divide the world. Von Hammer (according to Sprenger's Oriental Catalogue) speaks of Omar as "a Free-thinker, and *a great opponent of Sufism;*" perhaps because, while holding much of their Doctrine, he would not pretend to any inconsistent severity of morals. Sir W. Ouseley has written a Note to something of the same effect on the fly-leaf of the Bodleian MS. And in two Rubáiyát of Mons. Nicolas' own Edition Súf and Súfi are both disparagingly named.

No doubt many of these Quatrains seem unaccountable unless mystically interpreted; but many more as unaccountable unless literally. Were the Wine spiritual, for instance, how wash the Body with it when dead? Why make cups of the dead clay to be filled with—" La Divinité "—by some succeeding Mystic? Mons. Nicolas himself is puzzled by some "bizarres" and "trop Orientales" allusions and images—" d'une sensualité quelquefois revoltante " indeed—which "les convenances" do not permit him to translate; but still which the reader cannot but refer to "La Divinité."[1] No doubt also many of the Quatrains in the

---

[1] A Note to Quatrain 234 admits that, however clear the mystical meaning of such Images must be to Europeans, they are not quoted without " rougissant " even by laymen in Persia—" Quant aux termes de tendresse qui commencent ce quatrain, comme tant d'autres dans ce recueil, nos lecteurs, habitués maintenant à l'étrangeté des expressions si souvent employés par Khéyam pour rendre ses pensées sur l'amour divin, et à la singularité des images trop orientales, d'une sensualité quelquefois révoltante, n'auront pas de peine à se persuader qu'il s'agit de la Divinité, bien que cette conviction soit vivement dis-

Teheran, as in the Calcutta, Copies, are spurious; such *Rubáiyát* being the common form of Epigram in Persia. But this, at best, tells as much one way as another; nay, the Súfi, who may be considered the Scholar and Man of Letters in Persia, would be far more likely than the careless Epicure to interpolate what favours his own view of the Poet. I observe that very few of the more mystical Quatrains are in the Bodleian MS., which must be one of the oldest, as dated at Shiraz, A.H. 865, A.D. 1460. And this, I think, especially distinguishes Omar (I cannot help calling him by his—no, not Christian—familiar name) from all other Persian Poets: That, whereas with them the Poet is lost in his Song, the Man in Allegory and Abstraction; we seem to have the Man—the *Bonhomme*—Omar himself, with all his Humours and Passions, as frankly before us as if we were really at Table with him, after the Wine had gone round.

I must say that I, for one, never wholly believed in the Mysticism of Háfiz. It does not appear there was any danger in holding and singing Súfi Pantheism, so long as the Poet made his Salaam to Mohammed at the beginning and end of his Song. Under such conditions Jeláluddín, Jámi, Attár, and others sang; using Wine and Beauty indeed as Images to illustrate, not as a Mask to hide, the Divinity they were celebrating. Perhaps some Allegory less liable to mistake or abuse had been better among so inflam-

cutée par les moullahs musulmans, et même par beaucoup de laïques, qui rougissent véritablement d'une pareille licence de leur compatriote à l'égard des choses spirituelles."

mable a People: much more so when, as some think with Háfiz and Omar, the abstract is not only likened to, but identified with, the sensual Image; hazardous, if not to the Devotee himself, yet to his weaker Brethren; and worse for the Profane in proportion as the Devotion of the Initiated grew warmer. And all for what? To be tantalized with Images of sensual enjoyment which must be renounced if one would approximate a God, who, according to the Doctrine, *is* Sensual Matter as well as Spirit, and into whose Universe one expects unconsciously to merge after Death, without hope of any posthumous Beatitude in another world to compensate for all the self-denial of this. Lucretius' blind Divinity certainly merited, and probably got, as much self-sacrifice as this of the Súfi; and the burden of Omar's Song—if not "Let us eat"—is assuredly— "Let us drink, for Tomorrow we die!" And if Háfiz meant quite otherwise by a similar language, he surely miscalculated when he devoted his Life and Genius to so equivocal a Psalmody as, from his Day to this, has been said and sung by any rather than spiritual Worshippers.

However, it may remain an Open Question, both with regard to Háfiz and Omar: the reader may understand them either way, literally or mystically, as he chooses. Whenever Wine, Wine-bearer, Cypress, &c., are named, he has only to suppose "La Divinité;" and when he has done so with Omar, I really think he may proceed to the same Interpretation of Anacreon—and even Anacreon Moore.

RUBÁIYÁT

OF

OMAR KHAYYÁM OF NAISHAPÚR.

I.

Wake! For the Sun behind yon Eastern height
Has chased the Session of the Stars from Night;
  And, to the field of Heav'n ascending, strikes
The Sultán's Turret with a Shaft of Light.

II.

Before the phantom of False morning died,[1]
Methought a Voice within the Tavern cried,
  "When all the Temple is prepared within,
"Why lags the drowsy Worshipper outside?"

III.

And, as the Cock crew, those who stood before
The Tavern shouted—"Open then the door!
  "You know how little while we have to stay,
"And, once departed, may return no more."

IV.

Now the New Year reviving old Desires,[2]
The thoughtful Soul to Solitude retires,
   Where the WHITE HAND OF MOSES on the Bough
Puts out, and Jesus from the Ground suspires.[3]

V.

Iram indeed is gone with all his Rose,[4]
And Jamshýd's Sev'n-ring'd Cup where no one knows;
   But still a Ruby gushes from the Vine,
And many a Garden by the Water blows.

VI.

And David's lips are lockt; but in divine[5]
High-piping Péhlevi, with "Wine! Wine! Wine!
   Red Wine!"—the Nightingale cries to the Rose
That sallow cheek[6] of her's to incarnadine.

VII.

Come, fill the Cup, and in the fire of Spring
Your Winter-garment of Repentance fling:
   The Bird of Time has but a little way
To flutter—and the Bird is on the Wing.

VIII.

Whether at Naishápúr or Babylon,
Whether the Cup with sweet or bitter run,
   The Wine of Life keeps oozing drop by drop,
The Leaves of Life keep falling one by one.

IX.

Morning a thousand Roses brings, you say;
Yes, but where leaves the Rose of yesterday?
    And this first Summer month that brings the Rose
Shall take Jamshýd and Kaikobád away.

X.

Well, let it take them! What have we to do
With Kaikobád the Great, or Kaikhosrú?
    Let Rustum cry "To Battle!" as he likes,[7]
Or Hátim Tai "To Supper!"—heed not you.

XI.

With me along the strip of Herbage strown
That just divides the desert from the sown,
    Where name of Slave and Sultán is forgot—
And Peace to Máhmúd on his golden Throne!

XII.

Here with a little Bread beneath the Bough,
A Flask of Wine, a Book of Verse—and Thou
    Beside me singing in the Wilderness—
Oh, Wilderness were Paradise enow!

XIII.

Some for the Glories of This World; and some
Sigh for the Prophet's Paradise to come;
    Ah, take the Cash, and let the Promise go,
Nor heed the music of a distant Drum![8]

XIV.

Were it not Folly, Spider-like to spin
The Thread of present Life away to win—
   What? for ourselves, who know not if we shall
Breathe out the very Breath we now breathe in!

XV.

Look to the blowing Rose about us—"Lo,
"Laughing," she says, "into the world I blow:
   "At once the silken tassel of my Purse
"Tear, and its Treasure on the Garden throw."⁹

XVI.

For those who husbanded the Golden grain,
And those who flung it to the winds like Rain,
   Alike to no such aureate Earth are turn'd
As, buried once, Men want dug up again.

XVII.

The Worldly Hope men set their Hearts upon
Turns Ashes—or it prospers; and anon,
   Like Snow upon the Desert's dusty Face,
Lighting a little hour or two—was gone.

XVIII.

Think, in this batter'd Caravanserai
Whose Portals are alternate Night and Day,
   How Sultán after Sultán with his Pomp
Abode his destin'd Hour, and went his way.

XIX.

They say the Lion and the Lizard keep
The Courts where Jamshýd gloried and drank deep :[10]
   And Bahrám, that great Hunter—the Wild Ass
Stamps o'er his Head, but cannot break his Sleep.

XX.

The Palace that to Heav'n his pillars threw,
And Kings the forehead on his threshold drew—
   I saw the solitary Ringdove there,
And "Coo, coo, coo," she cried; and "Coo, coo, coo."[11]

XXI.

Ah, my Belovéd, fill the Cup that clears
To-DAY of past Regret and future Fears :
   To-morrow !—Why, To-morrow I may be
Myself with Yesterday's Sev'n thousand Years.[12]

XXII.

For some we loved, the loveliest and the best
That from his Vintage rolling Time has prest,
   Have drunk their Cup a Round or two before,
And one by one crept silently to rest.

XXIII.

And we, that now make merry in the Room
They left, and Summer dresses in new bloom,
   Ourselves must we beneath the Couch of Earth
Descend, ourselves to make a Couch—for whom ?

XXIV.

I sometimes think that never blows so red
The Rose as where some buried Cæsar bled;
   That every Hyacinth the Garden wears
Dropt in her Lap from some once lovely Head.

XXV.

And this delightful Herb whose living Green
Fledges the River's Lip on which we lean—
   Ah, lean upon it lightly! for who knows
From what once lovely Lip t springs unseen!

XXVI.

Ah, make the most of what we yet may spend,
Before we too into the Dust descend;
   Dust into Dust, and under Dust, to lie,
Sans Wine, sans Song, sans Singer, and—sans End!

XXVII.

Alike for those who for To-DAY prepare,
And those that after some To-MORROW stare,
   A Muezzín from the Tower of Darkness cries,
"Fools! your Reward is neither Here nor There!"

XXVIII.

Another Voice, when I am sleeping, cries,
" The Flower should open with the Morning skies."
   And a retreating Whisper, as I wake—
" The Flower that once has blown for ever dies."

XXIX.

Why, all the Saints and Sages who discuss'd
Of the Two Worlds so learnedly, are thrust
   Like foolish Prophets forth; their Words to Scorn
Are scatter'd, and their Mouths are stopt with Dust.

XXX.

Myself when young did eagerly frequent
Doctor and Saint, and heard great argument
   About it and about: but evermore
Came out by the same door as in I went.

XXXI.

With them the seed of Wisdom did I sow,
And with my own hand wrought to make it grow:
   And this was all the Harvest that I reap'd—
"I came like Water, and like Wind I go."

XXXII.

Into this Universe, and *Why* not knowing,
Nor *Whence*, like Water willy-nilly flowing:
   And out of it, as Wind along the Waste,
I know not *Whither*, willy-nilly blowing.

XXXIII.

What, without asking, hither hurried *Whence?*
And, without asking, *Whither* hurried hence!
   Ah, contrite Heav'n endowed us with the Vine
To drug the memory of that insolence!

XXXIV.

Up from Earth's Centre through the Seventh Gate
I rose, and on the Throne of Saturn sate,[13]
   And many Knots unravel'd by the Road;
But not the Master-knot of Human Fate.

XXXV.

There was the Door to which I found no Key:
There was the Veil through which I could not see:
   Some little talk awhile of ME and THEE
There was—and then no more of THEE and ME.[14]

XXXVI.

Earth could not answer; nor the Seas that mourn
In flowing Purple, of their Lord forlorn;
   Nor Heaven, with those eternal Signs reveal'd
And hidden by the sleeve of Night and Morn.

XXXVII.

Then of the THEE IN ME who works behind
The Veil of Universe I cried to find
   A Lamp to guide me through the darkness; and
Something then said—" An Understanding blind."

XXXVIII.

Then to the Lip of this poor earthen Urn
I lean'd, the secret Well of Life to learn:
   And Lip to Lip it murmur'd—" While you live,
" Drink!—for, once dead, you never shall return."

XXXIX.

I think the Vessel, that with fugitive
Articulation answer'd, once did live,
   And drink; and that impassive Lip I kiss'd,
How many Kisses might it take—and give!

XL.

For I remember stopping by the way
To watch a Potter thumping his wet Clay:
   And with its all-obliterated Tongue
It murmur'd—" Gently, Brother, gently, pray!"

XLI.

For has not such a Story from of Old
Down Man's successive generations roll'd
   Of such a clod of saturated Earth
Cast by the Maker into Human mould?

XLII.

And not a drop that from our Cups we throw[15]
On the parcht herbage but may steal below
   To quench the fire of Anguish in some Eye
There hidden—far beneath, and long ago.

XLIII.

As then the Tulip for her wonted sup
Of Heavenly Vintage lifts her chalice up,
   Do you, twin offspring of the soil, till Heav'n
To Earth invert you like an empty Cup.

XLIV.

Do you, within your little hour of Grace,
The waving Cypress in your Arms enlace,
   Before the Mother back into her arms
Fold, and dissolve you in a last embrace.

XLV.

And if the Cup you drink, the Lip you press,
End in what All begins and ends in—Yes;
   Imagine then you *are* what heretofore
You *were*—hereafter you shall not be less.

XLVI.

So when at last the Angel of the drink [16]
Of Darkness finds you by the river-brink,
   And, proffering his Cup, invites your Soul
Forth to your Lips to quaff it—do not shrink.

XLVII.

And fear not lest Existence closing *your*
Account, should lose, or know the type no more;
   The Eternal Sáki from that Bowl has pour'd
Millions of Bubbles like us, and will pour.

XLVIII.

When You and I behind the Veil are past,
Oh but the long long while the World shall last,
   Which of our Coming and Departure heeds
As much as Ocean of a pebble-cast.

XLIX.

One Moment in Annihilation's Waste,
One Moment, of the Well of Life to taste—
   The Stars are setting, and the Caravan[17]
Draws to the Dawn of Nothing—Oh make haste!

L.

Would you that spangle of Existence spend
About THE SECRET—quick about it, Friend!
   A Hair, they say, divides the False and True—
And upon what, prithee, does Life depend?

LI.

A Hair, they say, divides the False and True;
Yes; and a single Alif were the clue,
   Could you but find it, to the Treasure-house,
And peradventure to THE MASTER too;

LII.

Whose secret Presence, through Creation's veins
Running, Quicksilver-like eludes your pains:
   Taking all shapes from Máh to Máhi;[18] and
They change and perish all—but He remains;

LIII.

A moment guess'd—then back behind the Fold
Immerst of Darkness round the Drama roll'd
   Which, for the Pastime of Eternity,
He does Himself contrive, enact, behold.

LIV.

But if in vain, down on the stubborn floor
Of Earth, and up to Heav'n's unopening Door,
   You gaze To-day, while You are You—how then
To-morrow, You when shall be You no more?

LV.

Oh, plagued no more with Human or Divine,
To-morrow's tangle to itself resign,
   And lose your fingers in the tresses of
The Cypress-slender Minister of Wine.

LVI.

Waste not your Hour, nor in the vain pursuit
Of This and That endeavour and dispute;
   Better be merry with the fruitful Grape
Than sadden after none, or bitter, Fruit.

LVII.

You know, my Friends, how bravely in my House
For a new Marriage I did make Carouse:
   Divorced old barren Reason from my Bed,
And took the Daughter of the Vine to Spouse.

LVIII.

For "Is" and "Is-not" though with Rule and Line,[19]
And "Up-and-down" by Logic I define,
   Of all that one should care to fathom, I
Was never deep in anything but—Wine.

LIX.

Ah, but my Computations, People say,
Have squared the Year to human compass, eh?
　　If so, by striking from the Calendar
Unborn To-morrow, and dead Yesterday.

LX.

And lately, by the Tavern Door agape,
Came shining through the Dusk an Angel Shape
　　Bearing a Vessel on his Shoulder; and
He bid me taste of it; and 'twas—the Grape!

LXI.

The Grape that can with Logic absolute
The Two-and-Seventy jarring Sects confute:[20]
　　The sovereign Alchemist that in a trice
Life's leaden metal into Gold transmute:

LXII.

The mighty Mahmúd, Allah-breathing Lord,
That all the misbelieving and black Horde[21]
　　Of Fears and Sorrows that infest the Soul
Scatters before him with his whirlwind Sword.

LXIII.

Why, be this Juice the growth of God, who dare
Blaspheme the twisted tendril as a Snare?
　　A Blessing, we should use it, should we not?
And if a Curse—why, then, Who set it there?

LXIV.

I must abjure the Balm of Life, I must,
Scared by some After-reckoning ta'en on trust,
   Or lured with Hope of some Diviner Drink,
When the frail Cup is crumbled into Dust!

LXV.

If but the Vine and Love-abjuring Band
Are in the Prophet's Paradise to stand,
   Alack, I doubt the Prophet's Paradise
Were empty as the hollow of one's Hand.

LXVI.

Oh threats of Hell and Hopes of Paradise!
One thing at least is certain—*This* Life flies:
   One thing is certain and the rest is Lies;
The Flower that once is blown for ever dies.

LXVII.

Strange, is it not? that of the myriads who
Before us pass'd the door of Darkness through
   Not one returns to tell us of the Road,
Which to discover we must travel too.

LXVIII.

The Revelations of Devout and Learn'd
Who rose before us, and as Prophets burn'd,
   Are all but Stories, which, awoke from Sleep
They told their fellows, and to Sleep return'd.

LXIX.

Why, if the Soul can fling the Dust aside,
And naked on the Air of Heaven ride,
   Is't not a shame—is't not a shame for him
So long in this Clay suburb to abide!

LXX.

But that is but a Tent wherein may rest
A Sultan to the realm of Death addrest;
   The Sultan rises, and the dark Ferrásh
Strikes, and prepares it for another guest.

LXXI.

I sent my Soul through the Invisible,
Some letter of that After-life to spell:
   And after many days my Soul return'd
And said, "Behold, Myself am Heav'n and Hell:"

LXXII.

Heav'n but the Vision of fulfill'd Desire,
And Hell the Shadow of a Soul on fire,
   Cast on the Darkness into which Ourselves,
So late emerg'd from, shall so soon expire.

LXXIII.

We are no other than a moving row
Of visionary Shapes that come and go
   Round with this Sun-illumin'd Lantern held
In Midnight by the Master of the Show;[22]

LXXIV.

Impotent Pieces of the Game He plays
Upon this Chequer-board of Nights and Days;
   Hither and thither moves, and checks, and slays;
And one by one back in the Closet lays.

LXXV.

The Ball no question makes of Ayes and Noes,
But Right or Left as strikes the Player goes;
   And He that toss'd you down into the Field,
He knows about it all—HE knows—HE knows! [23]

LXXVI.

The Moving Finger writes; and, having writ,
Moves on: nor all your Piety nor Wit
   Shall lure it back to cancel half a Line,
Nor all your Tears wash out a Word of it.

LXXVII.

For let Philosopher and Doctor preach
Of what they will, and what they will not—each
   Is but one Link in an eternal Chain
That none can slip, nor break, nor over-reach.

LXXVIII.

And that inverted Bowl we call The Sky,
Whereunder crawling coop'd we live and die,
   Lift not your hands to *It* for help—for It
As impotently rolls as you or I.

LXXIX.

With Earth's first Clay They did the Last Man knead,
And there of the Last Harvest sow'd the Seed:
   And the first Morning of Creation wrote
What the Last Dawn of Reckoning shall read.

LXXX.

Yesterday *This* Day's Madness did prepare;
To-morrow's Silence, Triumph, or Despair:
   Drink! for you know not whence you came, nor why:
Drink! for you know not why you go, nor where.

LXXXI.

I tell you this—When, started from the Goal,
Over the flaming shoulders of the Foal
   Of Heav'n Parwín and Mushtari they flung,[24]
In my predestin'd Plot of Dust and Soul

LXXXII.

The Vine had struck a fibre: which about
If clings my Being—let the Dervish flout;
   Of my Base metal may be filed a Key,
That shall unlock the Door he howls without.

LXXXIII.

And this I know: whether the one True Light,
Kindle to Love, or Wrath-consume me quite,
   One Flash of It within the Tavern caught
Better than in the Temple lost outright.

LXXXIV.

What! out of senseless Nothing to provoke
A conscious Something to resent the yoke
   Of unpermitted Pleasure, under pain
Of Everlasting Penalties, if broke!

LXXXV.

What! from his helpless Creature be repaid
Pure Gold for what he lent us dross-allay'd—
   Sue for a Debt we never did contract,
And cannot answer—Oh the sorry trade!

LXXXVI.

Nay, but, for terror of his wrathful Face,
I swear I will not call Injustice Grace;
   Not one Good Fellow of the Tavern but
Would kick so poor a Coward from the place.

LXXXVII.

Oh Thou, who didst with pitfall and with gin
Beset the Road I was to wander in,
   Thou wilt not with Predestin'd Evil round
Enmesh, and then impute my Fall to Sin?

LXXXVIII.

Oh Thou, who Man of baser Earth didst make,
And ev'n with Paradise devise the Snake:
   For all the Sin the Face of wretched Man
Is black with—Man's Forgiveness give—and take!

* * * * * * *

LXXXIX.

As under cover of departing Day
Slunk hunger-stricken Ramazán away,
   Once more within the Potter's house alone
I stood, surrounded by the Shapes of Clay.

XC.

And once again there gather'd a scarce heard
Whisper among them; as it were, the stirr'd
   Ashes of some all but extinguisht Tongue,
Which mine ear kindled into living Word.

XCI.

Said one among them—" Surely not in vain,
" My Substance from the common Earth was ta'en,
   " That He who subtly wrought me into Shape
" Should stamp me back to shapeless Earth again?"

XCII.

Another said—" Why, ne'er a peevish Boy
" Would break the Cup from which he drank in Joy;
   " Shall He that of his own free Fancy made
" The Vessel, in an after-rage destroy!"

XCIII.

None answer'd this; but after silence spake
Some Vessel of a more ungainly Make;
   "They sneer at me for leaning all awry;
"What! did the Hand then of the Potter shake?"

XCIV.

Thus with the Dead as with the Living, *What?*
And *Why?* so ready, but the *Wherefor* not,
   One on a sudden peevishly exclaim'd,
"Which is the Potter, pray, and which the Pot?"

XCV.

Said one—"Folks of a surly Master tell,
"And daub his Visage with the Smoke of Hell;
   "They talk of some sharp Trial of us—Pish!
"He's a Good Fellow, and 'twill all be well."

XCVI.

"Well," said another, "Whoso will, let try,
"My Clay with long oblivion is gone dry:
   "But, fill me with the old familiar Juice,
"Methinks I might recover by-and-bye!"

XCVII.

So while the Vessels one by one were speaking,
One spied the little Crescent all were seeking:[25]
   And then they jogg'd each other, "Brother! Brother!
"Now for the Porter's shoulder-knot a-creaking!"

* * * * * * *

XCVIII.

Ah, with the Grape my fading Life provide,
And wash my Body whence the Life has died,
   And lay me, shrouded in the living Leaf,
By some not unfrequented Garden-side.

XCIX.

Whither resorting from the vernal Heat
Shall Old Acquaintance Old Acquaintance greet,
   Under the Branch that leans above the Wall
To shed his Blossom over head and feet.

C.

Then ev'n my buried Ashes such a snare
Of Vintage shall fling up into the Air,
   As not a True-believer passing by
But shall be overtaken unaware.

CI.

Indeed the Idols I have loved so long
Have done my credit in Men's eye much wrong:
   Have drown'd my Glory in a shallow Cup,
And sold my Reputation for a Song.

CII.

Indeed, indeed, Repentance oft before
I swore—but was I sober when I swore?
   And then and then came Spring, and Rose-in-hand
My thread-bare Penitence apieces tore.

CIII.

And much as Wine has play'd the Infidel,
And robb'd me of my Robe of Honour—Well,
   I often wonder what the Vintners buy
One half so precious as the ware they sell.

CIV.

Yet Ah, that Spring should vanish with the Rose!
That Youth's sweet-scented manuscript should close!
   The Nightingale that in the branches sang,
Ah whence, and whither flown again, who knows!

CV.

Would but the Desert of the Fountain yield
One glimpse—if dimly, yet indeed reveal'd,
   Toward which the fainting Traveller might spring,
As springs the trampled herbage of the field!

CVI.

Oh if the World were but to re-create,
That we might catch ere closed the Book of Fate,
   And make The Writer on a fairer leaf
Inscribe our names, or quite obliterate!

CVII.

Better, oh better, cancel from the Scroll
Of Universe one luckless Human Soul,
   Than drop by drop enlarge the Flood that rolls
Hoarser with Anguish as the Ages roll.

CVIII.

Ah Love! could you and I with Fate conspire
To grasp this sorry Scheme of Things entire,
   Would not we shatter it to bits—and then
Re-mould it nearer to the Heart's Desire!

CIX.

But see! The rising Moon of Heav'n again
Looks for us, Sweet-heart, through the quivering Plane:
   How oft hereafter rising will she look
Among those leaves—for one of us in vain!

CX.

And when Yourself with silver Foot shall pass
Among the Guests Star-scatter'd on the Grass,
   And in your joyous errand reach the spot
Where I made One—turn down an empty Glass!

TAMÁM.

NOTES.

[1] The "*False Dawn;*" *Subhi Kázib*, a transient Light on the Horizon about an hour before the *Subhi sádik*, or True Dawn; a well-known Phenomenon in the East.

[2] New Year. Beginning with the Vernal Equinox, it must be remembered; and (howsoever the old Solar Year is practically superseded by the clumsy *Lunar* Year that dates from the Mohammedan Hijra) still commemorated by a Festival that is said to have been appointed by the very Jamshyd whom Omar so often talks of, and whose yearly Calendar he helped to rectify.

"The sudden approach and rapid advance of the Spring," says Mr Binning, "are very striking. Before the Snow is well off the Ground, the Trees burst into Blossom, and the Flowers start from the Soil. At *Naw Rooz* (*their* New Year's Day) the Snow was lying in patches on the Hills and in the shaded Vallies, while the Fruit-trees in the Garden were budding beautifully, and green Plants and Flowers springing upon the Plains on every side—

'And on old Hyems' Chin and icy Crown
'An odorous Chaplet of sweet Summer buds
'Is, as in mockery, set—'—

Among the Plants newly appear'd I recognized some old Acquaintances I had not seen for many a Year : among these, two varieties of the Thistle; a coarse species of the Daisy, like the Horse-gowan; red and white Clover; the Dock; the blue Corn-flower; and that vulgar Herb the Dandelion rearing its yellow crest on the Banks of the Watercourses." The Nightingale was not yet heard, for the Rose was not yet blown : but an almost identical Blackbird and Woodpecker helped to make up something of a North-country Spring.

[3] Exodus iv. 6; where Moses draws forth his Hand—not, according to the Persians, "*leprous as Snow,*"—but *white,* as our May-Blossom in Spring perhaps. According to them also the Healing Power of Jesus resided in his Breath.

[4] Iram, planted by King Shaddád, and now sunk somewhere in the Sands of Arabia. Jamshyd's Seven-ring'd Cup was typical of the 7 Heavens, 7 Planets, 7 Seas, &c., and was a *Divining Cup*.

[5] *Péhlevi,* the old Heroic *Sanskrit* of Persia. Háfiz also speaks of the Nightingale's *Péhlevi,* which did not change with the People's.

[6] I am not sure if this refers to the Red Rose looking sickly, or the Yellow Rose that ought to be Red; Red, White, and Yellow Roses all common in Persia. I think Southey, in his Common-Place Book, quotes from some Spanish author about a Rose being White till 10 o'clock; "Rosa perfecta" at 2; and "perfecta incarnada" at 5.

[7] Rustum, the "Hercules" of Persia, whose exploits are among the most celebrated in the Sháh-náma. Hátim Tai, a well-known Type of Oriental Generosity.

⁸ A Drum—beaten outside a Palace.

⁹ That is, the Rose's Golden Centre.

¹⁰ Persepolis: call'd also *Takht'i Jamshyd*—THE THRONE OF JAMSHYD, "*King-Splendid*," of the mythical *Peeshdádian* Dynasty, and supposed (according to the Sháh-náma) to have been founded and built by him. Others refer it to the Work of the Genie King, Ján Ibn Ján—who also built the Pyramids—before the time of Adam.

BAHRÁM GÚR—*Bahrám of the Wild Ass*—a Sassanian Sovereign—had also his Seven Castles (like the King of Bohemia!) each of a different Colour; each with a Royal Mistress within; each of whom tells him a Story, as told in one of the most famous Poems of Persia, written by Amír Khusraw: all these Sevens also figuring (according to Eastern Mysticism) the Seven Heavens, and perhaps the Book itself that Eighth, into which the mystical Seven transcend, and within which they revolve. The Ruins of Three of these Towers are yet shown by the Peasantry; as also the Swamp in which Bahrám sunk, like the Master of Ravenswood, while pursuing his *Gúr*.

¹¹ This Quatrain Mr Binning found, among several of Háfiz and others, inscribed by some stray hand among the ruins of Persepolis. The Ringdove's ancient *Péhlevi, Coo, Coo, Coo*, signifies also in Persian *"Where? Where? Where?"* In Attár's "Bird-parliament" she is reproved by the Leader of the Birds for sitting still, and for ever harping on that one note of lamentation for her lost Yúsuf.

¹² A thousand years to each Planet.

¹³ Saturn, Lord of the Seventh Heaven.

[14] Me-and-Thee: some dividual Existence or Personality distinct from the Whole.

[15] The custom of throwing a little Wine on the ground before drinking still continues in Persia, and perhaps generally in the East. Mons. Nicolas considers it "un signe de liberalité, et en même temps un avertissement que le buveur doit vider sa coupe jusqu' à la dernière goutte." Is it not more likely an ancient Superstition; a Libation to propitiate Earth, or make her an Accomplice in the illicit Revel? Or, perhaps, to divert the Jealous Eye by some sacrifice of superfluity, as with the Ancients of the West? With Omar we see something more is signified; the precious Liquor is not lost, but sinks into the ground to refresh the dust of some poor Wine-worshipper foregone.

Thus Háfiz, copying Omar in so many ways: "When thou drinkest Wine pour a draught on the ground. Wherefore fear the Sin which brings to another Gain?"

[16] According to one beautiful Oriental Legend, Azräel accomplishes his mission by holding to the nostril an Apple from the Tree of Life.

[17] The Caravans travelling by night, after the Vernal Equinox—their New Year's Day. This was ordered by Mohammed himself, I believe.

[18] From Máh to Máhi; from Fish to Moon.

[19] A Jest, of course, at his Studies. A curious mathematical Quatrain of Omar's has been pointed out to me; the more curious because almost exactly parallel'd by some Verses of Doctor Donne's, and quoted in Izaak Walton's Lives! Here is Omar: "You and I are the image of a pair of compasses; though we have two heads (sc. our

feet) we have one body; when we have fixed the centre for our circle, we bring our heads (sc. feet) together at the end." Dr Donne:

> If we be two, we two are so
> > As stiff twin-compasses are two;
> Thy Soul, the fixt foot, makes no show
> > To move, but does if the other do.
>
> And though thine in the centre sit,
> > Yet when my other far does roam,
> Thine leans and hearkens after it,
> > And grows erect as mine comes home.
>
> Such thou must be to me, who must
> > Like the other foot obliquely run;
> Thy firmness makes my circle just,
> > And me to end where I begun.

[20] The Seventy-two Religions supposed to divide the World: *including* Islamism, as some think: but others not.

[21] Alluding to Sultan Mahmúd's Conquest of India and its dark people.

[22] *Fánúsi khiyál*, a Magic-lanthorn still used in India; the cylindrical Interior being painted with various Figures, and so lightly poised and ventilated as to revolve round the lighted Candle within.

[23] A very mysterious Line in the Original:

> O dánad O dánad O dánad O ——

breaking off something like our Wood-pigeon's Note, which she is said to take up just where she left off.

[24] Parwín and Mushtari—The Pleiads and Jupiter.

[25] At the Close of the Fasting Month, Ramazán (which

makes the Musulman unhealthy and unamiable), the first Glimpse of the New Moon (who rules their Division of the Year), is looked for with the utmost Anxiety, and hailed with Acclamation. Then it is that the Porter's Knot may be heard—toward the *Cellar,* perhaps. Omar has elsewhere a pretty Quatrain about this same Moon—

> " Be of Good Cheer—the sullen Month will die,
> " And a young Moon requite us by and bye :
>   " Look how the Old one meagre, bent, and wan
> " With Age and Fast, is fainting from the Sky ! "

FINIS.

RUBÁIYÁT

OF

OMAR KHAYYÁM,

THE ASTRONOMER-POET OF PERSIA.

Rendered into English Verse.

THIRD EDITION.

LONDON:
BERNARD QUARITCH,
PICCADILLY.
1872.

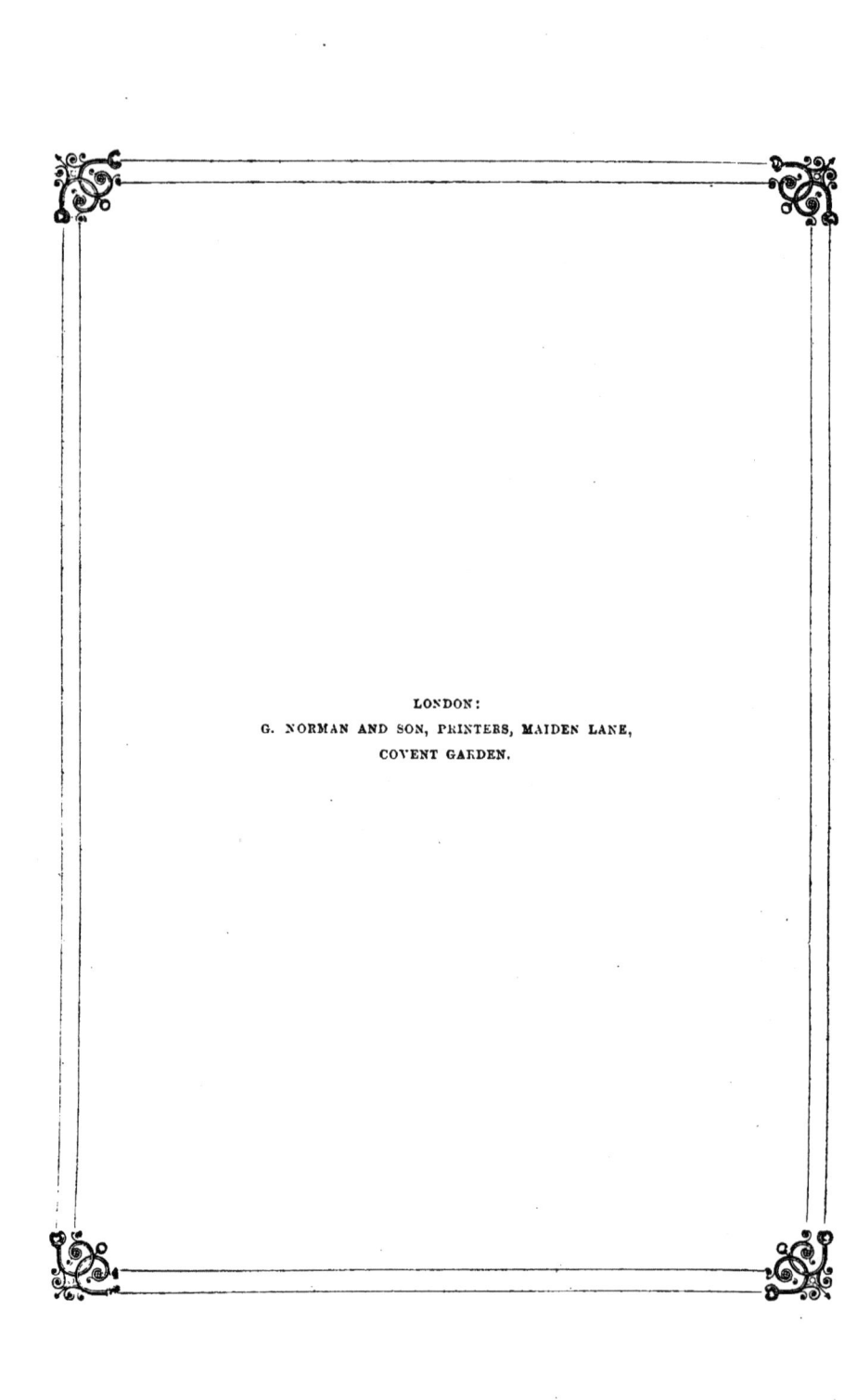

LONDON:
G. NORMAN AND SON, PRINTERS, MAIDEN LANE,
COVENT GARDEN.

OMAR KHAYYÁM,

THE

ASTRONOMER-POET OF PERSIA.

OMAR KHAYYÁM was born at Naishápúr in Khorasan in the latter half of our Eleventh, and died within the First Quarter of our Twelfth Century. The slender Story of his Life is curiously twined about that of two other very considerable Figures in their Time and Country: one of whom tells the Story of all Three. This was Nizám ul Mulk, Vizyr to Alp Arslan the Son, and Malik Shah the Grandson, of Toghrul Beg the Tartar, who had wrested Persia from the feeble Successor of Mahmúd the Great, and founded that Seljukian Dynasty which finally roused Europe into the Crusades. This Nizám ul Mulk, in his *Wasiyat*—or *Testament*—which he wrote and left as a Memorial for future Statesmen—relates the following, as quoted in the Calcutta Review, No. 59, from Mirkhond's History of the Assassins.

"'One of the greatest of the wise men of Khorassan 'was the Imám Mowaffak of Naishápúr, a man highly 'honoured and reverenced,—may God rejoice his soul; 'his illustrious years exceeded eighty-five, and it was 'the universal belief that every boy who read the Koran 'or studied the traditions in his presence, would as- 'suredly attain to honour and happiness. For this 'cause did my father send me from Tús to Naishápúr 'with Abd-us-samad, the doctor of law, that I might 'employ myself in study and learning under the guid- 'ance of that illustrious teacher. Towards me he ever 'turned an eye of favour and kindness, and as his pupil 'I felt for him extreme affection and devotion, so that 'I passed four years in his service. When I first came 'there, I found two other pupils of mine own age newly 'arrived, Hakim Omar Khayyám, and the ill-fated Ben 'Sabbáh. Both were endowed with sharpness of wit 'and the highest natural powers; and we three formed

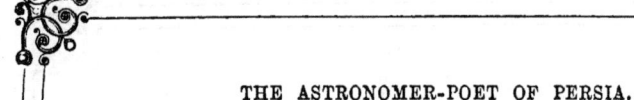

'a close friendship together. When the Imám rose
'from his lectures, they used to join me, and we re-
'peated to each other the lessons we had heard. Now
'Omar was a native of Naishápúr, while Hasan Ben
'Sabbáh's father was one Ali, a man of austere life and
'practice, but heretical in his creed and doctrine. One
'day Hasan said to me and to Khayyám, 'It is a uni-
'versal belief that the pupils of the Imám Mowaffak
'will attain to fortune. Now, even if we *all* do not
'attain thereto, without doubt one of us will; what then
'shall be our mutual pledge and bond?' We answered
'Be it what you please.' 'Well,' he said, 'let us make
'a vow, that to whomsoever this fortune falls, he shall
'share it equally with the rest, and reserve no pre-
'eminence for himself.' 'Be it so,' we both replied, and
'on those terms we mutually pledged our words. Years
'rolled on, and I went from Khorassan to Transoxiana,
'and wandered to Ghazni and Cabul; and when I
'returned, I was invested with office, and rose to be
'administrator of affairs during the Sultanate of Sultan
'Alp Arslán.'

"He goes on to state, that years passed by, and both his old school-friends found him out, and came and claimed a share in his good fortune, according to the school-day vow. The Vizier was generous and kept his word. Hasan demanded a place in the government, which the Sultan granted at the Vizier's request; but discontented with a gradual rise, he plunged into the maze of intrigue of an oriental court, and, failing in a base attempt to supplant his benefactor, he was disgraced and fell. After many mishaps and wanderings, Hasan became the head of the Persian sect of the *Ismailians*,—a party of fanatics who had long murmured in obscurity, but rose to an evil eminence under the guidance of his strong and evil will. In A.D. 1090, he seized the castle of Alamút, in the province of Rúdbar, which lies in the mountainous tract, south of the Caspian Sea; and it was from this mountain home he obtained that evil celebrity among the Crusaders as the OLD MAN OF THE MOUNTAINS, and spread terror through the Mohammedan world; and it is yet disputed whether the word *Assassin*, which they have left in the language of modern Europe as their dark memorial, is derived from the *hashish*, or opiate of hemp-leaves (the Indian *bhang*), with which they maddened themselves to the sullen pitch of oriental desperation, or from the name of the founder of the dynasty, whom we have seen in his quiet collegiate days, at Naishápúr. One of the countless victims of the Assassin's dagger was Nizám-ul-mulk himself, the old school-boy friend.[1]

"Omar Khayyám also came to the Vizier to claim the share; but not to ask for title or office. 'The greatest 'boon you can confer on me,' he said, 'is to let me live 'in a corner under the shadow of your fortune, to spread 'wide the advantages of Science, and pray for your 'long life and prosperity.' The Vizier tells us, that, when he found Omar was really sincere in his refusal, he pressed him no further, but granted him a yearly

[1] Some of Omar's Rubáiyát warn us of the danger of Greatness, the instability of Fortune, and while advocating Charity to all Men, recommending us to be too intimate with none. Attár makes Nizám-ul-mulk use the very words of his friend Omar [Rub. xxviii.], "When Nizám-ul-Mulk was in the Agony (of Death) he said, 'Oh God! I am passing away in the hand of the Wind.'"

pension of 1200 *mithkáls* of gold, from the treasury of Naishápúr.

"'At Naishápúr thus lived and died Omar Khayyám, 'busied,' adds the Vizier, 'in winning knowledge of 'every kind, and especially in Astronomy, wherein he 'attained to a very high pre-eminence. Under the Sul- 'tanate of Malik Shah, he came to Merv, and obtained 'great praise for his proficiency in science, and the 'Sultan showered favours upon him.'

"When Malik Shah determined to reform the calendar, Omar was one of the eight learned men employed to do it; the result was the *Jaláli* era (so called from *Jalal-u-din*, one of the king's names)—'a computation of time,' says Gibbon, 'which surpasses the Julian, and approaches the accuracy of the Gregorian style.' He is also the author of some astronomical tables, entitled Zíji-Maliksháhí," and the French have lately republished and translated an Arabic Treatise of his on Algebra.

"His Takhallus or poetical name (Khayyám) signifies a Tent-maker, and he is said to have at one time exercised that trade, perhaps before Nizám-ul-Mulk's generosity raised him to independence. Many Persian poets similarly derive their names from their occupations; thus we have Attár, 'a druggist,' Assár, 'an oil presser,' &c.[1] Omar himself alludes to his name in the following whimsical lines:—

> 'Khayyám, who stitched the tents of science,
> Has fallen in grief's furnace and been suddenly burned;
> The shears of Fate have cut the tent ropes of his life,
> And the broker of Hope has sold him for nothing!'

"We have only one more anecdote to give of his Life, and that relates to the close; it is told in the anonymous preface which is sometimes prefixed to his poems; it has been printed in the Persian in the appendix to Hyde's *Veterum Persarum Religio*, p. 499; and D'Herbelot alludes to it in his Bibliothèque, under *Khiam*:[2]—

"'It is written in the chronicles of the ancients that 'this King of the Wise, Omar Khayyám, died at

---

[1] Though all these, like our Smiths, Archers, Millers, Fletchers, &c., may simply retain the Surname of an hereditary calling.

[2] "Philosophe Musulman qui a vécu en Odeur de Sainteté dans la Fin du premier et le Commencement du second Siècle," no part of which, except the "Philosophe," can apply to *our* Khayyám.

'Naishápúr in the year of the Hegira, 517 (A.D. 1123);
'in science he was unrivalled,—the very paragon of his
'age. Khwájah Nizámi of Samarcand, who was one
'of his pupils, relates the following story: 'I often
'used to hold conversations with my teacher, Omar
'Khayyám, in a garden; and one day he said to me,
'"My tomb shall be in a spot where the north wind may
'scatter roses over it.' I wondered at the words he spake,
'but I knew that his were no idle words.[1] Years after,

---

[1] The Rashness of the Words, according to D'Herbelot, consisted in being so opposed to those in the Korán: "No Man knows where he shall die."—This story of Omar reminds me of another so naturally—and, when one remembers how wide of his humble mark the noble sailor aimed—so pathetically told by Captain Cook—not by Doctor Hawkesworth—in his Second Voyage. When leaving Ulietea, "Oreo's last request was for me to return. When he saw he could not obtain that promise, he asked me the name of my *Marai*—Burying place. As strange a question as this was, I hesitated not a moment, to tell him 'Stepney,' the parish in which I live when in London. I was made to repeat it several times over till they could pronounce it; and then 'Stepney Marai no Tootee' was echoed through a hundred mouths at once. I afterwards found the same question had been put to Mr. Forster by a man on shore; but he gave a different and indeed more proper answer, by saying, 'No man who used the sea could say where he should be buried.'"

'when I chanced to revisit Naishápúr, I went to his
'final resting-place, and lo! it was just outside a garden,
'and trees laden with fruit stretched their boughs over
'the garden wall, and dropped their flowers upon his
'tomb, so as the stone was hidden under them.'"

Thus far—without fear of Trespass—from the Calcutta Review. The writer of it, on reading in India this story of Omar's Grave, was reminded, he says, of Cicero's Account of finding Archimedes' Tomb at Syracuse, buried in grass and weeds. I think Thorwaldsen desired to have roses grow over him; a wish religiously fulfilled for him to the present day, I believe. However, to return to Omar.

Though the Sultan "shower'd Favours upon him," Omar's Epicurean Audacity of Thought and Speech caused him to be regarded askance in his own Time and Country. He is said to have been especially hated and dreaded by the Súfis, whose Practice he ridiculed, and whose Faith amounts to little more than his own when stript of the Mysticism and formal recognition of Islamism under which Omar would not hide. Their

Poets, including Háfiz, who are (with the exception of Firdausi) the most considerable in Persia, borrowed largely, indeed, of Omar's material, but turning it to a mystical Use more convenient to Themselves and the People they addressed; a People quite as quick of Doubt as of Belief; as keen of Bodily Sense as of Intellectual; and delighting in a cloudy composition of both, in which they could float luxuriously between Heaven and Earth, and this World and the Next, on the wings of a poetical expression, that might serve indifferently for either. Omar was too honest of Heart as well as of Head for this. Having failed (however mistakenly) of finding any Providence but Destiny, and any World but This, he set about making the most of it; preferring rather to soothe the Soul through the Senses into Acquiescence with Things as he saw them, than to perplex it with vain disquietude after what they *might be*. It has been seen, however, that his Worldly Ambition was not exorbitant; and he very likely takes a humorous or perverse pleasure in exalting the gratification of Sense above that of the Intellect, in which he must have taken great delight, although it failed to answer the Questions in which he, in common with all men, was most vitally interested.

For whatever Reason, however, Omar, as before said, has never been popular in his own Country, and therefore has been but scantily transmitted abroad. The MSS. of his Poems, mutilated beyond the average Casualties of Oriental Transcription, are so rare in the East as scarce to have reacht Westward at all, in spite of all the acquisitions of Arms and Science. There is no copy at the India House, none at the Bibliothèque Imperiále of Paris. We know but of one in England: No. 140 of the Ouseley MSS. at the Bodleian, written at Shiraz, A.D. 1460. This contains but 158 Rubáiyát. One in the Asiatic Society's Library at Calcutta (of which we have a Copy), contains (and yet imcomplete) 516, though swelled to that by all kinds of Repetition and Corruption. So Von Hammer speaks of *his* Copy as containing about 200, while Dr. Sprenger catalogues the Lucknow MS. at double that Number.[1] The Scribes,

[1] " Since this Paper was written (adds the Reviewer in a note),

too, of the Oxford and Calcutta MSS. seem to do their Work under a sort of Protest; each beginning with a Tetrastich (whether genuine or not), taken out of its alphabetical order; the Oxford with one of Apology; the Calcutta with one of Expostulation, supposed (says a Notice prefixed to the MS.) to have risen from a Dream, in which Omar's mother asked about his future fate. It may be rendered thus:—

> " Oh Thou who burn'st in Heart for those who burn
> " In Hell, whose fires thyself shall feed in turn ;
> " How long be crying, ' Mercy on them, God !'
> " Why, who art Thou to teach, and He to learn ?"

The Bodleian Quatrain pleads Pantheism by way of Justification.

> "If I myself upon a looser Creed
> " Have loosely strung the Jewel of Good deed,
> " Let this one thing for my Atonement plead :
> " That One for Two I never did mis-read."

The Reviewer, to whom I owe the Particulars of Omar's Life, concludes his Review by comparing him

" we have met with a Copy of a very rare Edition, printed at Calcutta in 1836. This contains 438 Tetrastichs, with an Appendix containing 54 others not found in some MSS."

with Lucretius, both as to natural Temper and Genius, and as acted upon by the Circumstances in which he lived. Both indeed were men of subtle, strong, and cultivated Intellect, fine Imagination, and Hearts passionate for Truth and Justice; who justly revolted from their Country's false Religion, and false, or foolish, Devotion to it; but who yet fell short of replacing what they subverted by such better *Hope* as others, with no better Revelation to guide them, had yet made a Law to themselves. Lucretius, indeed, with such material as Epicurus furnished, satisfied himself with the theory of so vast a machine fortuitously constructed, and acting by a Law that implied no Legislator; and so composing himself into a Stoical rather than Epicurean severity of Attitude, sat down to contemplate the mechanical Drama of the Universe which he was part Actor in; himself and all about him (as in his own sublime description of the Roman Theatre) discoloured with the lurid reflex of the Curtain suspended between the Spectator and the Sun. Omar, more desperate, or more careless of any so complicated System as resulted in nothing but hopeless Necessity, flung his own Genius and Learning with a bitter or humorous jest into the general Ruin which their insufficient glimpses only served to reveal; and, pretending sensual pleasure as the serious purpose of Life, only *diverted* himself with speculative problems of Deity, Destiny, Matter and Spirit, Good and Evil, and other such questions, easier to start than to run down, and the pursuit of which becomes a very weary sport at last!

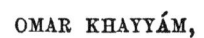

With regard to the present Translation. The original Rubáiyát (as, missing an Arabic Guttural, these *Tetrastichs* are more musically called) are independent Stanzas, consisting each of four Lines of equal, though varied, Prosody; sometimes *all* rhyming, but oftener (as here imitated) the third line a blank. Something as in the Greek Alcaic, where the penultimate line seems to lift and suspend the Wave that falls over in the last. As usual with such kind of Oriental Verse, the Rubáiyát follow one another according to Alphabetic Rhyme—a strange succession of Grave and Gay.

Those here selected are strung into something of an Eclogue, with perhaps a less than equal proportion of the "Drink and make-merry," which (genuine or not) recurs over-frequently in the Original. Either way, the Result is sad enough: saddest perhaps when most ostentatiously merry: more apt to move Sorrow than Anger toward the old Tentmaker, who, after vainly endeavouring to unshackle his Steps from Destiny, and to catch some authentic Glimpse of TOMORROW, fell back upon TODAY (which has out-lasted so many Tomorrows!) as the only Ground he got to stand upon, however momentarily slipping from under his Feet.

While the second Edition of this version of Omar was preparing, Monsieur Nicolas, French Consul at Resht, published a very careful and very good Edition of the Text, from a lithograph copy at Teheran, comprising 464 Rubáiyát, with translation and notes of his own.

Mons. Nicolas, whose Edition has reminded me of

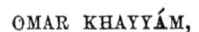

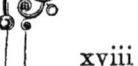

several things, and instructed me in others, does not consider Omar to be the material Epicurean that I have literally taken him for, but a Mystic, shadowing the Deity under the figure of Wine, Wine-bearer, &c., as Háfiz is supposed to do; in short, a Súfi Poet like Háfiz and the rest.

I cannot see reason to alter my opinion, formed as it was more than a dozen years ago when Omar was first shown me by one to whom I am indebted for all I know of Oriental, and very much of other, literature. He admired Omar's Genius so much, that he would gladly have adopted any such Interpretation of his meaning as Mons. Nicolas' if he could.[1] That he could not, appears by his Paper in the Calcutta Review already so largely quoted; in which he argues from the Poems themselves, as well as from what records remain of the Poet's Life.

And if more were needed to disprove Mons. Nicolas'

---

[1] Perhaps would have edited the Poems himself some years ago. He may now as little approve of my Version on one side, as of Mons. Nicolas' Theory on the other.

Theory, there is the Biographical Notice which he himself has drawn up in direct contradiction to the Interpretation of the Poems given in his Notes. (See pp. 13-14 of his Preface.) Indeed I hardly knew poor Omar was so far gone till his Apologist informed me. For here we see that, whatever were the Wine that Háfiz drank and sang, the veritable Juice of the Grape it was which Omar used, not only when carousing with his friends, but (says Mons. Nicolas) in order to excite himself to that pitch of Devotion which others reached by cries and "hurlemens." And yet, whenever Wine, Wine-bearer, &c. occur in the Text—which is often enough—Mons. Nicolas carefully annotates "Dieu," "La Divinité," &c.: so carefully indeed that one is tempted to think that he was indoctrinated by the Súfi with whom he read the Poems. (Note to Rub. ii. p. 8.) A Persian would naturally wish to vindicate a distinguished Countryman; and a Súfi to enrol him in his own sect, which already comprises all the chief Poets of Persia.

What historical Authority has Mons. Nicolas to show

that Omar gave himself up "avec passion à l'étude de la philosophie des Soufis"? (Preface, p. xiii.) The Doctrines of Pantheism, Materialism, Necessity, &c., were not peculiar to the Súfi; nor to Lucretius before them; nor to Epicurus before him; probably the very original Irreligion of Thinking men from the first; and very likely to be the spontaneous growth of a Philosopher living in an Age of social and political barbarism, under shadow of one of the Two and Seventy Religions supposed to divide the world. Von Hammer (according to Sprenger's Oriental Catalogue) speaks of Omar as "a Free-thinker, and *a great opponent of Sufism;*" perhaps because, while holding much of their Doctrine, he would not pretend to any inconsistent severity of morals. Sir W. Ouseley has written a note to something of the same effect on the fly-leaf of the Bodleian MS. And in two Rubáiyát of Mons. Nicolas' own Edition Súf and Súfi are both disparagingly named.

No doubt many of these Quatrains seem unaccountable unless mystically interpreted; but many more as unaccountable unless literally. Were the Wine spiritual, for instance, how wash the Body with it when dead? Why make cups of the dead clay to be filled with—"La Divinité"—by some succeeding Mystic? Mons. Nicolas himself is puzzled by some "bizarres" and "trop Orientales" allusions and images—"d'une sensualité quelquefois révoltante" indeed—which "les convenances" do not permit him to translate; but still which the reader cannot but refer to "La Divinité."[1] No doubt also many of the Quatrains in the Teheran, as in the Calcutta, Copies, are spurious; such *Rubáiyát* being the common form of Epigram in Persia. But this, at best, tells as much one way as another; nay, the

[1] A Note to Quatrain 234 admits that, however clear the mystical meaning of such Images must be to Europeans, they are not quoted without "rougissant" even by laymen in Persia—" Quant aux termes de tendresse qui commencent ce quatrain, comme tant d'autres dans ce recueil, nos lecteurs, habitués maintenant á l'étrangeté des expressions si souvent employés par Khéyam pour rendre ses pensées sur l'amour divin, et à la singularité des images trop orientales, d'une sensualité quelquefois révoltante, n'auront pas de peine à se persuader qu'il s'agit de la Divinité, bien que cette conviction soit vivement discutée par les moullahs musulmans, et même par beaucoup de laïques, qui rougissent véritablement d'une pareille licence de leur compatriote à l'égard des choses spirituelles."

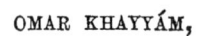

Súfi, who may be considered the Scholar and Man of Letters in Persia, would be far more likely than the careless Epicure to interpolate what favours his own view of the Poet. I observe that very few of the more mystical Quatrains are in the Bodleian MS. which must be one of the oldest, as dated at Shiraz, A.H. 865, A.D. 1460. And this, I think, especially distinguishes Omar (I cannot help calling him by his—no, not Christian—familiar name) from all other Persian Poets: That, whereas with them the Poet is lost in his Song, the Man in Allegory and Abstraction; we seem to have the Man—the *Bonhomme*—Omar himself, with all his Humours and Passions, as frankly before us as if we were really at Table with him, after the Wine had gone round.

I must say that I, for one, never wholly believed in the Mysticism of Háfiz. It does not appear there was any danger in holding and singing Súfi Pantheism, so long as the Poet made his Salaam to Mohammed at the beginning and end of his Song. Under such conditions Jeláluddín, Jámi, Attár, and others sang; using Wine and Beauty indeed as Images to illustrate, not as a Mask to hide, the Divinity they were celebrating. Perhaps some Allegory less liable to mistake or abuse had been better among so inflammable a People: much more so when, as some think with Háfiz and Omar, the abstract is not only likened to, but identified with, the sensual Image; hazardous, if not to the Devotee himself, yet to his weaker Brethren; and worse for the Profane in proportion as the Devotion of the Initiated grew warmer. And all for what? To be tantalized with Images of sensual enjoyment which must be renounced if one would approximate a God, who according to the Doctrine, *is* Sensual Matter as well as Spirit, and into whose Universe one expects unconsciously to merge after Death, without hope of any posthumous Beatitude in another world to compensate for all one's self-denial in this. Lucretius' blind Divinity certainly merited, and probably got, as much self-sacrifice as this of the Súfi; and the burden of Omar's Song—if not "Let us eat"—is assuredly—"Let us drink, for Tomorrow we die!" And if Háfiz meant quite otherwise by a similar language, he surely miscalculated when he devoted his Life and Genius to so equivocal a Psalmody as, from his Day to this, has been said and sung by any rather than spiritual Worshippers.

However, as there is some traditional presumption, and certainly the opinion of some learned men, in favour of Omar's being a Súfí—and even something of a Saint—those who please may so interpret his Wine and Cup-bearer. On the other hand, as there is far more historical certainty of his being a Philosopher, of scientific Insight and Ability far beyond that of the Age and Country he lived in; of such moderate worldly Ambition as becomes a Philosopher, and such moderate wants as rarely satisfy a Debauchee; other readers may be content to believe with me that, while the Wine Omar celebrates is simply the Juice of the Grape, he bragg'd more than he drank of it, in very defiance perhaps of that Spiritual Wine which left its Votaries sunk in Hypocrisy or Disgust.

RUBÁIYÁT

OF

OMAR KHAYYÁM OF NAISHAPUR.

I.

WAKE! For the Sun who scatter'd into flight
The Stars before him from the Field of Night,
   Drives Night along with them from Heav'n, and
      strikes
The Sultán's Turret with a Shaft of Light.

II.

Before the phantom of False morning died,[1]
Methought a Voice within the Tavern cried,
   "When all the Temple is prepared within,
"Why nods the drowsy Worshipper outside?"

III.

And, as the Cock crew, those who stood before
The Tavern shouted—" Open then the door !
" You know how little while we have to stay,
" And, once departed, may return no more."

IV.

Now the New Year reviving old Desires,[2]
The thoughtful Soul to Solitude retires,
  Where the WHITE HAND OF MOSES on the Bough
Puts out, and Jesus from the Ground suspires.[3]

V.

Iram indeed is gone with all his Rose,[4]
And Jamshyd's Sev'n-ring'd Cup where no one knows;
  But still a Ruby gushes from the Vine,
And many a Garden by the Water blows.

VI.

And David's lips are lockt; but in divine[5]
High-piping Péhlevi, with " Wine ! Wine ! Wine !
  " Red Wine !"—the Nightingale cries to the Rose
That sallow cheek[6] of her's to'incarnadine.

VII.

Come, fill the Cup, and in the fire of Spring
Your Winter-garment of Repentance fling:
　　The Bird of Time has but a little way
To flutter—and the Bird is on the Wing.

VIII.

Whether at Naishápúr or Babylon,
Whether the Cup with sweet or bitter run,
　　The Wine of Life keeps oozing drop by drop,
The Leaves of Life keep falling one by one.

IX.

Each Morn a thousand Roses brings, you say;
Yes, but where leaves the Rose of Yesterday?
　　And this first Summer month that brings the Rose
Shall take Jamshyd and Kaikobád away.

X.

Well, let it take them! What have we to do
With Kaikobád the Great, or Kaikhosrú?
　　Let Zál and Rustum thunder as they will,[7]
Or Hátim call to Supper—heed not you.

XI.

With me along the strip of Herbage strown
That just divides the desert from the sown,
   Where name of Slave and Sultán is forgot—
And Peace to Máhmúd on his golden Throne!

XII.

A Book of Verses underneath the Bough,
A Jug of Wine, a Loaf of Bread—and Thou
   Beside me singing in the Wilderness—
Oh, Wilderness were Paradise enow!

XIII.

Some for the Glories of This World; and some
Sigh for the Prophet's Paradise to come;
   Ah, take the Cash, and let the Credit go,
Nor heed the rumble of a distant Drum![8]

XIV.

Look to the blowing Rose about us—Lo,
"Laughing," she says, "into the world I blow,
   " At once the silken tassel of my Purse
"Tear, and its Treasure on the Garden throw."[9]

XV.

And those who husbanded the Golden grain,
And those who flung it to the winds like Rain,
 Alike to no such aureate Earth are turn'd
As, buried once, Men want dug up again.

XVI.

The Worldly Hope men set their Hearts upon
Turns Ashes—or it prospers; and anon,
 Like Snow upon the Desert's dusty Face,
Lighting a little hour or two—was gone.

XVII.

Think, in this batter'd Caravanserai
Whose Portals are alternate Night and Day,
 How Sultán after Sultán with his Pomp
Abode his destin'd Hour, and went his way.

XVIII.

They say the Lion and the Lizard keep
The Courts where Jamshyd gloried and drank deep;[10]
 And Bahrám, that great Hunter—the Wild Ass
Stamps o'er his Head, but cannot break his Sleep.

XIX.

I sometimes think that never blows so red
The Rose as where some buried Cæsar bled;
  That every Hyacinth the Garden wears
Dropt in her Lap from some once lovely Head.

XX.

And this reviving Herb whose tender Green
Fledges the River-Lip on which we lean—
  Ah, lean upon it lightly! for who knows
From what once lovely Lip it springs unseen!

XXI.

Ah, my Belovéd, fill the Cup that clears
To-day of past Regret and future Fears:
  To-morrow!—Why, To-morrow I may be
Myself with Yesterday's Sev'n thousand Years.[11]

XXII.

For some we loved, the loveliest and the best
That from his Vintage rolling Time has prest,
  Have drunk their Cup a Round or two before,
And one by one crept silently to rest.

XXIII.

And we, that now make merry in the Room
They left, and Summer dresses in new bloom,
   Ourselves must we beneath the Couch of Earth
Descend—ourselves to make a Couch—for whom?

XXIV.

Ah, make the most of what we yet may spend,
Before we too into the Dust descend;
   Dust into Dust, and under Dust, to lie,
Sans Wine, sans Song, sans Singer, and—sans End!

XXV.

Alike for those who for To-day prepare,
And those that after some To-morrow stare,
   A Muezzín from the Tower of Darkness cries,
"Fools! your Reward is neither Here nor There."

XXVI.

Why, all the Saints and Sages who discuss'd
Of the Two Worlds so learnedly are thrust
   Like foolish Prophets forth; their Words to Scorn
Are scatter'd, and their Mouths are stopt with Dust.

XXVII.

Myself when young did eagerly frequent
Doctor and Saint, and heard great argument
   About it and about: but evermore
Came out by the same door where in I went.

XXVIII.

With them the seed of Wisdom did I sow,
And with my own hand wrought to make it grow;
   And this was all the Harvest that I reap'd—
"I came like Water, and like Wind I go."

XXIX.

Into this Universe, and *Why* not knowing,
Nor *Whence*, like Water willy-nilly flowing;
   And out of it, as Wind along the Waste,
I know not *Whither*, willy-nilly blowing.

XXX.

What, without asking, hither hurried *Whence?*
And, without asking, *Whither* hurried hence!
   Oh, many a Cup of this forbidden Wine
Must drown the memory of that insolence!

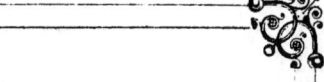

XXXI.

Up from Earth's Centre through the Seventh Gate
I rose, and on the Throne of Saturn sate,[12]
    And many a Knot unravel'd by the Road;
But not the Master-knot of Human Fate.

XXXII.

There was the Door to which I found no Key;
There was the Veil through which I could not see:
    Some little talk awhile of ME and THEE
There was—and then no more of THEE and ME.[13]

XXXIII.

Earth could not answer; nor the Seas that mourn
In flowing Purple, of their Lord forlorn;
    Nor rolling Heaven, with all his Signs reveal'd
And hidden by the sleeve of Night and Morn.

XXXIV.

Then of the THEE IN ME who works behind
The Veil, I lifted up my hands to find
    A Lamp amid the Darkness; and I heard,
As from Without—"THE ME WITHIN THEE BLIND!"

XXXV.

Then to the Lip of this poor earthen Urn
I lean'd, the Secret of my Life to learn :
   And Lip to Lip it murmur'd—"While you live,
"Drink!—for, once dead, you never shall return."

XXXVI.

I think the Vessel, that with fugitive
Articulation answer'd, once did live,
   And drink ; and Ah! the passive Lip I kiss'd,
How many Kisses might it take—and give!

XXXVII.

For I remember stopping by the way
To watch a Potter thumping his wet Clay,
   And with its all-obliterated Tongue
It murmur'd—"Gently, Brother, gently, pray?"[14]

XXXVIII.

Listen—a moment listen!—Of the same
Poor Earth from which that Human Whisper came
   The luckless Mould in which Mankind was cast
They did compose, and call'd him by the name.

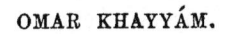

XXXIX.

And not a drop that from our Cups we throw[15]
For Earth to drink of, but may steal below
　　To quench the fire of Anguish in some Eye
There hidden—far beneath, and long ago.

XL.

As then the Tulip for her morning sup
Of Heav'nly Vintage from the soil looks up,
　　Do you devoutly do the like, till Heav'n
To Earth invert you like an empty Cup.

XLI.

Perplext no more with Human or Divine,
To-morrow's tangle to the winds resign,
　　And lose your fingers in the tresses of
The Cypress-slender Minister of Wine.

XLII.

And if the Wine you drink, the Lip you press,
End in what All begins and ends in—Yes;
　　Think then you are TO-DAY what YESTERDAY
You were—TO-MORROW you shall not be less.

XLIII.

So when the Angel of the darker Drink
At last shall find you by the river-brink,
   And, offering his Cup, invite your Soul
Forth to your Lips to quaff—you shall not shrink.[16]

XLIV.

Why, if the Soul can fling the Dust aside,
And naked on the Air of Heaven ride,
   Wer't not a Shame—wer't not a Shame for him
In this clay carcase crippled to abide?

XLV.

'Tis but a Tent where takes his one-day's rest
A Sultan to the realm of Death addrest;
   The Sultan rises, and the dark Ferrásh
Strikes, and prepares it for another Guest.

XLVI.

And fear not lest Existence closing your
Account, and mine, should know the like no more;
   The Eternal Sáki from that Bowl has pour'd
Millions of Bubbles like us, and will pour.

XLVII.

When You and I behind the Veil are past,
Oh but the long long while the World shall last,
   Which of our Coming and Departure heeds
As the SEV'N SEAS should heed a pebble-cast.

XLVIII.

A Moment's Halt—a momentary taste
Of BEING from the Well amid the Waste—
   And Lo!—the phantom Caravan has reach'd
The NOTHING it set out from—Oh, make haste!

XLIX.

Would you that spangle of Existence spend
About THE SECRET—quick about it, Friend!
   A Hair perhaps divides the False and True—
And upon what, prithee, does Life depend?

L.

A Hair perhaps divides the False and True;
Yes; and a single Alif were the clue—
   Could you but find it—to the Treasure-house,
And peradventure to THE MASTER too;

LI.

Whose secret Presence, through Creation's veins
Running Quicksilver-like eludes your pains;
   Taking all shapes from Máh to Máhi;[17] and
They change and perish all—but He remains;

LII.

A moment guess'd—then back behind the Fold
Immerst of Darkness round the Drama roll'd
   Which, for the Pastime of Eternity,
He does Himself contrive, enact, behold.

LIII.

But if in vain, down on the stubborn floor
Of Earth, and up to Heav'n's unopening Door,
   You gaze TO-DAY, while You are You—how then
TO-MORROW, You when shall be You no more?

LIV.

Waste not your Hour, nor in the vain pursuit
Of This and That endeavour and dispute;
   Better be jocund with the fruitful Grape
Than sadden after none, or bitter, Fruit.

LV.

You know, my Friends, with what a brave Carouse
I made a Second Marriage in my house;
   Divorced old barren Reason from my Bed,
And took the Daughter of the Vine to Spouse.

LVI.

For " Is" and " Is-not" though with Rule and Line,[18]
And " Up-and-down" by Logic I define
   Of all that one should care to fathom, I
Was never deep in anything but—Wine.

LVII.

Ah, but my Computations, People say,
Reduced the Year to better reckoning?—Nay,
   'Twas only striking from the Calendar
Unborn To-morrow, and dead Yesterday.

LVIII.

And lately, by the Tavern Door agape,
Came shining through the Dusk an Angel Shape
   Bearing a Vessel on his Shoulder; and
He bid me taste of it; and 'twas—the Grape!

LIX.

The Grape that can with Logic absolute
The Two-and-Seventy jarring Sects confute :[19]
   The sovereign Alchemist that in a trice
Life's leaden metal into Gold transmute :

LX.

The mighty Mahmúd, Allah-breathing Lord,
That all the misbelieving and black Horde[20]
   Of Fears and Sorrows that infest the Soul
Scatters before him with his whirlwind Sword.

LXI.

Why, be this Juice the growth of God, who dare
Blaspheme the twisted tendril as a Snare?
   A Blessing, we should use it, should we not?
And if a Curse—why, then, Who set it there?

LXII.

I must abjure the Balm of Life, I must,
Scared by some After-reckoning ta'en on trust,
   Or lured with Hope of some Diviner Drink,
To fill the Cup—when crumbled into Dust!

LXIII.

Oh threats of Hell and Hopes of Paradise!
One thing at least is certain—*This* Life flies;
   One thing is certain and the rest is Lies;
The Flower that once has blown for ever dies.

LXIV.

Strange, is it not? that of the myriads who
Before us pass'd the door of Darkness through
   Not one returns to tell us of the Road,
Which to discover we must travel too.

LXV.

The Revelations of Devout and Learn'd
Who rose before us, and as Prophets burn'd,
   Are all but Stories, which, awoke from Sleep
They told their fellows, and to Sleep return'd.

LXVI.

I sent my Soul through the Invisible,
Some letter of that After-life to spell:
   And by and by my Soul return'd to me,
And answer'd "I Myself am Heav'n and Hell:"

LXVII.

Heav'n but the Vision of fulfill'd Desire,
And Hell the Shadow of a Soul on fire,
   Cast on the Darkness into which Ourselves,
So late emerg'd from, shall so soon expire.

LXVIII.

We are no other than a moving row
Of Magic Shadow-shapes that come and go
   Round with this Sun-illumin'd Lantern held
In Midnight by the Master of the Show;[21]

LXIX.

Impotent Pieces of the Game He plays
Upon this Chequer-board of Nights and Days;
   Hither and thither moves, and checks, and slays,
And one by one back in the Closet lays.

LXX.

The Ball no question makes of Ayes and Noes,
But Right or Left as strikes the Player goes;
   And He that toss'd you down into the Field,
He knows about it all—HE knows—HE knows![22]

LXXI.

The Moving Finger writes; and, having writ,
Moves on: nor all your Piety and Wit
   Shall lure it back to cancel half a Line,
Nor all your Tears wash out a Word of it.

LXXII.

And that inverted Bowl they call the Sky,
Whereunder crawling coop'd we live and die,
   Lift not your hands to *It* for help—for It
As impotently rolls as you or I.

LXXIII.

With Earth's first Clay They did the Last Man knead,
And there of the Last Harvest sow'd the Seed:
   And the first Morning of Creation wrote
What the Last Dawn of Reckoning shall read.

LXXIV.

YESTERDAY *This* Day's Madness did prepare;
To-MORROW's Silence, Triumph, or Despair:
   Drink! for you know not whence you came, nor why:
Drink! for you know not why you go, nor where.

LXXV.

I tell you this—When, started from the Goal,
Over the flaming shoulders of the Foal
    Of Heav'n Parwín and Mushtari they flung,[23]
In my predestin'd Plot of Dust and Soul.

LXXVI.

The Vine had struck a fibre: which about
If clings my Being—let the Dervish flout;
    Of my Base metal may be filed a Key,
That shall unlock the Door he howls without.

LXXVII.

And this I know: whether the one True Light
Kindle to Love, or Wrath-consume me quite,
    One Flash of It within the Tavern caught
Better than in the Temple lost outright.

LXXVIII.

What! out of senseless Nothing to provoke
A conscious Something to resent the yoke
    Of unpermitted Pleasure, under pain
Of Everlasting Penalties, if broke!

LXXIX.

What! from his helpless Creature be repaid
Pure Gold for what he lent us dross-allay'd—
　　Sue for a Debt we never did contract,
And cannot answer—Oh the sorry trade!

LXXX.

Oh Thou, who didst with pitfall and with gin
Beset the Road I was to wander in,
　　Thou wilt not with Predestin'd Evil round
Enmesh, and then impute my Fall to Sin!

LXXXI.

Oh Thou, who Man of baser Earth didst make,
And ev'n with Paradise devise the Snake:
　　For all the Sin wherewith the Face of Man
Is blacken'd—Man's Forgiveness give—and take!

*　*　*　*　*　*

LXXXII.

As under cover of departing Day
Slunk hunger-stricken Ramazán away,
  Once more within the Potter's house alone
I stood, surrounded by the Shapes of Clay.

LXXXIII.

Shapes of all Sorts and Sizes, great and small,
That stood along the floor and by the wall;
  And some loquacious Vessels were; and some
Listen'd perhaps, but never talk'd at all.

LXXXIV.

Said one among them—" Surely not in vain
My substance of the common Earth was ta'en
  And to this Figure moulded, to be broke,
Or trampled back to shapeless Earth again."

LXXXV.

Then said a Second—" Ne'er a peevish Boy
" Would break the Bowl from which he drank in joy;
  " And He that with his hand the Vessel made
" Will surely not in after Wrath destroy."

LXXXVI.

After a momentary silence spake
Some Vessel of a more ungainly Make;
  "They sneer at me for leaning all awry:
"What! did the Hand then of the Potter shake?"

LXXXVII.

Whereat some one of the loquacious Lot—
I think a Súfi pipkin—waxing hot—
  "All this of Pot and Potter—Tell me then,
"Who makes—Who sells—Who buys—Who *is* the Pot?"[24]

LXXXVIII.

"Why," said another, "Some there are who tell
"Of one who threatens he will toss to Hell
  "The luckless Pots he marr'd in making—Pish!
"He's a Good Fellow, and 'twill all be well."

LXXXIX.

"Well," murmur'd one, "Let whoso make or buy,
"My Clay with long Oblivion is gone dry:
  "But fill me with the old familiar Juice,
"Methinks I might recover by and by."

XC.

So while the Vessels one by one were speaking,
The little Moon look'd in that all were seeking :[25]
    And then they jogg'd each other, "Brother! Brother!
"Now for the Porter's shoulder-knot a-creaking!"

      *   *   *   *   *   *

XCI.

Ah, with the Grape my fading Life provide,
And wash the Body whence the Life has died,
    And lay me, shrouded in the living Leaf,
By some not unfrequented Garden-side.

XCII.

That ev'n my buried Ashes such a snare
Of Vintage shall fling up into the Air
    As not a True-believer passing by
But shall be overtaken unaware.

XCIII.

Indeed the Idols I have loved so long
Have done my credit in Men's eye much wrong:
   Have drown'd my Glory in a shallow Cup,
And sold my Reputation for a Song.

XCIV.

Indeed, indeed, Repentance oft before
I swore—but was I sober when I swore?
   And then and then came Spring, and Rose-in-hand
My thread-bare Penitence apieces tore.

XCV.

And much as Wine has play'd the Infidel,
And robb'd me of my Robe of Honour—Well,
   I wonder often what the Vintners buy
One half so precious as the stuff they sell.

XCVI.

Yet Ah, that Spring should vanish with the Rose!
That Youth's sweet-scented manuscript should close!
   The Nightingale that in the branches sang,
Ah whence, and whither flown again, who knows!

XCVII.

Would but the Desert of the Fountain yield
One glimpse—if dimly, yet indeed, reveal'd,
   To which the fainting Traveller might spring,
As springs the trampled herbage of the field!

XCVIII.

Would but some wingéd Angel ere too late
Arrest the yet unfolded Roll of Fate,
   And make the stern Recorder otherwise
Enregister, or quite obliterate!

XCIX.

Ah Love! could you and I with Him conspire
To grasp this sorry Scheme of Things entire,
   Would not we shatter it to bits—and then
Re-mould it nearer to the Heart's Desire!

*   *   *   *   *   *

C.

Yon rising Moon that looks for us again—
How oft hereafter will she wax and wane;
  How oft hereafter rising look for us
Through this same Garden—and for *one* in vain!

CI.

And when like her, oh Sáki, you shall pass
Among the Guests Star-scatter'd on the Grass,
  And in your blissful errand reach the spot
Where I made One—turn down an empty Glass!

TAMÁM.

NOTES.

[1] The "*False Dawn;*" *Subhi Kázib*, a transient Light on the Horizon about an hour before the *Subhi sádik*, or True Dawn; a well-known Phenomenon in the East.

[2] New Year. Beginning with the Vernal Equinox, it must be remembered; and (howsoever the old Solar Year is practically superseded by the clumsy *Lunar* Year that dates from the Mohammedan Hijra) still commemorated by a Festival that is said to have been appointed by the very Jamshyd whom Omar so often talks of, and whose yearly Calendar he helped to rectify.

"The sudden approach and rapid advance of the Spring," says Mr. Binning, "are very striking. Before the Snow is well off the Ground, the Trees burst into Blossom, and the Flowers start from the Soil. At *Naw Rooz* (*their* New Year's Day) the Snow was lying in patches on the Hills and in the shaded Vallies, while the Fruit-trees in the Garden were budding beautifully, and green Plants and Flowers springing upon the Plains on every side—

'And on old Hyems' Chin and icy Crown
'An odorous Chaplet of sweet Summer buds
'Is, as in mockery, set—'—

Among the Plants newly appear'd I recognized some Acquaintances I had not seen for many a Year; among these, two varieties of the Thistle; a coarse species of the Daisy, like the Horse-gowan; red and white Clover; the Dock; the blue Corn-flower; and that vulgar Herb the Dandelion rearing its yellow crest on the Banks of the Watercourses." The Nightingale was not yet heard, for the Rose was not yet blown: but an almost identical Blackbird and Woodpecker helped to make up something of a North-country Spring.

[3] Exodus iv. 6; where Moses draws forth his Hand—not, according to the Persians, "*leprous as Snow*,"—but *white*, as our May-blossom in Spring perhaps. According to them also the Healing Power of Jesus resided in his Breath.

[4] Iram, planted by King Shaddád, and now sunk somewhere in the Sands of Arabia. Jamshyd's Seven-ring'd Cup was typical of the 7 Heavens, 7 Planets, 7 Seas, &c., and was a *Divining Cup*.

[5] *Péhlevi*, the old Heroic *Sanskrit* of Persia. Háfiz also speaks of the Nightingale's *Péhlevi*, which did not change with the People's.

[6] I am not sure if this refers to the Red Rose looking sickly, or the Yellow Rose that ought to be Red; Red, White, and Yellow Roses all common in Persia. I think Southey, in his Common-Place Book, quotes from some

Spanish author about Rose being White till 10 o'clock; "Rosa Perfecta" at 2; and "perfecta incarnada" at 5.

[7] Rustum, the "Hercules" of Persia, and Zál his Father, whose exploits are among the most celebrated in the Sháh-náma. Hátim Tai, a well-known Type of Oriental Generosity.

[8] A Drum—beaten outside a Palace.

[9] That is, the Rose's Golden Centre.

[10] Persepolis: call'd also *Takht'i Jamshyd* — THE THRONE OF JAMSHYD, "*King Splendid*," of the mythical *Peeshdádian* Dynasty, and supposed (according to the Sháh-náma) to have been founded and built by him. Others refer it to the Work of the Genie King, Ján Ibn Ján—who also built the Pyramids—before the time of Adam.

BAHRÁM GÚR—*Bahram of the Wild Ass*—a Sassanian Sovereign—had also his Seven Castles (like the King of Bohemia!) each of a different Colour: each with a Royal Mistress within; each of whom tells him a Story, as told in one of the most famous Poems of Persia, written by Amír Khusraw: all these Sevens also figuring (according to Eastern Mysticism) the Seven Heavens; and perhaps the Book itself that Eighth, into which the mystical Seven transcend, and within which they revolve. The Ruins of Three of these Towers are yet shown by the Peasantry; as also the Swamp in which Bahrám sunk, like the Master of Ravenswood, while pursuing his *Gúr*.

> The Palace that to Heav'n his pillars threw,
> And Kings the forehead on his threshold drew—
>   I saw the solitary Ringdove there,
> And " Coo, coo, coo," she cried ; and " Coo, coo, coo."

This Quatrain Mr. Binning found, among several of Háfiz and others, inscribed by some stray hand among the ruins of Persepolis. The Ringdove's ancient *Péhlevi Coo, Coo, Coo,* signifies also in Persian " *Where ? Where ? Where ?* " In Attár's "Bird-parliament" she is reproved by the Leader of the Birds for sitting still, and for ever harping on that one note of lamentation for her lost Yúsuf.

Apropos of Omar's Red Roses in Stanza xix, I am reminded of an old English Superstition, that our Anemone Pulsatilla, or purple " Pasque Flower," (which grows plentifully about the Fleam Dyke, near Cambridge), grows only where Danish Blood has been spilt.

[11] A thousand years to each Planet.

[12] Saturn, Lord of the Seventh Heaven.

[13] ME-AND-THEE: some dividual Existence or Personality distinct from the Whole.

[14] One of the Persian Poets—Attár, I think—has a pretty story about this. A thirsty Traveller dips his hand into a Spring of Water to drink from. By

and by comes another who draws up and drinks from an earthen Bowl, and then departs, leaving his Bowl behind him. The first Traveller takes it up for another draught; but is surprised to find that the same Water which had tasted sweet from his own hand tastes bitter from the earthen Bowl. But a Voice—from Heaven, I think—tells him the Clay from which the Bowl is made was once *Man;* and, into whatever shape renew'd, can never lose the bitter flavour of Mortality.

[15] The custom of throwing a little Wine on the ground before drinking still continues in Persia, and perhaps generally in the East. Mons. Nicolas considers it " un signe de libéralité, et en même temps un avertissement que le buveur doit vider sa coupe jusqu'à la dernière goutte." Is it not more likely an ancient Superstition; a Libation to propitiate Earth, or make her an Accomplice in the illicit Revel ? Or, perhaps, to divert the Jealous Eye by some sacrifice of superfluity, as with the Ancients of the West ? With Omar we see something more is signified; the precious Liquor is not lost, but sinks into the ground to refresh the dust of some poor Wine-worshipper foregone.

Thus Háfiz, copying Omar in so many ways : " When thou drinkest Wine pour a draught on the ground. Wherefore fear the Sin which brings to another Gain ?"

[16] According to one beautiful Oriental Legend, Azräel

accomplishes his mission by holding to the nostril an Apple from the Tree of Life.

This, and the two following Stanzas would have been withdrawn, as somewhat *de trop*, from the Text but for advice which I least like to disregard.

[17] From Máh to Máhi; from Fish to Moon.

[18] A Jest, of course, at his Studies. A curious mathematical Quatrain of Omar's has been pointed out to me; the more curious because almost exactly parallel'd by some Verses of Doctor Donne's, that are quoted in Izaak Walton's Lives! Here is Omar: "You and I are the image of a pair of compasses; though we have two heads (sc. our *feet*) we have one body; when we have fixed the centre for our circle, we bring our heads (sc. feet) together at the end." Dr. Donne:

>If we be two, we two are so
> As stiff twin-compasses are two;
>Thy Soul, the fixt foot, makes no show
> To move, but does if the other do.
>
>And though thine in the centre sit,
> Yet when my other far does roam,
>Thine leans and hearkens after it,
> And grows erect as mine comes home.
>
>Such thou must be to me, who must
> Like the other foot obliquely run;
>Thy firmness makes my circle just,
> And me to end where I begun.

[19] The Seventy-two Religions supposed to divide the World, *including* Islamism, as some think : but others not.

[20] Alluding to Sultan Mahmúd's Conquest of India and its dark people.

[21] *Fánúsi khiyàl*, a Magic-lanthorn still used in India; the cylindrical Interior being painted with various Figures, and so lightly poised and ventilated as to revolve round the lighted candle within.

[22] A very mysterious Line in the Original :

O dánad O dánad O dánad O——

breaking off something like our Wood-pigeon's Note, which she is said to take up just where she left off.

[23] Parwín and Mushtari—The Pleiads and Jupiter.

[24] This Relation of Pot and Potter to Man and his Maker figures far and wide in the Literature of the World, from the time of the Hebrew Prophets to the present; when it may finally take the name of "Pot-theism," by which Mr. Carlyle ridiculed Sterling's "Pantheism." *My* Sheikh, whose knowledge flows in from all quarters, writes to me—

"Apropos of old Omar's Pots, did I ever tell you the sentence I found in 'Bishop Pearson on the Creed'?" "Thus are we wholly at the disposal of His will, and our present and future condition, framed and ordered by His free, but wise and just, decrees. "*Hath not the potter power over the clay, of the same lump to make one vessel unto honour, and another unto dishonour?*" (Rom. ix. 21). And can that earth-artificer have a freer power over his *brother potsherd* (both being made of the same metal), than God hath over him, who, by the strange fecundity of His omnipotent power, first made the clay out of nothing, and then him out of that?"

And again—from a very different quarter—" I had to refer the other day to Aristophanes, and came by chance on a curious Speaking-pot story in the Vespæ, which I had quite forgotten.

Φιλοκλεων.   Ἄκουε, μὴ φεῦγ'· ἐν Συβάρει γυνή ποτε   l. 1435
κατέαξ' ἐχῖνον.

Κατηγορος.   Ταῦτ' ἐγὼ μαρτύρομαι.

Φι.   Οὐχῖνος οὖν ἔχων τιν' ἐπεμαρτύρατο·
           Εἶθ' ἡ Συβαρῖτις εἶπεν, ἒι ναὶ τὰν κόραν
           τὴν μαρτυρίαν ταύτην ἐάσας, ἐν τάχει
           ἐπίδεσμον ἐπρίω, νοῦν ἂν εἶχες πλείονα.

"The Pot calls a bystander to be a witness to his bad treatment. The woman says, 'If, by Proserpine, instead of all this 'testifying' (comp. Cuddie and his mother in 'Old Mortality!') you would buy yourself a trivet, it would show more sense in you!' The Scholiast explains *echinus* as ἄγγος τι ἐκ κεράμου."

[25] At the Close of the Fasting Month, Ramazán, (which makes the Musulman unhealthy and unamiable), the first Glimpse of the New Moon (who rules their division of the Year), is looked for with the utmost Anxiety, and hailed with Acclamation. Then it is that the Porter's Knot may be heard—toward the *Cellar*. Omar has elsewhere a pretty Quatrain about this same Moon—

> "Be of Good Cheer—the sullen Month will die,
> " And a young Moon requite us by and by :
> " Look how the Old one meagre, bent, and wan
> " With Age and Fast, is fainting from the Sky !"

FINIS.

POEMS

FROM THE

PERSIAN.

شهسوار اغوش میدان آمدی گوی بزن

Welcome, Prince of Horsemen, welcome!
Ride a field, and strike the Ball!

RUBÁIYÁT

OF

OMAR KHAYYÁM;

AND THE

SALÁMÁN AND ÁBSÁL

OF

JÁMÍ;

RENDERED INTO ENGLISH VERSE.

BERNARD QUARITCH; 15 PICCADILLY, LONDON.

1879.

LONDON:
G. NORMAN AND SON, PRINTERS, MAIDEN LANE,
COVENT GARDEN.

RUBÁIYÁT

OF

OMAR KHAYYÁM,

THE ASTRONOMER-POET OF PERSIA.

𝔎𝔢𝔫𝔡𝔢𝔯𝔢𝔡 𝔦𝔫𝔱𝔬 𝔈𝔫𝔤𝔩𝔦𝔰𝔥 𝔙𝔢𝔯𝔰𝔢.

FOURTH EDITION.

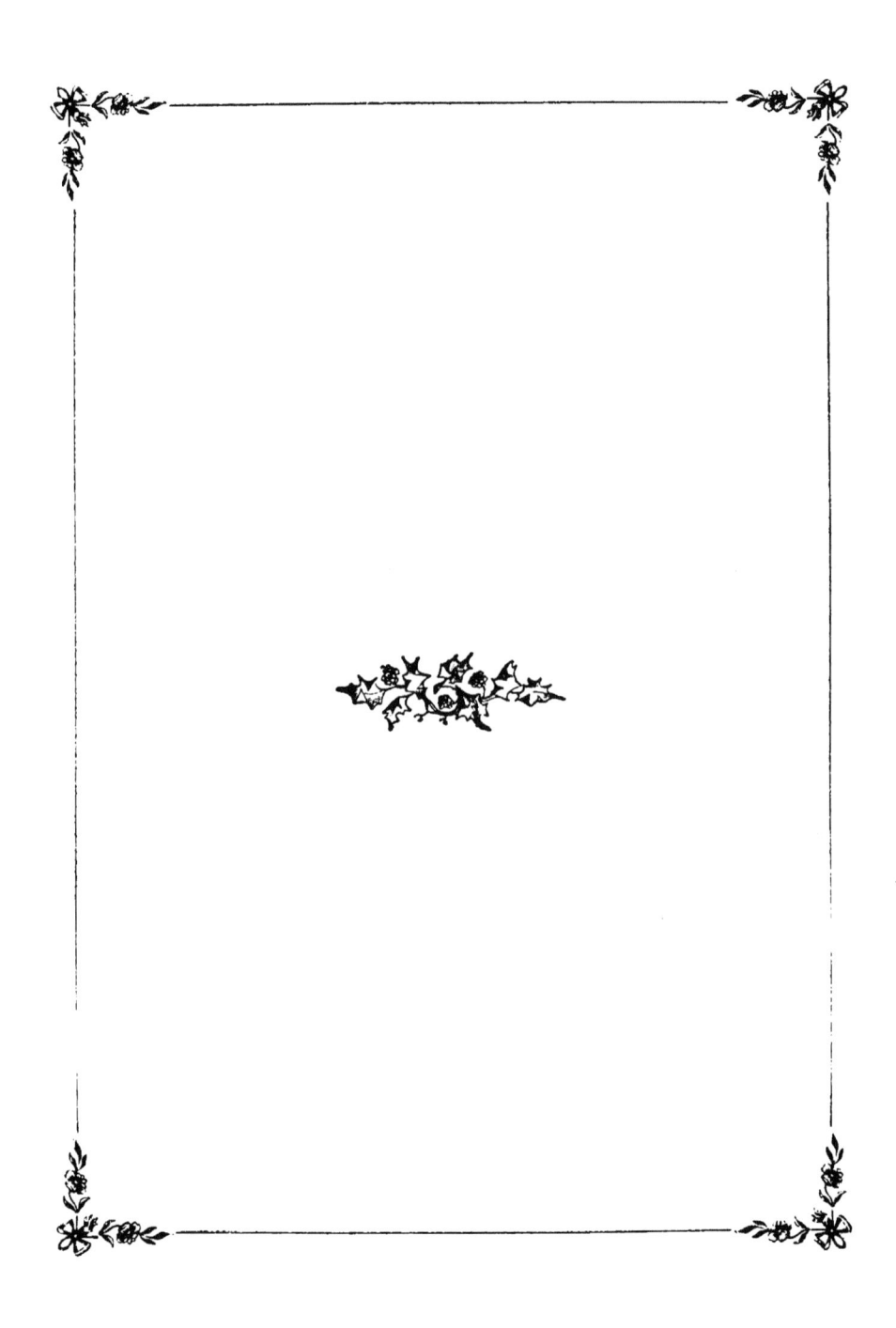

OMAR KHAYYÁM,

THE

Astronomer-Poet of Persia.

OMAR KHAYYÁM was born at Naishápúr in Khorasan in the latter half of our Eleventh, and died within the First Quarter of our Twelfth Century. The slender Story of his Life is curiously twined about that of two other very considerable Figures in their Time and Country: one of whom tells the Story of all Three. This was Nizám ul Mulk, Vizyr to Alp Arslan the Son, and Malik Shah the Grandson, of Toghrul Beg the Tartar, who had wrested Persia from the feeble Successor of Mahmúd the Great, and founded that Seljukian Dynasty which finally roused Europe into the Crusades. This Nizám ul Mulk, in his *Wasiyat*—or *Testament*—which he wrote and left as a Memorial for future Statesmen—relates the following, as quoted in the *Calcutta Review*, No. 59, from Mirkhond's History of the Assassins.

"'One of the greatest of the wise men of Khorassan

'was the Imám Mowaffak of Naishápúr, a man
'highly honoured and reverenced,—may God rejoice
'his soul; his illustrious years exceeded eighty-five,
'and it was the universal belief that every boy who
'read the Koran or studied the traditions in his
'presence, would assuredly attain to honour and
'happiness. For this cause did my father send me
'from Tús to Naishápúr with Abd-us-samad, the
'doctor of law, that I might employ myself in study
'and learning under the guidance of that illustrious
'teacher. Towards me he ever turned an eye of
'favour and kindness, and as his pupil I felt for him
'extreme affection and devotion, so that I passed
'four years in his service. When I first came there,
'I found two other pupils of mine own age newly
'arrived, Hakim Omar Khayyám, and the ill-fated
'Ben Sabbáh. Both were endowed with sharpness
'of wit and the highest natural powers; and we three
'formed a close friendship together. When the
'Imám rose from his lectures, they used to join
'me, and we repeated to each other the lessons we
'had heard. Now Omar was a native of Naishápúr,
'while Hasan Ben Sabbáh's father was one Ali, a
'man of austere life and practice, but heretical in
'his creed and doctrine. One day Hasan said to me
'and to Khayyám, 'It is a universal belief that the

'pupils of the Imám Mowaffak will attain to fortune.
'Now, even if we *all* do not attain thereto, without
'doubt one of us will; what then shall be our mutual
'pledge and bond?' We answered, 'Be it what you
'please.' 'Well,' he said, 'let us make a vow, that
'to whomsoever this fortune falls, he shall share it
'equally with the rest, and reserve no pre-eminence
'for himself.' 'Be it so,' we both replied, and on
'those terms we mutually pledged our words. Years
'rolled on, and I went from Khorassan to Trans-
'oxiana, and wandered to Ghazni and Cabul; and
'when I returned, I was invested with office, and
'rose to be administrator of affairs during the
'Sultanate of Sultan Alp Arslán.'

"He goes on to state, that years passed by, and both his old school-friends found him out, and came and claimed a share in his good fortune, according to the school-day vow. The Vizier was generous and kept his word. Hasan demanded a place in the government, which the Sultan granted at the Vizier's request; but discontented with a gradual rise, he plunged into the maze of intrigue of an oriental court, and, failing in a base attempt to supplant his benefactor, he was disgraced and fell. After many mishaps and wanderings, Hasan became the head of the Persian sect of the *Ismailians*,—a party of fanatics who had long murmured in obscurity, but rose to an evil eminence under the guidance of his strong and evil will. In A.D. 1090, he seized the castle of Alamút, in the province of Rúdbar, which lies in the mountainous tract south of the Caspian Sea; and it was from this mountain home he obtained that evil celebrity among the Crusaders as the OLD MAN OF THE MOUNTAINS, and spread terror through the Mohammedan world; and it is yet disputed whether the word *Assassin*, which they have left in the language of modern Europe as their dark memorial, is derived from the *hashish*, or opiate of hemp-leaves (the Indian *bhang*), with which they maddened themselves to the sullen pitch of oriental desperation, or from the name of the founder of the dynasty, whom we have seen in his quiet collegiate days, at Naishápúr. One of the countless victims of the Assassin's dagger was Nizám-ul-Mulk himself, the old school-boy friend.[1]

[1] Some of Omar's Rubáiyát warn us of the danger of Greatness, the instability of Fortune, and while advocating Charity to all Men, recommending us to be too intimate with none. Attár makes Nizám-ul-Mulk use the very words of his friend Omar [Rub. xxviii.], "When Nizám-ul-Mulk was in the Agony (of Death) he said, 'Oh God! I am passing away in the hand of the Wind.'"

"Omar Khayyám also came to the Vizier to claim the share; but not to ask for title or office. 'The 'greatest boon you can confer on me,' he said, 'is to 'let me live in a corner under the shadow of your 'fortune, to spread wide the advantages of Science, 'and pray for your long life and prosperity.' The Vizier tells us, that, when he found Omar was really sincere in his refusal, he pressed him no further, but granted him a yearly pension of 1200 *mithkáls* of gold, from the treasury of Naishápur.

"At Naishápúr thus lived and died Omar Khayyám, 'busied,' adds the Vizier, 'in winning 'knowledge of every kind, and especially in Astro-'nomy, wherein he attained to a very high pre-'eminence. Under the Sultanate of Malik Shah, he 'came to Merv, and obtained great praise for his 'proficiency in science, and the Sultan showered 'favours upon him.'

"When Malik Shah determined to reform the calendar, Omar was one of the eight learned men employed to do it; the result was the *Jaláli* era (so called from *Jalal-u-din*, one of the king's names)—'a computation of time,' says Gibbon, 'which surpasses the Julian, and approaches the accuracy of the Gregorian style.' He is also the author of some astronomical tables, entitled Zíji-Malikshahí," and the French have lately republished and translated an Arabic Treatise of his on Algebra.

"His Takhallus or poetical name (Khayyám) signifies a Tent-maker, and he is said to have at one time exercised that trade, perhaps before Nizám-ul-Mulk's generosity raised him to independence. Many Persian poets similarly derive their names from their occupations; thus we have Attár, 'a druggist,' Assár, 'an oil presser,' &c.[1] Omar himself alludes to his name in the following whimsical lines:—

> 'Khayyám, who stitched the tents of science,
>   Has fallen in grief's furnace and been suddenly burned;
>   The shears of Fate have cut the tent ropes of his life,
>   And the broker of Hope has sold him for nothing!'

"We have only one more anecdote to give of his Life, and that relates to the close; it is told in the anonymous preface which is sometimes prefixed to his poems; it has been printed in the Persian in the appendix to Hyde's *Veterum Persarum Religio*, p. 529; and D'Herbelot alludes to it in his Bibliothèque, under *Khiam*:[2]—

---

[1] Though all these, like our Smiths, Archers, Millers, Fletchers, &c., may simply retain the Surname of an hereditary calling.

[2] "Philosophe Musulman qui a vécu en Odeur de Sainteté vers la Fin du premier et le Commencement du second Siècle," no part of which, except the "Philosophe," can apply to *our* Khayyám.

"'It is written in the chronicles of the ancients 'that this King of the Wise, Omar Khayyám, died 'at Naishápúr in the year of the Hegira, 517 '(A.D. 1123); in science he was unrivalled,—the very 'paragon of his age. Khwájah Nizámi of Samar-'cand, who was one of his pupils, relates the 'following story: 'I often used to hold conversations 'with my teacher, Omar Khayyám, in a garden; and 'one day he said to me, 'My tomb shall be in a spot 'where the north wind may scatter roses over it.' I 'wondered at the words he spake, but I knew that his 'were no idle words.[1] Years after, when I chanced 'to revisit Naishápúr, I went to his final resting-'place, and lo! it was just outside a garden, and 'trees laden with fruit stretched their boughs over the 'garden wall, and dropped their flowers upon his 'tomb, so as the stone was hidden under them.'"

[1] The Rashness of the Words, according to D'Herbelot, consisted in being so opposed to those in the Korán: "No Man knows where he shall die."—This Story of Omar reminds me of another so naturally—and, when one remembers how wide of his humble mark the noble sailor aimed—so pathetically told by Captain Cook—not by Doctor Hawkesworth—in his Second Voyage. When leaving Ulietea, "Oreo's last request was for me to return. When he saw he could not obtain that promise, he asked the name of my *Marai*—Burying-place. As strange a question as this was, I hesitated not a moment to tell him

Thus far—without fear of Trespass—from the *Calcutta Review*. The writer of it, on reading in India this story of Omar's Grave, was reminded, he says, of Cicero's Account of finding Archimedes' Tomb at Syracuse, buried in grass and weeds. I think Thorwaldsen desired to have roses grow over him; a wish religiously fulfilled for him to the present day, I believe. However, to return to Omar.

Though the Sultan "shower'd Favours upon him," Omar's Epicurean Audacity of Thought and Speech caused him to be regarded askance in his own Time and Country. He is said to have been especially hated and dreaded by the Súfis, whose Practice he ridiculed, and whose Faith amounts to little more than his own when stript of the Mysticism and formal recognition of Islamism under which Omar would not hide. Their Poets, including Háfiz, who are (with the exception of Firdausi) the most considerable in Persia, borrowed largely, indeed, of

'Stepney,' the parish in which I live when in London. I was made to repeat it several times over till they could pronounce it; and then 'Stepney Marai no Toote' was echoed through a hundred mouths at once. I afterwards found the same question had been put to Mr. Forster by a man on shore; but he gave a different, and indeed more proper answer, by saying, ' No man who used the sea could say where he should be buried.' "

Omar's material, but turning it to a mystical Use more convenient to Themselves and the People they addressed; a People quite as quick of Doubt as of Belief; as keen of Bodily Sense as of Intellectual; and delighting in a cloudy composition of both, in which they could float luxuriously between Heaven and Earth, and this World and the Next, on the wings of a poetical expression, that might serve indifferently for either. Omar was too honest of Heart as well as of Head for this. Having failed however mistakenly of finding any Providence but Destiny, and any World but This, he set about making the most of it; preferring rather to soothe the Soul through the Senses into Acquiescence with Things as he saw them, than to perplex it with vain disquietude after what they *might* be. It has been seen, however, that his Worldly Ambition was not exorbitant; and he very likely takes a humorous or perverse pleasure in exalting the gratification of Sense above that of the Intellect, in which he must have taken great delight, although it failed to answer the Questions in which he, in common with all men, was most vitally interested.

For whatever Reason, however, Omar, as before said, has never been popular in his own Country, and therefore has been but scantily transmitted abroad. The MSS. of his Poems, mutilated beyond the average Casualties of Oriental Transcription, are so rare in the East as scarce to have reacht Westward at all, in spite of all the acquisitions of Arms and Science. There is no copy at the India House, none at the Bibliothèque Nationale of Paris. We know but of one in England: No. 140 of the Ouseley MSS. at the Bodleian, written at Shiraz, A.D. 1460. This contains but 158 Rubáiyát. One in the Asiatic Society's Library at Calcutta (of which we have a Copy), contains (and yet incomplete) 516, though swelled to that by all kinds of Repetition and Corruption. So Von Hammer speaks of *his* Copy as containing about 200, while Dr. Sprenger catalogues the Lucknow MS. at double that number.[1] The Scribes, too, of the Oxford and Calcutta MSS. seem to do their Work under a sort of Protest; each beginning with a Tetrastich (whether genuine or not), taken out of its alphabetical order; the Oxford with one of Apology; the Calcutta with one of Expostulation, supposed (says a Notice prefixed to the MS.) to have arisen from a Dream, in which Omar's

---

[1] "Since this Paper was written (adds the Reviewer in a note), "we have met with a Copy of a very rare Edition, printed at Calcutta in 1836. This contains 438 Tetrastichs, with an Appendix containing 54 others not found in some MSS."

mother asked about his future fate. It may be rendered thus :—

> "Oh Thou who burn'st in Heart for those who burn
> "In Hell, whose fires thyself shall feed in turn;
> "How long be crying, 'Mercy on them, God!'
> "Why, who art Thou to teach, and He to learn?"

The Bodleian Quatrain pleads Pantheism by way of Justification.

> "If I myself upon a looser Creed
> "Have loosely strung the Jewel of Good deed,
> "Let this one thing for my Atonement plead :
> "That One for Two I never did mis-read."

The Reviewer, to whom I owe the Particulars of Omar's Life, concludes his Review by comparing him with Lucretius, both as to natural Temper and Genius, and as acted upon by the Circumstances in which he lived. Both indeed were men of subtle, strong, and cultivated Intellect, fine Imagination, and Hearts passionate for Truth and Justice; who justly revolted from their Country's false Religion, and false, or foolish, Devotion to it; but who fell short of replacing what they subverted by such better *Hope* as others, with no better Revelation to guide them, had yet made a Law to themselves. Lucretius, indeed, with such material as Epicurus furnished, satisfied himself with the theory of a vast machine fortuitously constructed, and acting by a Law that implied no Legislator; and so composing himself into a Stoical rather than Epicurean severity of Attitude, sat down to contemplate the mechanical Drama of the Universe which he was part Actor in; himself and all about him (as in his own sublime description of the Roman Theatre) discoloured with the lurid reflex of the Curtain suspended between the Spectator and the Sun. Omar, more desperate, or more careless of any so complicated System as resulted in nothing but hopeless Necessity, flung his own Genius and Learning with a bitter or humorous jest into the general Ruin which their insufficient glimpses only served to reveal; and, pretending sensual pleasure as the serious purpose of Life, only *diverted* himself with speculative problems of Deity, Destiny, Matter and Spirit, Good and Evil, and other such questions, easier to start than to run down, and the pursuit of which becomes a very weary sport at last!

With regard to the present Translation. The original Rubáiyát (as, missing an Arabic Guttural, these *Tetrastichs* are more musically called) are independent Stanzas, consisting each of four Lines of equal, though varied, Prosody; sometimes *all* rhyming, but oftener (as here imitated) the third line a blank. Sometimes as in the Greek Alcaic, where the penultimate line seems to lift and suspend the Wave that falls over in the last. As usual with such kind of Oriental Verse, the Rubáiyát follow one another according to Alphabetic Rhyme—a strange succession of Grave and Gay. Those here selected are strung into something of an Eclogue, with perhaps a less than equal proportion of the "Drink and make-merry," which (genuine or not) recurs over-frequently in the Original. Either way, the Result is sad enough: saddest perhaps when most ostentatiously merry: more apt to move Sorrow than Anger toward the old Tentmaker, who, after vainly endeavouring to unshackle his Steps from Destiny, and to catch some authentic Glimpse of TO-MORROW, fell back upon TO-DAY (which has outlasted so many To-morrows!) as the only Ground he got to stand upon, however momentarily slipping from under his Feet.

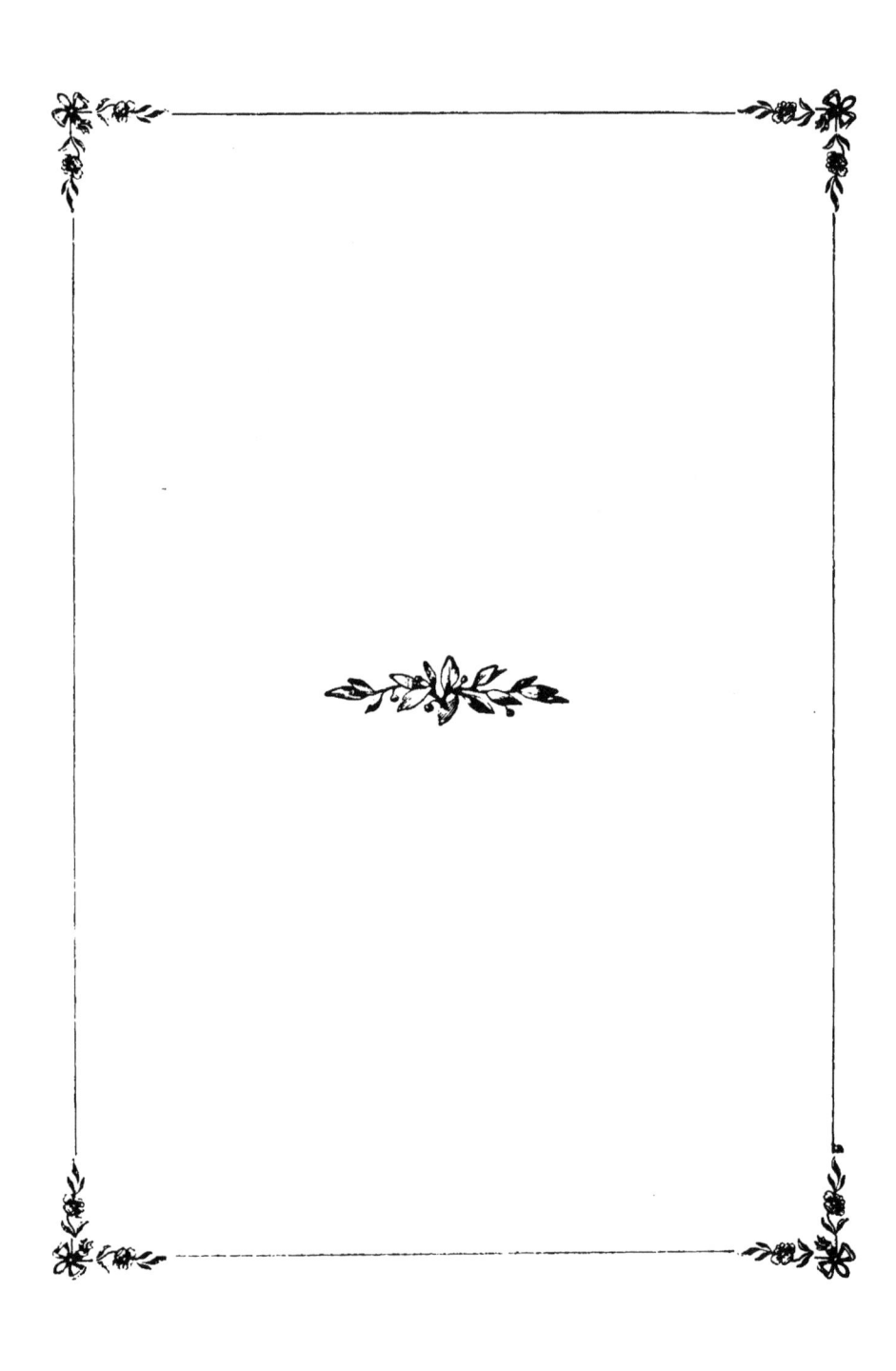

RUBÁIYÁT

OF

OMAR KHAYYÁM OF NAISHÁPÚR.

I.

WAKE! For the Sun who scatter'd into flight
The Stars before him from the Field of Night,
   Drives Night along with them from Heav'n, and
      strikes
The Sultán's Turret with a Shaft of Light.

II.

Before the phantom of False morning died,
Methought a Voice within the Tavern cried,
   "When all the Temple is prepared within,
"Why nods the drowsy Worshipper outside?"

III.

And, as the Cock crew, those who stood before
The Tavern shouted—"Open then the Door!
   "You know how little while we have to stay,
"And, once departed, may return no more."

IV.

Now the New Year reviving old Desires,
The thoughtful Soul to Solitude retires,
   Where the WHITE HAND OF MOSES on the Bough
Puts out, and Jesus from the Ground suspires.

V.

Iram indeed is gone with all his Rose,
And Jamshyd's Sev'n-ring'd Cup where no one knows;
   But still a Ruby kindles in the Vine,
And many a Garden by the Water blows.

VI.

And David's lips are lockt; but in divine
High-piping Pehleví, with "Wine! Wine! Wine!
   "Red Wine!"—the Nightingale cries to the Rose
That sallow cheek of her's to' incarnadine.

VII.

Come, fill the Cup, and in the fire of Spring
Your Winter-garment of Repentance fling:
   The Bird of Time has but a little way
To flutter—and the Bird is on the Wing.

VIII.

Whether at Naishápúr or Babylon,
Whether the Cup with sweet or bitter run,
 The Wine of Life keeps oozing drop by drop,
The Leaves of Life keep falling one by one.

IX.

Each Morn a thousand Roses brings, you say;
Yes, but where leaves the Rose of Yesterday?
 And this first Summer month that brings the Rose
Shall take Jamshyd and Kaikobád away.

X.

Well, let it take them! What have we to do
With Kaikobád the Great, or Kaikhosrú?
 Let Zál and Rustum bluster as they will,
Or Hátim call to Supper—heed not you.

XI.

With me along the strip of Herbage strown
That just divides the desert from the sown,
 Where name of Slave and Sultán is forgot—
And Peace to Mahmúd on his golden Throne!

XII.

A Book of Verses underneath the Bough,
A Jug of Wine, a Loaf of Bread—and Thou
   Beside me singing in the Wilderness—
Oh, Wilderness were Paradise enow!

XIII.

Some for the Glories of This World; and some
Sigh for the Prophet's Paradise to come;
   Ah, take the Cash, and let the Credit go,
Nor heed the rumble of a distant Drum!

XIV.

Look to the blowing Rose about us—" Lo,
" Laughing," she says, " into the world I blow,
   " At once the silken tassel of my Purse
" Tear, and its Treasure on the Garden throw."

XV.

And those who husbanded the Golden grain,
And those who flung it to the winds like Rain,
   Alike to no such aureate Earth are turn'd
As, buried once, Men want dug up again.

XVI.

The Worldly Hope men set their Hearts upon
Turns Ashes—or it prospers; and anon,
   Like Snow upon the Desert's dusty Face,
Lighting a little hour or two—was gone.

XVII.

Think, in this batter'd Caravanserai
Whose Portals are alternate Night and Day,
   How Sultán after Sultán with his Pomp
Abode his destin'd Hour, and went his way.

XVIII.

They say the Lion and the Lizard keep
The Courts where Jamshyd gloried and drank deep:
   And Bahrám, that great Hunter—the Wild Ass
Stamps o'er his Head, but cannot break his Sleep.

XIX.

I sometimes think that never blows so red
The Rose as where some buried Cæsar bled;
   That every Hyacinth the Garden wears
Dropt in her Lap from some once lovely Head.

XX.

And this reviving Herb whose tender Green
Fledges the River-Lip on which we lean—
   Ah, lean upon it lightly! for who knows
From what once lovely Lip it springs unseen!

XXI.

Ah, my Belovéd, fill the Cup that clears
To-day of past Regret and future Fears:
   To-morrow!—Why, To-morrow I may be
Myself with Yesterday's Sev'n thousand Years.

XXII.

For some we loved, the loveliest and the best
That from his Vintage rolling Time hath prest,
   Have drunk their Cup a Round or two before,
And one by one crept silently to rest.

XXIII.

And we, that now make merry in the Room
They left, and Summer dresses in new bloom,
   Ourselves must we beneath the Couch of Earth
Descend—ourselves to make a Couch—for whom?

XXIV.

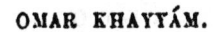

Ah, make the most of what we yet may spend,
Before we too into the Dust descend;
    Dust into Dust, and under Dust, to lie,
Sans Wine, sans Song, sans Singer, and—sans End!

XXV.

Alike for those who for TO-DAY prepare,
And those that after some TO-MORROW stare,
    A Muezzín from the Tower of Darkness cries,
"Fools! your Reward is neither Here nor There."

XXVI.

Why, all the Saints and Sages who discuss'd
Of the Two Worlds so wisely—they are thrust
    Like foolish Prophets forth; their Words to Scorn
Are scatter'd, and their Mouths are stopt with Dust.

XXVII.

Myself when young did eagerly frequent
Doctor and Saint, and heard great argument
    About it and about: but evermore
Came out by the same door where in I went.

XXVIII.

With them the seed of Wisdom did I sow,
And with mine own hand wrought to make it grow;
  And this was all the Harvest that I reap'd—
"I came like Water, and like Wind I go."

XXIX.

Into this Universe, and *Why* not knowing
Nor *Whence*, like Water willy-nilly flowing;
  And out of it, as Wind along the Waste,
I know not *Whither*, willy-nilly blowing.

XXX.

What, without asking, hither hurried *Whence*?
And, without asking, *Whither* hurried hence!
  Oh, many a Cup of this forbidden Wine
Must drown the memory of that insolence!

XXXI.

Up from Earth's Centre through the Seventh Gate
I rose, and on the Throne of Saturn sate,
  And many a Knot unravel'd by the Road;
But not the Master-knot of Human Fate.

XXXII.

There was the Door to which I found no Key;
There was the Veil through which I might not see:
   Some little talk awhile of ME and THEE
There was—and then no more of THEE and ME.

XXXIII.

Earth could not answer; nor the Seas that mourn
In flowing Purple, of their Lord forlorn;
   Nor rolling Heaven, with all his Signs reveal'd
And hidden by the sleeve of Night and Morn.

XXXIV.

Then of the THEE IN ME who works behind
The Veil, I lifted up my hands to find
   A Lamp amid the Darkness; and I heard,
As from Without—"THE ME WITHIN THEE BLIND!"

XXXV.

Then to the Lip of this poor earthern Urn
I lean'd, the Secret of my Life to learn:
   And Lip to Lip it murmur'd—"While you live,
"Drink!—for, once dead, you never shall return."

XXXVI.

I think the Vessel, that with fugitive
Articulation answer'd, once did live,
   And drink; and Ah! the passive Lip I kiss'd,
How many Kisses might it take—and give!

XXXVII.

For I remember stopping by the way
To watch a Potter thumping his wet Clay:
   And with its all-obliterated Tongue
It murmur'd—" Gently, Brother, gently, pray!"

XXXVIII.

And has not such a Story from of Old
Down Man's successive generations roll'd
   Of such a clod of saturated Earth
Cast by the Maker into Human mould?

XXXIX.

And not a drop that from our Cups we throw
For Earth to drink of, but may steal below
   To quench the fire of Anguish in some Eye
There hidden—far beneath, and long ago.

XL.

As then the Tulip for her morning sup
Of Heav'nly Vintage from the soil looks up,
   Do you devoutly do the like, till Heav'n
To Earth invert you—like an empty Cup.

XLI.

Perplext no more with Human or Divine,
To-morrow's tangle to the winds resign,
   And lose your fingers in the tresses of
The Cypress-slender Minister of Wine.

XLII.

And if the Wine you drink, the Lip you press,
End in what All begins and ends in—Yes;
   Think then you are To-day what Yesterday
You were—To-morrow you shall not be less.

XLIII.

So when the Angel of the darker Drink
At last shall find you by the river-brink,
   And, offering his Cup, invite your Soul
Forth to your Lips to quaff—you shall not shrink.

XLIV.

Why, if the Soul can fling the Dust aside,
And naked on the Air of Heaven ride,
   Wer't not a Shame—wer't not a Shame for him
In this clay carcase crippled to abide?

XLV.

'Tis but a Tent where takes his one day's rest
A Sultán to the realm of Death addrest;
   The Sultán rises, and the dark Ferrásh
Strikes, and prepares it for another Guest.

XLVI.

And fear not lest Existence closing your
Account, and mine, should know the like no more;
   The Eternal Sákí from that Bowl has pour'd
Millions of Bubbles like us, and will pour.

XLVII.

When You and I behind the Veil are past,
Oh, but the long, long while the World shall last,
   Which of our Coming and Departure heeds
As the Sea's self should heed a pebble-cast.

XLVIII.

A Moment's Halt—a momentary taste
Of BEING from the Well amid the Waste—
    And Lo!—the phantom Caravan has reacht
The NOTHING it set out from—Oh, make haste!

XLIX.

Would you that spangle of Existence spend
About THE SECRET—quick about it, Friend!
    A Hair perhaps divides the False and True—
And upon what, prithee, does life depend?

L.

A Hair perhaps divides the False and True;
Yes; and a single Alif were the clue—
    Could you but find it—to the Treasure-house,
And peradventure to THE MASTER too;

LI.

Whose secret Presence, through Creation's veins
Running Quicksilver-like eludes your pains;
    Taking all shapes from Máh to Máhi; and
They change and perish all—but He remains;

LII.

A moment guess'd—then back behind the Fold
Immerst of Darkness round the Drama roll'd
   Which, for the Pastime of Eternity,
He doth Himself contrive, enact, behold.

LIII.

But if in vain, down on the stubborn floor
Of Earth, and up to Heav'n's unopening Door,
   You gaze To-day, while You are You—how then
To-morrow, You when shall be You no more?

LIV.

Waste not your Hour, nor in the vain pursuit
Of This and That endeavour and dispute;
   Better be jocund with the fruitful Grape
Than sadden after none, or bitter, Fruit.

LV.

You know, my Friends, with what a brave Carouse
I made a Second Marriage in my house;
   Divorced old barren Reason from my Bed,
And took the Daughter of the Vine to Spouse.

LVI.

For "Is" and "Is-not" though with Rule and Line,
And " Up-and-down" by Logic I define,
  Of all that one should care to fathom, I
Was never deep in anything but—Wine.

LVII.

Ah, but my Computations, People say,
Reduced the Year to better reckoning?—Nay,
  'Twas only striking from the Calendar
Unborn To-morrow, and dead Yesterday.

LVIII.

And lately, by the Tavern Door agape,
Came shining through the Dusk an Angel Shape
  Bearing a Vessel on his Shoulder; and
He bid me taste of it; and 'twas—the Grape!

LIX.

The Grape that can with Logic absolute
The Two-and-Seventy jarring Sects confute:
  The sovereign Alchemist that in a trice
Life's leaden metal into Gold transmute:

LX.

The mighty Mahmúd, Allah-breathing Lord,
That all the misbelieving and black Horde
   Of Fears and Sorrows that infest the Soul
Scatters before him with his whirlwind Sword.

LXI.

Why, be this Juice the growth of God, who dare
Blaspheme the twisted tendril as a Snare?
   A Blessing, we should use it, should we not?
And if a Curse—why, then, Who set it there?

LXII.

I must abjure the Balm of Life, I must,
Scared by some After-reckoning ta'en on trust,
   Or lured with Hope of some Diviner Drink,
To fill the Cup—when crumbled into Dust!

LXIII.

Oh threats of Hell and Hopes of Paradise!
One thing at least is certain—*This* Life flies;
   One thing is certain and the rest is Lies;
The Flower that once has blown for ever dies.

LXIV.

Strange, is it not? that of the myriads who
Before us pass'd the door of Darkness through,
   Not one returns to tell us of the Road,
Which to discover we must travel too.

LXV.

The Revelations of Devout and Learn'd
Who rose before us, and as Prophets burn'd,
   Are all but Stories, which, awoke from Sleep
They told their comrades, and to Sleep return'd.

LXVI.

I sent my Soul through the Invisible,
Some letter of that After-life to spell:
   And by and by my Soul return'd to me,
And answer'd "I Myself am Heav'n and Hell:"

LXVII.

Heav'n but the Vision of fulfill'd Desire,
And Hell the Shadow from a Soul on fire
   Cast on the Darkness into which Ourselves,
So late emerg'd from, shall so soon expire.

LXVIII.

We are no other than a moving row
Of Magic Shadow-shapes that come and go
   Round with the Sun-illumin'd Lantern held
In Midnight by the Master of the Show;

LXIX.

But helpless Pieces of the Game He plays
Upon this Chequer-board of Nights and Days;
   Hither and thither moves, and checks, and slays,
And one by one back in the Closet lays.

LXX.

The Ball no question makes of Ayes and Noes,
But Here or There as strikes the Player goes;
   And He that toss'd you down into the Field,
He knows about it all—HE knows—HE knows!

LXXI.

The Moving Finger writes; and, having writ,
Moves on: nor all your Piety nor Wit
   Shall lure it back to cancel half a Line,
Nor all your Tears wash out a Word of it.

LXXII.

And that inverted Bowl they call the Sky,
Whereunder crawling coop'd we live and die,
   Lift not your hands to *It* for help—for It
As impotently moves as you or I.

LXXIII.

With Earth's first Clay They did the Last Man knead,
And there of the Last Harvest sow'd the Seed:
   And the first Morning of Creation wrote
What the Last Dawn of Reckoning shall read.

LXXIV.

YESTERDAY *This* Day's Madness did prepare;
TO-MORROW'S Silence, Triumph, or Despair:
   Drink! for you know not whence you came, nor why:
Drink! for you know not why you go, nor where.

LXXV.

I tell you this—When, started from the Goal,
Over the flaming shoulders of the Foal
   Of Heav'n Parwín and Mushtarí they flung,
In my predestin'd Plot of Dust and Soul

LXXVI.

The Vine had struck a fibre: which about
If clings my Being—let the Dervish flout;
   Of my Base metal may be filed a Key,
That shall unlock the Door he howls without.

LXXVII.

And this I know: whether the one True Light
Kindle to Love, or Wrath-consume me quite,
   One Flash of It within the Tavern caught
Better than in the Temple lost outright.

LXXVIII.

What! out of senseless Nothing to provoke
A conscious Something to resent the yoke
   Of unpermitted Pleasure, under pain
Of Everlasting Penalties, if broke!

LXXIX.

What! from his helpless Creature be repaid
Pure Gold for what he lent him dross-allay'd—
   Sue for a Debt we never did contract,
And cannot answer—Oh the sorry trade!

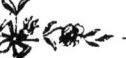

LXXX.

Oh Thou, who didst with pitfall and with gin
Beset the Road I was to wander in,
   Thou wilt not with Predestin'd Evil round
Enmesh, and then impute my Fall to Sin!

LXXXI.

Oh Thou, who Man of baser Earth didst make,
And ev'n with Paradise devise the Snake:
   For all the Sin wherewith the Face of Man
Is blacken'd—Man's forgiveness give—and take!

*   *   *   *   *   *

LXXXII.

As under cover of departing Day
Slunk hunger-stricken Ramazán away,
   Once more within the Potter's house alone
I stood, surrounded by the Shapes of Clay.

LXXXIII.

Shapes of all Sorts and Sizes, great and small,
That stood along the floor and by the wall;
   And some loquacious Vessels were; and some
Listen'd perhaps, but never talk'd at all.

LXXXIV.

Said one among them—" Surely not in vain
My substance of the common Earth was ta'en
   And to this Figure moulded, to be broke,
Or trampled back to shapeless Earth again."

LXXXV.

Then said a Second—" Ne'er a peevish Boy
" Would break the Bowl from which he drank in joy;
   " And He that with his hand the Vessel made
" Will surely not in after Wrath destroy."

LXXXVI.

After a momentary silence spake
Some Vessel of a more ungainly Make;
   " They sneer at me for leaning all awry:
" What! did the Hand then of the Potter shake?"

LXXXVII.

Whereat some one of the loquacious Lot—
I think a Súfi pipkin—waxing hot—
   "All this of Pot and Potter—Tell me then,
"Who is the Potter, pray, and who the Pot?"

LXXXVIII.

"Why," said another, "Some there are who tell
"Of one who threatens he will toss to Hell
   "The luckless Pots he marr'd in making—Pish!
"He's a Good Fellow, and 't will all be well."

LXXXIX.

"Well," murmur'd one, "Let whoso make or buy,
"My Clay with long Oblivion is gone dry:
   "But fill me with the old familiar Juice,
"Methinks I might recover by and by."

XC.

So while the Vessels one by one were speaking,
The little Moon look'd in that all were seeking:
   And then they jogg'd each other, "Brother! Brother!
"Now for the Porter's shoulder-knot a-creaking!"

* * * * * *

XCI.

Ah, with the Grape my fading Life provide,
And wash the Body whence the Life has died,
　　And lay me, shrouded in the living Leaf,
By some not unfrequented Garden-side.

XCII.

That ev'n my buried Ashes such a snare
Of Vintage shall fling up into the Air
　　As not a True-believer passing by
But shall be overtaken unaware.

XCIII.

Indeed the Idols I have loved so long
Have done my credit in this World much wrong:
　　Have drown'd my Glory in a shallow Cup,
And sold my Reputation for a Song.

XCIV.

Indeed, indeed, Repentance oft before
I swore—but was I sober when I swore?
   And then and then came Spring, and Rose-in-hand
My thread-bare Penitence apieces tore.

XCV.

And much as Wine has play'd the Infidel,
And robb'd me of my Robe of Honour—Well,
   I wonder often what the Vintners buy
One half so precious as the stuff they sell.

XCVI.

Yet Ah, that Spring should vanish with the Rose!
That Youth's sweet-scented manuscript should close!
   The Nightingale that in the branches sang,
Ah whence, and whither flown again, who knows!

XCVII.

Would but the Desert of the Fountain yield
One glimpse—if dimly, yet indeed, reveal'd,
   To which the fainting Traveller might spring,
As springs the trampled herbage of the field!

XCVIII.

Would but some wingéd Angel ere too late
Arrest the yet unfolded Roll of Fate,
　And make the stern Recorder otherwise
Enregister, or quite obliterate!

XCIX.

Ah Love! could you and I with Him conspire
To grasp this sorry Scheme of Things entire,
　Would not we shatter it to bits—and then
Re-mould it nearer to the Heart's Desire!

*　　*　　*　　*　　*　　*

C.

Yon rising Moon that looks for us again—
How oft hereafter will she wax and wane;
　How oft hereafter rising look for us
Through this same Garden—and for *one* in vain!

CI.

And when like her, oh Sákí, you shall pass
Among the Guests Star-scatter'd on the Grass,
    And in your joyous errand reach the spot
Where I made One—turn down an empty Glass!

TAMÁM.

NOTES.

(Stanza II.) The "*False Dawn ;*" *Subhi Kázib*, a transient Light on the Horizon about an hour before the *Subhi sádik*, or True Dawn ; a well-known Phenomenon in the East.

(IV.) New Year. Beginning with the Vernal Equinox, it must be remembered ; and (howsoever the old Solar Year is practically superseded by the clumsy *Lunar* Year that dates from the Mohammedan Hijra) still commemorated by a Festival that is said to have been appointed by the very Jamshyd whom Omar so often talks of, and whose yearly Calendar he helped to rectify.

"The sudden approach and rapid advance of the Spring," says Mr. Binning, "are very striking. Before the Snow is well off the Ground, the Trees burst into Blossom, and the Flowers start from the Soil. At *Naw Rooz* (*their* New Year's Day) the Snow was lying in patches on the Hills and in the shaded Vallies, while the Fruit-trees in the Garden were budding beautifully, and green Plants and Flowers springing upon the Plains on every side—

> ' And on old Hyems' Chin and icy Crown
> ' An odorous Chaplet of sweet Summer buds
> ' Is, as in mockery, set—' —

Among the Plants newly appear'd I recognized some Acquaintances I had not seen for many a Year: among these, two varieties of the Thistle ; a coarse species of the Daisy, like the Horse-gowan ; red and white Clover ; the Dock ; the blue Corn-flower ; and that vulgar Herb the Dandelion rearing its yellow crest on the Banks of the Water-courses." The Nightingale was not yet heard, for the Rose was not yet blown: but an almost identical Blackbird and Woodpecker helped to make up something of a North-country Spring.

"The White Hand of Moses." Exodus iv. 6; where Moses draws forth his Hand—not, according to the Persians, "*leprous as Snow*,"—but *white,* as our May-blossom in Spring perhaps. According to them also the Healing Power of Jesus resided in his Breath.

(V.) Iram, planted by King Shaddád, and now sunk somewhere in the Sands of Arabia. Jamshyd's Seven-ring'd Cup was typical of the 7 Heavens, 7 Planets, 7 Seas, &c., and was a *Divining Cup.*

(VI.) *Pehlevi,* the old Heroic *Sanskrit* of Persia. Háfiz also speaks of the Nightingale's *Pehlevi,* which did not change with the People's.

I am not sure if the fourth line refers to the Red Rose looking sickly, or to the Yellow Rose that ought to be Red; Red, White, and Yellow Roses all common in Persia. I think that Southey, in his Common-Place Book, quotes from some Spanish author about the Rose being White till 10 o'clock; "Rosa Perfecta" at 2; and "perfecta incarnada" at 5.

(X.) Rustum, the "Hercules" of Persia, and Zál his Father, whose exploits are among the most celebrated in the Sháh-náma. Hátim Tai, a well-known type of Oriental Generosity.

(XIII.) A Drum—beaten outside a Palace.

(XIV.) That is, the Rose's Golden Centre.

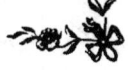

(XVIII.) Persepolis: call'd also *Takht-i-Jamshyd*—THE THRONE OF JAMSHYD, "*King Splendid,*" of the mythical *Peshdádian* Dynasty, and supposed (according to the Sháh-náma) to have been founded and built by him. Others refer it to the Work of the Genie King, Ján Ibn Ján—who also built the Pyramids—before the time of Adam.

BAHRÁM GÚR—*Bahram of the Wild Ass*—a Sassanian Sovereign—had also his Seven Castles (like the King of Bohemia!) each of a different Colour: each with a Royal Mistress within; each of whom tells him a Story, as told in one of the most famous Poems of Persia, written by Amír Khusraw: all these Sevens also figuring (according to Eastern Mysticism) the Seven Heavens; and perhaps the Book itself that Eighth, into which the mystical Seven transcend, and within which they revolve. The Ruins of Three of those Towers are yet shown by the Peasantry; as also the Swamp in which Bahrám sunk, like the Master of Ravenswood, while pursuing his *Gúr*.

> The Palace that to Heav'n his pillars threw,
> And Kings the forehead on his threshold drew—
> I saw the solitary Ringdove there,
> And "Coo, coo, coo," she cried; and "Coo, coo, coo."

This Quatrain Mr. Binning found, among several of Háfiz and others, inscribed by some stray hand among the ruins of Persepolis. The Ringdove's ancient *Pehlevi Coo, Coo, Coo*, signifies also in Persian "*Where? Where? Where?*" In Attár's "Bird-parliament" she is reproved by the Leader of the Birds for sitting still, and for ever harping on that one note of lamentation for her lost Yúsuf.

Apropos of Omar's Red Roses in Stanza xix, I am reminded of an old English Superstition, that our Anemone Pulsatilla, or purple "Pasque Flower," (which grows plentifully about the Fleam Dyke, near Cambridge), grows only where Danish Blood has been spilt.

(XXI.) A thousand years to each Planet.

(XXXI.) Saturn, Lord of the Seventh Heaven.

(XXXII.) ME-AND-THEE: some dividual Existence or Personality distinct from the Whole.

(XXXVII.) One of the Persian Poets—Attár, I think—has a pretty story about this. A thirsty Traveller dips his hand into a Spring of Water to drink from. By-and-by comes another who draws up and drinks from an earthen Bowl, and then departs, leaving his Bowl behind him. The first Traveller takes it up for another draught; but is surprised to find that the same Water which had tasted sweet from his own hand tastes bitter from the earthen Bowl. But a Voice—from Heaven, I think—tells him the clay from which the Bowl is made was once *Man*; and, into whatever shape renew'd, can never lose the bitter flavour of Mortality.

(XXXIX.) The custom of throwing a little Wine on the ground before drinking still continues in Persia, and perhaps generally in the East. Mons. Nicolas considers it " un signe de libéralité, et en même temps un avertissement que le buveur doit vider sa coupe jusqu'à la dernière goutte." Is it not more likely an ancient Superstition; a Libation to propitiate Earth, or make her an Accomplice in the illicit Revel? Or, perhaps, to divert the Jealous Eye by some sacrifice of superfluity, as with the Ancients of the West? With Omar we see something more is signified; the precious Liquor is not lost, but sinks into the ground to refresh the dust of some poor Wine-worshipper foregone.

Thus Háfiz, copying Omar in so many ways: " When thou drinkest Wine pour a draught on the ground. Wherefore fear the Sin which brings to another Gain?"

(XLIII.) According to one beautiful Oriental Legend, Azräel accomplishes his mission by holding to the nostril an Apple from the Tree of Life.

This, and the two following Stanzas would have been withdrawn, as somewhat *de trop*, from the Text, but for advice which I least like to disregard.

(LI.) From Máh to Máhi; from Fish to Moon.

(LVI.) A Jest, of course, at his Studies. A curious mathematical Quatrain of Omar's has been pointed out to me; the more curious because almost exactly parallel'd by some Verses of Doctor Donne's, that are quoted in Izaak Walton's Lives! Here is Omar: "You and I are the image of a pair of compasses; though we have two heads (sc. our *feet*) we have one body; when we have fixed the centre for our circle, we bring our heads (sc. feet) together at the end." Dr. Donne:

> If we be two, we two are so
>   As stiff twin-compasses are two;
> Thy Soul, the fixt foot, makes no show
>   To move, but does if the other do.
>
> And though thine in the centre sit,
>   Yet when my other far does roam,
> Thine leans and hearkens after it,
>   And grows erect as mine comes home.
>
> Such thou must be to me, who must
>   Like the other foot obliquely run;
> Thy firmness makes my circle just,
>   And me to end where I begun.

(LIX.) The Seventy-two Religions supposed to divide the World, *including* Islamism, as some think: but others not.

(LX.) Alluding to Sultan Mahmúd's Conquest of India and its dark people.

(LXVIII.) *Fánúsi khiyál*, a Magic-lanthorn still used in India; the cylindrical Interior being painted with various Figures, and so lightly poised and ventilated as to revolve round the lighted Candle within.

(LXX.) A very mysterious Line in the Original:

O dánad O dánad O dánad O ——

breaking off something like our Wood-pigeon's Note, which she is said to take up just where she left off.

(LXXV.) Parwín and Mushtarí—The Pleiads and Jupiter.

(LXXXVII.) This Relation of Pot and Potter to Man and his Maker figures far and wide in the Literature of the World, from the time of the Hebrew Prophets to the present; when it may finally take the name of "Pot theism," by which Mr. Carlyle ridiculed Sterling's "Pantheism." *My* Sheikh, whose knowledge flows in from all quarters, writes to me—

"Apropos of old Omar's Pots, did I ever tell you the sentence I found in 'Bishop Pearson on the Creed'? 'Thus are we wholly at the disposal of His will, and our present and future condition framed and ordered by His free, but wise and just, decrees. *Hath not the potter power over the clay, of the same lump to make one vessel unto honour, and another unto dishonour!* (Rom. ix. 21.) And can that earth-artificer have a freer power over his *brother potsherd* (both being made of the same metal), than God hath over him, who, by the strange fecundity of His omnipotent power, first made the clay out of nothing, and then him out of that?'"

And again—from a very different quarter—"I had to refer the other day to Aristophanes, and came by chance on a curious Speaking-pot story in the Vespæ, which I had quite forgotten.

4

Φιλοκλέων. Ἄκουε, μὴ φεῦγ'· ἐν Συβάρει γυνή ποτε 1. 1435
κατέαξ' ἐχῖνον.

Κατήγορος. Ταῦτ' ἐγὼ μαρτύρομαι.

Φι. Οὐχῖνος οὖν ἔχων τιν' ἐπεμαρτύρατο·
Εἶθ' ἡ Συβαρῖτις εἶπεν, ἒ ναὶ τὰν κόραν
τὴν μαρτυρίαν ταύτην ἐάσας, ἐν τάχει
ἐπίδεσμον ἐπρίω, νοῦν ἂν εἶχες πλείονα.

"The Pot calls a bystander to be a witness to his bad treatment. The woman says, 'If, by Proserpine, instead of all this 'testifying' (comp. Cuddie and his mother in ' Old Mortality !') you would buy yourself a rivet, it would show more sense in you !' The Scholiast explains *echinus* as ἄγγος τι ἐκ κεράμου."

One more illustration for the oddity's sake from the " Autobiography of a Cornish Rector," by the late James Hamley Tregenna. 1871.

" There was one old Fellow in our Company—he was so like a Figure in the ' Pilgrim's Progress ' that Richard always called him the ' ALLEGORY, ' with a long white beard—a rare Appendage in those days—and a Face the colour of which seemed to have been baked in, like the Faces one used to see on Earthenware Jugs. In our Country-dialect Earthenware is called ' *Clome* '; so the Boys of the Village used to shout out after him—' Go back to the Potter, Old Clome-face, and get baked over again.' For the ' Allegory,' though shrewd enough in most things, had the reputation of being ' *saift-baked*,' i.e., of weak intellect.

(XC.) At the Close of the Fasting Month, Ramazán (which makes the Musulman unhealthy and unamiable), the first Glimpse of the New Moon (who rules their division of the Year), is looked for with the utmost Anxiety, aud hailed with Acclamation. Then it is that the Porter's Knot may be heard—toward the *Cellar*. Omar has elsewhere a pretty Quatrain about the same Moon—

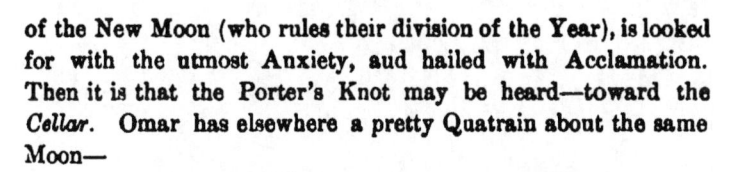

" Be of Good Cheer—the sullen Month will die,
" And a young Moon requite us by and by :
   " Look how the Old one meagre, bent, and wan
" With Age and Fast, is fainting from the Sky !"

FINIS.

شهسوار انجو شش بمیدان آ می گویی زنا

Welcome, Prince of Horsemen, welcome!
Ride a field, and strike the Ball!

LETTERS

AND

LITERARY REMAINS

OF

EDWARD FITZGERALD

EDITED BY

WILLIAM ALDIS WRIGHT

IN THREE VOLUMES.

VOL. III.

London:
MACMILLAN AND CO.
AND NEW YORK.
1889

[All Rights reserved.]

RUBÁIYÁT

OF

OMAR KHAYYÁM,

THE

ASTRONOMER-POET OF PERSIA.

𝕽𝖊𝖓𝖉𝖊𝖗𝖊𝖉 𝖎𝖓𝖙𝖔 𝕰𝖓𝖌𝖑𝖎𝖘𝖍 𝖁𝖊𝖗𝖘𝖊.

OMAR KHAYYÁM,

THE

ASTRONOMER-POET OF PERSIA.

OMAR KHAYYÁM was born at Naishápúr in Khorassán in the latter half of our Eleventh, and died within the First Quarter of our Twelfth Century. The slender Story of his Life is curiously twined about that of two other very considerable Figures in their Time and Country: one of whom tells the Story of all Three. This was Nizám ul Mulk, Vizyr to Alp Arslan the Son, and Malik Shah the Grandson, of Toghrul Beg the Tartar, who had wrested Persia from the feeble Successor of Mahmúd the Great, and founded that Seljukian Dynasty which finally roused Europe into the Crusades. This Nizám ul Mulk, in his *Wasiyat*—or *Testament*—which he wrote and left as a Memorial for future Statesmen—relates the following, as quoted in the *Calcutta Review*, No 59, from Mirkhond's History of the Assassins.

"'One of the greatest of the wise men of Khorassan 'was the Imám Mowaffak of Naishápúr, a man highly 'honoured and reverenced,—may God rejoice his soul;

'his illustrious years exceeded eighty-five, and it was the 'universal belief that every boy who read the Koran or 'studied the traditions in his presence, would assuredly 'attain to honour and happiness. For this cause did my 'father send me from Tús to Naishápúr with Abd-us-samad, 'the doctor of law, that I might employ myself in study 'and learning under the guidance of that illustrious teacher. 'Towards me he ever turned an eye of favour and kindness, 'and as his pupil I felt for him extreme affection and 'devotion, so that I passed four years in his service. When 'I first came there, I found two other pupils of mine own 'age newly arrived, Hakim Omar Khayyám, and the ill-fated 'Ben Sabbáh. Both were endowed with sharpness of wit 'and the highest natural powers; and we three formed a 'close friendship together. When the Imám rose from his 'lectures, they used to join me, and we repeated to each 'other the lessons we had heard. Now Omar was a native 'of Naishápúr, while Hasan Ben Sabbáh's father was one 'Ali, a man of austere life and practice, but heretical in his 'creed and doctrine. One day Hasan said to me and to 'Khayyám, 'It is a universal belief that the pupils of the 'Imám Mowaffak will attain to fortune. Now, even if we '*all* do not attain thereto, without doubt one of us will; what 'then shall be our mutual pledge and bond?' We answered, ''Be it what you please.' 'Well,' he said, 'let us make a vow, 'that to whomsoever this fortune falls, he shall share it 'equally with the rest, and reserve no pre-eminence for him-'self.' 'Be it so,' we both replied, and on those terms we 'mutually pledged our words. Years rolled on, and I went 'from Khorassan to Transoxiana, and wandered to Ghazni 'and Cabul; and when I returned, I was invested with 'office, and rose to be administrator of affairs during the 'Sultanate of Sultan Alp Arslán.'

"He goes on to state, that years passed by, and both his old school-friends found him out, and came and claimed a share in his good fortune, according to the school-day vow. The Vizier was generous and kept his word. Hasan demanded a place in the government, which the Sultan granted at the Vizier's request; but discontented with a gradual rise, he plunged into the maze of intrigue of an oriental court, and, failing in a base attempt to supplant his benefactor, he was disgraced and fell. After many mishaps and wanderings, Hasan became the head of the Persian sect of the *Ismailians*, —a party of fanatics who had long murmured in obscurity, but rose to an evil eminence under the guidance of his strong and evil will. In A.D. 1090, he seized the castle of Alamút, in the province of Rúdbar, which lies in the mountainous tract south of the Caspian Sea; and it was from this mountain home he obtained that evil celebrity among the Crusaders as the OLD MAN OF THE MOUNTAINS, and spread terror through the Mohammedan world; and it is yet disputed whether the word *Assassin*, which they have left in the language of modern Europe as their dark memorial, is derived from the *hashish*, or opiate of hemp-leaves (the Indian *bhang*), with which they maddened themselves to the sullen pitch of oriental desperation, or from the name of the founder of the dynasty, whom we have seen in his quiet collegiate days, at Naishápúr. One of the countless victims of the Assassin's dagger was Nizám-ul-Mulk himself, the old school-boy friend *.

* Some of Omar's Rubáiyát warn us of the danger of Greatness, the instability of Fortune, and while advocating Charity to all Men, recommending us to be too intimate with none. Attár makes Nizám-ul-Mulk use the very words of his friend Omar [Rub. xxviii.], "When Nizám-ul-Mulk was in the Agony (of Death) he said, 'Oh God! I am passing away in the hand of the Wind.'"

"Omar Khayyám also came to the Vizier to claim his share; but not to ask for title or office. 'The greatest boon 'you can confer on me,' he said, 'is to let me live in a corner 'under the shadow of your fortune, to spread wide the 'advantages of Science, and pray for your long life and 'prosperity.' The Vizier tells us, that, when he found Omar was really sincere in his refusal, he pressed him no further, but granted him a yearly pension of 1200 *mithkáls* of gold, from the treasury of Naishápúr.

"At Naishápúr thus lived and died Omar Khayyám, 'busied,' adds the Vizier, 'in winning knowledge of every kind, 'and especially in Astronomy, wherein he attained to a very 'high pre-eminence. Under the Sultanate of Malik Shah, he 'came to Merv, and obtained great praise for his proficiency 'in science, and the Sultan showered favours upon him.'

"When Malik Shah determined to reform the calendar, Omar was one of the eight learned men employed to do it; the result was the *Jaláli* era (so called from *Jalál-ud-din*, one of the king's names)—'a computation of time,' says Gibbon, 'which surpasses the Julian, and approaches the accuracy of the Gregorian style.' He is also the author of some astronomical tables, entitled Zíji-Malikshahí," and the French have lately republished and translated an Arabic Treatise of his on Algebra.

"His Takhallus or poetical name (Khayyám) signifies a Tent-maker, and he is said to have at one time exercised that trade, perhaps before Nizám-ul-Mulk's generosity raised him to independence. Many Persian poets similarly derive their names from their occupations; thus we have Attár, 'a druggist,' Assár, 'an oil presser,' &c.* Omar himself alludes to his name in the following whimsical lines:—

* Though all these, like our Smiths, Archers, Millers, Fletchers, &c., may simply retain the Surname of an hereditary calling.

'Khayyám, who stitched the tents of science,
Has fallen in grief's furnace and been suddenly burned;
The shears of Fate have cut the tent ropes of his life,
And the broker of Hope has sold him for nothing!'

"We have only one more anecdote to give of his Life, and that relates to the close; it is told in the anonymous preface which is sometimes prefixed to his poems; it has been printed in the Persian in the Appendix to Hyde's *Veterum Persarum Religio*, p. 499; and D'Herbelot alludes to it in his Bibliothèque, under *Khiam* *:—

"'It is written in the chronicles of the ancients that this 'King of the Wise, Omar Khayyám, died at Naishápúr in 'the year of the Hegira, 517 (A.D. 1123); in science he was 'unrivalled,—the very paragon of his age. Khwájah Nizámi 'of Samarcand, who was one of his pupils, relates the 'following story: 'I often used to hold conversations with 'my teacher, Omar Khayyám, in a garden; and one day he 'said to me, 'My tomb shall be in a spot where the north 'wind may scatter roses over it.' I wondered at the words 'he spake, but I knew that his were no idle words †. Years 'after, when I chanced to revisit Naishápúr, I went to his 'final resting-place, and lo! it was just outside a garden, and

---

* "Philosophe Musulman qui a vécu en Odeur de Sainteté dans sa Religion, vers la Fin du premier et le Commencement du second Siècle," no part of which, except the " Philosophe," can apply to our Khayyám.

† The Rashness of the Words, according to D'Herbelot, consisted in being so opposed to those in the Korán: "No Man knows where he shall die."—This story of Omar reminds me of another so naturally—and when one remembers how wide of his humble mark the noble sailor aimed—so pathetically told by Captain Cook—not by Doctor Hawkesworth—in his Second Voyage (i. 374). When leaving Ulietea, "Oreo's last request was for me to return. When he saw he could not obtain that promise, he asked the name of my *Marai* (burying-place).

'trees laden with fruit stretched their boughs over the garden 'wall, and dropped their flowers upon his tomb, so that the 'stone was hidden under them.'"

Thus far—without fear of Trespass—from the *Calcutta Review*. The writer of it, on reading in India this story of Omar's Grave, was reminded, he says, of Cicero's Account of finding Archimedes' Tomb at Syracuse, buried in grass and weeds. I think Thorwaldsen desired to have roses grow over him; a wish religiously fulfilled for him to the present day, I believe. However, to return to Omar.

Though the Sultan "shower'd Favours upon him," Omar's Epicurean Audacity of Thought and Speech caused him to be regarded askance in his own Time and Country. He is said to have been especially hated and dreaded by the Súfis, whose Practice he ridiculed, and whose Faith amounts to little more than his own, when stript of the Mysticism and formal recognition of Islamism under which Omar would not hide. Their Poets, including Háfiz, who are (with the exception of Firdausi) the most considerable in Persia, borrowed largely, indeed, of Omar's material, but turning it to a mystical Use more convenient to Themselves and the People they addressed; a People quite as quick of Doubt as of Belief; as keen of Bodily Sense as of Intellectual; and delighting in a cloudy composition of both, in which they could float luxuriously between Heaven and Earth, and this

---

As strange a question as this was, I hesitated not a moment to tell him 'Stepney;' the parish in which I live when in London. I was made to repeat it several times over till they could pronounce it; and then 'Stepney Marai no Toote' was echoed through an hundred mouths at once. I afterwards found the same question had been put to Mr Forster by a man on shore; but he gave a different, and indeed more proper answer, by saying, 'No man who used the sea could say where he should be buried.'"

World and the Next, on the wings of a poetical expression, that might serve indifferently for either. Omar was too honest of Heart as well as of Head for this. Having failed (however mistakenly) of finding any Providence but Destiny, and any World but This, he set about making the most of it; preferring rather to soothe the Soul through the Senses into Acquiescence with Things as he saw them, than to perplex it with vain disquietude after what they *might* be. It has been seen, however, that his Worldly Ambition was not exorbitant; and he very likely takes a humorous or perverse pleasure in exalting the gratification of Sense above that of the Intellect, in which he must have taken great delight, although it failed to answer the Questions in which he, in common with all men, was most vitally interested.

For whatever Reason, however, Omar, as before said, has never been popular in his own Country, and therefore has been but scantily transmitted abroad. The MSS. of his Poems, mutilated beyond the average Casualties of Oriental Transcription, are so rare in the East as scarce to have reacht Westward at all, in spite of all the acquisitions of Arms and Science. There is no copy at the India House, none at the Bibliothèque Nationale of Paris. We know but of one in England: No. 140 of the Ouseley MSS. at the Bodleian, written at Shiráz, A.D. 1460. This contains but 158 Rubáiyát. One in the Asiatic Society's Library at Calcutta (of which we have a Copy), contains (and yet incomplete) 516, though swelled to that by all kinds of Repetition and Corruption. So Von Hammer speaks of *his* Copy as containing about 200, while Dr. Sprenger catalogues the Lucknow MS. at double that number*. The Scribes,

---

* "Since this Paper was written (adds the Reviewer in a note), " we have met with a Copy of a very rare Edition, printed at Calcutta

too, of the Oxford and Calcutta MSS. seem to do their Work under a sort of Protest; each beginning with a Tetrastich (whether genuine or not), taken out of its alphabetical order; the Oxford with one of Apology; the Calcutta with one of Expostulation, supposed (says a Notice prefixed to the MS.) to have arisen from a Dream, in which Omar's mother asked about his future fate. It may be rendered thus:—

"Oh Thou who burn'st in Heart for those who burn
"In Hell, whose fires thyself shall feed in turn;
 "How long be crying, 'Mercy on them, God!'
"Why, who art Thou to teach, and He to learn?"

The Bodleian Quatrain pleads Pantheism by way of Justification.

"If I myself upon a looser Creed
"Have loosely strung the Jewel of Good deed,
"Let this one thing for my Atonement plead:
"That One for Two I never did mis-read."

The Reviewer*, to whom I owe the Particulars of Omar's Life, concludes his Review by comparing him with Lucretius, both as to natural Temper and Genius, and as acted upon by the Circumstances in which he lived. Both indeed were men of subtle, strong, and cultivated Intellect, fine Imagination, and Hearts passionate for Truth and Justice; who justly revolted from their Country's false Religion, and false, or foolish, Devotion to it; but who fell short of replacing what they subverted by such better *Hope* as others, with no better Revelation to guide them, had yet made a Law to themselves. Lucretius, indeed, with such material as

in 1836. This contains 438 Tetrastichs, with an Appendix containing 54 others not found in some MSS."

* Professor Cowell.

Epicurus furnished, satisfied himself with the theory of a vast machine fortuitously constructed, and acting by a Law that implied no Legislator; and so composing himself into a Stoical rather than Epicurean severity of Attitude, sat down to contemplate the mechanical Drama of the Universe which he was part Actor in; himself and all about him (as in his own sublime description of the Roman Theatre) discoloured with the lurid reflex of the Curtain suspended between the Spectator and the Sun. Omar, more desperate, or more careless of any so complicated System as resulted in nothing but hopeless Necessity, flung his own Genius and Learning with a bitter or humorous jest into the general Ruin which their insufficient glimpses only served to reveal; and, pretending sensual pleasure as the serious purpose of Life, only *diverted* himself with speculative problems of Deity, Destiny, Matter and Spirit, Good and Evil, and other such questions, easier to start than to run down, and the pursuit of which becomes a very weary sport at last!

With regard to the present Translation. The original Rubáiyát (as, missing an Arabic Guttural, these *Tetrastichs* are more musically called) are independent Stanzas, consisting each of four Lines of equal, though varied, Prosody; sometimes *all* rhyming, but oftener (as here imitated) the third line a blank. Somewhat as in the Greek Alcaic, where the penultimate line seems to lift and suspend the Wave that falls over in the last. As usual with such kind of Oriental Verse, the Rubáiyát follow one another according to Alphabetic Rhyme—a strange succession of Grave and Gay. Those here selected are strung into something of an Eclogue, with perhaps a less than equal proportion of the "Drink and make-merry," which (genuine or not) recurs over-frequently in the Original. Either way, the Result is sad enough: saddest perhaps when most ostentatiously merry: more apt to move Sorrow than Anger toward the old Tentmaker, who, after vainly endeavouring to unshackle his Steps from Destiny, and to catch some authentic Glimpse of To-morrow, fell back upon To-day (which has outlasted so many To-morrows!) as the only Ground he had got to stand upon, however momentarily slipping from under his Feet.

While the second Edition of this version of Omar was preparing, Monsieur Nicolas, French Consul at Resht, published a very careful and very good Edition of the Text, from a lithograph copy at Teheran, comprising 464 Rubáiyát, with translation and notes of his own.

Mons. Nicolas, whose Edition has reminded me of several things, and instructed me in others, does not consider Omar to be the material Epicurean that I have literally taken him for, but a Mystic, shadowing the Deity under the figure of Wine, Wine-bearer, &c., as Háfiz is supposed to do; in short, a Súfi Poet like Háfiz and the rest.

I cannot see reason to alter my opinion, formed as it was more than a dozen years ago* when Omar was first shown me by one to whom I am indebted for all I know of Oriental, and very much of other, literature. He admired Omar's Genius so much, that he would gladly have adopted any such Interpretation of his meaning as Mons. Nicolas' if he could†. That he could not, appears by his Paper in the Calcutta Review already so largely quoted; in which he

---

* [This was written in 1868. W. A. W.]

† Perhaps would have edited the Poems himself some years ago. He may now as little approve of my Version on one side, as of Mons. Nicholas' Theory on the other.

argues from the Poems themselves, as well as from what records remain of the Poet's Life.

And if more were needed to disprove Mons. Nicolas' Theory, there is the Biographical Notice which he himself has drawn up in direct contradiction to the Interpretation of the Poems given in his Notes. (See pp. xiii–xiv. of his Preface.) Indeed I hardly knew poor Omar was so far gone till his Apologist informed me. For here we see that, whatever were the Wine that Háfiz drank and sang, the veritable Juice of the Grape it was which Omar used, not only when carousing with his friends, but (says Mons. Nicolas) in order to excite himself to that pitch of Devotion which others reached by cries and "hurlemens." And yet, whenever Wine, Wine-bearer, &c. occur in the text—which is often enough—Mons. Nicolas carefully annotates "Dieu," "La Divinité," &c.: so carefully indeed that one is tempted to think that he was indoctrinated by the Súfi with whom he read the Poems. (Note to Rub. ii. p. 8.) A Persian would naturally wish to vindicate a distinguished Countryman; and a Súfi to enrol him in his own sect, which already comprises all the chief Poets of Persia.

What historical Authority has Mons. Nicolas to show that Omar gave himself up "avec passion à l'étude de la philosophie des Soufis"? (Preface, p. xiii.) The Doctrines of Pantheism, Materialism, Necessity, &c., were not peculiar to the Súfi; nor to Lucretius before them; nor to Epicurus before him; probably the very original Irreligion of Thinking men from the first; and very likely to be the spontaneous growth of a Philosopher living in an Age of social and political barbarism, under shadow of one of the Two and Seventy Religions supposed to divide the world. Von Hammer (according to Sprenger's Oriental Catalogue) speaks of Omar as "a Free-thinker, and *a great opponent of Sufism;*" perhaps because, while holding much of their Doctrine, he would not pretend to any inconsistent severity of morals. Sir W. Ouseley has written a note to something of the same effect on the fly-leaf of the Bodleian MS. And in two Rubáiyát of Mons. Nicolas' own Edition Súf and Súfi are both disparagingly named.

No doubt many of these Quatrains seem unaccountable unless mystically interpreted; but many more as unaccountable unless literally. Were the Wine spiritual, for instance, how wash the Body with it when dead? Why make cups of the dead clay to be filled with—" La Divinité"—by some succeeding Mystic? Mons. Nicolas himself is puzzled by some "bizarres" and "trop Orientales" allusions and images—" d'une sensualité quelquefois révoltante" indeed— which "les convenances" do not permit him to translate; but still which the reader cannot but refer to "La Divinité*." No doubt also many of the Quatrains in the Teheran, as in the Calcutta, Copies, are spurious; such *Rubáiyát* being the common form of Epigram in Persia. But this, at best, tells as much one way as another; nay, the Súfi, who may be considered the Scholar and Man of Letters in Persia, would be far more likely than the careless Epicure to inter-

---

* A Note to Quatrain 234 admits that, however clear the mystical meaning of such Images must be to Europeans, they are not quoted without "rougissant" even by laymen in Persia—"Quant aux termes de tendresse qui commencent ce quatrain, comme tant d'autres dans ce recueil, nos lecteurs, habitués maintenant á l'étrangeté des expressions si souvent employés par Khéyam pour rendre ses pensées sur l'amour divin, et à la singularité de ses images trop orientales, d'une sensualité quelquefois révoltante, n'auront pas de peine à se persuader qu'il s'agit de la Divinité, bien que cette conviction soit vivement discutée par les moullahs musulmans et même par beaucoup de laïques, qui rougissent véritablement d'une pareille licence de leur compatriote à l'égard des choses spirituelles."

polate what favours his own view of the Poet. I observe that very few of the more mystical Quatrians are in the Bodleian MS. which must be one of the oldest, as dated at Shiraz, A.H. 865, A.D. 1460. And this, I think, especially distinguishes Omar (I cannot help calling him by his—no, not Christian—familiar name) from all other Persian Poets: That, whereas with them the Poet is lost in his Song, the Man in Allegory and Abstraction; we seem to have the Man—the *Bonhomme*—Omar himself, with all his Humours and Passions, as frankly before us as if we were really at Table with him, after the Wine had gone round.

I must say that I, for one, never wholly believed in the Mysticism of Háfiz. It does not appear there was any danger in holding and singing Súfi Pantheism, so long as the Poet made his Salaam to Mohammed at the beginning and end of his Song. Under such conditions Jeláluddín, Jámí, Attár, and others sang; using Wine and Beauty indeed as Images to illustrate, not as a Mask to hide, the Divinity they were celebrating. Perhaps some Allegory less liable to mistake or abuse had been better among so inflammable a People: much more so when, as some think with Háfiz and Omar, the abstract is not only likened to, but identified with, the sensual Image; hazardous, if not to the Devotee himself, yet to his weaker Brethren; and worse for the Profane in proportion as the Devotion of the Initiated grew warmer. And all for what? To be tantalized with Images of sensual enjoyment which must be renounced if one would approximate a God, who according to the Doctrine, *is* Sensual Matter as well as Spirit, and into whose Universe one expects unconsciously to merge after Death, without hope of any posthumous Beatitude in another world to compensate for all one's self-denial in this. Lucretius' blind Divinity certainly merited, and probably got, as much self-sacrifice as this of the Súfi; and the burden of Omar's Song—if not " Let us eat"—is assuredly—" Let us drink, for Tomorrow we die!" And if Háfiz meant quite otherwise by a similar language, he surely miscalculated when he devoted his Life and Genius to so equivocal a Psalmody as, from his Day to this, has been said and sung by any rather than Spiritual Worshippers.

However, as there is some traditional presumption, and certainly the opinion of some learned men, in favour of Omar's being a Súfí—and even something of a Saint—those who please may so interpret his Wine and Cup-bearer. On the other hand, as there is far more historical certainty of his being a Philosopher, of scientific Insight and Ability far beyond that of the Age and Country he lived in; of such moderate worldly Ambition as becomes a Philosopher, and such moderate wants as rarely satisfy a Debauchee; other readers may be content to believe with me that, while the Wine Omar celebrates is simply the Juice of the Grape, he bragged more than he drank of it, in very defiance perhaps of that Spiritual Wine which left its Votaries sunk in Hypocrisy or Disgust.

RUBÁIYÁT

OF

OMAR KHAYYÁM OF NAISHÁPÚR.

I.

WAKE! For the Sun, who scatter'd into flight
The Stars before him from the Field of Night,
  Drives Night along with them from Heav'n, and strikes
The Sultán's Turret with a Shaft of Light.

II.

Before the phantom of False morning died,
Methought a Voice within the Tavern cried,
  "When all the Temple is prepared within,
"Why nods the drowsy Worshipper outside?"

III.

And, as the Cock crew, those who stood before
The Tavern shouted—"Open then the Door!
  "You know how little while we have to stay,
"And, once departed, may return no more."

IV.

Now the New Year reviving old Desires,
The thoughtful Soul to Solitude retires,
  Where the WHITE HAND OF MOSES on the Bough
Puts out, and Jesus from the Ground suspires.

V.

Iram indeed is gone with all his Rose,
And Jamshyd's Sev'n-ring'd Cup where no one knows;
  But still a Ruby kindles in the Vine,
And many a Garden by the Water blows.

VI.

And David's lips are lockt; but in divine
High-piping Pehleví, with "Wine! Wine! Wine!
  "Red Wine!"—the Nightingale cries to the Rose
That sallow cheek of hers to' incarnadine.

VII.

Come, fill the Cup, and in the fire of Spring
Your Winter-garment of Repentance fling:
  The Bird of Time has but a little way
To flutter—and the Bird is on the Wing.

VIII.

Whether at Naishápúr or Babylon,
Whether the Cup with sweet or bitter run,
  The Wine of Life keeps oozing drop by drop,
The Leaves of Life keep falling one by one.

IX.

Each Morn a thousand Roses brings, you say;
Yes, but where leaves the Rose of Yesterday?
  And this first Summer month that brings the Rose
Shall take Jamshyd and Kaikobád away.

X.

Well, let it take them! What have we to do
With Kaikobád the Great, or Kaikhosrú?
   Let Zál and Rustum bluster as they will,
Or Hátim call to Supper—heed not you.

XI.

With me along the strip of Herbage strown
That just divides the desert from the sown,
   Where name of Slave and Sultán is forgot—
And Peace to Mahmúd on his golden Throne!

XII.

A Book of Verses underneath the Bough,
A Jug of Wine, a Loaf of Bread—and Thou
   Beside me singing in the Wilderness—
Oh, Wilderness were Paradise enow!

XIII.

Some for the Glories of This World; and some
Sigh for the Prophet's Paradise to come;
   Ah, take the Cash, and let the Credit go,
Nor heed the rumble of a distant Drum!

XIV.

Look to the blowing Rose about us—"Lo,
"Laughing," she says, "into the world I blow,
   "At once the silken tassel of my Purse
"Tear, and its Treasure on the Garden throw."

XV.

And those who husbanded the Golden grain,
And those who flung it to the winds like Rain,
   Alike to no such aureate Earth are turn'd
As, buried once, Men want dug up again.

XVI.

The Worldly Hope men set their Hearts upon
Turns Ashes—or it prospers; and anon,
   Like Snow upon the Desert's dusty Face,
Lighting a little hour or two—is gone.

XVII.

Think, in this batter'd Caravanserai
Whose Portals are alternate Night and Day,
   How Sultán after Sultán with his Pomp
Abode his destined Hour, and went his way.

XVIII.

They say the Lion and the Lizard keep
The Courts where Jamshyd gloried and drank deep:
   And Bahrám, that great Hunter—the Wild Ass
Stamps o'er his Head, but cannot break his Sleep.

XIX.

I sometimes think that never blows so red
The Rose as where some buried Cæsar bled;
   That every Hyacinth the Garden wears
Dropt in her Lap from some once lovely Head.

XX.

And this reviving Herb whose tender Green
Fledges the River-Lip on which we lean—
   Ah, lean upon it lightly! for who knows
From what once lovely Lip it springs unseen!

XXI.

Ah, my Belovéd, fill the Cup that clears
TO-DAY of past Regrets and future Fears:
   To-morrow!—Why, To-morrow I may be
Myself with Yesterday's Sev'n thousand Years.

XXII.

For some we loved, the loveliest and the best
That from his Vintage rolling Time hath prest,
  Have drunk their Cup a Round or two before,
And one by one crept silently to rest.

XXIII.

And we, that now make merry in the Room
They left, and Summer dresses in new bloom,
  Ourselves must we beneath the Couch of Earth
Descend—ourselves to make a Couch—for whom?

XXIV.

Ah, make the most of what we yet may spend,
Before we too into the Dust descend;
  Dust into Dust, and under Dust to lie,
Sans Wine, sans Song, sans Singer, and—sans End!

XXV.

Alike for those who for To-day prepare,
And those that after some To-morrow stare,
  A Muezzín from the Tower of Darkness cries,
"Fools! your Reward is neither Here nor There."

XXVI.

Why, all the Saints and Sages who discuss'd
Of the Two Worlds so wisely—they are thrust
  Like foolish Prophets forth; their Words to Scorn
Are scatter'd, and their Mouths are stopt with Dust.

XXVII.

Myself when young did eagerly frequent
Doctor and Saint, and heard great argument
  About it and about: but evermore
Came out by the same door where in I went.

XXVIII.

With them the seed of Wisdom did I sow,
And with mine own hand wrought to make it grow;
   And this was all the Harvest that I reap'd—
"I came like Water, and like Wind I go."

XXIX.

Into this Universe, and *Why* not knowing
Nor *Whence*, like Water willy-nilly flowing;
   And out of it, as Wind along the Waste,
I know not *Whither*, willy-nilly blowing.

XXX.

What, without asking, hither hurried *Whence?*
And, without asking, *Whither* hurried hence!
   Oh, many a Cup of this forbidden Wine
Must drown the memory of that insolence!

XXXI.

Up from Earth's Centre through the Seventh Gate
I rose, and on the Throne of Saturn sate,
   And many a Knot unravel'd by the Road;
But not the Master-knot of Human Fate.

XXXII.

There was the Door to which I found no Key;
There was the Veil through which I might not see:
   Some little talk awhile of ME and THEE
There was—and then no more of THEE and ME.

XXXIII.

Earth could not answer; nor the Seas that mourn
In flowing Purple, of their Lord forlorn;
   Nor rolling Heaven, with all his Signs reveal'd
And hidden by the sleeve of Night and Morn.

OMAR KHAYYÁM.

XXXIV.

Then of the THEE IN ME who works behind
The Veil, I lifted up my hands to find
   A lamp amid the Darkness; and I heard,
As from Without—"THE ME WITHIN THEE BLIND!"

XXXV.

Then to the Lip of this poor earthen Urn
I lean'd, the Secret of my Life to learn:
   And Lip to Lip it murmur'd—"While you live,
"Drink!—for, once dead, you never shall return."

XXXVI.

I think the Vessel, that with fugitive
Articulation answer'd, once did live,
   And drink; and Ah! the passive Lip I kiss'd,
How many Kisses might it take—and give!

XXXVII.

For I remember stopping by the way
To watch a Potter thumping his wet Clay:
   And with its all-obliterated Tongue
It murmur'd—"Gently, Brother, gently, pray!"

XXXVIII.

And has not such a Story from of Old
Down Man's successive generations roll'd
   Of such a clod of saturated Earth
Cast by the Maker into Human mould?

XXXIX.

And not a drop that from our Cups we throw
For Earth to drink of, but may steal below
   To quench the fire of Anguish in some Eye
There hidden—far beneath, and long ago.

XL.

As then the Tulip for her morning sup
Of Heav'nly Vintage from the soil looks up,
  Do you devoutly do the like, till Heav'n
To Earth invert you—like an empty Cup.

XLI.

Perplext no more with Human or Divine,
To-morrow's tangle to the winds resign,
  And lose your fingers in the tresses of
The Cypress-slender Minister of Wine.

XLII.

And if the Wine you drink, the Lip you press,
End in what All begins and ends in—Yes;
  Think then you are TO-DAY what YESTERDAY
You were—TO-MORROW you shall not be less.

XLIII.

So when that Angel of the darker Drink
At last shall find you by the river-brink,
  And, offering his Cup, invite your Soul
Forth to your Lips to quaff—you shall not shrink.

XLIV.

Why, if the Soul can fling the Dust aside,
And naked on the Air of Heaven ride,
  Were't not a Shame—were't not a Shame for him
In this clay carcase crippled to abide?

XLV.

'Tis but a Tent where takes his one day's rest
A Sultán to the realm of Death addrest;
  The Sultán rises, and the dark Ferrásh
Strikes, and prepares it for another Guest.

XLVI.

And fear not lest Existence closing your
Account, and mine, should know the like no more;
   The Eternal Sákí from that Bowl has pour'd
Millions of Bubbles like us, and will pour.

XLVII.

When You and I behind the Veil are past,
Oh, but the long, long while the World shall last,
   Which of our Coming and Departure heeds
As the Sea's self should heed a pebble-cast.

XLVIII.

A Moment's Halt—a momentary taste
Of BEING from the Well amid the Waste—
   And Lo!—the phantom Caravan has reach'd
The NOTHING it set out from—Oh, make haste!

XLIX.

Would you that spangle of Existence spend
About THE SECRET—quick about it, Friend!
   A Hair perhaps divides the False and True—
And upon what, prithee, may life depend?

L.

A Hair perhaps divides the False and True;
Yes; and a single Alif were the clue—
   Could you but find it—to the Treasure-house,
And peradventure to THE MASTER too;

LI.

Whose secret Presence, through Creation's veins
Running Quicksilver-like eludes your pains;
   Taking all shapes from Máh to Máhi; and
They change and perish all—but He remains;

LII.

A moment guess'd—then back behind the Fold
Immerst of Darkness round the Drama roll'd
  Which, for the Pastime of Eternity,
He doth Himself contrive, enact, behold.

LIII.

But if in vain, down on the stubborn floor
Of Earth, and up to Heav'n's unopening Door,
  You gaze TO-DAY, while You are You—how then
TO-MORROW, You when shall be You no more?

LIV.

Waste not your Hour, nor in the vain pursuit
Of This and That endeavour and dispute;
  Better be jocund with the fruitful Grape
Than sadden after none, or bitter, Fruit.

LV.

You know, my Friends, with what a brave Carouse
I made a Second Marriage in my house;
  Divorced old barren Reason from my Bed,
And took the Daughter of the Vine to Spouse.

LVI.

For "Is" and "IS-NOT" though with Rule and Line
And "UP-AND-DOWN" by Logic I define,
  Of all that one should care to fathom, I
Was never deep in anything but—Wine.

LVII.

Ah, but my Computations, People say,
Reduced the Year to better reckoning?—Nay,
  'Twas only striking from the Calendar
Unborn To-morrow, and dead Yesterday.

LVIII.

And lately, by the Tavern Door agape,
Came shining through the Dusk an Angel Shape
   Bearing a Vessel on his Shoulder; and
He bid me taste of it; and 'twas—the Grape!

LIX.

The Grape that can with Logic absolute
The Two-and-Seventy jarring Sects confute:
   The sovereign Alchemist that in a trice
Life's leaden metal into Gold transmute:

LX.

The mighty Mahmúd, Allah-breathing Lord,
That all the misbelieving and black Horde
   Of Fears and Sorrows that infest the Soul
Scatters before him with his whirlwind Sword.

LXI.

Why, be this Juice the growth of God, who dare
Blaspheme the twisted tendril as a Snare?
   A Blessing, we should use it, should we not?
And if a Curse—why, then, Who set it there?

LXII.

I must abjure the Balm of Life, I must,
Scared by some After-reckoning ta'en on trust,
   Or lured with Hope of some Diviner Drink,
To fill the Cup—when crumbled into Dust!

LXIII.

Oh threats of Hell and Hopes of Paradise!
One thing at least is certain—*This* Life flies;
   One thing is certain and the rest is Lies;
The Flower that once has blown for ever dies.

LXIV.

Strange, is it not? that of the myriads who
Before us pass'd the door of Darkness through,
 Not one returns to tell us of the Road,
Which to discover we must travel too.

LXV.

The Revelations of Devout and Learn'd
Who rose before us, and as Prophets burn'd,
 Are all but Stories, which, awoke from Sleep
They told their comrades, and to Sleep return'd.

LXVI.

I sent my Soul through the Invisible,
Some letter of that After-life to spell:
 And by and by my Soul return'd to me,
And answer'd "I Myself am Heav'n and Hell:"

LXVII.

Heav'n but the Vision of fulfill'd Desire,
And Hell the Shadow from a Soul on fire,
 Cast on the Darkness into which Ourselves,
So late emerged from, shall so soon expire.

LXVIII.

We are no other than a moving row
Of Magic Shadow-shapes that come and go
 Round with the Sun-illumined Lantern held
In Midnight by the Master of the Show;

LXIX.

But helpless Pieces of the Game He plays
Upon this Chequer-board of Nights and Days;
 Hither and thither moves, and checks, and slays,
And one by one back in the Closet lays.

LXX.

The Ball no question makes of Ayes and Noes,
But Here or There as strikes the Player goes;
   And He that toss'd you down into the Field,
He knows about it all—HE knows—HE knows!

LXXI.

The Moving Finger writes; and, having writ,
Moves on: nor all your Piety nor Wit
   Shall lure it back to cancel half a Line,
Nor all your Tears wash out a Word of it.

LXXII.

And that inverted Bowl they call the Sky,
Whereunder crawling coop'd we live and die,
   Lift not your hands to *It* for help—for It
As impotently moves as you or I.

LXXIII.

With Earth's first Clay They did the Last Man knead,
And there of the Last Harvest sow'd the Seed:
   And the first Morning of Creation wrote
What the Last Dawn of Reckoning shall read.

LXXIV.

YESTERDAY *This* Day's Madness did prepare;
TO-MORROW'S Silence, Triumph, or Despair:
   Drink! for you know not whence you came, nor why:
Drink! for you know not why you go, nor where.

LXXV.

I tell you this—When, started from the Goal,
Over the flaming shoulders of the Foal
   Of Heav'n Parwín and Mushtarí they flung,
In my predestined Plot of Dust and Soul

LXXVI.

The Vine had struck a fibre: which about
If clings my Being—let the Dervish flout;
  Of my Base metal may be filed a Key,
That shall unlock the Door he howls without.

LXXVII.

And this I know: whether the one True Light
Kindle to Love, or Wrath-consume me quite,
  One Flash of It within the Tavern caught
Better than in the Temple lost outright.

LXXVIII.

What! out of senseless Nothing to provoke
A conscious Something to resent the yoke
  Of unpermitted Pleasure, under pain
Of Everlasting Penalties, if broke!

LXXIX.

What! from his helpless Creature be repaid
Pure Gold for what he lent him dross-allay'd—
  Sue for a Debt he never did contract,
And cannot answer—Oh the sorry trade!

LXXX.

Oh Thou, who didst with pitfall and with gin
Beset the Road I was to wander in,
  Thou wilt not with Predestined Evil round
Enmesh, and then impute my Fall to Sin!

LXXXI.

Oh Thou, who Man of baser Earth didst make,
And ev'n with Paradise devise the Snake:
  For all the Sin wherewith the Face of Man
Is blacken'd—Man's forgiveness give—and take!

* * * * * *

LXXXII.

As under cover of departing Day
Slunk hunger-stricken Ramazán away,
　Once more within the Potter's house alone
I stood, surrounded by the Shapes of Clay.

LXXXIII.

Shapes of all Sorts and Sizes, great and small,
That stood along the floor and by the wall;
　And some loquacious Vessels were; and some
Listen'd perhaps, but never talk'd at all.

LXXXIV.

Said one among them—"Surely not in vain
"My substance of the common Earth was ta'en
　"And to this Figure moulded, to be broke,
"Or trampled back to shapeless Earth again."

LXXXV.

Then said a Second—"Ne'er a peevish Boy
"Would break the Bowl from which he drank in joy;
　"And He that with his hand the Vessel made
"Will surely not in after Wrath destroy."

LXXXVI.

After a momentary silence spake
Some Vessel of a more ungainly Make;
　"They sneer at me for leaning all awry:
"What! did the Hand then of the Potter shake?"

LXXXVII.

Whereat some one of the loquacious Lot—
I think a Súfi pipkin—waxing hot—
 "All this of Pot and Potter—Tell me then,
"Who is the Potter, pray, and who the Pot?"

LXXXVIII.

"Why," said another, "Some there are who tell
"Of one who threatens he will toss to Hell
 "The luckless Pots he marr'd in making—Pish!
"He's a Good Fellow, and 't will all be well."

LXXXIX.

"Well," murmur'd one, "Let whoso make or buy,
"My Clay with long Oblivion is gone dry:
 "But fill me with the old familiar Juice,
"Methinks I might recover by and by."

XC.

So while the Vessels one by one were speaking,
The little Moon look'd in that all were seeking:
 And then they jogg'd each other, "Brother! Brother!
"Now for the Porter's shoulder-knot a-creaking!"

* * * * * *

XCI.

Ah, with the Grape my fading Life provide,
And wash the Body whence the Life has died,
 And lay me, shrouded in the living Leaf,
By some not unfrequented Garden-side.

XCII.

That ev'n my buried Ashes such a snare
Of Vintage shall fling up into the Air
   As not a True-believer passing by
But shall be overtaken unaware.

XCIII.

Indeed the Idols I have loved so long
Have done my credit in this World much wrong:
   Have drown'd my Glory in a shallow Cup,
And sold my Reputation for a Song.

XCIV.

Indeed, indeed, Repentance oft before
I swore—but was I sober when I swore?
   And then and then came Spring, and Rose-in-hand
My thread-bare Penitence apieces tore.

XCV.

And much as Wine has play'd the Infidel,
And robb'd me of my Robe of Honour—Well,
   I wonder often what the Vintners buy
One half so precious as the stuff they sell.

XCVI.

Yet Ah, that Spring should vanish with the Rose!
That Youth's sweet-scented manuscript should close!
   The Nightingale that in the branches sang,
Ah whence, and whither flown again, who knows!

XCVII.

Would but the Desert of the Fountain yield
One glimpse—if dimly, yet indeed, reveal'd,
   To which the fainting Traveller might spring,
As springs the trampled herbage of the field!

XCVIII.

Would but some wingéd Angel ere too late
Arrest the yet unfolded Roll of Fate,
  And make the stern Recorder otherwise
Enregister, or quite obliterate!

XCIX.

Ah Love! could you and I with Him conspire
To grasp this sorry Scheme of Things entire,
  Would not we shatter it to bits—and then
Re-mould it nearer to the Heart's Desire!

*   *   *   *   *   *

C.

Yon rising Moon that looks for us again—
How oft hereafter will she wax and wane;
  How oft hereafter rising look for us
Through this same Garden—and for *one* in vain!

CI.

And when like her, oh Sákí, you shall pass
Among the Guests Star-scatter'd on the Grass,
  And in your joyous errand reach the spot
Where I made One—turn down an empty Glass!

TAMAM.

NOTES.

(Stanza II.) The "*False Dawn;*" *Subhi Kázib*, a transient Light on the Horizon about an hour before the *Subhi sádik*, or True Dawn; a well-known Phenomenon in the East.

(IV.) New Year. Beginning with the Vernal Equinox, it must be remembered; and (howsoever the old Solar Year is practically superseded by the clumsy *Lunar* Year that dates from the Mohammedan Hijra) still commemorated by a Festival that is said to have been appointed by the very Jamshyd whom Omar so often talks of, and whose yearly Calendar he helped to rectify.

"The sudden approach and rapid advance of the Spring," says Mr Binning[1], "are very striking. Before the Snow is well off the Ground, the Trees burst into Blossom, and the Flowers start forth from the Soil. At *Now Rooz* [*their* New Year's Day] the Snow was lying in patches on the Hills and in the shaded Vallies, while the Fruit-trees in the Gardens were budding beautifully, and green Plants and Flowers springing up on the Plains on every side—

> 'And on old Hyems' Chin and icy Crown
> 'An odorous Chaplet of sweet Summer buds
> 'Is, as in mockery, set.'—

Among the Plants newly appeared I recognised some old Acquaintances I had not seen for many a Year: among these, two varieties of the Thistle—a coarse species of Daisy like the 'Horse-gowan'—red and white Clover—the Dock—the blue Corn-flower—and that vulgar Herb the Dandelion rearing its yellow crest on the Banks of the Watercourses." The Nightingale was not yet heard, for the Rose was not yet blown: but an almost identical Blackbird and Woodpecker helped to make up something of a North-country Spring.

[1] *Two Years' Travel in Persia*, &c. i. 165.

"The White Hand of Moses." Exodus iv. 6; where Moses draws forth his Hand—not, according to the Persians, "*leprous as Snow*,"—but *white*, as our May-blossom in Spring perhaps. According to them also the Healing Power of Jesus resided in his Breath.

(v.) Iram, planted by King Shaddád, and now sunk somewhere in the Sands of Arabia. Jamshyd's Seven-ring'd Cup was typical of the 7 Heavens, 7 Planets, 7 Seas, &c., and was a *Divining Cup*.

(vi.) *Pehlevi*, the old Heroic *Sanskrit* of Persia. Háfiz also speaks of the Nightingale's *Pehlevi*, which did not change with the People's.

I am not sure if the fourth line refers to the Red Rose looking sickly, or to the Yellow Rose that ought to be Red; Red, White, and Yellow Roses all common in Persia. I think that Southey, in his Common-Place Book, quotes from some Spanish author about the Rose being White till 10 o'clock; "Rosa Perfecta" at 2; and "perfecta incarnada" at 5.

(x.) Rustum, the "Hercules" of Persia, and Zál his Father, whose exploits are among the most celebrated in the Sháh-náma. Hátim Tai, a well-known type of Oriental Generosity.

(xiii.) A Drum—beaten outside a Palace.

(xiv.) That is, the Rose's Golden Centre.

(xviii.) Persepolis: call'd also *Takht-i-Jamshyd*—THE THRONE OF JAMSHYD, "*King Splendid*," of the mythical *Peshdádian* Dynasty, and supposed (according to the Sháh-náma) to have been founded and built by him. Others refer it to the Work of the Genie King, Ján Ibn Ján—who also built the Pyramids—before the time of Adam.

BAHRÁM GÚR—*Bahram of the Wild Ass*—a Sassanian Sovereign—had also his Seven Castles (like the King of Bohemia!) each of a different Colour: each with a Royal Mistress within; each of whom tells him a Story, as told in one of the most famous Poems of Persia, written by Amír Khusraw: all these Sevens also figuring (according to Eastern Mysticism) the Seven Heavens; and perhaps the Book itself that Eighth, into which the mystical Seven transcend, and within which they revolve. The Ruins of Three of those Towers are yet shown by the Peasantry; as also the Swamp in which Bahrám sunk, like the Master of Ravenswood, while pursuing his *Gúr*.

> The Palace that to Heav'n his pillars threw,
> And Kings the forehead on his threshold drew—
> I saw the solitary Ringdove there,
> And "Coo, coo, coo," she cried; and "Coo, coo, coo."

NOTES. 369

This Quatrain Mr Binning found, among several of Háfiz and others, inscribed by some stray hand among the ruins of Persepolis. The Ringdove's ancient *Pehlevi Coo, Coo, Coo*, signifies also in Persian "*Where? Where? Where?*" In Attár's "Bird-parliament" she is reproved by the Leader of the Birds for sitting still, and for ever harping on that one note of lamentation for her lost Yúsuf.

Apropos of Omar's Red Roses in Stanza xix, I am reminded of an old English Superstition, that our Anemone Pulsatilla, or purple "Pasque Flower" (which grows plentifully about the Fleam Dyke, near Cambridge), grows only where Danish Blood has been spilt.

(XXI.)   A thousand years to each Planet.

(XXXI.)   Saturn, Lord of the Seventh Heaven.

(XXXII.)   ME-AND-THEE: some dividual Existence or Personality distinct from the Whole.

(XXXVII.)   One of the Persian Poets—Attár, I think—has a pretty story about this. A thirsty Traveller dips his hand into a Spring of Water to drink from. By-and-by comes another who draws up and drinks from an earthen Bowl, and then departs, leaving his Bowl behind him. The first Traveller takes it up for another draught; but is surprised to find that the same Water which had tasted sweet from his own hand tastes bitter from the earthen Bowl. But a Voice—from Heaven, I think—tells him the clay from which the Bowl is made was once *Man;* and, into whatever shape renewed, can never lose the bitter flavour of Mortality.

(XXXIX.)   The custom of throwing a little Wine on the ground before drinking still continues in Persia, and perhaps generally in the East. Mons. Nicolas considers it "un signe de libéralité, et en même temps un avertissement que le buveur doit vider sa coupe jusqu'à la dernière goutte." Is it not more likely an ancient Superstition; a Libation to propitiate Earth, or make her an Accomplice in the illicit Revel? Or, perhaps, to divert the Jealous Eye by some sacrifice of superfluity, as with the Ancients of the West? With Omar we see something more is signified; the precious Liquor is not lost, but sinks into the ground to refresh the dust of some poor Wine-worshipper foregone.

Thus Háfiz, copying Omar in so many ways: "When thou drinkest Wine pour a draught on the ground. Wherefore fear the Sin which brings to another Gain?"

(XLIII.)   According to one beautiful Oriental Legend, Azräel accomplishes his mission by holding to the nostril an Apple from the Tree of Life.

This and the two following Stanzas would have been withdrawn, as somewhat *de trop*, from the Text, but for advice which I least like to disregard.

(LI.) From Máh to Máhi; from Fish to Moon.

(LVI.) A Jest, of course, at his Studies. A curious mathematical Quatrain of Omar's has been pointed out to me; the more curious because almost exactly parallel'd by some Verses of Doctor Donne's, that are quoted in Izaak Walton's Lives! Here is Omar: "You and I are the image of a pair of compasses; though we have two heads (sc. our *feet*) we have one body; when we have fixed the centre for our circle, we bring our heads (sc. feet) together at the end." Dr Donne:

> If we be two, we two are so
>   As stiff twin-compasses are two;
> Thy Soul, the fixt foot, makes no show
>   To move, but does if the other do.
>
> And though thine in the centre sit,
>   Yet when my other far does roam,
> Thine leans and hearkens after it,
>   And grows erect as mine comes home.
>
> Such thou must be to me, who must
>   Like the other foot obliquely run;
> Thy firmness makes my circle just,
>   And me to end where I begun.

(LIX.) The Seventy-two Religions supposed to divide the World, *including* Islamism, as some think: but others not.

(LX.) Alluding to Sultan Mahmúd's Conquest of India and its dark people.

(LXVIII.) *Fánúsi khiyál*, a Magic-lantern still used in India; the cylindrical Interior being painted with various Figures, and so lightly poised and ventilated as to revolve round the lighted Candle within.

(LXX.) A very mysterious Line in the Original:

> O dánad O dánad O dánad O ——

breaking off something like our Wood-pigeon's Note, which she is said to take up just where she left off.

(LXXV.) Parwín and Mushtarí—The Pleiads and Jupiter.

(LXXXVII.) This Relation of Pot and Potter to Man and his Maker figures far and wide in the Literature of the World, from the time of the Hebrew Prophets to the present; when it may finally take the name of "Pot theism," by which Mr Carlyle ridiculed Sterling's "Pantheism." *My* Sheikh, whose knowledge flows in from all quarters, writes to me—

"Apropos of old Omar's Pots, did I ever tell you the sentence I found in 'Bishop Pearson on the Creed'? 'Thus are we wholly at the disposal of His will, and our present and future condition framed and ordered by His free, but wise and just, decrees. *Hath not the potter power over the clay, of the same lump to make one vessel unto honour, and another unto dishonour?* (Rom. ix. 21.) And can that earth-artificer have a freer power over his *brother potsherd* (both being made of the same metal), than God hath over him, who, by the strange fecundity of His omnipotent power, first made the clay out of nothing, and then him out of that?'"

And again—from a very different quarter—"I had to refer the other day to Aristophanes, and came by chance on a curious Speaking-pot story in the Vespæ, which I had quite forgotten.

Φιλοκλέων.	Ἄκουε, μὴ φεῦγ'· ἐν Συβάρει γυνή ποτε κατέαξ' ἐχῖνον.	l. 1435
Κατήγορος.	Ταῦτ' ἐγὼ μαρτύρομαι.	
Φι.	Οὐχῖνος οὖν ἔχων τιν' ἐπεμαρτύρατο· Εἶθ' ἡ Συβαρῖτις εἶπεν, εἰ ναὶ τὰν κόραν τὴν μαρτυρίαν ταύτην ἐάσας, ἐν τάχει ἐπίδεσμον ἐπρίω, νοῦν ἂν εἶχες πλείονα.	

"The Pot calls a bystander to be a witness to his bad treatment. The woman says, 'If, by Proserpine, instead of all this 'testifying' (comp. Cuddie and his mother in 'Old Mortality!') you would buy yourself a rivet, it would show more sense in you!' The Scholiast explains *echinus* as ἄγγος τι ἐκ κεράμου."

One more illustration for the oddity's sake from the "Autobiography of a Cornish Rector," by the late James Hamley Tregenna. 1871.

"There was one old Fellow in our Company—he was so like a Figure in the 'Pilgrim's Progress' that Richard always called him the 'ALLEGORY,' with a long white beard—a rare Appendage in those days—and a Face the colour of which seemed to have been baked in, like the Faces one used to see on Earthenware Jugs. In our Country-dialect Earthenware is called '*Clome*'; so the Boys of the Village used to shout out after him—'Go back to the Potter, old Clome-face, and get baked over again.' For the 'Allegory,' though shrewd enough in most things, had the reputation of being '*saift-baked*,' i.e., of weak intellect."

(XC.) At the Close of the Fasting Month, Ramazán (which makes the Musulman unhealthy and unamiable), the first Glimpse of the New Moon (who rules their division of the Year), is looked for with the utmost Anxiety, and hailed with Acclamation. Then it is that the Porter's Knot may be heard—toward the *Cellar*. Omar has elsewhere a pretty Quatrain about the same Moon—

> "Be of Good Cheer—the sullen Month will die,
> "And a young Moon requite us by and by:
> "Look how the Old one meagre, bent, and wan
> "With Age and Fast, is fainting from the Sky!"

[*The first Edition of the translation of Omar Khayyám, which appeared in 1859, differs so much from those which followed, that it has been thought better to print it in full, instead of attempting to record the differences.*]

I.

AWAKE! for Morning in the Bowl of Night
Has flung the Stone that puts the Stars to Flight:
　And Lo! the Hunter of the East has caught
The Sultán's Turret in a Noose of Light.

II.

Dreaming when Dawn's Left Hand was in the Sky
I heard a Voice within the Tavern cry,
　"Awake, my Little ones, and fill the Cup
"Before Life's Liquor in its Cup be dry."

III.

And, as the Cock crew, those who stood before
The Tavern shouted—"Open then the Door!
　"You know how little while we have to stay,
"And, once departed, may return no more."

IV.

Now the New Year reviving old Desires,
The thoughtful Soul to Solitude retires,
  Where the WHITE HAND OF MOSES on the Bough
Puts out, and Jesus from the Ground suspires.

V.

Irám indeed is gone with all its Rose,
And Jamshýd's Sev'n-ring'd Cup where no one knows;
  But still the Vine her ancient Ruby yields,
And still a Garden by the Water blows.

VI.

And David's Lips are lock't; but in divine
High piping Péhlevi, with "Wine! Wine! Wine!
  "*Red* Wine!"—the Nightingale cries to the Rose
That yellow Cheek of her's to'incarnadine.

VII.

Come, fill the Cup, and in the Fire of Spring
The Winter Garment of Repentance fling:
  The Bird of Time has but a little way
To fly—and Lo! the Bird is on the Wing.

VIII.

And look—a thousand Blossoms with the Day
Woke—and a thousand scatter'd into Clay:
  And this first Summer Month that brings the Rose
Shall take Jamshýd and Kaikobád away.

IX.

But come with old Khayyám, and leave the Lot
Of Kaikobád and Kaikhosrú forgot:
  Let Rustum lay about him as he will,
Or Hátim Tai cry Supper—heed them not.

X.

With me along some Strip of Herbage strown
That just divides the desert from the sown,
  Where name of Slave and Sultán scarce is known,
And pity Sultán Máhmúd on his Throne.

XI.

Here with a Loaf of Bread beneath the Bough,
A Flask of Wine, a Book of Verse—and Thou
  Beside me singing in the Wilderness—
And Wilderness is Paradise enow.

XII.

"How sweet is mortal Sovranty!"—think some:
Others—"How blest the Paradise to come!"
  Ah, take the Cash in hand and wave the Rest;
Oh, the brave Music of a *distant* Drum!

XIII.

Look to the Rose that blows about us—"Lo,
"Laughing," she says, "into the World I blow:
  "At once the silken Tassel of my Purse
"Tear, and its Treasure on the Garden throw."

XIV.

The Worldly Hope men set their Hearts upon
Turns Ashes—or it prospers; and anon,
  Like Snow upon the Desert's dusty Face
Lighting a little Hour or two—is gone.

XV.

And those who husbanded the Golden Grain,
And those who flung it to the Winds like Rain,
  Alike to no such aureate Earth are turn'd
As, buried once, Men want dug up again.

XVI.

Think, in this batter'd Caravanserai
Whose Doorways are alternate Night and Day,
  How Sultán after Sultán with his Pomp
Abode his Hour or two, and went his way.

XVII.

They say the Lion and the Lizard keep
The Courts where Jamshýd gloried and drank deep;
  And Bahrám, that great Hunter—the Wild Ass
Stamps o'er his Head, and he lies fast asleep.

XVIII.

I sometimes think that never blows so red
The Rose as where some buried Cæsar bled;
  That every Hyacinth the Garden wears
Dropt in its Lap from some once lovely Head.

XIX.

And this delightful Herb whose tender Green
Fledges the River's Lip on which we lean—
  Ah, lean upon it lightly! for who knows
From what once lovely Lip it springs unseen!

XX.

Ah, my Belovéd, fill the Cup that clears
TO-DAY of past Regrets and future Fears—
  To-morrow?—Why, To-morrow I may be
Myself with Yesterday's Sev'n Thousand Years.

XXI.

Lo! some we loved, the loveliest and best
That Time and Fate of all their Vintage prest,
  Have drunk their Cup a Round or two before,
And one by one crept silently to Rest.

XXII.

And we, that now make merry in the Room
They left, and Summer dresses in new Bloom,
  Ourselves must we beneath the Couch of Earth
Descend, ourselves to make a Couch—for whom?

XXIII.

Ah, make the most of what we yet may spend,
Before we too into the Dust descend;
  Dust into Dust, and under Dust, to lie,
Sans Wine, sans Song, sans Singer, and—sans End!

XXIV.

Alike for those who for TO-DAY prepare,
And those that after a TO-MORROW stare,
  A Muezzín from the Tower of Darkness cries
"Fools! your Reward is neither Here nor There!"

XXV.

Why, all the Saints and Sages who discuss'd
Of the Two Worlds so learnedly, are thrust
  Like foolish Prophets forth; their Words to Scorn
Are scatter'd, and their Mouths are stopt with Dust.

XXVI.

Oh, come with old Khayyám, and leave the Wise
To talk; one thing is certain, that Life flies;
  One thing is certain, and the Rest is Lies;
The Flower that once has blown for ever dies.

XXVII.

Myself when young did eagerly frequent
Doctor and Saint, and heard great Argument
  About it and about: but evermore
Came out by the same Door as in I went.

XXVIII.

With them the Seed of Wisdom did I sow,
And with my own hand labour'd it to grow:
  And this was all the Harvest that I reap'd—
"I came like Water, and like Wind I go."

XXIX.

Into this Universe, and *why* not knowing,
Nor *whence*, like Water willy-nilly flowing:
  And out of it, as Wind along the Waste,
I know not *whither*, willy-nilly blowing.

XXX.

What, without asking, hither hurried *whence?*
And, without asking, *whither* hurried hence!
  Another and another Cup to drown
The Memory of this Impertinence!

XXXI.

Up from Earth's Centre through the Seventh Gate
I rose, and on the Throne of Saturn sate,
  And many Knots unravel'd by the Road;
But not the Knot of Human Death and Fate.

XXXII.

There was a Door to which I found no Key:
There was a Veil past which I could not see:
  Some little Talk awhile of ME and THEE
There seem'd—and then no more of THEE and ME.

XXXIII.

Then to the rolling Heav'n itself I cried,
Asking, "What Lamp had Destiny to guide
  "Her little Children stumbling in the Dark?"
And—"A blind Understanding!" Heav'n replied.

XXXIV.

Then to this earthen Bowl did I adjourn
My Lip the secret Well of Life to learn:
    And Lip to Lip it murmur'd—"While you live
"Drink!—for once dead you never shall return."

XXXV.

I think the Vessel, that with fugitive
Articulation answer'd, once did live,
    And merry-make; and the cold Lip I kiss'd
How many Kisses might it take—and give!

XXXVI.

For in the Market-place, one Dusk of Day,
I watch'd the Potter thumping his wet Clay:
    And with its all obliterated Tongue
It murmur'd—"Gently, Brother, gently, pray!"

XXXVII.

Ah, fill the Cup:—what boots it to repeat
How Time is slipping underneath our Feet:
    Unborn TO-MORROW, and dead YESTERDAY,
Why fret about them if TO-DAY be sweet!

XXXVIII.

One Moment in Annihilation's Waste,
One Moment, of the Well of Life to taste—
    The Stars are setting and the Caravan
Starts for the Dawn of Nothing—Oh, make haste!

XXXIX.

How long, how long, in infinite Pursuit
Of This and That endeavour and dispute?
    Better be merry with the fruitful Grape
Than sadden after none, or bitter, Fruit.

XL.

You know, my Friends, how long since in my House
For a new Marriage I did make Carouse:
  Divorced old barren Reason from my Bed,
And took the Daughter of the Vine to Spouse.

XLI.

For "Is" and "Is-not" though *with* Rule and Line,
And "Up-and-down" *without*, I could define,
  I yet in all I only cared to know,
Was never deep in anything but—Wine.

XLII.

And lately, by the Tavern Door agape,
Came stealing through the Dusk an Angel Shape
  Bearing a Vessel on his Shoulder; and
He bid me taste of it; and 'twas—the Grape!

XLIII.

The Grape that can with Logic absolute
The Two-and-Seventy jarring Sects confute:
  The subtle Alchemist that in a Trice
Life's leaden Metal into Gold transmute.

XLIV.

The mighty Mahmúd, the victorious Lord,
That all the misbelieving and black Horde
  Of Fears and Sorrows that infest the Soul
Scatters and slays with his enchanted Sword.

XLV.

But leave the Wise to wrangle, and with me
The Quarrel of the Universe let be:
  And, in some corner of the Hubbub coucht,
Make Game of that which makes as much of Thee.

XLVI.

For in and out, above, about, below,
'Tis nothing but a Magic Shadow-show,
  Play'd in a Box whose Candle is the Sun,
Round which we Phantom Figures come and go.

XLVII.

And if the Wine you drink, the Lip you press,
End in the Nothing all Things end in—Yes—
  Then fancy while Thou art, Thou art but what
Thou shalt be—Nothing—Thou shalt not be less.

XLVIII.

While the Rose blows along the River Brink,
With old Khayyám the Ruby Vintage drink:
  And when the Angel with his darker Draught
Draws up to Thee—take that, and do not shrink.

XLIX.

'Tis all a Chequer-board of Nights and Days
Where Destiny with Men for Pieces plays:
  Hither and thither moves, and mates, and slays,
And one by one back in the Closet lays.

L.

The Ball no Question makes of Ayes and Noes,
But Right or Left, as strikes the Player goes;
  And He that toss'd Thee down into the Field,
He knows about it all—HE knows—HE knows!

LI.

The Moving Finger writes; and, having writ,
Moves on: nor all thy Piety nor Wit
  Shall lure it back to cancel half a Line,
Nor all thy Tears wash out a Word of it.

LII.

And that inverted Bowl we call The Sky,
Whereunder crawling coop't we live and die,
   Lift not thy hands to *It* for help—for It
Rolls impotently on as Thou or I.

LIII.

With Earth's first Clay They did the Last Man's knead,
And then of the Last Harvest sow'd the Seed:
   Yea, the first Morning of Creation wrote
What the Last Dawn of Reckoning shall read.

LIV.

I tell Thee this—When, starting from the Goal,
Over the shoulders of the flaming Foal
   Of Heav'n Parwín and Mushtara they flung,
In my predestin'd Plot of Dust and Soul

LV.

The Vine had struck a Fibre; which about
If clings my Being—let the Súfi flout;
   Of my Base Metal may be filed a Key,
That shall unlock the Door he howls without.

LVI.

And this I know: whether the one True Light,
Kindle to Love, or Wrathconsume me quite,
   One Glimpse of It within the Tavern caught
Better than in the Temple lost outright.

LVII.

Oh Thou, who didst with Pitfall and with Gin
Beset the Road I was to wander in,
   Thou wilt not with Predestination round
Enmesh me, and impute my Fall to Sin?

LVIII.

Oh, Thou, who Man of baser Earth didst make,
And who with Eden didst devise the Snake;
  For all the Sin wherewith the Face of Man
Is blacken'd, Man's Forgiveness give—and take!

* * * * * * * *

KÚZA-NÁMA.

LIX.

Listen again. One Evening at the Close
Of Ramazán, ere the better Moon arose,
  In that old Potter's Shop I stood alone
With the clay Population round in Rows.

LX.

And, strange to tell, among that Earthen Lot
Some could articulate, while others not:
  And suddenly one more impatient cried—
"Who *is* the Potter, pray, and who the Pot?"

LXI.

Then said another—"Surely not in vain
"My Substance from the common Earth was ta'en,
  "That He who subtly wrought me into Shape
"Should stamp me back to common Earth again."

LXII.

Another said—"Why, ne'er a peevish Boy,
"Would break the Bowl from which he drank in Joy;
  "Shall He that *made* the Vessel in pure Love
"And Fansy, in an after Rage destroy!"

LXIII.

None answer'd this; but after Silence spake
A Vessel of a more ungainly Make:
  "They sneer at me for leaning all awry;
"What! did the Hand then of the Potter shake?"

LXIV.

Said one—"Folks of a surly Tapster tell,
"And daub his Visage with the Smoke of Hell;
  "They talk of some strict Testing of us—Pish!
"He's a Good Fellow, and 'twill all be well."

LXV.

Then said another with a long-drawn Sigh,
"My Clay with long oblivion is gone dry:
  "But, fill me with the old familiar Juice,
"Methinks I might recover by-and-bye!"

LXVI.

So while the Vessels one by one were speaking,
One spied the little Crescent all were seeking:
  And then they jogg'd each other, "Brother! Brother!
"Hark to the Porter's Shoulder-knot a-creaking!"

* * * * * * * *

LXVII.

Ah, with the Grape my fading Life provide,
And wash my Body whence the Life has died,
  And in a Windingsheet of Vine-leaf wrapt,
So bury me by some sweet Garden-side.

LXVIII.

That ev'n my buried Ashes such a Snare
Of Perfume shall fling up into the Air,
  As not a True Believer passing by
But shall be overtaken unaware.

LXIX.

Indeed the Idols I have loved so long
Have done my Credit in Men's Eye much wrong:
  Have drown'd my Honour in a shallow Cup,
And sold my Reputation for a Song.

LXX.

Indeed, indeed, Repentance oft before
I swore—but was I sober when I swore?
  And then and then came Spring, and Rose-in-hand
My thread-bare Penitence apieces tore.

LXXI.

And much as Wine has play'd the Infidel,
And robb'd me of my Robe of Honour—well,
  I often wonder what the Vintners buy
One half so precious as the Goods they sell.

LXXII.

Alas, that Spring should vanish with the Rose!
That Youth's sweet-scented Manuscript should close!
  The Nightingale that in the Branches sang,
Ah, whence, and whither flown again, who knows!

LXXIII.

Ah Love! could thou and I with Fate conspire
To grasp this sorry Scheme of Things entire,
  Would not we shatter it to bits—and then
Re-mould it nearer to the Heart's Desire!

LXXIV.

Ah, Moon of my Delight who know'st no wane,
The Moon of Heav'n is rising once again:
  How oft hereafter rising shall she look
Through this same Garden after me—in vain!

LXXV.

And when Thyself with shining Foot shall pass
Among the Guests Star-scatter'd on the Grass,
  And in thy joyous Errand reach the Spot
Where I made one—turn down an empty Glass!

TAMÁM SHUD.

NOTE BY THE EDITOR.

IT must be admitted that FitzGerald took great liberties with the original in his version of Omar Khayyám. The first stanza is entirely his own, and in stanza XXXI. of the fourth edition (XXXVI. in the second) he has introduced two lines from Attár (See Letters p. 251). In stanza LXXXI. (fourth edition), writes Professor Cowell, 'There is no original for the line about the snake: I have looked for it in vain in Nicolas; but I have always supposed that the last line is FitzGerald's mistaken version of Quatr. 236 in Nicolas' ed. which runs thus:

  O thou who knowest the secrets of every one's mind,
  Who graspest every one's hand in the hour of weakness,
  O God, give me repentance and accept my excuses,
  O thou who givest repentance and acceptest the excuses of every one.

FitzGerald mistook the meaning of *giving* and *accepting* as used here, and so invented his last line out of his own mistake. I wrote to him about it when I was in Calcutta; but he never cared to alter it'.

VARIATIONS

BETWEEN THE SECOND, THIRD AND FOURTH EDITIONS OF

OMAR KHAYYÁM.

STANZA

I.   In ed. 2:
Wake! For the Sun behind yon Eastern height
Has chased the Session of the Stars from Night;
  And, to the field of Heav'n ascending, strikes
The Sultán's Turret with a Shaft of Light.

    In the first draught of ed. 3 the first and second lines stood thus:

Wake! For the Sun before him into Night
A Signal flung that put the Stars to flight.

II.   In ed. 2:
Why lags the drowsy Worshipper outside?

V.   In edd. 2 and 3:
But still a Ruby gushes from the Vine.

IX.   In edd. 2 and 3:
Morning a thousand Roses brings, you say.

X.   In ed. 2:
Let Rustum cry "To battle!" as he likes,
Or Hátim Tai "To Supper!"—heed not you.

    In ed. 3:
Let Zál and Rustum thunder as they will.

STANZA

XII. In ed. 2:
Here with a little Bread beneath the Bough,
A Flask of Wine, a Book of Verse—and Thou &c.

XIII. In ed. 2:
Ah, take the Cash, and let the Promise go,
Nor heed the music of a distant Drum!

XX. In ed. 2:
And this delightful Herb whose living Green.

XXII. In edd. 2 and 3:
That from his Vintage rolling Time has prest.

XXVI. In edd. 2 and 3:
Of the Two Worlds so learnedly, are thrust.

XXVII. In ed. 2:
Came out by the same door as in I went.

XXVIII. In edd. 2 and 3:
And with my own hand wrought to make it grow.

XXX. In ed. 2:
Ah, contrite Heav'n endowed us with the Vine
To drug the memory of that insolence!

XXXI. In ed. 2:
And many Knots unravel'd by the Road.

XXXII. In edd. 2 and 3:
There was the Veil through which I could not see.

XXXIII. In ed. 2:
Nor Heav'n, with those eternal Signs reveal'd.

XXXIV. In ed. 2:
Then of the THEE IN ME who works behind
The Veil of Universe I cried to find
  A Lamp to guide me through the darkness; and
Something then said—"An Understanding blind."

XXXV. In ed. 2:
I lean'd, the secret Well of Life to learn.

AND FOURTH EDITIONS OF OMAR KHAYYÁM. 389

STANZA

XXXVI. In ed. 2:

And drink; and that impassive Lip I kiss'd.

XXXVIII. In ed. 2 the only difference is 'For' instead of 'And' in the first line; but in the first draught of ed. 3 the stanza appeared thus:

For, in your Ear a moment—of the same
Poor Earth from which that Human Whisper came,
  The luckless Mould in which Mankind was cast
They did compose, and call'd him by the name.

In ed. 3 the first line was altered to

Listen—a moment listen!—Of the same &c.

XXXIX. In ed. 2:

On the parcht herbage but may steal below.

XL. In ed. 2:

As then the Tulip for her wonted sup
Of Heavenly Vintage lifts her chalice up,
  Do you, twin offspring of the soil, till Heav'n
To Earth invert you like an empty Cup.

In the first draught of ed. 3 the stanza is the same as in edd. 3 and 4, except that the second line is

Of Wine from Heav'n her little Tass lifts up.

XLI. In ed. 2 and the first draught of ed. 3:

Oh, plagued no more with Human or Divine
To-morrow's tangle to itself resign.

XLII. In ed. 2:

And if the Cup you drink, the Lip you press,
End in what All begins and ends in—Yes;
  Imagine then you *are* what heretofore
You *were*—hereafter you shall not be less.

The first draught of ed. 3 agrees with edd. 3 and 4 except that the first line is

And if the Cup, and if the Lip you press.

STANZA

XLIII. In ed. 2:

So when at last the Angel of the drink
Of Darkness finds you by the river-brink,
  And, proffering his Cup, invites your Soul
Forth to your Lips to quaff it—do not shrink.

> In the first draught of ed. 3 the only change made was from 'proffering' to 'offering', but in ed. 3 the stanza assumed the form in which it also appeared in ed. 4. The change from 'the Angel' to 'that Angel' was made in MS. by FitzGerald in a copy of ed. 4.

XLIV. In ed. 2:

Is't not a shame—is't not a shame for him
So long in this Clay suburb to abide!

XLV. In ed. 2:

But that is but a Tent wherein may rest.

XLVI. In ed. 2:

And fear not lest Existence closing *your*
Account, should lose, or know the type no more.

XLVII. In ed. 2:

As much as Ocean of a pebble-cast.

In ed. 3:

As the SEV'N SEAS should heed a pebble-cast.

XLVIII. In ed. 2:

One Moment in Annihilation's Waste,
One Moment, of the Well of Life to taste—
  The Stars are setting, and the Caravan
Draws to the 'Dawn of Nothing—Oh make haste'.

> In the first draught of ed. 3 line 3 originally stood:
>
> Before the starting Caravan has reach'd
>
> the rest of the stanza being as in edd. 3 and 4.

XLIX. In ed. 2:

A Hair, they say, divides the False and True.

> The change from 'does' to 'may' in the last line was made by FitzGerald in MS.

AND FOURTH EDITIONS OF OMAR KHAYYÁM. 391

STANZA
L.   In ed. 2:
        A Hair, they say, divides the False and True.

LII.   In edd. 2 and 3:
        He does Himself contrive, enact, behold.

LIII.   In the first draught of ed. 3:
        To-morrow, when You shall be You no more.

LIV.   In ed. 2:
        Better be merry with the fruitful Grape.

LV.   In ed. 2:
        You know, my Friends, how bravely in my House
        For a new Marriage I did make Carouse.

LVII.   In ed. 2:
        Have squared the Year to Human Compass, eh?
        If so, by striking from the Calendar.

LXII.   In ed. 2:
        When the frail Cup is crumbled into Dust!

LXIII. In ed. 2:
        The Flower that once is blown for ever dies.

LXV.   In edd. 2 and 3:
        They told their fellows, and to Sleep return'd.

LXVI.   In ed. 2:
            And after many days my Soul return'd
        And said, 'Behold, Myself am Heav'n and Hell'.

LXVII. In ed. 2:
        And Hell the Shadow of a Soul on fire.

LXVIII. In ed. 2:
        Of visionary Shapes that come and go
        Round with this Sun-illumin'd Lantern held.

LXIX.   In ed. 2:
        Impotent Pieces of the Game He plays.

LXX.   In ed. 2:
        But Right or Left as strikes the Player goes.

STANZA

LXXII. In ed. 2 and the first draught of ed. 3:
And that inverted Bowl we call The Sky.
In edd. 2 and 3:
As impotently rolls as you or I.

LXXIX. In ed. 2:
Pure Gold for what he lent us dross-allay'd.

LXXXI. In ed. 2:
For all the Sin the Face of wretched Man
Is black with—Man's Forgiveness give—and take!

LXXXIII. In ed. 2:
And once again there gather'd a scarce heard
Whisper among them; as it were, the stirr'd
Ashes of some all but extinguisht Tongue
Which mine ear kindled into living Word.

LXXXIV. In ed. 2:
My Substance from the common Earth was ta'en,
That He who subtly wrought me into Shape
Should stamp me back to shapeless Earth again?

LXXXV. In ed. 2:
Another said—'Why, ne'er a peevish Boy
'Would break the Cup from which he drank in Joy;
'Shall He that of his own free Fancy made
The Vessel, in an after-rage destroy!'

LXXXVI. In ed. 2:
None answer'd this; but after silence spake.

LXXXVII. In ed. 2:
Thus with the Dead as with the Living, *What?*
And *Why?* so ready, but the *Wherefor* not,
One on a sudden peevishly exclaim'd,
'Which is the Potter, pray, and which the Pot?

LXXXVIII. In ed. 2:
Said one—'Folks of a surly Master tell,
'And daub his Visage with the Smoke of Hell;
'They talk of some sharp Trial of us—Pish!
'He's a Good Fellow, and 'twill all be well.'

STANZA

LXXXIX. In ed. 2:
'Well,' said another, 'Whoso will, let try.'

XC. In ed. 2:
One spied the little Crescent all were seeking.

XCI. In ed. 2:
And wash my Body whence the Life has died.

XCIII. In ed. 2:
Have done my credit in Men's eye much wrong.

XCV. In ed. 2:
One half so precious as the ware they sell.

XCVII. In ed. 2:
Toward which the fainting Traveller might spring.

XCVIII. In ed. 2:
Oh if the World were but to re-create,
That we might catch ere closed the Book of Fate,
And make The Writer on a fairer leaf
Inscribe our names, or quite obliterate!

XCIX. In ed. 2:
Ah Love! could you and I with Fate conspire.

C. In ed. 2:
But see! The rising Moon of Heav'n again
Looks for us, Sweet-heart, through the quivering Plane:
How oft hereafter rising will she look
Among those leaves—for one of us in vain!

CI. In ed. 3:
And when Yourself with silver Foot shall pass.

In the first draught of ed. 3 'Foot' is changed to 'step'.

In ed. 3:
And in your blissful errand reach the spot.

STANZAS WHICH APPEAR IN THE SECOND EDITION ONLY.

XIV. Were it not Folly, Spider-like to spin
The Thread of present Life away to win—
 What? for ourselves, who know not if we shall
Breathe out the very Breath we now breathe in!

XX. (This stanza is quoted in the note to stanza XVIII. in the third and fourth editions.)

XXVIII. Another Voice, when I am sleeping, cries,
"The Flower should open with the Morning skies."
 And a retreating Whisper, as I wake—
"The Flower that once has blown for ever dies."

XLIV. Do you, within your little hour of Grace,
The waving Cypress in your Arms enlace,
 Before the Mother back into her arms
Fold, and dissolve you in a last embrace..

LXV. If but the Vine and Love-abjuring Band
Are in the Prophet's Paradise to stand,
 Alack, I doubt the Prophet's Paradise
Were empty as the hollow of one's Hand.

LXXVII. For let Philosopher and Doctor preach
Of what they will, and what they will not—each
 Is but one Link in an eternal Chain
That none can slip, nor break, nor over-reach.

LXXXVI. Nay, but, for terror of his wrathful Face,
I swear I will not call Injustice Grace;
 Not one Good Fellow of the Tavern but
Would kick so poor a Coward from the place.

XC.   And once again there gather'd a scarce heard
        Whisper among them; as it were, the stirr'd
          Ashes of some all but extinguisht Tongue,
        Which mine ear kindled into living Word.

(In the third and fourth editions stanza LXXXIII. takes the place of this.)

XCIX. Whither resorting from the vernal Heat
        Shall Old Acquaintance Old Acquaintance greet,
          Under the Branch that leans above the Wall
        To shed his Blossom over head and feet.

CVII. Better, oh better, cancel from the Scroll
        Of Universe one luckless Human Soul,
          Than drop by drop enlarge the Flood that rolls
        Hoarser with Anguish as the Ages roll.

COMPARATIVE TABLE OF STANZAS IN THE FOUR EDITIONS.

Ed. 1	Ed. 2	Edd. 3 & 4	Ed. 1	Ed. 2	Edd. 3 & 4
I	I	I	XVII	XIX	XVIII
II	II	II	XVIII	XXIV	XIX
III	III	III	XIX	XXV	XX
IV	IV	IV	XX	XXI	XXI
V	V	V	XXI	XXII	XXII
VI	VI	VI	XXII	XXIII	XXIII
VII	VII	VII	XXIII	XXVI	XXIV
VIII	IX	IX	XXIV	XXVII	XXV
IX	X	X	XXV	XXIX	XXVI
X	XI	XI	XXVI	LXVI	LXIII
XI	XII	XII	XXVII	XXX	XXVII
XII	XIII	XIII	XXVIII	XXXI	XXVIII
XIII	XV	XIV	XXIX	XXXII	XXIX
XIV	XVII	XVI	XXX	XXXIII	XXX
XV	XVI	XV	XXXI	XXXIV	XXXI
XVI	XVIII	XVII	XXXII	XXXV	XXXII

COMPARATIVE TABLE.

Ed. 1	Ed. 2	Edd. 3 & 4	Ed. 1	Ed. 2	Edd. 3 & 4
XXXIII	XXXVII	XXXIV	LXXIV	CIX	C
XXXIV	XXXVIII	XXXV	LXXV	CX	CI
XXXV	XXXIX	XXXVI		VIII	VIII
XXXVI	XL	XXXVII		XIV	
XXXVII				XX	Note on XVIII
XXXVIII	XLIX	XLVIII			
XXXIX	LVI	LIV		XXVIII	
XL	LVII	LV		XXXVI	XXXIII
XLI	LVIII	LVI		XLI	XXXVIII
XLII	LX	LVIII		XLII	XXXIX
XLIII	LXI	LIX		XLIII	XL
XLIV	LXII	LX		XLIV	
XLV				XLVII	XLVI
XLVI	LXXIII	LXVIII		XLVIII	XLVII
XLVII	XLV	XLII		L	XLIX
XLVIII	XLVI	XLIII		LI	L
XLIX	LXXIV	LXIX		LII	LI
L	LXXV	LXX		LIII	LII
LI	LXXVI	LXXI		LIV	LIII
LII	LXXVIII	LXXII		LV	XLI
LIII	LXXIX	LXXIII		LIX	LVII
LIV	LXXXI	LXXV		LXIII	LXI
LV	LXXXII	LXXVI		LXIV	LXII
LVI	LXXXIII	LXXVII		LXV	
LVII	LXXXVII	LXXX		LXVII	LXIV
LVIII	LXXXVIII	LXXXI		LXVIII	LXV
LIX	LXXXIX	LXXXII		LXIX	XLIV
LX	XCIV	LXXXVII		LXX	XLV
LXI	XCI	LXXXIV		LXXI	LXVI
LXII	XCII	LXXXV		LXXII	LXVII
LXIII	XCIII	LXXXVI		LXXVII	
LXIV	XCV	LXXXVIII		LXXX	LXXIV
LXV	XCVI	LXXXIX		LXXXIV	LXXVIII
LXVI	XCVII	XC		LXXXV	LXXIX
LXVII	XCVIII	XCI		LXXXVI	
LXVIII	C	XCII		XC	LXXXIII
LXIX	CI	XCIII		XCIX	
LXX	CII	XCIV		CV	XCVII
LXXI	CIII	XCV		CVI	XCVIII
LXXII	CIV	XCVI		CVII	
LXXIII	CVIII	XCIX			

菲譯第五版魯拜集

菲译第五版鲁拜集

译　序

　　汇刊菲兹杰拉德的五个《鲁拜集》译本,分别配上五种中译:文言散文、七言绝句、集唐、集宋、白话诗。正常来说,白话诗译本一定是最重要的,七言绝句其次,文言散文又次,集唐、集宋其实只是个玩笑。但在我,白话诗译本却是副产品,仅仅比集唐、集宋的玩笑严肃点儿。先译了前四种,为凑成五个版本,我只好第一次用白话译诗。被逼出来的东西,不可能完美,更何况,我的白话又很差。

　　不论是阅读,还是写作,我和大家一样,白话肯定比文言的经验多。可是写文言,远比写白话愉快得多。苏东坡讲作文:"大略如行云流水,初无定质,但常行于所当行,常止于所不可不止,文理自然,姿态横生。"在写文言时偶有体会,可写白话时就从来没体会过。于是从小学写白话,就是负担。以后写作文,写论文,简直成了生活的噩梦。白话似乎只是个工具,你说它会带来什么样的愉快,除了工具的愉快,我想不出别的。这大概不得不归因于天分。我天生不适合白话文,勤能补拙,在这里起不到什么用处。

　　我白话之差,同样表现在翻译上。有过翻译经验的人大概都知道,译文很容易被原文的语言牵着走,就是因为你并没有掌握好用来翻译的语言。思果先生讲翻译理论,主要就讲怎么保持纯正的中文,这是极有眼光的。我对这一点虽然很明白,但是拿起笔来,就不知不觉跟着原文跑了。举个例子:

　　Towards me he ever turned an eye of favor and kindness, and as his pupil I felt for him extreme affection and devotion, so that I passed four years in his service.

这句子一点儿不难。但我怎么也搞不顺,只能译成这样:他对我多予垂青和慈爱,作为学生我对他无限尊敬和热爱,就这样我服侍了他四年。我几乎认为,翻译大概只能到这个地步了。等找出自己的文言译文一对,才知道,不是不能翻译,实在是自己的白话太糟了。文言如此译的:师于我特加垂青,而吾为弟子亦尽忠爱,亲侍讲席,四载于兹矣。基本做到思果先生纯正中文的要求。

可是,有人跟我说,不对,你主要是念头问题。你一用白话就贴原文,用文言就只顾译文。我说,还是能力问题。用文言不知不觉底气就足,不在乎贴不贴原文,一用白话自卑就暗暗作祟,不贴原文就不踏实。当然,我也常常怀疑,这能力不足的责任,究竟该由个人全部承担,还是白话自身也须承担些?

所以,我希望读者理解,我的白话译文只是极不成熟的习作,对待它需要多些包容。更何况,这种作即使不断习下去,也不大会成熟。那我要求的就不止是包容,而是宽大。

不过,有了两种语体的翻译经验,倒是使我更认真地反思了翻译学界的一种普遍看法。这似乎成了现在翻译界的共识:"翻译外国诗歌用中国古典诗体,又用文言,很难成功。"有这样的看法,其实和我的情况貌似相反实则一致,我是白话差,别人是文言不够好。其实只要很好地掌握了用来翻译的语言,成功都是可能的。特别是,诗里那些叙述质朴的句子,白话译出来欠缺诗味,文言却能很好地弥补。举个例子,《鲁拜集》第37首:

For I remember stopping by the way
To watch a Potter thumping his wet Clay:
　　And with its all-obliterated Tongue
It murmur'd—"Gently, Brother, gently, pray!"

白话译出来是:
我记得曾在路边停留,

看一个陶匠把陶泥使劲捣揉。
而它,用全已失传的语言低诉:
"轻点儿,兄弟,轻点儿,求求。"
文言译出来是:
记驻行途看冶陶,冶中陶土作悲号:"君当太古原吾与,今日君工且缓操。"

可以明显地看出,文言的古雅给予了质朴的叙述一种特别的味道,从内在精神上更好地还原了原诗的趣味。说文言翻译很难成功,实在应该更谨慎些。

自然,由于白话水平太低,我在这里不能像在文言译本的序言里那样,提出有自己创见的翻译理论。但在翻译过程中,关于韵律方面也有两点经验之谈。

先说押韵。任何语种成熟的诗都得押韵,比较起来,中文诗的押韵真算简单的,没有那么多复杂的韵式。可是很奇怪,写白话诗的越来越不愿意押韵了,大家似乎有个共识:白话诗押韵挺 low 的。说实话,这一点让我有些轻视白话诗,觉得它不够成熟。即使我这样写惯旧诗的人,一百零六部平水韵用起来捉襟见肘的时候也不是很多,但一写白话诗,用汉语拼音押个韵也觉得蛮困难。不是找不到韵字,那不是困难,关键白话很多字缺乏雅致,用了总不脱乡土小调的味道。这就是为什么白话诗押韵总给人挺 low 的感觉。大概因为白话还缺少历史的厚重,不及文言词汇的左右逢源。

尽管如此,我仍然坚持按旧诗的规矩,平上去三声绝不通押。写白话诗押韵的,这个好像还没见过。这倒不是我守旧,不信您可以自己读读,通押肯定不好听。余光中翻译洛尔迦,声韵极动听,比如这一节:
穿过原野,穿过烈风,
赤红的月亮,漆黑的马。
死亡正在俯视着我,
在戍楼上,在科尔多瓦。

可是余先生的原译文就没这么好听了。"科尔多瓦"台湾多译作"科尔多巴",到了大陆,改为通译的"科尔多瓦",和上面的"马",都是上声,押在一起的声音立刻不一样了。旧诗押韵的好处我不愿意放弃,道理就是如此。

诚然,困难不小,经常为了一个韵脚押不上,或是换来换去,或是调整句序,以至勉强,甚至错误,都顾不上了。大家有时嘲笑演员"宁穿错,不穿破",我这时竟然深深理解演员的苦衷了。

再说音步。这是黄杲炘先生译本最重要的特色之一。(另外一个特色大概就是"柔巴依集"的译名了。)我认为白话按着音步一念,尤其像乡土小调。音步表现诗的节奏,如旧诗里讲究的句式,五言的二三式,七言的二二三式。但文言凝练,容易形成自然的节奏,白话松散,节奏就显得不太自然。只要看看地方戏曲的唱词,就能体会那种不自然,但那是配乐不是诵念的,不自然并非问题。音步讲究过分了,就会出现通篇使用京剧十字句三三四式的极端例子,同时也就宣告了音步的破灭。

当然,我不是说白话诗不要节奏,白话的特色决定了它的节奏不能以音步这样死板的形式表现,而应该根据语调自然的抑扬顿挫。大概这样的节奏无法有确定的形式,但根据白话诗的发展,我们的确可以期待它的成熟。

同时,英文和中文各自的语法特征,也会使步趋英诗节奏的中文音步更加生硬。尽管习惯了旧诗在句式上又叠加平仄的严格规范,我还是放弃了音步的探索。必须说,尽管互相之间未必肯定,我始终非常尊重黄杲炘先生的努力,更乐于看到音步的成功。

这个白话译文是按照菲兹杰拉德的第五版翻译的。原版后面有四个附录:第一版译诗全文,第二、三、四版的译诗异文,第二版独有的译诗,各版编次对照表。这些附录是为了详细列出菲兹杰拉德各版译诗的细致差异,当然,译序和译注的不少异文就被忽略了。实际上很多英译的异文没有办法、也没有必要全部体现在中文里,我对四个附录做了不同的处理。从第一版译诗中,选译了18首异文较多的,作为附录一。第二版独有的译诗全部译出,(其中第 20 首已经出现在第五版第 18 首的译注里,所以略去了。)另外增加了一些异文较明显的译诗,一共 13 首,作为附录二。第三版第四版的异文基本不用再译,不过,附录保留了第三版第一首的初稿,还有第三十八首,差异比较大,译出作为附录三。各版编次对照表,将不易分辨的罗马数字换成阿拉伯数字,作为附录四。

  坦率的讲,菲兹杰拉德的文字并不好懂,很多地方我吃不准。不仅因为英文的古雅,也因为知识的背景。为此参考了名家译本,主要是郭沫若、梁实秋、黄杲炘三家,但三家歧异处我往往缺乏决断的能力。又去请教了很多朋友,深怕过多打扰,很多地方也还没能解决。因此,译文的准确性就会大打折扣,希望得到谅解,更希望得到指正。

2019 年 8 月 23 日,译者。

奥马尔·海亚姆:波斯的天文学家诗人

奥马尔·海亚姆在我们的11世纪后半叶生于呼罗珊的内沙普尔,死在我们的12世纪的第一个25年。他一生很少的故事却跟他们那个时代和国家两个非常重要的人物奇妙地联系在一起——他们三个中的一个讲述了那个故事,他就是尼查木·乌尔·莫尔克。莫尔克先后作了鞑靼人脱斡邻勒·伯克的儿子阿尔普·阿尔斯兰、孙子马立克·沙的维齐尔。脱斡邻勒·伯克从马赫穆德大帝无能的继承人手里夺得了波斯,建立塞尔柱王朝,它最终激起欧洲发动了十字军东征。这个尼查木·乌尔·莫尔克,写了一本《遗书》留给将来的政治家作借鉴,在书里有如下的说法。这里根据《加尔各答评论》第五十九号转引米尔克洪的《阿萨辛史》。

呼罗珊的智慧之人中最伟大的一个就是内沙普尔的伊玛目穆瓦法克,他是个备受尊崇的人——愿神赐福他的灵魂,他辉煌的岁月超过85年。人们普遍相信,在他面前诵读《可兰经》和学习传统的孩子,一定会得到荣耀和快乐。因为这个原因,我父亲把我从突斯送到了内沙普尔,和法学博士阿布德·乌斯·沙玛德一起,好让我在这位杰出老师的指导下全心学习。他对我多予垂青和慈爱,作为学生我对他无限尊敬和热爱,就这样在他那里我服侍了四年。我刚到那儿时,就发现另外两个新到的同龄学生,哈基姆·奥马尔·海亚姆和背运的本·萨巴赫。两个人才智聪敏天赋绝佳,于是我们三个结下了亲密的友情。每当伊玛目离开讲席,他们常常和我一起,共同复习学过的课程。奥马尔是内沙普尔当地人,哈桑·本·萨巴赫的父亲是个阿里,一个过着自我克制的生活且现实的人,但他的信仰和教条近于异端。一天哈桑对我和海亚姆说:"大家普遍相信伊玛目穆瓦法克的学生将会获得幸运。就算我们不会都获得,无疑其中的一个也会,那我们相互之间该有什么誓约?"我们回答:"照你喜欢的。""好,"他说:"让我们起誓,不论这幸运降临到谁,他都要跟其他人分享，没有任何特别的留给自己。""就这样。"我俩一起回答，于是照那个约定我们互相起誓。岁月如驰，我从呼罗珊去了中亚河中地区，又游历了伽兹尼和喀布尔。我返回时，被委以官职，后来在阿尔普·阿尔斯兰苏丹治下升任首相。

他继续叙述，又过了几年，他的老同学都找到了他，根据求学时代的誓言，来要求共享他的好运。维齐尔为人爽朗慷慨，遵守了誓言。哈桑要求一个官位，苏丹因维齐尔的请求同意了。但他不满足于渐次升迁，误入迷途，参与了一个东方宫廷的阴谋，他卑鄙地试图取代他的恩人，没有成功，因此失宠而遭放逐。在经过许多不幸和流离之后，哈桑成为亦思马因教波斯教派的领袖。这是一群狂热分子，经历长期的暗中酝酿，在哈桑强大而邪恶的意志引导下终于达致邪恶的巅峰。公元1090年，他占据鲁德巴省的阿剌模忒堡，地处里海南面的山区。正是由于这个山中据点，他在十字军中获得了邪恶的名号：山中老人，并让恐怖遍布伊斯兰世界。现代欧洲语言中的暗杀一词，就是他们遗留下的黑色记忆。其字源仍有争论，有的说来自 hashish，即从大麻叶中提炼的麻醉剂（印度文 bhang），用这个东西他们使自己痴狂，达到东方人绝望时抑郁的极点。有的说来自集团创始者的名字，我们在他平静的内沙普尔求学时代看到过这个名字。暗杀之刃的无数牺牲者之一，就是尼查木·乌尔·莫尔克他自己，幼学时的故友。①

奥马尔·海亚姆也来见维齐尔要求他的一份，但并不要求名位和官职。"你能给我的最大赐予，"他说，"就是让我生活在你好运庇护的一隅，广播科学之益，同时为你长寿大吉而祈祷。"维齐尔告诉我们，当他发现奥马尔的拒绝确实是真诚的，就不再强劝，而从内沙普尔的金库中每年支给他1200金币作为年金。

---

① 奥马尔《鲁拜集》的一些篇章警告我们盛时的危险、好运的无常，同时倡言对所有人友善，劝告我们不要跟任何人过于密切。阿塔尔让尼查木·乌尔·莫尔克使用了他朋友奥马尔的话（《鲁拜集》第二十八首）："尼查木·乌尔·莫尔克临死时呻吟说，哦，主啊，我正从风的手里消逝。"

"在内沙普尔奥马尔·海亚姆这样生活直至去世，"维齐尔又说，"他忙于获取各样的知识，尤其是天文学，在这一领域他已登峰造极。当马立克·沙苏丹治下，他来到谋夫，因为学问的精深享有盛誉，苏丹对他颇示恩宠。"

那时马立克·沙决定修历，奥马尔是从事此事的八位学者之一。其成果就是哲拉里历（这个称呼来自国王的一个名字哲拉鲁丁）。"在时间的推算上，"吉本说，"超过了凯撒历，接近格里高利历的精准。"他也是一些被命名为马立克·沙希星算表的天文图表的作者，法国人近来曾有重版，并且翻译了他的一篇阿拉伯文的代数论。

他写诗的用名海亚姆，意思是制帐篷者，据说他曾经干过这行，大概是在尼查木·乌尔·莫尔克的慷慨使他生活自主之前。很多波斯诗人都同样地因他们的职业得名，像我们知道的阿塔，是个药剂师；阿萨，是个榨油匠，等等。① 奥马尔自己在下面怪诞的诗行里暗指其名：

海亚姆，他缝制了科学的帐篷，
　　却很快被焚烧在忧患的炉火之中；
命运之剪剪断了他人生的帐篷绳索，
　　希望的商贩卖掉他也只为了虚空。

我们还有一件他的生平轶事要讲，关系到他的临终。这出自一篇佚名的序言，在某个时期被放在他的诗集前。其波斯原文印在海德《波斯古教》的附录，见第499页。戴波卢的《文库》，在海姆条下也曾提及。②

它被记录在古代的编年史里，这位智慧的王者，奥马尔·海亚姆，在海吉拉历517年（公元1123年）卒于内沙普尔。在科学上他无与伦比，是他那个时代的典范。撒马尔罕的尼札米和卓，他的学

---

① 不过这些就像我们的史密斯（铁匠）、阿切尔（射手）、米勒（磨工）、弗莱彻（箭工）等，只是简单地从世代传袭的称呼取得姓氏。

② "1世纪末2世纪初，这位伊斯兰教哲人有圣香的体验。"除了同为哲学家，没有其他任何一点，可以归于我们的海亚姆。

生,讲述了下面这个故事:"我经常跟我的老师,奥马尔·海亚姆,在花园里谈话。一天他对我说:'我的坟墓要置于北风吹落玫瑰于其上的地方。'我很惊诧他说出这样的话,但我知道他从不说空话。① 很多年过去,我有机会重访内沙普尔,我去了他最后的安息之地。看啊!它正好在一个花园外边,树上缀满果实,枝条伸过花园的围墙,把花朵撒在他的墓上,直到墓石被完全掩埋其下。"

我已不惮侵权从《加尔各答评论》大量征引。它的作者,用印度文读了奥马尔坟墓的故事,他说,让他想起西塞罗的记述,在叙拉古寻找到被杂草所掩埋的阿基米德坟墓。我想到多瓦尔德森希望种出的玫瑰可以掩盖他,我相信,直到今天他的愿望都得到了虔诚的满足。好了,回到奥马尔吧。

虽然苏丹"对他颇示恩宠",但奥马尔坦率的享乐主义思想和言论使他在自己的时代和国度为人所侧目。相传苏菲派尤其痛恨和惧怕他,他们的行事被他嘲笑,他们的信仰也根本不比他自己的多一点儿,如果除去神秘主义和伊斯兰教义的形式认可,而奥马尔是不愿用这些来掩饰的。他们的诗人,包括哈菲兹,他是菲尔多西之外波斯最重要的诗人,确实都取资于奥马尔,但转而用作神秘的用途以便于他们自己和他们对之诵读的民族。这个民族怀疑和信仰都很容易,身体和理智都很敏锐,喜欢两者暧昧的结合,在其间他们

---

① 根据戴波卢,这段话的轻率在于跟《可兰经》中的话抵牾:"没有人能知道他将死在哪里。"——奥马尔这个故事,很自然地让我想起另外一个故事,特别是当一个人想起那位高贵的水手在设定自己卑微的目标时是多么茫然无绪——库克船长,而不是霍克沃斯博士,在他的《第二次航行》(第一卷第374页)一书里这样哀伤地写道。当离开乌列特亚时,奥瑞奥的最后一个请求是要我返回。当他发现他不能得到我的许诺时,就问我将来的安葬地的名称。虽说这个问题很奇怪,我还是毫不犹豫地告诉他:"斯特普尼。"这是我在伦敦时居住的教区。他们要求我重复念了好几遍,直到他们可以读出来。这时"斯特普尼的安葬地里没有图特"的声音立刻回响在上百人的口中。我后来发现一个海岸上的人也对福斯特先生问了同样的问题,但是他给出了一个不同却更恰当的回答,是这样说:"一个经常在海上的人是不能说出他会葬在哪里的。"

可以纵情浮游于天国尘世和今生来世之间,凭着诗句的翅膀,不在乎地投身于任何一方。奥马尔的心灵和头脑对此过于诚实。他(不管有多错误地)找不到任何神意除了命运,找不到任何世界除了此世,他就尽量抓住它,他宁肯通过感官来顺从他所见到的事物好让心灵平静,也不肯困惑于它们此后将会如何以致徒然扰乱。我们也看到,他世间的追求并不过度,他很像是在使人欣喜的感官满足中得到一种幽默的、乖张的乐趣,将之置于理智之上。其实在理智中他得到了极大的愉悦,尽管理智不能回答他的问题,和所有人一样,那些问题是最受关切的。

然而,不管什么原因,如之前所说,奥马尔从未在他自己的国家广受欢迎,因此也很少传至国外。他的诗集稿本《东方散佚抄本集》未收,在东方已很少见,就根本传不到西方了,虽说在武器和科学方面东西交流是很充分的。其复制本印度学堂没有,巴黎国家图书馆也没有。我们知道只有一本在英国,就是牛津包德勒图书馆编号乌斯利第 140 号的写本,公元 1460 年写于设拉子。这里包括 158 首鲁拜。有一本在加尔各答亚洲协会图书馆,我们得到一个副本,包括仍不完备的 516 首,还被各样的重出和劣制品种充斥。冯·海默尔说他的副本包括 200 首,施普伦格博士著录的鲁克诺稿本两倍于此。① 看来,牛津和加尔各答写本的抄写者,在从事这项工作时,也是很有点不情愿的。每一个都以一首四行诗(不论真伪)开始,从其字母次序的排列中抽出,牛津写本是一首忏悔诗,加尔各答写本是一首告诫诗。后者根据缀于稿本的说明被推测起因于一个梦,梦中奥马尔的母亲询问他未来的命运。可以这样来译述:

哦,你为那些在地狱被焚者忧心如焚,
你自己也得轮到在那火里焚身。
你要呼喊多久:"怜悯他们吧,上帝!"

---

① 评论者在注释里补充说:"写完这篇文章后,我们又碰上一个极其罕见版本的副本,1836 年在加尔各答印行。这里包括 438 首四行诗,附录中还包括另外不见于其他稿本的 54 首。"

啊，去教的，你是何人？来学的，他是何人？

包德勒写本的四行诗主张泛神论，以此表明正当：

如果我自己用松散的信念，

松散地把善行的珠宝来串，

就让这一件事替我恳求赎罪：

我从未把一当二讲乱。

评论者①——奥马尔生平的细节我都得益于他，在他评述的收束处比较了奥马尔和卢克莱修，二人的自然性情和天赋很相像，所遭遇的生存环境也很相像。都是敏锐、坚强的人，有经受训练的智力和良好的想象力，心灵渴求真理和正义。他们正当地反抗国家的虚伪宗教和委身于此的虚伪或愚昧。不过，他们不能像别人一样用更好的希望取代他们所推翻的，也没有更好的启示来引导他们，可也还是为自己订立了律法。卢克莱修确是靠着伊壁鸠鲁提供的那些材料，满足于自己认为的宇宙是偶然形成的巨大机械这一理论，它的运动虽循法则却找不出立法者。他把自己塑造成斯多葛式的，而非伊壁鸠鲁式的严肃态度。他坐下来凝视着宇宙的机械戏剧，在其中他也扮演了一个角色，他自己和围绕他的一切（就像他自己对罗马剧场的壮观描写）都在悬挂于观众和太阳之间的幕布的可怕反射下褪尽颜色。对于任何这样的复杂体系，其结果只是没有希望的必然性，奥马尔显得更悲观，或是更漫不在意。他把自己的天才和学问，伴以苦涩、幽默的玩笑，倾注在普遍的毁灭上，这毁灭在他们不完全的一瞥中仅仅有所显露而已。于是假装把人欲之乐当成人生的严肃目的，只是用神、命运、物质和精神、善和恶等这些理论问题让自己得到消遣，而这些问题开始要比继续下去容易，对它们的探索最终成为令人倦怠的游戏。

来看看现在的译本。开始的鲁拜（由于缺少一个阿拉伯语的喉音，这些四行诗的名称听起来更具音乐性）是单独的诗节，每节由四

---

① 考威尔教授。

行诗句组成,其韵律大致相同也偶有变化,有时全部押韵,但经常是(像现在所模拟的)第三句不押韵。有些类似古希腊的阿尔凯奥斯诗体,倒数第二行像是被提起来,暂停一下再如波浪般落在最后一行。就像一般常见的这类东方诗集一样,鲁拜集按照入韵字母的词序编排,这就看到死亡和欢乐被奇怪地接在一起了。那些被选出的诗歌恰好成为一组田园诗,这里东方诗歌中过于经常出现的"饮酒和作乐"的内容(真实或不真实)在比例上可能更少一些。不管如何,这结果是足够伤感的,最伤感的可能是最夸耀欢乐的时候,反使老帐篷匠容易哀伤过于愤怒。他徒然想让自己的脚步摆脱命运,能赶上真正瞥见明天,可还是跌回了今天(它延迟了那么多明天!)那是他唯一可以立足的地方,尽管也很快会从他脚下溜走。

当奥马尔这个译本的第二版正在准备时,法国驻雷什特总领事尼古拉斯先生也出版了一个非常仔细和完美的版本,底本是德黑兰的一个石印本,收有464首鲁拜,还附有他的翻译和注释。

尼古拉斯先生,他的版本在一些地方提示了我,在另一些地方指导了我,并不认为奥马尔是个物质的伊壁鸠鲁主义者,我倒是直接这么认为的。他认为奥马尔是一个神秘主义者,在酒、担酒者等形象下隐喻着神,如同我们猜想哈菲兹所做的,简单说,是一个像哈菲兹和其他诗人一样的苏菲诗人。

我没能看到我改变观点的理由,它在十几年前就形成了,当时有个人第一次把奥马尔拿给我看。我对东方的所有了解,以及大量其他的知识,包括文学,都受惠于这个人。他对奥马尔那么赞赏,如果他能认可,一定会愉快地征引像尼古拉斯先生那样关于他的意义的阐释。[①] 然而他不能,我已大量引用的他发表在《加尔各答评论》

[①] 大概多年前他自己也编辑了这部诗集。他现在可能很少会赞同我这一边的译文,对尼古拉斯先生那一边的理论也是一样。

上的文章能够表明，在那里他的论述或者根据诗本身，或者根据诗人生平的遗留记录。

如果需要进一步反驳尼古拉斯先生的理论，这有一条他自己写出的传记性附言（见他的序言第13、14页）和他在注释里给出的诗的解释直接相反。我真的几乎不知道可怜的奥马尔被引到这么远，直到替他辩解的人告诉我。在这里我们看到，不管哈菲兹喝的和歌唱的酒究竟是何物，唯有跟奥马尔经常在一起的才是真正出自葡萄汁的酒。不仅在和朋友畅饮时，甚至（如尼古拉斯先生所说）为了刺激他自己进入狂热的程度时，这在别人是通过哭喊叫骂达到的。然而，不管何时只要文本中出现酒、担酒者等，这又是很经常的，尼古拉斯先生都小心地注解为"神""神圣的"等。如此小心的行为，会引起人猜想他是被一个一起读诗的苏菲时时在灌输（《鲁拜集》第二首的注释，见第8页）。一个波斯人自然会希望维护一个杰出的本国人的声望，而一个苏菲也自然会把他纳入他自己的教派，在他的教派中，波斯所有重要的诗人都被纳入了。

尼古拉斯先生表示，奥马尔"酷嗜苏菲派的学说"（序言第八页）而沉溺其中，这一点有什么历史性的权威根据？泛神论、唯物论、必然性等原则，并不是苏菲派独有的，也不是他们之前的卢克莱修和他之前的伊壁鸠鲁独有的。它可能属于最早的思想者那种非常原始的无神论，更可能是一个社会和政治野蛮时代，在七十二宗的每一个都想分裂世界的阴影下，生活在其中的哲学家自发产生的。冯·海默尔（根据施普伦格的《东方目录》）说奥马尔是"自由思想者，苏菲派的伟大反对者"。大概是因为，当他掌握了很多他们的学说时，他就不会假装在道德上十分严苛，从而造成自己前后矛盾。乌斯利爵士在包德勒稿本的扉页上也写下了表示相同观点的题记。在尼古拉斯先生自己的版本里，也有两首鲁拜，苏弗和苏菲都是被贬抑地称呼的。

无疑很多这样的四行诗如果不作神秘解释看来无法理解，但更多的如果不是照字面解释也是无法理解的。比如，酒如果是精神性的,但一个人死后如何用它清洗身体?为什么用没有生命的泥土做酒杯,必须被一些后来的神秘主义者注入"神灵"?尼古拉斯先生自己看来被一些"奇异"和"过于东方"的暗示和形象所困扰,这些东西诚然"过于肉欲而有时使人起反感",这样的"方便语"不允许他把它们翻译出来,而读者只有指向"神圣性"而别无他法了。① 无疑在德黑兰写本中也有一些四行诗,就像在加尔各答写本中,都是伪作,这样的鲁拜其实是波斯短诗的常见形式。但这里至少同时揭示了事情的两个方面。虽然苏菲被看作波斯的学者和文学家,但他们比漫不经心的伊壁鸠鲁主义者更可能挟带有利于他自己的关于这位诗人的看法。我注意到,在包德勒抄本里很少有较为神秘的四行诗,它应该是最古老的抄本之一,在回历 865 年、公元 1460 年写于设拉子。这个,我认为,特别有助于将奥马尔(我忍不住使用他为人熟知的名字称呼他,而不是基督教的教名)与其他波斯诗人区别开来。这才是那位在寓言和玄境中的人,那位自放于自己的歌声里的诗人。我们好像和这个人相伴,那就是奥马尔本人,带着他所有的幽默和热情,坦率地在我们前面。我们好像真实地和他同桌共饮,酒已经开始轮流倒上了。

我必须说,就个人而言,我从来没有完全相信哈菲兹的神秘主义。只要这位诗人在他的歌曲开头和结尾向穆罕默德行额手礼,即便他持有和歌唱苏菲的泛神论,也似乎不会有什么危险。哲拉鲁

---

① 在第 234 首的注释他承认了这一点,不管这些意象的神秘意义对于欧洲人是多么显而易见,但它们即使被波斯的平信徒所引述,也不会不"脸红"。"当读到这首四行诗开头的欢爱之情时,一如读这本诗集中其他篇章时那样,我们的读者如今早已习惯于这些奇异的表达——海亚姆经常用这种方式来表达他对神圣之爱的思索。而对于那些太过东方化的意象所具有的特点,那种有时过于叛逆的肉欲,我们的读者可以毫无困难地将它们看作是指向神圣性的。然而这种信念在穆斯林毛拉间引起了激烈的争论,而且不少世俗信徒对此也颇有非议——其同胞们对于这些指向精神的事物一视同仁的许可令他们确实为之感到脸红。"

丁、贾米、阿塔，还有其他人，都是在这样的条件之下歌唱的，他们实际上是用酒和美人作为意象去阐明，而非作为面具去掩饰，他们赞颂的神明。也许用些不那么容易犯错或滥用的讽喻，对于容易激动的人民比较合适。在以下情况下更是如此：一些人认为对于哈菲兹和奥马尔，那种抽象不只是与肉欲形象相似，而且与之相同。这些都是危险的东西，即便对于虔诚教徒自身而言不是危险的，对于他的较脆弱的兄弟们而言却是危险的。对于刚入会的新的教徒，敬拜越是热烈，相应的亵渎就更加严重。这一切是因为什么呢？用官感愉悦的形象来诱惑，而如果一个人想接近神，这是必须弃绝的。根据教义，这位神既是官感物质亦是精神，人们期望在死后与其宇宙不知不觉地合而为一，而不去指望在此世的全部克己努力，可以在另一世界获得任何福祉的补偿。卢克莱修的盲目神性，显然值得人们付出而且很可能也确实获得了与苏菲的这种神性一样多的自我牺牲。而奥马尔的歌的主题，如果不是"让我们吃"，那一定是"让我们喝，因为明天我们就死了！"如果哈菲兹用相近的语言表达了完全不同的意思，那么当他把自己的生命和天才倾注在如此模棱两可的赞美诗时，他肯定失算了。因为从他那时候到现在，曾说过和唱过这些赞美诗的，都不是精神上的礼拜者。

然而，由于有一些传统的推测，当然还有一些有学问人的意见，赞成奥马尔是苏菲派，甚至是圣徒，因此，有些人乐于如此解释他的酒和担酒者。可是另一方面，也有大量的历史事实证明他是一个哲学家，他具有远超他所生活的时代和国家的科学洞见和能力，证明他节制的世俗抱负使他只想做个哲学家，节制的欲望使他只想做个容易知足的享乐者。其他的读者会同意我，相信奥马尔赞颂的酒只是葡萄的汁液，他的夸口远胜他的酒量，也许他只是为了表示对精神上的酒的蔑视，因为那让它的徒众陷入了虚伪或令人嫌恶之中。

1

醒来啊！太阳已让群星逃散，
从夜域之中，在他的前面，
　连夜也一起驱出天际，再举
光之长矢射中苏丹的塔殿。

2

那假晨光的幻色还没消褪，
似有声音喊来，从客舍之内：
　"寺里的一切都准备好了，
怎么礼拜者还在外昏昏思睡？"

3

鸡叫了，他们正在徘徊，
对着客舍大喊："快把门开开！
　知道吗？我们只能呆一小会儿，
一旦走了，也许不再回来。"

4

这时新年把旧愿重新唤起，
沉思的灵魂返归幽独，那里
　有摩西的白手伸在枝头，
还有耶稣的呼息吹来地底。

5

伊兰园和它的玫瑰都无踪迹，
也没人知道杰姆西王的七环杯哪里寻觅。
　然而仍有红宝石般的光焰闪耀藤间，
和许多繁花盛开的园子依傍水际。

6

大卫的唇紧锁;夜莺向玫瑰在叫,
用那神圣、高亮的巴列维语调:
　"酒!酒!酒!殷红的酒!"
唤起血色好把她脸颊的蔫黄去掉。

7

来,杯要斟满,悔当抛掷,
像冬衣欲弃,春火正炽。
　时之鸟,只有短短的路程,
而那鸟已经展翅。

8

不管是纳霞堡或巴比伦的岁月,
也别管杯里是甜汁还是苦液。
　那点点滴尽的,是生命之酒,
片片飘落的,是生命之叶。

9

你说,每个早晨带来玫瑰千花,
不错,可昨天的玫瑰落在谁家?
　而这带来玫瑰的第一个夏月,
也带走杰姆西和凯柯巴。

10

好吧,让它把他们带走!
凯柯巴和凯霍斯鲁于我们何有?
　让扎尔和鲁斯图姆纵情叫战,
让哈蒂姆命宴——你也没法插手。

11
沿着长满牧草的狭路,跟我来,
那儿正好把荒地从田亩隔开。
　但愿黄金宝座上的马穆德安泰,
而这里,奴隶和苏丹之名都已忘怀。

12
树下一壶酒,一块干粮,
一卷诗,还有你傍我身旁,
　放歌在荒野,
哦,荒野就是天堂。

13
有人为了现世的荣光,
有人祈盼先知的天堂;
　啊,先取现钱,别管债券,
也别管嘈嘈的鼓声在远方。

14
看那绽放的玫瑰在我们身边,
"看,"她说:"我含笑绽放世间,
　很快我锦囊的丝穗就被扯掉,
里面的珠宝遍落花园。"

15
那一些耕耘出金色的稻米,
那一些把它像雨点般抛在风里,
　他们都不会变成这金沙,
它一旦沉埋,还会被人再次掘起。

16

人们念兹在兹的俗世希望
成了灰烬——或者,它兴旺;
　之后,就像大漠沙面上的雪,
终归消逝,——只是一时明亮。

17

想想看,这商队旅舍任之凋敝,
它的门户就是昼夜交替。
　苏丹一个跟一个如何擅其声势,
而到了命定时刻,便自离去。

18

他们说狮子和蜥蜴正侵占
杰姆西王欢呼豪饮的官殿;
　　　　而巴拉姆王,那伟大的猎手,
不再醒来,任野驴在他头顶踏践。

19

我常想,没有哪儿的玫瑰花丛,
能像凯撒埋血处开出的一样红。
　而花园每一朵绽放的风信子,
都是从当年美人头上飘落随风。

20

这新草嫩青,毛羽般平铺
如唇的河畔,我们斜躺在绿芜——
　啊,躺下时要轻些,因为谁知道
它从当年的哪片娇唇悄然生出?

21
来,我亲爱的,倒满酒,今天
让它驱走以往的悔恨,将来的忧烦。
　　明天! 啊,到了明天,我也许
连自己也进入了昨天的七千年。

22
那些人为我们热爱,最是珍稀,
那滚动时光所压榨的陈酿之奇。
　　此前也不过喝得一巡两圈,
就一个跟一个默默地进去安息。

23
我们作乐在他们留下的空房,
夏日又穿起了新的鲜花衣裳。
　　我们也得躺到大地之床的底下,
为了谁? 把自己变成一张床。

24
啊,把我们还能花费的都用完,
在我们沦入尘土之前。
　　尘土进入尘土,在尘土下入睡,
无酒,无歌,无歌者,也无终端。

25
就像那些人,为了今天而筹备,
和那些人,因注目明天而宽慰。
　　　　　　报时人从黑暗之塔高喊,
"愚人! 这儿和那儿都没你的饷馈。"

26

为何,所有的圣徒和哲人,
那般智慧地就两个世界议论纷纭,
　像愚蠢的先知一样被置之不理,
他们的话遭唾弃,他们的嘴封了尘。

27

我自己年轻时经常热切造访
学者和圣人,听到高论宏讲,
　关于它反复申说;但终究
是从那同一个门来而复往。

28

跟着他们我把智慧的种子播在土中,
再用自己亲手的劳作使之长成。
　而这就是我得到的所有收获——
我来如水,我去如风。

29

进入这世界,不知缘由,
也不知源头,如水漫漫而流;
　再从它出离,像风沿着荒漠,
漫漫而吹,我不知尽头。

30

为什么,没问问,就从哪儿匆忙到这里?
也没问问,又从这儿匆忙去哪里!
　啊,这一杯杯遭禁的酒,
会淹没这记忆,关于那些无礼。

31

我从地心飞升,将第七门穿过,
稳踞在土星的宝座。
　　许多疑惑都已在路上解开,
只除了那人类命运的最大之惑。

32

这有门,我找不到钥匙,
这有帷幕,里面我不能窥知。
　　很少的话语匆匆谈到我和你,
而后,你和我存在不了几时。

33

地不能回答;海也不能,
哀哭着离弃他们的主,在涌动的紫色中;
　　旋转的天也不能,用夜和晨之袖,
来回隐现着他所有的十二宫。

34

幕后支配的我中之你,
我对之把双手举起,
　　去寻暗中之灯;而我听到,
似从外来的话语:"你中之我盲矣!"

35

我俯向这粗制陶罐的唇边,
想请教我生命的幽玄。
　　唇接唇时它咕哝道,"当你活着,
喝!因为,一旦死去,你永不回还。"

36

我想这酒器,用那咕哝的话语
回答,有过生命,饮过酒醴。
　哦,我吻着的这漠然的唇,
曾有过多少吻,它接受又给与!

37

我记得曾在路边停留,
看一个陶匠把陶泥使劲捣揉。
　而它,用全已失传的语言低诉:
"轻点儿,兄弟,轻点儿,求求。"

38

不就是这样的故事?从之前
很久的人们那里代代流传,
　就是这样湿透的土泥,
被造物者照人形而抟。

39

从我们酹酒的杯中,
每一滴渗入地下无息无声。
　去熄灭那眼中的愁苦之火,
很久以前,深埋重重。

40

郁金香在尘间仰沐朝晖,
渴望着那天赐的新醅。
　你可愿真心效仿?直到上天
把你翻倒地上,像一只空杯。

41
莫再困扰于天人之际,
明天的纠结任随风去。
　让你的手指在她发间放纵,
那身修如柏的行觞佳丽。

42
如果你喝的酒,你吻的唇,
其终结和所有的开始和终结俱存。
　是呀,想到今日之你既是
昨日之你——明天你不会减一分。

43
当天使手持浓黑的酒醴,
最终在河边看到了你,
　你不要颤栗,他会请你的灵魂
痛饮,把酒杯向你唇边举起。

44
如果灵魂能将躯壳抛在一边,
无牵挂地在天空盘桓,
　难道不羞愧,他难道不羞愧,
还在这泥土的遗骸里蹒跚?

45
这只是苏丹去死亡之域的途中,
作一日逗留的帐篷。
　一俟苏丹起驾,那黑暗的侍卫
就收拾起,准备另一个客人居停。

46

不用怕存在把你的账销掉,
还有我的;这样的事就不再知道。
　不死的酒侍从那碗里倒出
如我们一般的千万酒沫,还会再倒。

47

当你和我在那幕后消失,
哦,很久很久,这世界仍会维持;
　它对待我们的到来和离去,
就像大海自身对待一块投石。

48

片时的停留——片时的存在
之饮,从那荒漠中的清泉一脉。
　看!幻影般的商队已经到达
它从中出发的虚无。——哦,赶快!

49

你如果想把生存的珠片消耗,
朋友,快些去,为了探求那玄奥。
　是非或许就在毫发之间,
请问,人生能有什么依靠?

50

是非或许就在毫发之间,
是的,一个阿里夫就是肇端,
　只要你能找到,会通往宝库,
或许也通往真主面前。

51
他隐秘的有,运行于造物之脉,
水银般避于你的痛苦以外。
　赋予从鱼到月所有的形状,
他们都在变化和消亡,但他永在。

52
一时被猜疑——就返回后面,
环绕戏台,幕前尽成黑暗。
　为了永恒之娱,
他自己编导,演出,观看。

53
如果都是徒然,下是永锢的地面,
向上天堂的大门也被锁断,
　今天你还是你时,犹能瞩目,
而明天你不再是你,又怎么办?

54
别浪费时间,也别徒劳驱驰,
为了这样那样的努力与争执;
　欢享那繁实累累的葡萄,胜似
愁闷地追求虚无、或苦涩的果实。

55
你知道,我的朋友,怎样盛大的狂欢,
我举行第二次婚礼,在我的房间。
　老迈不育的理性离开了我的床榻,
我和葡萄的女儿新结了良缘。

56

为了是非而用直尺和墨线，
那升沉我依靠逻辑来判断。
　　在一个人所想探求的一切中，
除了酒，我从未在任何事上深陷。

57

啊，人们说，我的算制，
简化了岁时更好测算？——不是，
　　那只是从历书中删去了
未生的明天，和已死的昨日。

58

不久前，门户大开的酒店边上，
一人从暮色中闪闪而临，如天使之状，
　　他肩上扛着一个罐子，
请我来尝，那是——葡萄佳酿。

59

葡萄酒能以逻辑的绝对之真，
辩破七十二家教派的纷纭。
　　那至尊的炼金术士，
顷时把生命的铅水变作黄金。

60

强大的马穆德，如真主降临，
让所有邪教和黑色的族群，
　　其灵魂已为恐惧和悲伤遍布，
在他和他的旋风之剑前，四散纷纷。

61

这酒浆既是上帝的产物,
谁敢咒骂这缠绕的卷须如网布?
　是赐福,我们就该受用,为什么不?
若是诅咒,那要问问,谁置此处?

62

我必须弃绝这人生的陶醉,我必须,
为了相信那些后来的清算而惊疑,
　或是为了期待那些神酒而迷惑,
注满那杯子,——当零落在尘泥!

63

哦,地狱的威胁,天堂的期望!
一事至少是确定的——这生命如飞一样。
　一事是确定的,其它都是谎话,
花儿一次盛开,永远凋丧。

64

不是很奇怪?无数的人
在我们之前穿过那扇黑暗之门,
　那边是我们也得去走的路,
没有一个回来告诉我们。

65

那些虔诚和博学之士,
像被焚的先知,在我们前讲出的启示,
　不过就是他们才醒来,
和又睡去之际,讲给同伴的故事。

66

我让我的灵魂径入不可见之地,
去拼读生命之后的字句。
　　不久我的灵魂回来答复我:
"我自己就是天堂和地狱。"

67

天堂只是满足欲望的幻现,
而地狱是投在那片黑暗
　　之上焦灼心灵的虚影,我们
才从黑暗中显出,很快将在其中消散。

68

我们不过是转动的一排
幻化之影,去去来来,
　　绕着那太阳点亮的灯笼;
在半夜它被提着,由那演出的主裁。

69

那是无助的棋子,供他游戏消磨,
这棋盘由夜和日间隔,
　　在上面到处走,将,吃,
之后一个个放置回棋盒。

70

球没法表示同意和不同意,
这儿和那儿都由打球人打去;
　　他知道关于它的一切,他知道,
就是他把你抛落在地。

71

移动的手指在写,写完
继续移动;所有你的智慧和敬虔,
　都无法诱引它返回删去半行字迹,
所有你的泪水也无法将一字沉湮。

72

那倒扣的碗他们叫作天,
被扣住的我们,匍匐生死于其间。
　不必举手向它求助,
它同样无助地转动,如你我一般。

73

他们用最早的泥土抟成最后的人,
就这样为最后的收获将种子耕耘。
　末日清算时将要读到的,
已经写在创世的第一个早晨。

74

昨天,预备了今天的疯狂,
明天的沉默,失望,或者辉煌。
　喝!你不知道你从何来,为何来,
喝!你也不知道你为何去,去何方。

75

我告诉你这个:才从终点出发的时刻,
他们把昴星和木星抛过
　金牛星那如火焰般的肩头,
在我尘骸和灵魂的定命里坠落。

76

如果葡萄藤生出深深的根,
缠住了我的存在——让托钵僧怪嗔;
　用我这低贱的材料锉把钥匙,
就能打开那扇他叫嚣于外的大门。

77

我知道这个:不管是一道真实之光
点燃了爱,还是愤怒将我彻底毁亡,
　在酒店中看到它一闪,
也好过完全迷失在殿堂。

78

什么!从没有感知的虚无,
将那些有意识的事物生出,
　也会怨恨禁绝快乐的枷轭,
如果打破了,必受永罚之苦毒。

79

什么!他对无助的生物,
把借出的废材要求用纯金偿付?
　哦,这是悲哀的交易!不能答应,
我们要控告这从未签订的债务。

80

哦你,把酒浆和诱惑
在我去游荡的路上置设。
　你岂不是把注定的恶遍布,
再使我的陷落成为罪过!

81
哦你,用污泥把人来塑,
甚至造了乐园也把蛇相付。
 那一切的罪用来把人脸抹黑,
你给人宽恕,也得到宽恕。

82
像是被离去的白天所掩护,
为饥饿所困的斋月找到了逃路。
 我又独自站在陶匠的屋中,
被各种形状的陶坯围住。

83
各样的形状大小的尺寸,一道站立,
靠着墙,沿着地;
 有些是唠唠叨叨的家伙,
有些可能在听着,却绝不吭气。

84
他们中的一个说:"实非徒然,
选出我材质的泥土原本平凡,
 被塑成这个样子,再被毁掉,
或者又被踩成没有形状的泥团。"

85
第二个就说:"没有一个
顽皮的孩子会把他欢饮的碗打破;
 他也不会在发怒时毁坏陶器,
既然当初是他亲手制作。"

86

片刻的沉静之后,有一个开了口,
在那些陶器里它算做得比较丑:
　"他们都笑我歪歪斜斜地立着,
怎么,当时陶匠的手在发抖?"

87

这儿有个话多的家伙,
我想是个苏菲派的小罐,发了火,
　"这些个陶罐和陶工,
谁是陶工,谁是陶罐,请告诉我!"

88

"啊?"又一个讲,"有些说道,
他扬言要把那些个往地狱里丢掉,
　就是被他做坏了的不幸陶罐,
哼!他可是个好伙伴,绝不会胡闹。"

89

"好了,不管谁做谁买,"一个在呢喃,
"弃置了这么久,我的土质都已变干:
　不过,只要把过去熟悉的酒浆注满,
我想,我很快就能复元。"

90

陶器们正一个个地这样闲讲,
都在期待的一弯微月已可遥赏。
　他们就互相碰着,"兄弟,兄弟!
现在就等扛酒人的担子吱吱作响!"

91

啊,为我凋谢的生命准备葡萄酒浆,
好清洗我的身躯当生命消亡。
　用新鲜的叶子将我裹好,
葬在那并非少有人来的园子旁。

92

纵使我埋骨成灰,
也要把葡萄的网罗向空中抛飞。
　不会只有一个路过的信士,
将被它不知不觉地牵回。

93

真的,我热爱了这么久的偶像
耽误了我在这个世界的声望。
　淹没我的光荣在浅杯之中,
出卖我的体面为了一声低唱。

94

真的,真的,以前常常悔罪,
我发誓——可我发誓时不曾喝醉?
　然后春天一到,玫瑰在手,
我那褴褛的忏悔纷纷撕碎。

95

虽然酒扮演了没有信仰的角色,
还把我名誉的外衣撕破,
　我还是经常疑惑:卖酒的所买,
能否将他所卖的一半抵过。

96

啊,春天带着玫瑰去无踪迹,
韶年的芳馨篇页也将掩闭。
　那在枝头欢唱的夜莺,
谁知是哪里飞来,何处飞去?

97

沙漠里能够把泉水瞥见,
哪怕踪迹微茫,只要真的出现,
　虚弱的行人也会跃起,
就像踩倒的牧草又一次挺起地面。

98

只盼那些有翼的天使别来太迟,
赶上命运的书卷还在打开之时。
　让那严格的书记另外再写,
或者,把字迹涂抹严实。

99

啊,我爱,要是你我能跟他协力
去掌握万物所有的可悲设计,
　我们难道不会把它砸碎,
再重新塑造,使它最接近心中所欲?

100

那边升起的月亮又来寻找我们,
此后她还将几度圆缺,几度找寻?
　她升起,寻遍这同样的花园,
——却再也见不到那一个人。

101

啊,行觞人,你如果像她那样穿过
在草地上如星分散的宾客,
  在你这愉快的差使中,到了我
那块儿地方,请为我把杯中的酒倾落。

注释

（2）"虚假黎明"（Subhi Kazib），在真正的黎明（Subhi sadik）前大约一个小时，地平线上一瞬间的光线。在东方是个很常见的现象。

（4）"新年"。必须记得这里新年是从春分开始（无论如何旧太阳历实际上已经被极不方便的太阴历取代了，它的计日从穆罕默德迁居算起），这个日子据说是由杰姆西王指定为纪念节日的。杰姆西王是奥马尔经常提到的，其年历他也参与过修订。

宾宁说："春色突然到来，很快遍布，非常吸引人。田野才开始解冻，树木抽芽，土壤生花。在他们的元旦（Naw Rooz），雪在山上如补丁，在谷间像阴影，园中果树的新枝已很美丽，绿草杂花在平原到处都是。

'老迈的冬日之神戴着冰冠
夏天的蓓蕾做成一个芬芳的花环
嘲讽似地，放在——'

在新生的各种植物中我又认出一些多年未见的熟悉品种，有两种蓟；野雏菊，很像马头兰；红白三叶草；酸模；蓝色的矢车菊；水岸两边的野生草药蒲公英生出黄色的顶冠。"还听不到夜莺，看不到玫瑰，但是画眉鸟和啄木鸟已经唤起了北方乡村的春天。

"摩西的白色之手"。见《出埃及记》第四章第六节。那里说，摩西抽出他的手——根据波斯人，没有说"大麻疯像雪"，只说"白"——大概类似我们春天的山茶花。也是据他们说，耶稣的治愈能力就在他的气息中。

（5）伊兰园，为夏达德王所建，现在已经湮没在阿拉伯沙漠的某个位置。杰姆西王的七环杯象征七重天，七大行星，七个海等，是一只神杯。

（6）巴列维语，波斯古代英雄时代类似梵语的古老语言。哈菲兹也讲过夜莺的巴列维语没有跟着人类的一起改变。

我不能确定第四行所指,究竟是看起来很惨黄的红玫瑰,还是黄玫瑰本该为红色?红色、白色、黄色的玫瑰在波斯都很普遍。我想索西在他的《类纂》里,引用了一些西班牙作者的说法,说玫瑰在十点是白色,两点是黄色,五点是红色。

(10)鲁斯图姆,波斯的赫拉克利特,扎尔是他的父亲,《列王纪》里高度颂扬了他的功绩。哈蒂姆,东方式慷慨的闻名典范。

(13)这个鼓,是在宫外敲击的。

(14)那里是玫瑰的黄金中心。

(18)波斯波利斯,也被称作杰姆西王的宝座。杰姆西王是神话时代的俾什达迪王朝最杰出的国王,根据《列王纪》的说法,他被认为兴建了这座城。也有人说是妖王詹·伊卜·詹在亚当时代之前的工程,这位妖王也建造过金字塔。

巴拉姆·古尔,有野驴巴拉姆之称,萨珊王朝君主。像波西米亚王一样,也有他的七座城堡,每个城堡有不同的颜色,住着一位皇家公主,每个公主给他讲一个故事。这是波斯最著名的诗歌之一中所讲的,它的作者是阿米尔·霍斯陆。根据东方的神话,这些七城之类都象征七重天,大概这部诗自己就是八重天,它凌驾在神秘的七重之上,被它们围绕。那些塔楼还有三座遗址,由乡人开放参观。还有一个巴拉姆追猎野驴时陷入的沼泽,就像雷文斯伍德的主人一样。

宫殿把他的柱子向天空投出,

在门口曾有国王容貌的画图。

那儿我见到孤飞的鸽子,

"咕咕咕",她叫,"咕咕咕"。

这首是宾宁发现的,和哈菲兹等人的一些诗,被游人刻在波斯波利斯的遗址上。鸽子的"咕咕咕"像古代巴列维语,在波斯语里的意思是"哪里?哪里?哪里?"在阿塔尔的《百鸟朝凤》也提到鸽子被群鸟领袖责备,她一直停着不动,为了失去的优素福永远弹着忧伤的曲调。

（19）关于奥马尔第十九首里的红玫瑰，我想起一个英格兰的老迷信说法，我们的紫色白头翁（靠近剑桥的富利姆渠生长很多），只生在丹麦人洒血之地。

（21）每一个行星一千年。

（31）土星，第七重天的主宰。

（32）我和你，不同于全体的独立存在或单一体。

（37）一个波斯诗人，我想是阿塔尔，讲过一个与此相关的美丽故事。一个口渴的旅人从泉水里捧水喝。跟着又来了另一个，他拿了个陶碗舀水喝，然后把碗留在身后就离开了。第一个旅人拿起碗来再舀，他吃惊地发现，同样的水从他手里喝的是甜的，从陶碗里喝的就是苦的。这时有声音，我想从天上传来，告诉他：制碗的陶土曾经被做成人，现在形状换了样，但是必死者的苦味没有丢掉。

（39）饮酒前在地面洒一点儿酒的习俗在波斯还保留着，可能在东方都一样。尼古拉斯先生认为这是"表示慷慨豁达，同时劝说喝酒者应当一饮而尽，直到最后一滴"。这不是很像古代的迷信观点，奠酒以取悦地神，使她一起参与这违禁的狂欢？或者可能是用丰盛的祭品愉悦那些羡慕的眼睛，就像西方的古代人？而我们看到奥马尔还有另外的用意，珍贵的酒不能丢弃，让它渗入地下好使那些从前可怜的好酒者重新振作。

哈菲兹在很多方面都摹仿奥马尔，他说："当你喝酒时把一杯倾倒地上，难道不怕罪孽又会增长？"

（43）根据一个美丽的东方传奇，亚兹拉尔把生命之树的苹果放在鼻孔下面，就完成了他的使命。

这一首，和之后的两首，有人认为是多余的，应该从文本中删去，但我对此建议宁可忽视。

（51）From Máh to Máhi，从鱼到月。

（56）这当然是关于他学问的一个玩笑。奥马尔有一首奇妙的数学诗被指出给我，更奇妙的是它跟多恩博士的一些诗几乎完全可以类比,这些诗被艾萨克·沃尔顿的传记引用。奥马尔的诗是:"我和你可以和圆规的形象相比,虽然我们有两个头却是一个身体。在我们固定了圆周的中心,最终两个头合在了一起。"多恩博士:

如果我们是两个,我们两个
也像直直的圆规两脚相并。
你的灵魂,是固定的脚,不过,
只是看来不动,另一个动你就动。

虽然你在中心稳坐,
但当我,那另一个去远行,
你就倾听着我,把身斜侧,
等到我回家你才直起身形。

对我你正是这样,我也像
另外那只脚,跑时身子也斜着。
你的坚定使我的圆恰当,
我的终点与起点相合。

(59)七十二教派据说划分了世界,有些人认为包括了伊斯兰教,有些不这么认为。

(60)暗指马穆德苏丹征服印度和它的黑种人。

(68)魔灯(*Fanusi khiyal*)在印度仍在使用,一个圆筒形内芯上画着各种人物,小心地使之平稳和通风,围绕着里面点燃的蜡烛旋转。

(70)原文有一句很奇异,文词断续有些像我们的《木鸽笔记》,说是她总是从断掉的地方开始。

(75)Parwín and Mushtari,就是昴宿和木星。

(87)陶罐和陶匠跟人和造物主的比较关系,从希伯来先知时代到今天,在世界文学中流传既久且广。最后出现了"罐神论"这个名称,卡莱尔还用这个词揶揄斯特林的泛神论。我的教长,具有淹通

的学问,写信给我:

"至于老奥马尔的陶罐,我没有告诉你我在《皮尔森主教论信仰》一文中发现的意见?'我们全由他的意志处置,我们当前和将来境况的缔构和安排全由他智慧和公正的意志决裁。陶匠难道没有对陶土的权力,同一块土,或者做出一个高贵的器皿,或者做出一个低贱的器皿?(《罗马书》第九章第二十一节)制陶者对于他的陶片兄弟(都由同样的材料做成)不是有任意的权力,就像神对他?神用无所不能的权力去做奇妙的创造,先从虚无造出泥土,又从泥土造出他。'"

还有从一个非常不同的地方得到的。"我在以后的时候会提到阿里斯托芬,偶然想起他的《马蜂》一剧中有个惊奇的说话陶罐的故事,但现在完全忘记了。"

陶罐请旁观者给他的不好待遇作证。一个妇人说:"以普洛塞尔皮娜起誓,你如果不去作证,(像《清教徒》里卡迪和他的母亲)就去买个铆钉,倒是显得更聪明。"学者解释说,那个罐子就是陶匠做的碗。

为了猎奇可以再举个例子,见詹姆斯·哈姆雷·特雷格纳近作《康沃尔郡教士自传》。

在我的朋友里有个奇怪的家伙,他那么像《天路历程》里的一个人物,所以理查总是叫他"寓言"。他留着长长的白胡子,那个时期这是少见的附加物,脸的颜色像经过烘焙,像我们常在陶罐上见的面孔。在我们的方言里,把陶器叫"克娄",所以村里的孩子常常在他后面喊叫:"赶快回到陶匠那儿,老克娄脸,再烤一下。""寓言"在很多事上足够精明,就是对于这个"再烤一下"的名声显得很乏智数。

(90)在斋月结束的时候,新月(它决定着他们对一年的划分)的第一瞥早被焦急万分地等待,现在人们可以大声欢呼了。地窖里运酒者捆扎的声音也能听到了。奥马尔关于这同样的月亮还有另外一首很好的四行诗:

开心吧!郁闷的月份将要死去,

新月给我们的补偿不断持续。
看那老的,憔悴,佝偻,惨淡,
被时间和斋戒折磨,已奄奄在天际!

附录一：第一版译诗 18 首

原编辑者按语：

奥马尔·海亚姆翻译的初版，是在 1859 年，和后来的版本有很大的差异，我想还是把它全部印出来更好，而不再试图标出那些差异。

1

醒来啊！早晨把石子投入
夜天之碗，让群星飞出天幕：
　看！那东方的猎手，
用光之长索把苏丹的塔殿套住。

2

睡梦里黎明的左手已在天空，
我听见酒店里传来喊声，
　"起来吧，我的小家伙们，倒满杯子，
别等到生命之酒干涸在杯中。"

8

看，每天醒来了一千朵花，
一千朵花又飘落泥沙。
　而这带来玫瑰的第一个夏月，
也带走杰姆西和凯柯巴。

9

来,跟着我老海亚姆,
忘了凯柯巴和凯霍斯鲁。
　让鲁斯图姆为所欲为,
让哈蒂姆命宴——无预汝。

12

"人间的权力是惬意的!"有人想,
另有人——"天堂之临是何等安享!"
　啊,把现钱攥在手,丢开其余,
哦,那远方的鼓乐声威震响。

26

哦,跟着老海亚姆,让智者去辩言,
一事是确定的——这生命如飞一般。
　一事是确定的,其它都是谎话,
花儿一次盛开,永远凋残。

33

我就向着自转的上天呼喊,
问,"命运用什么样的灯盏
　把她在黑暗中摸爬的孩童引领?"
上天回答,"一种理智,昏昧如瞎眼!"

36

一天黄昏,我在市场上逗留,
看一个陶匠把陶泥使劲捣揉。
　而它,用全已失传的语言低诉:
"轻点儿,兄弟,轻点儿,求求。"

37

啊,倒满杯子,那样只会失落,
反复地讲时光从脚下溜过,
　未生的明日,和已死的昨日,
何必为它们烦恼,假如你今日欢乐。

38

等片刻在荒沙废碛的中间,
等片刻,一尝生命之泉——
　群星在沉没,商队已启程,
向着虚无之晨——哦,别拖延!

45

让智者去争辩,
让我跟宇宙的不和相伴:
　在喧嚣的某个角落,
跟那谑笑你的对着干。

46

进出不停,上下匆遽,
这只是幻影的灯戏。
　灯里的蜡烛是太阳,
周围是我们的虚形来来去去。

47

如果唇你曾吻,酒你曾喝,
都终结在万物所终结之无——是的,
　那想想当你在,你在不过是
你会——无——你只会不失不得。

48

当这河岸边的玫瑰遍开盛多,
跟老海亚姆把红酒一起喝。
　　等到天使手持浓黑的药液
走近你,——接过来,不要畏缩。

59

再听。斋月结束的那个晚天,
更美好的月亮升起之前,
　　那个老陶坊里我独自站立,
全部的陶器排成了一圈。

60

说来奇怪,那堆土罐子中,
有些能讲,有些不能:
　　忽然,一个更性急的叫喊:
"请说说,谁是陶罐,谁是陶工?"

64

一个说——"人们提起那乖张的酒保,
他用地狱的烟灰把脸瞎搞;
　　他们说我们可有了严酷的考验,
哼,他是个不错的家伙,一切会干得好。"

74

啊,可知我欢乐的明月长圆,
天空的明月又一次升起眼前。
　　此后她还会多少次升起,找我
找遍这同样的园子——只是徒然!

原编辑者后记：

必须承认，菲兹杰拉德在他的奥马尔·海亚姆的译本中，相对原文来说有很大的自由度。第一首全是他自己的，第四版的第三十三首，(第二版第三十六首。译按：原文误作三十一。)有两行取自阿塔尔，(见书信集，第一卷第251页)。关于第四版的第八十一首，考威尔教授写到："原文没有一句提到蛇，我找遍了尼古拉斯版也没有见到。我总是怀疑最后一行是尼古拉斯版第236首的误译，它是这样的：

你知道每个人的隐秘在他心里，

你会抓住他的手当他软弱颓靡。

神啊，让我悔改，给我宽恕，

会让每个人悔改，给每个人宽恕，啊你！

菲兹杰拉德弄错了这里'让'和'给'的意思，出于他自己的错误杜撰了最后一行。我在加尔各答时就此写信给他，但他从未注意改正。"

附录二:第二版译诗 13 首

1

醒来啊!太阳在东山的后面
把群星从夜色里驱散。
　然后,升到中天,再向
苏丹的塔楼射出光芒之箭。

14

还不愚蠢,像蜘蛛一样织着
这眼前的生命之丝去换取什么?
　我们自己,都不知道是否
将呼出的气息就是正吸进的!

28

在我睡时,另一个声音响亮,
"花朵要跟晨色一起开放。"
　之后是渐弱的呢喃,当我醒来——
"花朵一度盛开永成凋丧。"

44

你,还在短暂的恩宠之中,
手臂缠上柏树枝飘飘随风,
　趁地母用她的手臂抱入
之前,先消融在这最后一拥。

65

如果只是禁绝酒和爱的那帮
占据先知的天堂,
　悲夫,我疑惑先知的天堂
不过是把空拳一张。

77

就让哲人和博士去训诫
那他们愿意和不愿意的一切——
　都不过是永恒链条上的一环,
没有那个能脱节,也不能断掉,逾越。

86

不,哪怕,他怒容吓人,
我立誓不会把不公当施恩;
　没有一个酒店里的好汉
不把这样卑微的懦夫踢出门。

90

又一次,在他们中间,
聚起了几乎听不清的呢喃,
　像是拨动熄灭话语的死灰,
由我的耳朵点亮成活的语言。

94

如此对死者如同对生者,什么?
为什么? 问得现成,答却难说。
　忽然有个暴躁地叫嚷:"请回答,
哪个是陶匠,哪个又是陶罐呢?"

99

从春日的阳和到了那里,
老友会跟老友问候致礼。
　在斜出墙头的树枝下,
他的花朵把我头脚掩起。

106

哦,如果世界能重造,
命运书卷掩上之前我们能赶到,
　就让书写人把我们的名字
写上洁净的书页,或全都删掉。

107

更好一点,哦,更好一点,
从宇宙之卷把一个不幸灵魂删减,
　比起一滴一滴随着岁月滚动
最终涌成洪流嘶哑惨痛地翻卷。

109

看!亲爱的,天上月亮又升
来找我们,穿过扶疏的梧桐,
　以后她还会几度升起,从那叶间
来找我们中的一个——却将成空。

附录三:第三版译诗 2 首

1(初稿)
醒来啊!太阳腾跃到它前面
那夜空之中,迫使群星飞散,
　连夜也一起驱出天际,再举
光之长矢射中苏丹的塔殿。

38
好,你听一下吧,
人声来自这普通的泥巴,
　他们把人形投入这不幸的铸模
塑造了,再用这名字去叫它。

附录四：各版编次对照表

第一版	第二版	第三、四、五版
1	1	1
2	2	2
3	3	3
4	4	4
5	5	5
6	6	6
7	7	7
	8	8
8	9	9
9	10	10
10	11	11
11	12	12
12	13	13
	14	
13	15	14
15	16	15
14	17	16
16	18	17
17	19	18
	20	
20	21	21
21	22	22
22	23	23
18	24	19
19	25	20

23	26	24
24	27	25
26	28	
25	29	26
27	30	27
28	31	28
29	32	29
30	33	30
31	34	31
32	35	32
	36	33
	37	34
33		
34	38	35
35	39	36
36	40	37
37		
	42	39
	43	40
	44	
47	45	42
48	46	43
	47	46
	48	47
38	49	48
	50	49
	51	50
	52	51
	53	52

	54	53
	55	41
39	56	54
40	57	55
41	58	56
	59	57
42	60	58
43	61	59
44	62	60
	63	61
	64	62
	65	
	66	63
	67	64
	68	65
	69	44
	70	45
	71	66
	72	67
45		
49	74	69
50	75	70
51	76	71
	77	
52	78	72
53	79	73
	80	74
54	81	75
55	82	76

56	83	77
	84	78
	85	79
	86	
57	87	80
58	88	81
59	89	82
	90	83
61	91	84
62	92	84
63	93	84
60	94	84
64	95	84
65	96	84
66	97	84
67	98	91
	99	
68	100	92
69	101	93
70	102	94
71	103	95
72	104	96
	105	97
	106	98
	107	
73	108	99
74	109	100
75	110	101

其九十：齋月每令回教徒衆疲弱躁厲，將終，新月彼爲分年之度也，之初睹，久跂足待，而今爲一歡呼矣。窖中傭夫結束之聲亦可聞矣。奧瑪別有佳什言此月，曰：「悶時已過可爲歡，直待新光賣酒餐。老月不堪成禁斷，羸容慘色送將闌。歡兮，陰鬱之齋月已死，新月將來償吾。爲光陰、齋戒之困，老月已作羸弱、佝僂、蒼白之相，奄奄於天際。」

頓所撰之本傳。意堪並行。奧瑪詩曰：「規如吾汝形同有，共一身兮分二首。圓徑圓周果取中，相循終到長相守。吾汝如規之形，一身而二首。既定圓周之中心，吾汝之首終必相合。」多恩詩曰：「那用哀哀怨別離？吾身與汝合如規。汝心不動吾身運，情自相牽到處隨。」既定圓周之中心，吾汝之首終必相合。」多恩詩曰：「那用哀哀怨別離？吾身與汝合如規。汝心不動吾身運，情自相牽到處隨。莫道閨中晏坐安，閨心處處繫征鞍。側身待到歸來日，始得相迎直起看。君心相待感吾心，不計奔忙誓死尋。爲汝情堅何敢誤？重來定未負初吟。」

其五十九：七十二宗遍據此世，或言回教在其內，或言非也。

其六十：隱指馬穆德王征印度而役其黑民。

其六十八：幻燈今猶用之印度也，內置一柱筒，繪諸色人其上，巧使平穩，兼使風生，環其內之燭火旋焉。

其七十一：原文有一句甚詭，辭之斷續頗類吾國《木鳩記》，言伊每從中斷處重操也。

其七十五：二辭即昂宿與木星也。

其八十七：陶罐、陶匠之與吾人，造物者相媲也，自希伯來先知以來至於今日，見之天下文辭中，既久且廣也。終有「罐神論」之名，而卡萊爾以之譏斯特林之「泛神論」也。吾之謝赫，其學博通，嘗致吾書云：

「與老奧瑪陶罐之相類者，吾未嘗示汝得之《皮爾森主教信仰論》中者耶？『故吾人全由其志處置，吾當今與將來境況之締構悉付其獨運而審智、公正之裁。陶匠豈無權柄？於同一土也，或以爲貴器或以爲賤器。』（《羅馬書》九章二十一節）彼搏土者之於同產之碎陶，蓋皆自同質出者，豈不亦有獨運之權柄，一若神之於彼？神擅遍有之權柄，妙於創作，方自虛無造泥土，復自泥土造彼也。」

又有從絕不同之域中得者。「他日吾將言阿里斯托芬，偶憶彼《馬蜂》劇中有能言陶罐之奇事，而吾久忘之矣。」陶罐爲其惡遇請他罐爲證。婦言，以冥后爲誓，爾如不與其證，一若《清教徒》中卡迪並其母，市一釘，尤智。注疏者言其罐，是陶匠所制之碗也。

尚有一例尤奇，見詹姆斯·哈姆雷·特雷格納一八七一年近作《康沃爾郡教士自傳》。

「吾儕中有一奇人，頗似《天路歷程》中一人，故理查每呼之『寓言』」，蓄長鬚，盡白，時人中罕有，面色如經焙，見陶甌所繪人面也。在吾鄉之方言，呼陶器爲『克妻』，故村童常逐其後，嬉鬧曰：『老克妻面，往陶匠所，再焙之！』是『寓言』雖行事頗狡，而於待焙之名殊乏智數。」

菲兹杰拉德《鲁拜集》译本五版汇刊

巴拉姆，有野驢之號，薩珊朝帝君，亦有七城，若波希米亞王，而每城異彩，城居一妃，妃爲傳奇。此據阿米爾·霍斯陸所作之波斯名詩也。東國小說家云七城象七重天，霍斯陸之詩故名《八重天》也，既凌彼七重，遂使環之旋行。今尚遺廢址三、鄉人以爲名勝。亦有廢沼，巴拉姆王逐驢時陷焉，一若雷文斯伍德之主家。

「廢宮遺柱上淩空，日角龍顏想像中。我來惟見斑鳩孤飛，其聲咕咕然，哀呼不止。」在尼古拉斯版《鲁拜集》列第三百五十章，亦在温菲爾德之譯本。此章賓寧所得，爲瀉子刻諸波斯波利斯廢址，雜之哈菲兹諸人所作間。斑鳩聲若古巴列維語「咕，咕，咕」近波斯語「何處，何處，何處」也。

阿特《鳥會》亦言斑鳩，伊爲鳥首所責，蓋自失彼優素福，停而不飛，喃喃無休，恒作一悲調也。

其十九：奧瑪十九章之紅玫瑰，余憶一英倫舊日詭談，吾國之紫白頭翁，近劍橋之富利姆渠多有焉，惟生於丹麥人喋血處。

其二十一：一行星爲一千年也。

其三十一：土星，第七重天之君也。

其三十二：吾汝、獨、一之與全也。

其三十七：一波斯詩客，吾憶爲阿特，嘗述小說，可資比觀。一遊子渴，掬泉而飲。時有聲來，吾度之或自天也，語之曰：製碗之土嘗搏爲人，今雖易其形，無易其促命之苦。

其三十九：飲前酹酒於地之俗，今波斯猶是也，東方蓋皆如是。尼古拉斯以爲：「以示慷慨豁達，兼勸飲者飲必盡也。」抑或意同西方之古民，豐其祭品以娛慕者眼目耶？而吾人見奧瑪尚別有意在，蓋酒爲菁華，莫酒以媚地神，且使伊同此逸樂耶？殊類古俗，莫酒不能棄，將以滲之地下，欲使古昔之飲者復甦也。

哈菲兹多方擬奧瑪，其有詩曰：「惟汝傾此最佳釀，罪其增益慎勿忘。」

其四十三：東國有傳奇言，亞兹拉爾以生死樹之實置人鼻下，用踐其命。

其五十一：**From Máh to Máhi**，始乎魚終乎月也。

其五十六：此固言其學之滑稽語也。奧瑪有詩以算學爲喻，吾以爲奇，而更奇者，彼詩乃與多恩博士之詩，見艾薩克·沃爾

注釋

其二：所謂「幻曙」者，真曙前約一小時，天際頃刻之光芒也。此天象在東國人皆能詳。

其三：必知此新歲之始爲春分。蓋舊有之太陽曆久爲陋劣之太陰曆所替，彼計日起自穆罕默德之改邑。以春分爲元日佳節，傑姆西王之命也。奧瑪每言彼王，且嘗與其曆之修訂。

賓寧言：「春色忽來，頃時漸滿，殊動人也。冰雪方解，已見雜花生樹，新芽破土矣。元日之雪綴綴山際，明滅谷間，園樹萌蘗，郊青處處。『冰雪淺作冠，夏榮繁作飾。斯觀一何謔……』譯注：此出莎士比亞《仲夏夜夢》第二齣，蓋謂冬神毳毳，著淺冰冠，而綴夏榮以爲花環，譃飾其上也。群植新生者中，吾猶識數種，而頻年未睹矣。有薊二種，野春菊，頗類馬頭蘭，紅白之苜蓿，闊葉之酸模，藍矢車菊，黃華采采。」夜鶯未聞，玫瑰未放，然畫眉與啄木鳥固皆能喚北鄙之春矣。

「摩西白色之手」，見《出埃及記》四章六節。彼處言，摩西方出其手云云，而波斯人固未言痳瘋如雪，惟言色白耳，殆類吾地春日之山楂花耶？彼又云，耶穌愈病之力存乎其息中。

其五：伊蘭園，夏達德王之所建也，今湮於大食國沙磧中。傑姆西王之七環杯，以象七重天海、七耀星宿諸事，神杯也。

其六：巴列維語，古波斯雅言也。哈菲茲亦言夜鶯之巴列維語，未與吾人之語偕易。吾不能決四行中所言，究爲紅玫瑰帶慘色耶，抑彼黃玫瑰實應爲紅耶？蓋紅、白、黃之玫瑰，在波斯均常見者。索西之《類纂》徵諸西班牙著述，云玫瑰十時爲白，二時爲黃，五時爲紅。

其十：魯斯塔姆，波斯之赫拉克勒斯也，扎爾其父，《王書》盛言其績。哈蒂姆，以豪爽疏財聞名東國。

其十三：是鼓，宮外所擊者也。

其十四：彼處，玫瑰最盛地也。

其十八：波斯波利斯城，有傑姆西王御座之名。俾什達迪朝，傳同神古，其王之最稱者，即傑姆西王也。依《王書》說，是城即此王興築。又説爲精怪之跡，在生人之先，其遺跡尚有金字塔云。

其一百零一

百分勸酒不須愁（司馬光），挈榼攜棋得勝游（李光）。事往歲深無處問（曾旼），梅花明月爲誰留（王奕）。

其九十六

狂風浩蕩喚春歸（孔武仲），掩卷燈前淚滴衣（釋行海）。時有行雲自來去（王孝先），碧桃花外一鶯飛（趙汝回）。

其九十七

飄零沙漠若爲情（文天祥），泉本無貪人自清（方信孺）。僕木偃禾如不起（王陶），縈迂草徑少人行（王十朋）。

其九十八

九天使者號真王（王十朋），只放青蒼一冊方（楊萬里）。重待三長專筆削（強至），人間生死路茫茫（文天祥）。

其九十九

協力從今請共治（陳宓），了知造化最兒嬉（許月卿）。易如可毀乾坤熄（何夢桂），陶鑄蒼生盡未遲（翁合）。

其一百

星斗翻芒互降升（鄭獬），空園亦喜綠陰增（戴栩）。曾看清夜陪明月（萬規），不見斯人但服膺（趙蕃）。

其九十一
葡萄生摘薦新醅（王安禮），淨洗詩脾萬古埃（方岳）。死葬小園芳草地（楊億），每春顏色爲誰開（王禹偁）？

其九十二
後死猶來瘞骨灰（胡寅），野花閒抱故藤開（宋庠）。聖賢用策寧相遠（石介），盡逐羈愁入酒杯（王柏）。

其九十三
開盞時時中聖人（李光），可能熟醉巧謀身（郭印）。淺斟低唱癡兒女（仇遠），盡把功名付客塵（宋庠）。

其九十四
今年莫省是何年（陳著），未敢昏昏只醉眠（劉才邵）。誓酒不應忘此老（陳師道），一花消息小春前（錢時）。

其九十五
投名且向酒壺中（王洋），畢竟兩端皆是空（李綱）。世事不容輕易看（文天祥），人間天上此歡同（應廓）。

其八十六 天應不語悶應同（朱淑真），稍涉新奇卻未工（宋犖）。好醜元來都是幻（文天祥），難將此意問鴻蒙（楊時）。

其八十七 壺觴歌詠欲忘歸（楊冠卿），齊物名篇孰是非（劉弇）。欲默不能言不可（利登），各隨妍醜自芳菲（歐陽修）。

其八十八 更陶瓦缶作尊彝（趙良埈），仁暴由來各異施（劉克莊）。幸不幸間身且隱（方回），卻思公道即無疑（于觀文）。

其八十九 得失秋毫豈更嗟（王安石），貌枯神澤骨槎牙（艾性夫）。君來特地平分破（何夢桂），塊壘澆平酒自賒（宋祁）。

其九十 倚看新月露纖纖（王之道），霧拂青天幸一瞻（郭祥正）。明日陰晴真可卜（李質），夜深無處認青簾（劉學箕）。

其八十一

泥土相纏四百年（王質），秋蛇春蚓任人傳（王之道）。向來平實交相勉（陳著），罪福區區不足編（姜特立）。

其八十二

萬象鮮明禁火前（李龏），重尋勝處少留連（王洋）。從來造物陶甄手（陸遊），幻出壺中小有天（李洪）。

其八十三

紅泥俄見酒壺新（張鎡），品格高低各自春（董特立）。瓶缽剩添風月滿（蔡向），等閒語默見天真（黃履）。

其八十四

生涯身事任東西（晁補之），祇恐鈞陶意不齊（韋驤）。珍重一壺酬絕唱（徐鉉），是非千載逐芳泥（譚用之）。

其八十五

了知造化最兒嬉（許月卿），獨有癡頑二字奇（陸遊）。一怒赭山何所損（胡寅），斡回天地聾當時（劉效）。

其七十六

瓠壺藤蔓便相縈（辛棄疾），應與道人增笑聲（釋德洪）。好事還殊門外路（方大琮），崇朝開戶放身行（韓淲）。

其七十七

深自憐餘不及情（洪擬），故應天罰遣偏盲（劉克莊）。消愁亦有旗亭酒（孔平仲），廟祀何曾暫割牲（李覯）。

其七十八

太虛無實可追尋（王安石），情好相投歲月深（王邁）。靜土兀然方止酒（蘇籀），少狂費盡一生心（劉克莊）。

其七十九

石隕媧皇補後天（王禹偁），精金百鍊始知堅（陳宓）。悲哉易感精神往（王柏），好約抽毫玉陛前（文彥博）。

其八十

手把先天已後書（文天祥），江山酌酒尚無餘（孫子光）。我將乘興拚沉醉（吳芾），罪或無多乞赦除（劉宰）。

其七十一
恰見天書字數行（周文璞），再來方覺路歧長（孔文仲）。我今稽首虔誠禮（黃拱），千載仙居已渺茫（方信孺）。

其七十二
更於底處問穹蒼（張栻），下視人間有肺腸（陳傅良）。白髮來爲生死別（王銍），一元不動固安詳（徐僑）。

其七十三
媧皇得道自神仙（蘇軾），潛握人間造化權（史瑜）。天地有窮歸幻化（馬廷鸞），絕憐塵土過年年（黎廷瑞）。

其七十四
萬事紛紛醉即休（楊時），身名曾不問沈浮（趙挺之）。匆匆去日多於髮（陸游），今日那知明日愁（方一夔）？

其七十五
夜沖星斗落旄頭（何文季），快似神駒略九州（徐恢）。一石蒲桃先載酒（宋庠），紫微新命舊交遊（王禹偁）。

其六十六

初非恍惚與希夷（朱熹），文字當場莫好奇（吳泳）。上有天堂下地獄（趙炅），一身切莫計安危（趙蕃）。

其六十七

天堂地獄又重新（釋智愚），憂喜忘心即養神（徐鉉）。欲究本來源出處（王阮），無邊物色盡橫陳（王炎）。

其六十八

月起林間燈映紗（許月卿），大千俱屬眼中花（釋守卓）。何人幻此圓機妙（吳潛），來往同看本一家（王十朋）。

其六十九

烏飛兔走兩悠悠（柴元彪），不起爭心效弈秋（孫應時）。過眼浮雲翻覆易（范成大），一盤棋子情誰收（華岳）？

其七十

俠場星影鬥飛毬（宋祁），擊若無心可狎鷗（趙善括）。日月時同來去異（劉應鳳），長年報道不須愁（楊萬里）。

其六十一

年年專遣送蒲桃（蘇軾），生理應須問酒醪（王安石）。有命自知誰畏禍（徐積），人情只合醉陶陶（兜率長老）。

其六十二

沉湎應從通率論（陳棣），他年富貴豈須論（韋驤）。夫君泉下儻無憾（史堯弼），索酒得杯和月吞（華岳）。

其六十三

古今上下幾千年（文天祥），要信人生各有緣（陸游）。老去光陰如箭急（王柏），花開頃刻更堪憐（楊公遠）。

其六十四

冥心晦息掩柴關（馬廷鸞），元氣淋漓挽不還（王阮）。個裏竟能無一語（朱熹），前途事業自登山（孫應時）。

其六十五

士甘焚死不公侯（黃庭堅），更爲吟哦萬古愁（孔武仲）。人物熙熙醒醉裏（范成大），乘時談笑上瀛洲（韓淲）。

其五十六

夸谈名理浩无穷（张载），规矩乾坤心匠中（王义山）。今我到来都不问（毕仲游），便须索酒对东风（卫博）。

其五十七

我于推步亦留心（顾逢），穆穆无凶合在今（龙昌期）。去日背人来日逼（刘弇），惜春惟付酒杯深（韩淲）。

其五十八

柳边一点酒旗星（汪莘），何日相携双玉瓶（本之）？君若此时辞痛饮（吴芾），人间无路仰天庭（黄庭坚）。

其五十九

利名中伏祸机深（刘克庄），有酒何人可共斟（卢祖皋）？毕世谩求铅汞伏（张伯端），分明滴滴是黄金（赵崇森）。

其六十

愁城高耸酒难攻（吴潜），破贼须从此立功（李纲）。安得君王倚天剑（杨冠卿），扫除阴翳出长空（王遂）。

其五十一

汞内消停自合和(趙炅),百年流轉寄風波(彭汝礪)。魚遊碧沼涵靈德(歐陽修),月上松梢映綠蘿(王庭珪)。

其五十二

誰知真宰執天端(呂陶),只當空廬雜劇看(文天祥)。銀燭高張那得爾(周孚),一聲聲落曲屏閒(武衍)。

其五十三

地盡天窮草木愁(洪咨夔),塵塵何地不周流(韓淲)。明朝直向煙霞去(馬子嚴),一笑人間百事休(方岳)。

其五十四

買歡酤酒試春衣(張耒),世俗難論真是非(方岳)。不比芳春萬紅紫(劉學箕),隨階圓實似珠璣(孔平仲)。

其五十五

珠被齊光更合歡(張冕),何妨裛客自盤桓(王令)。吾儕自是生無智(王十朋),只作葡萄一斗看(張嵲)。

其四十六

名書鬼錄已經年（王十朋），但聽松風自得仙（陸游）。春醅如澠介眉壽（史浩），乾坤生意本無邊（方岳）。

其四十七

江湖吊影一身單（趙鼎），汝死那知世界寬（王安石）？海水如今平似掌（李覯），略無蹤跡到波瀾（賈收）。

其四十八

北望燕雲不盡頭（汪元量），胡沙漠漠去無休（葛天民）。峰前三尺寒泉水（蔡元厲），到處何妨為少留（朱熹）？

其四十九

生死應同晝與昏（楊萬里），是非一致亦何言（孔平仲）。百年身逐無涯智（彭汝礪），世味濃枯不見痕（魏了翁）。

其五十

是非一致亦何言（孔平仲），循取佳名睹聖門（何棄仲）。牆面豈能知奧義（王安石），皇天終不答根源（宋庠）。

其四十一

何須龜筴強稽疑（李之儀）？身後生前是兩岐（文天祥）。今日尊前休惜醉（吳芾），一雙青鬢綰青絲（項安世）。

其四十二

經年不識酒沾唇（劉敞），終作邙山一窖塵（陸游）。生死兩無纖芥恨（何基），區區翻覆亦何人（王安石）？

其四十三

一去空山竟杳然（姜特立），孟婆久送過河船（王奕）。相逢未暇聊持酒（韋驤），多病清羸挽不前（張擴）。

其四十四

倏然屍解去何之（虞儔），鵬鷃逍遥各自知（王安石）。下視塵寰真一撮（郭祥正），誰人不是塚纍纍（虞儔）？

其四十五

此去橫經涉遠途（連文鳳），遊魂多不返穹廬（劉克莊）。我今漂泊還相似（蘇轍），息念忘懷心晏如（李昉）。

其三十六

濡唇亦足荷深恩（馮時行），負爾商歌酒一樽（賀鑄）。閱盡輩流身獨健（陸游），死生契闊不堪論（李光）。

其三十七

賤非泥土貴非金（釋惟一），可惜良工苦片心（林用中）。生死已從前世定（宇文虛中），一門兄弟辱恩深（孔平仲）。

其三十八

女媧搏土費工夫（潘牥），休説衆生垢有無（王十朋）。四海流傳如見問（方岳），莫將名實自相誣（辛棄疾）。

其三十九

曾玄有酒酹淒涼（馬廷鸞），是處爲家莫斷腸（劉光祖）。天下共寃渠不恨（陳淵），一時煩濁變清涼（吳芾）。

其四十

泛艷金莖湛露濃（孫覿），長生空問茯苓松（張元幹）。鬱金香是蘭陵酒（王安石），只嗅清香醉殺儂（張道洽）。

其三十一

風馬雲車碧落翔（任希夷），鎮星合得配中央（陳楠）。周天一轂三十輻（王庭珪），應共白雲朝帝鄉（柳交）。

其三十二

直室深扃老氏關（宋祁），疎簾半捲鎮長閒（鄭鑑）。悟來不必多言語（邵雍），擺落塵埃步入山（王阮）。

其三十三

百頃滄波望似空（蘇洞），山河大地一無窮（彭汝礪）。悠悠天道推終始（王工部），五曜循環十二宮（王質）。

其三十四

夜深却見太陰虧（汪夢斗），閃閃青燈照薄帷（張耒）。欲問大鈞吾豈敢（李正民）？象名爲物本無知（陽枋）。

其三十五

至今笙鶴不歸來（方岳），牢落生涯泥一杯（歐陽修）。金斗倒垂交勸飲（孔平仲），人生常苦歲華催（李昭玘）。

其二十六

身後身前事莫猜（王寂），神通用盡却成獸（釋了惠），一朝人事淒涼改（歐陽修），零落殘碑半蝕苔（方岳）。

其二十七

問學淵源已造深（葛勝仲），不將生死動其心（葉茵）。微忱稱報慚無路（艾可叔），直自巢由錯到今（陸游）。

其二十八

愚智紛紛總一丘（陳宓），知君所得在無求（韓維）。殘紅併逐狂風去（張公庠），萬事不禁江水流（陸游）。

其二十九

從來宇宙一乾坤（王柟），此意微茫僅復存（韓淲）。莫問路頭何處去（劉克莊），皇天終不答根源（宋庠）。

其三十

問君何用惜居諸（林季仲）？來去須觀本一如（李綱）。止酒無聊還自笑（陸游），百金聊作杖頭沽（周紫芝）。

菲兹杰拉德《鲁拜集》译本五版汇刊

其二十一
今朝忽有酒如川（黄庭坚），昨日春风变旧年（王珪）。明日觉来浑不记（杨时），此身如在结绳前（陆游）。

其二十二
我有谪仙三百杯（文同），葡萄生摘荐新醅（王安礼）。只今醉倒君休笑（毕仲游），后死犹来瘗骨灰（胡寅）。

其二十三
当年宫殿赋昭阳（辛弃疾），却作游人歌舞场（方信孺）。今日难谋明日计（杨公远），纍纍邱陇水茫茫（卫泾）。

其二十四
一生享用四时春（史弥宁），莫待东风吹作尘（吴芾）。当日繁华今不见（刘宰），愁来无酒话无人（陈藻）。

其二十五
几年客路欢奔波（史弥宁），数听鸡人楼上歌（梅尧臣）。身后有名岂如酒（陆游），茫茫仙意果如何（洪炎）？

九八

其十六
榮華富貴各擾前（吳潛），石火光中又度年（孔武仲）。極目龍沙千里遠（廖行之），雪消羣醜只依然（王柏）。

其十七
逆旅浮雲自不知（蘇軾），君王安用獵熊羆（劉克莊）。雙丸倦擲羲和手（周密），影在窗前作麼移（方岳）？

其十八
陵墓猶含古木春（周文璞），豺狼當道實堪嗔（鄭清之）。至今風吼松聲怒（甘邦俊），猶說君王獵渭濱（劉望之）。

其十九
故國山河百戰侵（孫覿），何人塗血染楓林（劉過）？瓊幡第一番花信（方岳），彼美人兮無古今（馬廷鸞）。

其二十
溪頭青草弄春柔（劉跂），生物趨新曾未休（陳傑）。卻為有情人愛惜（胡宿），一身輕共野雲浮（李復）。

菲茲杰拉德《魯拜集》譯本五版匯刊

其十一

君王神武不開邊（周彥質），沉醉何人藉草眠（楊億）。漫說風沙臨瀚海（李光），濃陰滿目盡桑田（司馬光）。

其十二

一天清露屬園蔬（劉宰），酒裏功名定不虛（張侃）。小舞清歌元有興（馮時行），此中依約是華胥（孔武仲）。

其十三

榮華夢事付朱門（王灼），身後從誰問子孫（高翥）。惟是此生一杯酒（孫銳），不妨爲客任乾坤（陳知柔）。

其十四

從茲日月是青春（史浩），花意慇懃恰似人（范純仁）。吹盡玫瑰能底惜（張鎡），數他珍寶信非珍（舒亶）。

其十五

未應軒冕足關心（韋驤），縮伏蒿萊聽命沉（王令）。聞道江頭消息好（劉子翬），淘沙個個得精金（李之儀）。

九六

其六

雨晴禽哢是歌唇（方岳），天地應酬上國春（王珪）。面帶淒涼無酒色（王洋），薔薇紅透更精神（方回）。

其七

美景良辰定不空（王安石），是非已落酒杯中（方岳）。沉沉鳥沒天無盡（趙秉文），水色山光萬古同（陳省華）。

其八

尚自浮家客帝京（林洪），百年能病幾番醒（蘇元老）？花飄茵席三生淨（朱槔），翁棄人寰一葉輕（王洋）。

其九

千朵穠芳倚檻斜（向敏中），雨枝零落不成花（彭汝礪）。風流耆舊消沉盡（張致遠），有限光陰屬鬢華（趙蕃）。

其十

升平奚羨帝王功（文天祥），萬事浮雲過眼空（張綱）。大業豪華今寂寞（黃公度），古來虛死幾英雄（陸游）。

菲茲杰拉德《魯拜集》譯本五版匯刊

其一
星光欲沒曉光連，（黃大受），碧月團團墮九天（王安石）。日出東方塵滿眼（王炎），故都宮闕尚巍然（姚望之）。

其二
朝暉還復變濛濛（韋驤），喚醒昏昏嗜睡翁（蘇軾）。龍駕清都三境接（岳珂），南柯靈夢莫相通（劉兼）。

其三
天外雞鳴曉日初（許昌齡），故應有客問何如（王直方）。臨風不語空歸去（尤袤），從此身名與世疏（刁約）。

其四
一元不動固安詳（徐僑），嬾拙山林合退藏（李正民）。那與人間同日月（馬之純）？聖神深意念遐方（王拱辰）。

其五
園林猶認舊亭臺（元積中），更遣人間識玉杯（錢惟演）。明旦江頭倍惆悵（徐鉉），野花漂盡雪玫瑰（沈與求）。

莪默絕句搗宋集

譯 序

世罕雙全之法，每致狼跋。嘗集唐句迻譯《莪默絕句集》，蓋循不用唐以後事之通例。而莪默生當北宋，略晚於東坡，與山谷、後山相先後，似用宋人句爲尤宜也。復集宋句迻譯，附菲氏譯本四版行，循拗唐語例，名之《莪默絕句搗宋集》。既成集唐之譯本，心猶戚戚焉。復集宋句既成，與集唐本比觀，趣味迥然相異。俗論唐人韻多，宋人理勝，殆皮相耳。觀此二本中，言情說理，殊無唐宋之別。丰腴簡淡，或有高下之等。蓋時也，格也，其間消息，有不能以世法識之者。於是竊爲揣測，莪默與宋人，時既未遠，格乃相近耶？宋人學深，擺落凡豔，寫之于詩，易趨簡淡，固也。而莪默當回教苦禁之餘，忽返身欲，然性耽學術，未至放縱，酒色陶寫，時見高華，此隱然與宋人殊向而同致者也。雖波斯舊文，苦不能諳，征之菲氏英譯，固無歧耳。故以此集宋之句，參之英譯，得互彰焉。即以比觀乎集唐之本，相異處適足相發，亦得互彰焉。譬諸鏡鏡相照，還生境境，曰實曰虛，全在具眼。

己亥六月十二，我瞻室序。

戴黙絕句揭宋集

其一百零一

間世星郎夜宴時（方干），唯看新月吐蛾眉（王涯）。今來座上偏惆悵（張祜），賜酒盈杯誰共持（白居易）？

其九十六

枝上紅香片片飛（王周），夏鶯千囀弄薔薇（杜牧）。人間飛去猶堪恨（魏樸），無約無期春自歸（徐夤）。

其九十七

寧辭沙塞往來頻（韋應物）？待得甘泉渴殺人（殷堯藩）。纖草數莖勝靜地（劉禹錫），塵勞難索幻泡身（白居易）。

其九十八

仙使高臺十二重（蘇頲），人間無處更相逢（劉長卿）？如今悔恨將何益（韋莊），雙履難留去住蹤（齊己）。

其九十九

鴛侶先行是最榮（王甚夷），空山寂歷道心生（張說）。不須浪作縱山意（李商隱），見盡人間萬物情（劉禹錫）。

其一百

月到中宵始滿林（齊己），舊來行處好追尋（王仁裕）。一年十二度圓缺（李建樞），更入新年恐不禁（李商隱）。

其九十一
萬片香魂不可招（胡宿），靈華冷沁紫葡萄（趙鸞鸞）。已收身向園林下（白居易），還挈來時舊酒瓢（廖凝）。

其九十二
泉臺杳隔路茫茫（戴叔倫），遙囑高人未肯嘗（陸龜蒙）。還比蒲桃天上植（孟郊），九天仙樂送瓊漿（胡曾）。

其九十三
請贈劉伶作醉侯（皮日休），若無知薦一生休（王建）。不辭更住醒還醉（曹松），擾擾凡情逐水流（施肩吾）。

其九十四
苦心唯到醉中閑（貫休），省悟前非一息間（馬湘）。莫遣東風吹酒醒（許渾），不論時節請開關（劉禹錫）。

其九十五
再到仙簷憶酒壚（李商隱），也曾辜負酒家胡（元稹）。風流好愛杯中物（韓翃），便與人間衆寶殊（李涉）。

其八十六

應憐疏散任天真（羅隱），赤嶺前年泥土身。（白居易），今日更須詢哲匠（嚴維），忍將虛誕誤時人（呂温）？

其八十七

真宰無私造化均（李咸用），歡娛應逐使君新（白居易）。稱觴彼此情何異（元稹）？莫怨工人醜畫身（王睿）。

其八十八

是是非非竟不真（貫休），莫教猶作獨迷人（杜牧）。共歡天意如人意（王維），造化多情狀物親（楊巨源）。

其八十九

勞生何處是閒時（許渾），塵滿尊罍誰得知（方干）。今日龍鍾人共棄（劉長卿），百憂須賴酒醫治（吳融）。

其九十

乍捲簾帷月上時（元稹），再來相見是佳期（盧綸）。行杯且待終歌怨（羅隱），勞動春風颺酒旗（白居易）。

其八十一

豈知天道曲如弓（韋莊），世事如聞風裏風（李群玉）。平昔苦心何所恨（鄭谷）？牲牢郊祀信無窮（周曇）。

其八十二 下九首爲《甕歌集》

孤城楊柳晚來蟬（劉滄），閑出城南禁火天（殷堯藩）。何處最添詩客興（韋莊），一時傾望重陶甄（趙嘏）。

其八十三

千妖萬態逞妍姿（周曇），先者貪前後者遲（歐陽詹）。喧靜不由居遠近（元稹），相逢況是舊相知（方干）。

其八十四

價高磚瓦即黃金（李咸用），拋擲泥中一聽沈（雍陶）。陶冶性靈在底物（杜甫），先齊老少死生心（白居易）。

其八十五

吹噓成事古今同（方干），將示人間造化工（吳融）。莫倚兒童輕歲月（竇鞏），敗亡安可怨恩恩（韓偓）？

其七十六

翠蔓飄飄欲掛人（皮日休），近來方解惜青春（鄭谷），莫嫌恃酒輕言語（牛僧孺），笑脫袈裟得舊身（吳融）。

其七十七

尊前勸酒是春風（白居易），常說人間法自空（皎然）。聞道神仙不可接（張說），且陶真性一杯中（李咸用）。

其七十八

一一玄微縹緲成（李克恭），幻人哀樂繫何情（白居易）？九重每憶同仙禁（王起），暫謫歸天固有程（李翔）。

其七十九

名利塵隨日月長（許渾），用時應不稱媧皇（吳融）。絳紗凝焰開金像（李紳），焚盡星壇五夜香（李昭象）。

其八十

十分酒寫白金盂（薛逢），只自先天造化爐（薛逢）。流落天涯誰見問（韋莊），何妨相逐去清都（貫休）？

其七十一
天書遙借翠微宮（王維），蜀紙虛留小字紅（韓偓）。酒薄恨濃消不得（韋莊），百年哀樂又歸空（包佶）。

其七十二
誰向穹蒼問事由（方干）？早知皆是自拘囚（韓愈）。驚濤日夜兩翻覆（徐凝），應笑蹉跎身未酬（李中）。

其七十三
清晨相訪立門前（姚合），直取煙霞送百年（王績）。苔壁媧皇煉來處（盧元輔），黃塵初起此留連（羅隱）。

其七十四
感知大造竟無窮（劉耕），一縷鴻毛天地中（白居易）。石語花愁徒自詑（皎然），人間日月急如風（姚合）。

其七十五
太歲只遊桃李徑（盧仝），直須天畔落旄頭（李咸用）。六龍日馭天行健（鮑溶），貴賤同歸土一丘（薛逢）。

其六十六

終無形狀始無因（李山甫），今日他鄉獨爾身（劉長卿）。書信茫茫何處問（魚玄機）？昨宵魂夢到仙津（項斯）。

其六十七

天堂地獄總無情（龐蘊），猶在燈前禮佛名（白居易）。有路茫茫向誰問（靈一）？玉晨鐘磬兩三聲（元稹）。

其六十八

人間無路得相招（施肩吾），上帝高居絳節朝（杜甫）。銷聚本來皆是幻（韓偓），一燈懸影過中宵（齊己）。

其六十九

安排棋局就清涼（李中），都是人間戲一場（白居易）。直到劫餘還作陸（曹松），臣心日夜與天長（李咸用）。

其七十

杖底敲毬遠有聲（賈島），電腰風腳一何輕（羅隱）。不辭宛轉長隨手（魚玄機），天上人間莫問程（楊巨源）。

其六十一

開樽漫摘葡萄嘗（唐彥謙），飛上鰲頭侍玉皇（徐夤）。禍福細尋無會處（白居易），水雲先解傍壺觴（曹松）。

其六十二

踏翻王母九霞觴（許碏），直道忘憂也未忘（吳融）。欲問靈蹤無處所（韋莊），高天默默物茫茫（白居易）。

其六十三

一生年少幾多時（杜荀鶴）？身後傳誰庇蔭誰（白居易）？今日春光君不見（張籍），朝驚穠色暮空枝（許渾）。

其六十四

搜景馳魂入查冥（韓偓），誰同種玉驗僊經（高駢）？立班始得遙相見（王仁裕），且爲人間寄茯苓（張祜）。

其六十五

虔奉天尊與世尊（牛嶠），此心從此更何言（羅隱）。欲知火宅焚燒苦（白居易），宿習修來得慧根（劉禹錫）。

其五十六

野水浮雲處處秋（朱晦），欲回天地入扁舟（李商隱）。應須繩墨機關外（白居易），白玉尊前倒即休（徐凝）。

其五十七

天行時氣許教吞（李都），細落粗和忽復繁（薛能）。去日漸加餘日少（元稹），主司通處不須論（黃滔）。

其五十八

酒肆藏名三十春（李白），至今空感往來人（高駢）。霞光捧日登天上（棲白），時造玄微不趁新（周賀）。

其五十九

休將如意辯真空（唐求），酒伴衰顏只暫紅（白居易）。鉛汞此時為至藥（呂喦），時人何處覓金公（元陽子）。

其六十

倚天雙劍古今閑（來鵬），不遣胡兒匹馬還（戴叔倫）。功業要當垂永久（牟融），常經此地謁龍顏（董皎）。

其五十一

祇是操持造化爐（姚鵠），劃開元氣建洪樞（薛逢）。日爻陰耦生真汞（彭曉），便與人間眾寶殊（李涉）。

其五十二

一時驚喜見風儀（劉禹錫），曉月啼多錦幕垂（鄭谷）。莫遣洪爐曠真宰（薛逢），逢人劇戲不尋思（張鷟）。

其五十三

上窮碧落下黃泉（白居易），只是當時已惘然（李商隱）。魂夢不知身在路（胡令能），更從今日望明年（杜荀鶴）。

其五十四

莫向光陰惰寸功（杜荀鶴），衰顏宜解酒杯中（李絳）。談玄麈尾拋雲底（陸龜蒙），填海移山總是空（王建）。

其五十五

綵童交捧合歡杯（黃滔），笑映朱簾覷客來（盧綸）。讀易草玄人不會（韋莊），狂心醉眼共裴回（方干）。

其四十六
世間人事有何窮（劉禹錫），生死即應無異同（方干）。天上歡娛春有限（白居易），算程不怕酒觴空（翁承贊）。

其四十七
舞拂蒹葭倚翠帷（張蠙），隨風一去絕還期（錢起）。適來投石空江上（胡曾），貴賤人生自不知（李咸用）。

其四十八
羊角輕風旋細塵（元稹），韶光入隊影玢璘（徐商）。憐君未到沙丘日（羅隱），待得甘泉渴殺人（殷堯藩）。

其四十九
長年都不惜光陰（白居易），始覺玄門興味深（李中）。莫道人生難際會（韓偓），是非皆到此時心（李群玉）。

其五十
是非皆到此時心（李群玉），步繞池邊字印深（顧非熊）。但問主人留幾日（白居易），地藏方石恰如金（杜光庭）。

其四十一
天人不可怨而尤（賈島），明日愁來明日愁（羅隱）。傾國妖姬雲鬢重（林寬），尊前偏喜接君留（高璩）。

其四十二
明日誰爲今日看（黃滔）？浮生各自系悲歡（司空圖）。美人美酒長相逐（劉禹錫），眼界無窮世界寬（方干）。

其四十三
江邊尋得數株紅（于鵠），春酒相攜就竹叢（王昌齡）。今日舉觴君莫問（羅隱），世間人事有何窮（劉禹錫）？

其四十四
曾道逍遙第一篇（溫庭筠），凡襟洗去欲成仙（朱著）。不須倚向青山住（許渾），遙望齊州九點煙（李賀）。

其四十五
征途行色慘風煙（白居易），沙塞依稀落日邊（陳陶）。玉帳笙歌留盡日（齊己），君王且住一千年（知玄）。

其三十六
勸我春醪一兩杯（崔櫓），可能長誦免輪回（徐夤）？當筵芬馥歌唇動（劉兼），倘有風情或可來（白居易）。

其三十七
今日自為行路塵（李山甫），濁泥遺塊待陶鈞（徐夤）。不須並礙東西路（李商隱），節概猶誇似古人（高駢）。

其三十八
補天殘片女媧拋（姚合），翻向天涯困縶匏（韓偓）。回首便辭塵土世（韋莊），未嘗開口怨平交（杜荀鶴）。

其三十九
地勝難招自古魂（韓偓），斗醪何惜置盈尊（陸龜蒙）。不堪病渴仍多慮（司空圖），骨化重泉志尚存（周曇）。

其四十
蘭陵美酒鬱金香（李白），敢望青宮賜顯揚（錢弘俶）？滿院落花從覆地（姚鵠），一生心事住春光（徐夤）。

其三十一
积水仍将银汉连（张九龄），九重天近色弥鲜（姚合）。茫茫宇宙人无数（白居易），天命须知岂偶然（孙元晏）。

其三十二
高却垣墙鑰却门（冯道），此心难舍意难论（韦洵美）。归途休问从前事（刘沧），骨化重泉志尚存（周昙）。

其三十三
万古坤灵镇碧嵩（韦庄），海波摇动一杯中（方干）。六龙日驭天行健（鲍溶），造化无言自是功（杨巨源）。

其三十四
本约同来谒帝阊（韦庄），千途万辙乱真源（齐己）。莫言一片危基在（刘禹锡），暗室由来有祸门（李商隐）。

其三十五
衰荣閒事且持杯（王枢），此日平生眼豁开（师鼐）。从此当歌唯痛饮（司空图），不知冠盖几人回（许浑）。

其二十六

古來靈跡必通神（杜牧），不屬高談虛論人（周曇）。身死不知多少載（蔣吉），一分零落九成塵（方干）。

其二十七

一堂賢聖總虛空（李世民），道似危途動即窮（羅隱）。莫向人間爭勝負（牛嶠），往來殊已倦西東（齊己）。

其二十八

平生辛苦未能酬（杜荀鶴），巧者焦勞智者愁（白居易）。銷聚本來皆是幻（韓偓），西風澹澹水悠悠（許渾）。

其二十九

白雲常在水潺潺（許渾），縱目聊窮宇宙間（周樸）。今日舉觴君莫問（羅隱），春風吹盡不同攀（白居易）。

其三十

自由歸去竟何因（齊己）？與世滔滔莫問津（徐鉉）。不飲一杯聽一曲（白居易），人間疏散更無人（鄭谷）。

其二十一

玉杯春暖許同傾（方干），碧落歸時莫問程（趙嘏）。天地有鑪長鑄物（徐夤），劫灰飛盡古今平（李賀）。

其二十二

何曾得見此風流（王昌齡）？不覺年華似箭流（方干）。酒盡露零賓客散（劉駕），衣冠千古漫荒丘（唐彥謙）。

其二十三

百花飛盡柳花初（劉禹錫），林苑園亭興有餘（吉皎）。惆悵卻愁明日別（韋莊），此身長短是空虛（白居易）。

其二十四

且門樽前見在身（牛僧孺），十千沽酒莫辭貧（崔敏童）。九層黃土是何物（李山甫）？不見當時勸酒人（曹唐）。

其二十五

羲和辛苦送朝陽（李商隱），顯得蓬萊日月長（程太虛）。何事欲休休不得（韋莊）？古來今往盡茫茫（吳融）。

其十六
道情虛遣俗情悲（張祜），昨日榮華今日衰（白居易）。風捲暮沙和雪起（許渾），到頭能得幾多時（孫元晏）。

其十七
閒銷日月兩輪空（歐陽炯），猶寄形於逆旅中（白居易）。定恐故園留不住（黃滔），天涯此別恨無窮（劉長卿）。

其十八
吳苑荒涼故國名（羅隱），滿川狐兔當頭行（張祜）。寒驢放飽騎將出（張籍），可要王侯知姓名（方干）？

其十九
美人千里思何窮（李羣玉），借問誰家花最紅（白居易）？只有花知啼血處（吳融），年年先發館娃宮（陳羽）。

其二十
江頭爭看碧油新（崔道融），草岸斜鋪翡翠茵（白居易）。因問館娃何所恨（李紳），朱脣不動翠眉顰（李涉）。

菲茲杰拉德《魯拜集》譯本五版匯刊

其十一

野田極目草茫茫（胡曾），西過流沙歸路長（陳羽）。醉臥醒吟都不覺（魚玄機），解將惆悵感君王（韋莊）？

其十二

詩酒能消一半春（趙嘏），盤蔬餅餌逐時新（白居易）。靜酬嘉唱對幽景（李山甫），鳴鳳樓中天上人（沈佺期）。

其十三

生前富貴非吾願（李濤），洞裏朝元去不逢（白居易）。無限玄言一杯酒（皮日休），夢長先斷景陽鐘（吳融）。

其十四

好與玫瑰作近鄰（張泌），年年含笑舞青春（張說）。莫愁紅豔風前散（武元衡），且作花間共醉人（元積）。

其十五

長與耕耘致歲豐（李頻），奢雲豔雨祇悲風（陸龜蒙）。一朝若也無常至（陳裕），填海移山總是空（王建）。

其六

莫向春風唱鷓鴣（鄭谷），喜聞春鳥勸提壺（白居易）。庭前惟有薔薇在（劉商），數調持觴興有無（杜牧）？

其七

強偷春力報年華（司空圖），先脫寒衣送酒家（崔道融）。桃李光陰流似水（崔覲），今朝青鳥使來賒（李商隱）。

其八

酒伴歡娛久不同（白居易），浮生何處問窮通（翁洮）？天知惜日遲遲暮（徐夤），笑指生涯樹樹紅（陸龜蒙）。

其九

一樹繁花一畝宮（薛能），牆頭風急數枝空（韓偓）。三千年後知誰在（羅隱）？花在舊時紅處紅（懷浚）。

其十

山河無力為英雄（歸仁），今古由來事不同（白居易）。四海風雲難際會（李山甫），不如沈醉臥春風（徐夤）。

菲茲傑拉德《魯拜集》譯本五版匯刊

其一

陽精欲出陰精落（韓偓），星斗離披煙靄收（褚載）。待得華胥春夢覺（吳融），朝光瑞氣滿宮樓（張籍）。

其二

臥穩昏昏睡到明（白居易），遙聞別院喚人聲（王建）。道場齋戒今初服（韋應物），牢落煙霞夢不成（譚用之）。

其三

良久遠雞方報晨（方干），酒旗相伴惹行人（段成式）。經過此地無窮事（劉滄），漫苦如今有限身（元稹）。

其四

每歲東來助發生（羅鄴），感通今日見神明（熊皎）。永和春色千年在（劉長卿），始信幽人不愛榮（盧綸）。

其五

春堤繚繞水徘徊（劉禹錫），誰見當初泛玉杯（李昌符）？惟有年光堪自惜（劉滄），九華紅艷吐玫瑰（徐夤）。

七〇

視神也，靈肉一同，乃惟期身終投世潛與相合，而以他世福祉償此世克己之望遂絕矣。盧克萊修之視神爲盲也誠有所長，然其自屬也乃與蘇菲輩等。惟奧瑪所歌者，若非使吾食，必使吾飲，蓋爲明日之定死也。若哈菲茲以相類之辭述相異之義，彼之所度必誤矣。彼傾其生與才付諸若此隱微之頌詩，自其生之日至於今，言之歌之者恐多非純信者也。

然頗有博學之鴻儒持成見、采學說，許奧瑪爲一蘇菲，甚乃一聖徒，故樂由是而詮其酒與提壺之辭也。而又有更多之史事足徵彼哲人也，具學力，逾世代，但謙謙乎欲爲一世間之智者、一知足之縱樂者耳。故必有人也同乎吾，以奧瑪所頌者實出葡萄之酒漿也，而其所誇實過所飲，蓋欲蔑棄酒之神明，以其驅彼徒衆胥淪於僞善與嫌惡也。

「獨行之士，蘇菲輩讎對之雄也。」蓋因所知教義既多，不能故視矛盾不見以觸峻德也。烏西利爵士於飽盡樓寫本之扉頁，亦題識類似之辭。即尼君自刊本，亦有魯拜二章，直以貶抑之辭氣呼彼蘇菲輩也。確有詩章，非作玄釋，似無可解。然更多者，非依文釋，亦無可解。何故以無生之陶土作杯，必由後來玄家注以神靈？蓋尼君每爲諸廋辭意象所擾，身終將何能以之浴體？何故以無生之陶土作杯，必由後來玄家注以神靈？蓋尼君每爲諸廋辭意象所擾，身終將何異而著東國之色彩，誠欲之甚以致人厭者，故臨其文而躊躇不敢譯。無已，乃爲讀之者委諸神靈也。第二百三十四章之注可徵，彼言其詩意象之玄義雖於歐人也昭然，而彼儕於此俗人也猶不免乎赧然。「此章開端述濃情之語，集中甚多，讀之者亦已習之。雖珈音繁言以喻慕神之思者極異，雖其意象過著東國色彩而時因身欲致人非議，然使吾人信其事涉神聖固無難也。此固每爲回教賢哲所辯，亦偶爲俗人所議，然彼儕於此俱無間言，雖其事涉神思，尚足令彼色赧也。」德黑蘭鈔本中諸多詩章，一如加爾各答鈔本，顯爲贋作，貌若魯拜，實則波斯刺詩習見之短章耳。然吾從此贋作中實有所窺，見尼君之説誤也。蓋在波斯，蘇菲輩多學者文人，實較漠然之伊壁鳩魯輩更易以能助其説之論竄亂原意也。吾見飽盡樓寫本中罕有稍涉玄秘之詩章，蓋最古鈔本之一也，回曆八百六十五年，西元一千四百六十年寫於設拉子。吾以爲此足別奧瑪與波斯他詩客。吾尤喜以奧瑪呼之，此固非教名，人皆熟知之也。較之諸詩客，見彼常處於玄隱之際，而此自放乎歌吟之間也。我輩遂宛然似與奧瑪同坐，彼坦然席前，令睹其人，習其滑稽，會其高興，而酒已巡矣。

吾尚須言此，自我見之，固未盡信哈菲茲之玄義妙蘊也。詩客但於始歌終曲之際額手頌穆罕默德，縱以泛神持論而詠歌之，殊無傷也。類是者，哲拉魯丁、賈米、阿特與他歌者，誠以醇酒婦人爲意象，用昭其所贊之神明，非故爲覆冪以掩蔽之也。然恐置諸血氣賁張者前，以不易致誤致濫之譬説爲較善也。茲雖於持信者無傷，然於弱信之民有視哈菲茲與奧瑪之玄思，非僅擬喻，正爲身欲，方此之時尤若是也。甚者新徒愈激，褻玩愈劇。何者？身欲之樂誠可致亂，必欲近神，決須棄此。且夫律則之胞或恐有害。

費氏結樓三版序

吾方預此奧瑪譯本之再版，法國駐臘什特總領事尼古拉斯君刊一校勘甚備之善本，影德黑蘭鈔本爲底本，凡魯拜四百六十四章，並其所譯與所注。

尼古拉斯版，或以發我，或以益我。然吾誠視奧瑪爲耽耳目之伊壁鳩魯輩，而尼君必欲歸之玄門，其言酒也提壺也皆隱指神，一若哈菲茲之所素行者。蓋視奧瑪爲蘇菲詩客，與哈菲茲諸人等也。

吾未見有以易吾說之由也。吾說之成，肇在十數年前，時有人初以奧瑪示我。吾於東國及其文學故實所知獨多，皆得是人之賜。彼激賞奧瑪之才，若能有所與，必樂援若蘇菲君之義詮也。數年間，其或亦編訂此集竟，恐今於吾譯與尼古拉斯之說皆少有所許矣。

其所述皆據詩作及詩客生平之遺錄也。然不能與也。其刊於《加爾各答評論》之文，吾嘗備引者，可以爲徵。

倘更須一證以攻尼君之說，彼序之第十三十四頁有類傳記之附筆一則，其自寫者也，決與其詮詩之齟齬。非有辯說者相曉，吾誠不知其不幸致奧瑪之入歧途也一至於此。茲須識之，無論哈菲茲所飲所歌之酒竟爲何物，惟奧瑪所言之酒實出葡萄之漿者無虛。非但與諸友酣樂時如是也，即如尼君所言，赴身幻虔之境時亦如是也，而他人則徒賴呼號耳。然尼君一俟見詩中有酒與提壺字，即以「神」「神屬」釋之。其如是之謹也，頗疑有一蘇菲輩人從其共讀，時訓導之。若《魯拜集》第二章注，第八頁。

尼君言奧瑪之棄己說而從蘇菲也，見序文第八頁，果以何文獻徵之？泛神之則、唯物之論、必然之法，非蘇菲輩之獨有也，亦非前此盧克萊修、伊壁鳩魯之獨有也。或太始冥想者初無崇信，或立政生民猶乏文明，七十二宗欲裂天下，遂令哲人神機潛運，自然而萌耶？馮・海默爾之言奧瑪，據《施普倫格東方目錄》，

法，遊戲生焉。集句其一也。宋之荊公，尤好爲之，而明清以降，工巧極其至。而復狎其法，遊戲中復有遊戲生焉。集句詩鐘其一也。近人有張叢碧，優爲之。若集杜甫、李商隱句之分詠庸醫，卜者云：「新鬼煩冤舊鬼哭，他生未卜此生休。」猶稱善謔。至集韓偓、杜甫句之合詠老夫、少妻云：「陽精欲出陰精落，黃鳥時兼白鳥飛。」則褻而虐矣。

余嘗論逸譯之法，亦江西派之詩法也。雖其變也屢，而其法也固一，皆江西派之詩法之不同耳。余譯莪默之絕句，其四十四云：「吾魂如能棄其軀也，則擺落牽掛，凌虛而行。視向者之輾轉塵下屍骸間，寧無愧耶？」譯之曰：「多慚客養千金體，長在齊州九點煙。」此江西法也。其二十二云：「明日耶？明日之吾，恐已在七千年前之昨日矣。」蓋莪默之時，波斯人以地球之齡爲七千年也。余直以長吉詩譯之曰：「劫灰飛盡古今平。」是江西法浸而爲集句也。余固非才，特以嘗試之心，黽勉集句而逸譯之，居然集事。而竟似集句詩鐘矣。於逸譯之事，亦見合於詩史者。理之自相推衍，其中固有冥冥者在，豈人能干之耶？

余所集句必唐人，循不用唐以後事之通例也。其法有三焉：上者意相合也，次者意可曲通也，最下但烘托其意耳。等而下之者，固有天之所不能完，亦有人之所不能致者也。然猶得陳逸雲兄「搜韻」之助，索之機械間矣。讀之者易其遊戲，恕其荒殖，毋深責可也。

續溪汪時甫，有《麝塵蓮寸集》，集宋詞之作也。用飛卿「搗麝成塵香不滅，拗蓮作寸絲難絕」之句。今此集附菲氏譯本三版行，竊用汪氏意，顏曰《莪默絕句拗唐集》。

己亥六月十二，我瞻室序。

莪默絕句拗唐集

譯　序

康德云：「見聞之際或有法焉，其爲數二，稍多亦無不可，其質異。置諸一理之下，見涵而和。方吾人之識之也，可以成吾之悅，甚乃吾之奇。其奇之也，雖習焉而不止。」此江西派詩法也。山谷曰：「古之能爲文章者，眞能陶冶萬物，雖取古人之陳言入於翰墨，如靈丹一粒，點鐵成金也。」夫鐵之成金，陳言而新意也。彼陳言自有意，人所共知，吾雖言之不足奇。以之出吾新意，則必與舊意異其質，因其言而涵容之，且使和之，於是而悅焉，而奇焉。山谷自負其「我居北海君南海」。此《經》語也，而《經》之意不必是山谷意。蓋彼言其不相及，此言其遙隔也。一爲山谷牽合之，奇意生焉。此點鐵成金之法，而與康德之論符契若是。

此又非江西派一家之法也，宋以後人類知用是。蓋生唐人之後，不資書以爲詩，無以逾唐人也。東坡嘲孟浩然「韻高而才短，如造內法酒手而無材料」，其隱衷在焉。故宋之後，詩法一變，文辭必以古雅爲宗。元人稍不如是，譏之似詞。明人言性靈者，視同野狐，即清之袁簡齋，雖竊大名，難逃其議也。雖然，辭之古雅，不害其時新。以見聞之際，其法實繁。一意也，運之法或不能窮。才人之心也黠，乃狎其

義默絕句拗唐集

菲兹杰拉德《鲁拜集》譯本五版匯刊

同為塵土更伶俜,若有微言誰肯聽。
一入模間真鑄錯,以人呼我豈叨榮? 二版其四十一

四版五版有異譯八首:

其一
東君長矢舉遙空,直迫星芒夜色窮。
為喚人間新睡覺,金光看射素檀宮。 二版其一

其三十
長疑何事不先詢,遣作匆匆來去身。
持酒連杯須莫禁,酒淫豈復憶狂嗔? 二版其三十三

其四十八
沙磧清泉甘有餘,暫留遽飲信非虛。
起看商隊遙如幻,直往無中復太初。 二版其四十九

其八十三
罍甕瓶壺色樣齊,沿牆匝地各高低。
彼方饒舌此傾耳,妙理沈浮何易稽? 二版其九十

其八十七
時有能言小缶來,善齊物論語相開:
「若知天下無同異,瓷器何輸大匠才?」 二版其九十四

其八十八
又一前云莫妄疑,物無美惡不相遺。
誰言地獄將投畀?直以仁心翊化基。 二版其九十五

其九十八
天使翩翩舒翼來,金縢密冊尚全開。
不聞簿吏矜嚴酷,筆削相煩曷敢推。 二版其一百零六

其一百
明月尋人夜夜來,盈虛不改此追陪。
淒涼知有誰相遇?只向空園照冷杯。 二版其一百零九

己亥七月廿一,我瞻室識。

天外朝曦左手臨，酒翁喝破夢沈沈：「兒生未似杯常滿，莫負及時來一斟。」二版其二

其三十三

潛運高天一任呼，更無燈火指明途。嬰孩匍匐原非惜，直日智兮盲且愚。二版其三十七

其四十六

馬騎燈裏影迴旋，儘自紛紛幻大千。一點孤明陽燧火，是誰取向正中懸？二版其七十三

其四十七

酒有竭時唇有枯，不疑萬物盡歸無。汝今倘在終難在，那見其間得喪殊？二版其四十五

其四十八

江邊共我老珈音，花下尊前興不禁。莫畏他年逢帝使，持來黑酒徑須斟。二版其四十六

其五十九

臨夕全非禁食天，陶家舊肆月初懸。獨來側耳重相覓，一衆成行繞我前。二版其八十九

其六十

頗怪其間語默殊，一坯不耐奮相呼：「孰爲工匠孰爲器，辨得環中同異無？」二版其九十四

其七十四

所歡明月幾曾虛？又向中天光景舒。從此園林多遍照，年年只是不逢予。二版其一百零九

其一（初稿）

三版有異譯二首：

其三十八

金光長矢擲遙空，直迫星芒夜色窮。喚得華胥春夢醒，輝煌齊指大明宮。二版其一

跋

予用七字絶句迻譯菲氏《魯拜集》，既梓行，或病其不能盡與原作意合，予曰：使意與原作合，且不與格律違，吾無難也。其難，失雅度神韻也。聞者以爲誇，予亦無辯。然於舊譯殊未愜意，非意之不相合，辭之未渾成也。每思更作，因循未就。今歲適當菲氏譯本之行百六十年，專力半載成之，視舊譯易其十之七八矣。斟酌之際，譯法不期而變，昔之似與不似，今爲漸合也。亦偶有不合者，不欲盡爲原文轉，固亦菲氏法吾於迻譯之道，至此一進。非敢謂之盡善，庶可爲誇辯。蓋前無辯者，井蛙、夏蟲本無足與言耳。予所譯菲氏《魯拜集》五種，惟此爲經意之作。今附菲氏第二版行，他版刪餘、異譯者，亦皆譯出，不忍遽棄，錄之於此。

一版有刪餘二首：

其三十七

來將美酒滿吾杯，莫恨光陰去不回。後日未生前日死，那妨今日笑顏開？

其四十五

智如相辯即成訛，天地不和吾與和。甕內一隅箕踞坐，戲從肝膽起風波。

又有異譯九首：

其一

夜天如盌日如璆，星斗紛紛避一投。醒見東君遙出獵，金光長索罥官樓。二版其一

其二

之形，一身而二首。既定圓周之中心，吾汝之首終必相合。」多恩詩曰：「那用哀哀怨別離？吾身與汝合如規。汝心不動吾身運，情自相牽到處隨。莫道閨中晏坐安，閨心處處繫征鞍。側身待到歸來日，始得相迎直起看。君心相待感吾心，不計奔忙誓死尋。為汝情堅何敢誤？重來定未負初吟。」

其六十二行：七十二宗遍據此世，或言回教在其內，或言非也。

其六十三行：隱指馬穆德王征印度而役其黑民。

其七十四行：幻燈今猶用之印度也，內置一柱筒，繪諸色人其上，巧使平穩，兼使風生，環其內之燭火旋焉。

其七十五行：原文有一句甚詭，辭之斷續頗類吾國《木鴿記》，言伊每從中斷處重操也。

其八十一行：二辭即昂宿與木星也。

其九十二行：齋月每令回教徒衆疲弱躁厲，將終，新月彼為分年之度也，之初睹，久跂足待，而今為一歡呼矣。窖中傭夫結束之聲亦可聞矣。奧瑪別有佳什言此月，曰：「悶時已過可為歡，直待新光黃酒餐。老月不堪成禁斷，羸容慘色送將闌。歡兮，陰鬱之齋月已死，新月將來償吾。為光陰，齋戒之困，老月已作羸弱、佝僂、蒼白之相，奄奄於天際。

菲兹杰拉德《鲁拜集》译本五版汇刊

其十九二行：波斯波利斯城，有傑姆西王御座之名。俾什達迪朝，傳同神古，其王之最稱者，即傑姆西王也。依《王書》說，是城即此王興築。又說爲精怪之跡，在生人之先，其遺跡尚有金字塔云。

巴拉姆，有野驢之號，薩珊朝帝君，亦有七城，若波希米亞王，而每城異彩，城居一妃，妃爲說一傳奇。此據阿米爾·霍斯陸所作之波斯名詩也。東國小說家云七城象七重天，霍斯陸之詩故名《八重天》也，既凌彼七重，遂使環之旋行。今尚遺廢址三，鄉人以爲名勝。亦有廢沼，巴拉姆王逐驢時陷焉，一若雷文斯伍德之主家。

其二十四行：「廢宮遺柱上凌空，日角龍顏想像中。惟有斑鳩偏稱意，自來自去叫春風。廢殿荒蕪，惟遺柱高矗，上指蒼穹。我來惟見斑鳩孤飛，其聲咕咕然，哀呼不止。」在尼古拉斯版《鲁拜集》列第三百五十章，亦在溫菲爾德之譯本。此章實寧所得，爲蕩子刻諸波斯利斯廢址，雜之哈菲茲諸人所作間。斑鳩聲若古巴列維語「咕，咕，咕」近波斯語「何處，何處，何處」也。阿特《鳥會》亦言斑鳩，伊爲鳥首所責，蓋自失彼優素福，停而不飛，喃喃無休，恆作一悲調也。

其二十一四行：一行星爲一千年也。

其三十一二行：土星，第七重天之君也。

其三十四行：吾汝，獨，一之與全也。

其四十二一行：飲前酹酒於地之俗，今波斯猶是也，東方蓋如是。尼古拉斯以爲：「以示慷慨豁達，兼勸飲者飲必盡也。」不殊類古俗，莫酒以媚地神，且使伊同此逸樂耶？抑或意同西方之古民，豐其祭品以娛羨者眼目耶？而吾人見奧瑪尚別有意在，蓋酒爲菁華，殊不能棄，將以滲之地下，欲使古昔之飲者復甦也。

其四十二二行：飲前酹酒之俗，今波斯猶是也，東方蓋如是。哈菲茲多方擬奧瑪，其有詩曰：「惟汝傾此最佳釀，罪其增益愼勿忘。」

其四十六一行：東國有傳奇言，亞茲拉爾以生死樹之實置人鼻下，或言此章及下二章宜刪，然吾殊不爲意。

其四十九三行：吾以爲商隊在元日即春分日後夜行，蓋贅餘之詞也，蓋穆罕默德之命也。

其五十二三行：From Máh to Máhi，始乎魚終乎月也。

其五十八一行：此固言其學之滑稽語也。奧瑪有詩以算學爲喻，吾以爲奇，而更奇者，彼詩乃與多恩博士之詩，見艾薩克·沃爾頓所撰之本傳。意堪並行。奧瑪詩曰：「規如吾汝形同有，共一身兮分二首。圓徑圓周果取中，相循終到長相守。吾汝如規

五八

注釋

其二一行：所謂「幻曙」者，真曙前約一小時，天際頃刻之光芒也。此天象在東國人皆能詳。

其四一行：必知此新歲之始爲春分。蓋舊有之太陽曆久爲陋劣之太陰曆所替，彼計日起自穆罕默德之改邑。以春分爲元日佳節，傑姆西王之命也。奧瑪每言彼王，且嘗與其曆之修訂。

賓寧《波斯二歲遊歷》卷一第一六五頁言：「春色忽來，頃時漸滿，殊動人也。冰雪淺作冠，夏榮繁作飾。斯觀一何諡……」譯注：此出莎士比亞《仲夏夜夢》第二齣，蓋謂冬神毫盡，著淺冰冠，而綴夏榮以爲花環，譔飾其上也。『冰雪淺作冠，夏榮繁作飾。』群植新生者中，吾猶識數種，而頻年未睹矣。有薊二種，野春菊，頗類馬頭蘭，闊葉之酸模，藍矢車菊。而沿水岸，遍蒲公英，黃華采采。」夜鶯未聞，玫瑰未放，然畫眉與啄木鳥固皆能喚北鄙之春矣。

四行：見《出埃及記》四章六節。彼處言，摩西方出其手云云，而波斯人固未言痲瘋如雪，惟言色白耳，殆類吾地春日之山楂花耶？彼又云，耶穌愈病之力存乎其息中。

其五一行：伊蘭園，夏達德王之所建也，今湮於大食國沙磧中。傑姆西王之七環杯，以象七重天海、七耀星宿諸事，神杯也。

其六一行：巴列維言，古波斯雅言也。哈菲茲亦言夜鶯之巴列維語，未與吾人之語偕易。

四行：吾不能決四行中所言，究爲紅玫瑰帶慘色耶，抑彼黃玫瑰實應爲紅耶？蓋紅、白、黃之玫瑰，在波斯均常見者。索西之《類纂》徵諸西班牙著述，云玫瑰十時爲白，二時爲黃，五時爲紅。

其十三行：魯斯塔姆，波斯之赫拉克勒斯也，扎爾其父，《王書》盛言其績。哈蒂姆，以豪爽疏財聞名東國。

其十四行：是鼓，宮外所擊者也。

其十五四行：彼處，玫瑰最盛地也。

波斯短歌行

五七

其一百零九
同看尋人月色來,梧桐影裏漫徘徊。明朝萬一成孤另,葉葉枝枝空照哀。

其一百一十
誰伴名園露飲來,翩如星裏月徘徊。歡時請向淒涼處,爲我殷勤酹一杯。

其一百零三

行既淫淫名既諠，事猶不解酒家胡。卿來賣此忘憂物，一世歡顏買得無？

其一百零四

花自飄零春自歸，錦年香稿掩依依。枝頭聽得鶯啼盡，誰曉去來何處飛？

其一百零五

疲人一瞥起相招，沙自茫茫泉自遙。應似牧場青草偃，百蹄過盡復揚翹。

其一百零六

乾坤開闢得重期，尚及天書未掩時。名字欲添新樣紙，或央簿吏徑除之。

其一百零七

皇天注冊本無親，何事畸零托此身？歲久涓流成恨海，滄波湧處盡顰呻。

其一百零八

憫此不仁予美呼，一同造化運靈樞。政須宇宙俱顛覆，始得從心鑄作殊。

其九十七
言時新月露纖纖，甕缶紛然引領瞻。喜若不禁相倚語，今期擔上一聲添。

其九十八
葡萄佳釀請先陳，一日云姐用洗身。其葉菁菁相就殮，不妨葬近滿園春。

其九十九
將辭春暖赴佳城，誰與殷勤指舊盟？正有斜枝牆外出，一身都爲覆花英。

其一百
瘞骨成灰正未甘，葡萄生出蔓先罩。中天網得聖徒在，相視欣欣殊不諳。

其一百零一
長向樽前中聖賢，人間名譽轉難全。一杯足使浮榮沒，一曲拚教令聞捐。

其一百零二
人生多悔誓多申，只向從前夢夢身。誰復單絲牽一懺？萬花盈手正臨春。

其九十一
一云製作豈無功，拔我凡常泥土中。旋復成形旋復毀，蹴回泥土亦何忡？

其九十二
次云彼自手親為，孰謂怒來將毀之？雖是狡童貪渴飲，一杯猶解緩相持。

其九十三
時則諸壺默不言，忽聞窯器苦鳴冤：「人皆笑我形枯槁，失手誰於大匠論？」

其九十四
曰死曰生常有言，談因談果竟無門。一坯不耐語多躁：「匠器區區何待論？」

其九十五
一云地獄取煙塵，汙面來為惡主人。大任於斯憂不識，勞其筋骨顯諸仁。

其九十六
孰陶孰市一長呀，久置塵間身欲枯。但取舊家陳釀到，頃時沾潤得全蘇。

其八十五
大鈞造物信難任，予以泥沙索以金。此責不聞相約束，悲哉那肯更來尋？

其八十六
落落由他怒目瞋，豈將大偽喚為真？筵前賓客多剛直，正怕相逢罵座人。

其八十七
人生漂蕩苦消魂，處處相逢有酒樽。使我樽前沉湎盡，更言天罰是奇冤。

其八十八
搏土絙泥意已差，力窮竟未拔其蛇。人神從此交相怨，黥面誅心漫正邪。

其八十九　下九首為《甕歌行》
齋月久為饑餒勞，蔽諸去日得潛逃。我來又向陶坊立，百狀胚腪擁四遭。

其九十
相與私言微若摧，譬之聲熄冷於灰。我今聞語明如在，疑是銀缸故照來。

其七十九
太初摶土盡成人,便是浮生代代塵。笑爾身終憂會計,不知註定在茲晨。

其八十
昨日預爲今日狂,明朝得喪轉茫茫。人生自是無根蒂,莫問去來揮汝觴。

其八十一
直掠烏鳶火色肩,旄頭太歲墜長天。黃塵定命輕拋擲,枉説初行泰始前。

其八十二
葡萄藤蔓結吾生,一任賤身修士輕。能啟玄關爲管籥,外邊留爾起囂聲。

其八十三
靈光燭起遍生春,失計無憂天殭身。過眼旗亭才一瞥,絕勝禮拜久迷真。

其八十四
莫向虛無怨不仁,化生人物具形神。禁歡一軛休思脫,若被天刑長苦辛。

其七十三
何人夜半力無雙,提得紗籠日作釭。環以往來虛幻相,大千世界看幢幢。

其七十四
身如戲弄在圍棋,晝夜為枰安所之?任爾推移爭劫罷,不過一一笥中遺。

其七十五
玉勒金鞍笑打毬,一杆擊處看星流。偶然墮地真遊戲,怨甚君身不自由?

其七十六
神指常書更不居,空勞虔智挽其徂。半行一字揮毫定,傾淚休期得湔除。

其七十七
且從賢哲道相傳,稱意違心只未全。枉向環中求一節,無逾無脫守無愆。

其七十八
蒼然覆盌指為天,下者芸芸劇可憐。舉手遙呼休乞援,一般無奈自迴旋。

其六十七
每奇先我入冥關，過者憧憧無一還。前路懸知終要赴，不來相告爾何慳？

其六十八
先知焚死士何期？虔智空傳開示詞。不過都將枕中記，篝燈夜話賺癡兒。

其六十九
君若去為屍解仙，御風直上自泠然。多慚客養千金體，長在齊州九點煙。

其七十
大行途上一穹廬，冥侍迎王暫駐輿。王去自將收拾起，明朝過客尚堪居。

其七十一
遣教魂魄往幽途，異世書文辨得無？魂魄頃時還報語：「天堂地獄正為吾。」

其七十二
心足神勞幻妄生，天堂地獄本虛名。暗投莫怨浮沈在，但遣人間嗜欲平。

其六十一
辯盡無涯辯有涯，不如全付酒仙家。能收君淚如鉛水，鍊作黃金買歲華。

其六十二
君王赫赫儼如神，驚走玄膚外道民。魂魄未憐憂懼在，劍鋒四運劇風輪。

其六十三
既云酒醴作由神，敢指葡萄藤蔓嗔？苦說陷人誰設置，如為天賜正須親。

其六十四
人生沈緬禁無難，說到天刑慘不歡。仍待長承神液滿，粉身碎骨化杯盤。

其六十五
先知苦說竟何功？無酒無歡興已窮。若此天堂寧待問，張拳一看是空空。

其六十六
上窮碧落下黃泉，惟此常遷是不遷。好記萬花開頃刻，休教賺作一生顛。

其五十五
人天有惑再無憂，明日風前萬事休。爲喚酒姬修若柏，青絲一握戀溫柔。

其五十六
此攻彼守漫徒勞，有限生涯偶值遭。結實非空即爲苦，何如歡壓萬葡萄？

其五十七
何期再赴合歡宮，賓客喧闐高興同。虛廓天成離婦恨，蒲桃酒是女兒紅。

其五十八
尺墨須能繩是非，形名亦得測沈飛。一生苦恨鈎玄客，不解杯中妙理微。

其五十九
歲時不贅始稱佳，推算工夫以簡誇。後日未生前日死，那須更向曆書加？

其六十
曾記前時暮色青，長天遙墜酒旗星。蓬門未入先呼飲，自向肩頭解玉瓶。

其四十九
一脈沙間司命泉，相呼速飲在窮邊。即催商隊虛無去，星斗離披曙色懸。

其五十
君如不惜擲韶華，徑指玄關道路賒。性命空餘百年在，是非惟間一毫差。

其五十一
是非惟間一毫差，直借神名引路邪。若過寶山無妄喜，許能邅造主人家。

其五十二
象外環中動不居，退藏冥宰莫仁予。魚而至月形俱賦，變滅由之但自如。

其五十三
一晌登場解意無？幕垂燈燼暗紅氍。也知真宰恒遊戲，譜得傳奇漫自娛。

其五十四
地鋼天遙願已違，汝能爲汝日常稀。莫辭上下窮瞻顧，待得明朝事事非。

其四三
擎杯當學鬱金香，朝露擎來作酒漿。身不覆時杯不覆，百年三萬六千場。

其四四
應知天眷不多時，呕嘹招招柏樹枝。未及坤靈先攬入，終身一擁且銷之。

其四五
醇酒婦人安所終，從來終始只爲空。計今之汝誠如昨，何事長憂明日窮？

其四六
逢迎終自在河濱，黑酒高持儼若神。滿引向前邀汝魄，徑須歡飲莫逡巡。

其四七
百年有死若爲驚？天地無窮德日生。君看盌中千萬沫，神姬長在宴前傾。

其四八
靈帷偕入渺無痕，空見綿綿天地存。來去但如投一石，微瀾不改海波翻。

其三十七
向彼天帷汝在吾，冥行直把一燈呼。遂而似若聞相語：「惟見智兮盲且愚。」

其三十八
側身試就紫泥杯，待問吾生大惑來。相接如言及時飲，一朝歸去不能回。

其三十九
器物喁喁若起予，戀生嗜酒必其初。唇間授受應無度，今更接時情已疏。

其四十
記駐行途看冶陶，冶中陶土作悲號：「君當太古原吾與，今日君工且緩操。」

其四十一
此說孰云非是焉？古人以降代相傳。即斯泥土成生類，塑作功由造化全。

其四十二
滿引休辭金葉蕉，持來一酹泯然消。土中埋眼憂如火，長在冥昏待酒澆。

其三十一
相從植慧待其豐，手自澆培久用功。竟至穫時惟是此，我來如水去如風。

其三十二
來時無故亦無方，一水悠悠天地長。莫問泠然安所適，如風吹過磧沙旁。

其三十三
長疑何事不先詢，遣作匆匆來去身。應是天公深悔在，解憂爲賜萬藤春。

其三十四
人間渺渺鎮星尊，直上遙天第七門。終是命途難借問，群疑破盡一身存。

其三十五
高門扃閉鑰難尋，望極空愁簾幕深。片語微聞及吾汝，那知倏忽已同沈？

其三十六
地惟淵默海嚶呻，遙失滄波舊主人。天自頻翻晨夕袖，星躔顯晦與同循。

其二十五
春來河畔草如茵，攜得同心緩倚身。愛惜一彎真媚態，多應憶著美人唇。

其二十六
且鬥樽前見在身，一錢猶在莫辭貧。明朝黃土壟中臥，無酒無歌無再晨。

其二十七
他生未卜此生勞，齊拜森森殿塔高。上有雞人呼一語：「愚夫去住總無褒。」

其二十八
睡裏先聞傳語來，花顏應逐曉天開。不知爭發終何益？一寸春心一寸灰。

其二十九
聖徒雄辯究天人，誰謂愚同術士倫？土掩塵封終不語，至今貽笑說通神。

其三十
玄談聖論昔能尊，直欲因之窮道根。其我獨芒終未達，出時仍在入時門。

其十九
獅據蜥盤天地窮,宮陵蕪沒宴歌空。野驢踏得骷髏破,不遇君王射虎弓。

其二十
廢宮遺柱上凌空,日角龍顏想像中。惟有斑鳩偏稱意,自來自去叫春風。

其二十一
殷勤把酒勸卿卿,來日須同去日傾。萬一明朝天地改,劫灰飛盡古今平。

其二十二
年華醞釀出醇濃,同是精英世所鍾。持酒數行依次去,一眠泉下不來逢。

其二十三
昔人別館作歡場,仍看薰風新弄妝。我自將眠塵土下,為誰身亦是眠床?

其二十四
玫瑰紅艷世難偕,開處英雄碧血埋。一一園中風信子,料應先在美人釵。

其十三
人間天上說榮華，笑爾區區計已差。且典春衣拚一醉，晨鐘暮鼓兩俱遐。

其十四
效彼蜘蛛寧不愚，生絲命縷費工夫。吾人日夜勞呼吸，氣息方同知得無？

其十五
玫瑰開遍遶吾身，道是嫣然同世塵。囊裏珍奇應不惜，傾來爲續滿園春。

其十六
瓦缶黃鐘一例沉，當時枉自費行吟。江頭誰問懷沙恨？淘盡江沙只見金。

其十七
一世浮華幻樂哀，熾於炎火冷於灰。消除終似龍沙雪，誰見當時明滅來？

其十八
天地何妨逆旅看？門前日月轉雙丸。榮華多少逢迎盡，一樣匆匆遣素檀。

其七

春火先燔冬日衣,杯中問甚去年非。好知萬古無多路,過眼長空一鳥飛。

其八

朝野未應妨性殊,苦甘一例得心娛。莫辭淺把涓涓酒,便好深憐葉葉梧。

其九

朝來千朵一時開,零落誰將昨日哀?同是催花風信在,無端曾把哲王催。

其十

哲王催老只由他,天地徒勞涕淚多。誰見大人龍戰怒?誰聞小雅《鹿鳴》歌?

其十一

牧草逶迤一帶青,恰分窮壤與新町。偕來肯較君王業?聊祝承平到帝廷。

其十二

袖詩一卷傍高株,食一簞兮酒一壺。得汝清歌相媚嫵,荒郊那與樂郊殊?

菲茲杰拉德《魯拜集》譯本五版匯刊

其一
日出東山夜色澄，盡驅星斗轉高昇。金光長矢中天舉，遙射宮樓最上層。

其二
虛晨幻色未明前，客舍先聞高語傳：「早向堂前歌樂聖，何爲枕上夢遊仙？」

其三
雄雞一叫客來呼，直到門前索酒沽：「萬歲千秋君莫問，此回歸去更來無？」

其四
萬象更新始一元，幽人觀化到無言。白華如手綴枝遍，淑氣發春生物繁。

其五
磧中帝苑逐時窮，海外神杯照世空。惟有年年溪水畔，等閒紅紫盡春風。

其六
詩律長瘖似凍烏，殷勤誰解勸提壺？不辭唱盡春風媚，添與薔薇一點朱。

「獨行之士，蘇菲輩讎對之雄也。」蓋因所知教義既多，不能故視矛盾不見以觸峻德也。烏西利爵士於飽蠹樓寫本之扉頁，亦題識類似之辭。即尼君自刊本，亦有魯拜二章，直以貶抑之辭氣呼彼蘇菲輩也。確有詩章，非作玄釋，似無可解。何故以無生之陶土作杯，必由後來玄家注以神靈？然更多者，非依文釋，亦無可解。蓋尼君每爲諸廋辭意象所擾，身終將何能以之浴體？何故以無生之陶土作杯，必由後來玄家注以神靈？彼皆極異而著東國之色彩，誠欲之甚以致人厭者，故臨其文而躊躇不敢譯。無已，乃爲讀之者委諸神靈也。第二百三十四章之注可徵，彼言其詩意象之玄義雖於歐人也昭然，而玄辭之微述即於波斯之俗人也猶不免乎赧然。「此章開端述濃情之語，集中甚多，讀之者亦已習之。雖珈音繁言以喻慕神之思者極異，雖其意象過著東國色彩而時因身欲致人非議，然使吾人信其事涉神聖固無難也。此固每爲回教賢哲所辯，亦偶爲俗人所議，然彼儕輩於此俱無間言，雖其事涉神思，尚足令彼色報也。」德黑蘭鈔本中諸多詩章，一如加爾各答鈔本，顯爲贗作，貌若魯拜，實則波斯刺詩習見之短章耳。然吾從此贗作中實有所窺，見尼君之說誤也。蓋在波斯，蘇菲輩多學者文人，實較漠然之伊壁鳩魯輩更易以能助其說之論竄亂原意也。吾見飽蠹樓寫本中罕有稍涉玄秘之詩章，蓋最古鈔本之一也，回曆八百六十五年，西元一千四百六十年寫於設拉子。吾以爲此足別奧瑪與波斯他詩客。吾尤喜以奧瑪呼之，此固非教名，而人皆熟知之也。較之諸詩客，見彼常處於玄隱之際，而此自放乎歌吟之間也。我輩遂宛然似與奧瑪同坐，彼坦然席前，令睹其人，習其滑稽，會其高興，而酒已巡矣。

然則究當如何詮哈菲茲與奧瑪之詩，吾無斷語焉，玄釋文解，惟讀者自擇之。睹酒、提壺、翠柏之辭，以爲其語神可也。親事之而如見奧瑪在側，吾誠以爲繼阿那克里翁，抑阿那克里翁‧莫爾而作同解亦可也。

其所述皆據詩作及詩客生平之遺錄也。

倘更須一證以攻尼君之說，彼序之第十三四頁有類傳記之附筆一則，其自寫者也，決與其詮詩之說齟齬。此其相示軼聞之一也。「其時世亂兵荒，詭詐間作，惟珈音避身鄉土，樂學蘇菲。每與諸友飲，酒佐其思，如顛如樂。而他人抵此境，多以爲在呼號時耳。」「波斯編年史家言，珈音尤喜宴飲，夜中月華如水，流照露臺，歌樂方作，行觴已巡。忽有風至，堂中燭滅，臺前缶側，酒漿遍地。珈音微慍，即席賦詩，未免瀆神之過也。其詩曰：『碎我壺罌絕我歡，威儀抑抑諒無端。不妨泥土填吾口，問主真曾到醉闌？汝敗我缶，吾主。吾惟飲，緬淫在汝。呀，其使土掩吾口，汝亦醉耶？吾主。』

「作詩已，珈音忽睹鏡中，面如炭矣。以爲天之罰也，遂更作一章，語益肆。曰：『孰能無過在人間，無過身應逝不還。過惡如須惡相易，將非汝我一般頑？在人間者誰無罪歟？汝言。無罪者焉得生？汝言。汝以惡易惡，與我將無同？汝言。』」

非有辯説者相曉，吾誠不知其不幸致奧瑪之入歧途也一至於此。茲須識之，無論哈菲兹所飲所歌之酒竟爲何物，惟奧瑪所言之酒實出葡萄之漿者無虛。非但與諸友酣樂時如是也，即如尼君所言，赴身幻虐之境時亦如是也，而他人則徒賴呼號耳。然尼君一俟見詩中有酒與提壺字，即以「神」「神屬」釋之。若《魯拜集》第二章注，第八頁。其如是之謹也，頗疑有一蘇菲輩人從其共讀，時訓導之。一波斯人必與其同族之傑出者，一蘇菲亦必黨之，而況波斯名詩客固多入其彀中歟？

尼君言奧瑪之棄己説而從蘇菲也，見序文第八頁，果以何文獻徵之？泛神之則、唯物之論、必然之法，非蘇菲輩之獨有也，亦非前此盧克萊修、伊壁鳩魯之獨有也。或太始冥想者初無崇信，或立政生民猶乏文明，七十二宗欲裂天下，遂令哲人神機潛運，自然而萌耶？馮·海默爾之言奧瑪，據《施普倫格東方目錄》

度，而無制之者。然其處身也，殊近斯多葛，較伊壁鳩魯尤嚴苛。獨坐凝視，觀宇宙之運行，如機械之戲劇，自身亦在戲劇中，並相環者，一若其壯詞所賦之羅馬歌臺，俱爲帷幕慘色之映而黯然，彼帷懸諸天日與觀劇者間。奧瑪並此繁瑣之統系亦無所跂，或直漠視之，蓋此統系惟無望之定命也。乃付其深學富才於萬有之遍壞，此遍壞但於一瞥之際有所現耳，且出之以苦澀、滑稽之談笑。聊作玩世之態，正言生惟逸樂，徒爲遣興之故，始語神語命，判物靈，辨善惡，繼則難，終則殆矣。

厥述今之所譯。魯拜之名，奪回文之一音，增英言之搖曳。本一子立之短章，章四句，皆律句，時有變化，而格度略同。四句或皆入韻，然第三句多不入韻，若今所擬者是也。此略似希臘阿爾凱奧斯之體，不入韻處逆挽其韻，令其稍止，復墜於末句也。東國之詩卷，胥依入韻字母次序，《魯拜集》亦是也。故墓與樂竟成詭列，爲其首字母之同也。今所選者，適成一田園詩集。「醇酒婦人」本東國詩人屢愛言之者，雖未知果出其誠否，而今所删餘者於比率則殊少矣。然此終爲悲懷詩也。悲之甚者，無過於名矜逸樂，而實則令彼老廬帳工能傷不能怒也。蓋徒然欲步出定命，往瞥明朝，然復墮今日，又將無盡遲明朝也。

彼惟能於今日立足，而今日又轉瞬從足下逝矣。

吾方預此奧瑪之新版，法國駐臘什特總領事尼古拉斯君刊一校勘甚備之善本，影德黑蘭鈔本爲底本，凡魯拜四百六十四章，並其所譯與所注。

尼古拉斯版，或以發我，或以益我。然吾誠視奧瑪爲耽耳目之伊壁鳩魯輩，而尼君必欲歸之玄門，其言酒也提壺也皆隱指神，一若哈菲茲之所素行者。蓋視奧瑪爲蘇菲詩客，與哈菲茲諸人等也。吾未見有以易吾說之由也。吾說之成，肇在十數年前，時有人初以奧瑪示我。吾於東國及其文學故實所知獨多，皆得是人之賜。彼激賞奧瑪之才，若能有所與，必樂援若尼君之義詮也。數年間，其或亦編訂此集

世極其所有，用所遇諸物娛六欲而撫一心，不徒擾擾於將來之憂也。然吾人亦見其於俗世之求實不逾其度。於感官之娛也，得滑稽乖張之趣，用以尚心智，亦頗有足樂者。然心智不足解其惑，其惑正人人所同者，攸關甚大。

無問何故，前已言奧瑪之詩向未馳聲國中，亦眇傳海外。其詩集稿本，支離不全，通行《東方散佚抄本集》中未錄。雖在東國猶稱罕覯，況傳乎西海耶？然西人每能盡得東國之兵械與技巧也。其副本，印度學舍無有也，巴黎之國家圖書館亦無有也。吾知英倫存一寫本，在牛津飽蠹樓，標識號烏斯利一四零，西元一千四百六十年寫於設拉子，凡詩一百五十八章。加爾各答之亞細亞社會圖書館藏一本，吾得錄副焉，存五百一十六章，亦非完本，然重見與妄擬者已充斥其間。而馮·海默爾言其有副本約存二百，施普倫格著錄之魯克諾寫本又倍其數。

評論者附言曰：「寫此文竟，吾等又遇一極罕版本之副本，一千八百三十六年加爾各答刊行。凡四行詩四百三十八章，附錄中尚有五十四章不見諸他寫本中。」牛津與加爾各答寫本之抄手，其寫此也，似均出所迫。卷首皆有四行詩一章，先毋問其真贗，實自原字母之排序中別出。牛津寫本為懺辭。加爾各答寫本為誠辭，依是本前綴之語，詩蓋肇因於一夢，夢中奧瑪母氏詢其將來之運命。可如是譯：「火生地獄每焚心，說到焚身汝亦臨。上帝枉呼垂憫念，遞相教授遣誰任？」汝為地獄中焚身者而焚汝心，而汝身亦終須為獄火所焚。汝之呼「神其憫彼也」何久！呼，教者汝為誰，學者彼為誰？飽蠹樓寫本之詩，論近泛神，以直相徵。詩云：「我如約束不堅牢，善行成珠竟散條。幸是一元無二讀，即逢天譴可相逃。」倘吾以無力之約束，漫爾串善行之珠玉，吾將因此一事而禱：吾終未稱一為二也。

評論者考威爾教授，奧瑪生平盡從之而得也。於文末以盧克萊修譬奧瑪，蓋二人不但氣稟與天才相近，即所遭亦相近也。皆敏於見，勇於行，學深才富，求是慕義。國有偽信，愚人竭誠，俱能以正相斥。既敗偽信，雖無能正之，亦無能得真信，然猶有則守。盧克萊修得伊壁鳩魯之學，視宇宙為運數所成之機械，雖循法

三四

其軼事尚有一可述者，宜綴篇末。「見之其詩集之序文，文出何人手、出何世，均莫能詳。海德有書名《波斯古教》，附錄之四百九十九頁，有其波斯原文。戴波盧之《文庫》，海音目下亦有之。「回教哲人，約當一世紀末二世紀初，專力精修，住於神聖之香境，珈音之與彼也，但同爲哲人耳，外皆無所類。」

古之編年史有言，智之王者奧瑪於海吉拉曆五百一十七年，西元一千一百二十三年，卒於納霞堡，學邁往古，範垂當世。撒馬爾罕之長者尼札米，嘗從其學，有言：「吾每與吾師奧瑪珈音語於園中，一日，謂我：『吾墓所在，當有北風飄玫瑰於其上。』我固訝其言，然知非謾語也。戴波盧以此文辭氣近率，與《可蘭經》之言相悖，蓋經言：『無人能知其將死何地。』奧瑪之軼事使吾憶及另一事，此庫克而非霍克沃思之《再航記》第一章三七四頁所述者，彼尊貴倫敦所隸失卑微之的，其言也哀。『方辭烏列特亞，奧瑞奧惟欲吾返。知不可必，遂問吾葬所。雖所問甚詭，吾仍徑告之曰斯特普尼，蓋吾居倫敦所隸之教區也。』彼衆乞吾數言之，俾彼亦能言，頃時百人齊呼：『斯特普尼墓間無圖特。』吾後知福斯特亦在水濱遇此問，彼所答異，然尤當也。彼云：『無長處海上者能言其將葬何地也。』」數年後，吾重過納霞堡，弔其葬處，正鄰一園，園中橫枝逾牆，結實纍纍，而傾其朵墓上，墓石爲盡覆焉。」

吾不憚剽奪之嫌繁録《加爾各答評論》之文如右。其作者既從印度語讀奧瑪墓事，言令彼憶及西塞羅之述，蓋於敘拉古見阿基米德墓掩於草叢間。而吾則念多瓦爾德森，彼欲玫瑰生時能覆其身，吾信至今尚得隨時饜其心也。然請再言奧瑪。

雖王甚致恩寵，而奧瑪於逸樂之坦然根於思、形諸言，多爲時人側目。蓋彼輩之踐行，常爲奧瑪所嘲；彼輩之信仰，若去其爲奧瑪不屑之玄秘與虛飾，又實無以過之也。彼國詩客多取資奧瑪，雖哈菲茲亦猶是也，蓋自菲爾多西外，哈菲茲實波斯最可矚目者也。然盡轉而爲玄秘之用，俾其詩於已於衆實有所便。蓋彼衆輕於疑信，敏於形神，愉於二者之冥合，遂藉詩句爲羽翼，恣遊乎天國凡塵，今世來生，不執一端。惟奧瑪知命而疑天，重生而輕死，雖云過，想思盡出乎誠。故寧於今

波斯亦思马因教魁首。亦思马因教人皆狂信，陰蓄已久，得哈桑行其凶強之志，遂成極惡。西元之一千零九十年，哈桑竟取魯德巴省之阿剌模忒堡，在里海之南，亂山之間，號曰「山中丈人」。其大行畏怖，幾遍回教之地。今歐人語中行刺一詞，疑其凶念之子遺也。其字源或出哈石失，蓋大麻葉所制之煙食也，印度語謂之 bhang，服之能致人迷幻，陰鬱顛倒，失志走險。或出彼魁首名，納霞堡志學之日，固已識之矣。被行刺之害者固多，其同學故交，尼查木‧烏爾‧莫爾克其一也。莫爾克用其友奧瑪語《魯拜集》頗有詩譽居高之易危，淑命之不固，倡言與人人為善而莫與人密邇。阿特嘗使尼查木‧烏爾‧莫爾克之垂死也，號曰：天乎！吾從風之手中逝矣！」

「尼查木‧烏爾‧莫爾克之垂死也，號曰：天乎！吾從風之手中逝矣！」

奧瑪珈音亦往見相君請其所有，然非名位也。曰：「君所能惠莫若處我於一隅，為君佳運所蔭，廣播學問之澤，吾兼為君之福壽祈。」相君告吾輩曰，既知奧瑪之卻名位實出其誠，乃不復勸，即敕納霞堡公庫，年予之一千二百金。

奧瑪珈音遂居納霞堡，亦卒於是。相君言其汲汲乎博學，而於天學尤精，實造極焉。馬立克‧沙王時，嘗至謀夫，以學問之湛深得盛譽，王甚致恩寵。

時馬立克‧沙王修曆法，八人與其事，奧瑪其一也。遂制哲拉里曆，用王之一名哲拉魯丁焉。吉本曰：「其算精於凱撒曆，而近乎格列高里曆。」又嘗繪星圖，題曰馬立克沙希星算表，近法人重印之，且譯其回文之代數論焉。

珈音者，蓋其賦詩之別號也，考其義，厥為制盧帳者，傳其嘗事此業，殆在尼查木‧烏爾‧莫爾克殁恩厚予使能自立之前歟？波斯詩客例以所業為名，若阿特為方劑師、阿薩為榨油匠也。亦若吾英倫之史密斯（鐵匠）、阿切爾（射手）、米勒（磨工）、弗萊徹（箭工）等，不過呼先世之業為姓氏耳。

奧瑪嘗有奧句隱括其名，曰：「珈音既作知之帳廬，而終為憂患之爐火所爍。運命之織穹廬，何事忽投憂患火？命剪其絲今世哀，望虛其報來生左。

奧瑪珈音：波斯之天學詩客

奧瑪珈音者，呼羅珊省之納霞堡城人也。生當十一世紀之後半，卒在十二世紀之前二十五年。生平甚略，獨與當時國中二顯人頗相糾葛。其一名尼查木‧烏爾‧莫爾克，烏瑪德自突斯往納霞堡，期從明師，沉潛於學。師於我特加垂青，而吾為弟子亦盡忠愛，親侍講席，四載於茲矣。我初至此，即見年相仿者二人，哈基姆‧奧瑪‧珈音與厄運之本‧薩巴赫，皆新來從學者。二人常共我遊處，溫故時習。奧瑪固納霞堡人也，哈桑‧本‧薩巴赫父為阿里，屬行而務實，然所遵信多近異端。一日，哈桑語吾與珈音曰：「皆以為從伊瑪目莫瓦法克學者必致淑命。雖三人俱致，或有所疑，必有一人焉。如將相約，當有何誓？」吾與珈音曰：「從君所願。」彼曰：「善，請為此誓：淑命天降，必與共之，毋得專！」吾與珈音曰：「必如是。」誓遂定。日居月諸，吾自呼羅珊往河中，且遊伽茲尼與喀布爾。既返，被命入宮，旋相阿爾普‧阿爾斯蘭王。越數年，二同學循之至，因昔日之誓請同此淑命。相君踐誓，無少吝。哈桑求一官，王因相君之請予之。然不饜於遞遷，遂與東國之亂謀，擬代恩相之位。謀既不成，失王寵，竟遭斥。屢經困躓顛沛，終為

伯克子阿爾普‧阿爾斯蘭、孫馬立克‧沙。初，馬赫穆德大帝之後寡能，脫幹鄰勒‧伯克遂有波斯，是為塞爾柱朝，終致歐人十字軍之役。莫爾克之書曰《遺書》，蓋遺後之為政者為鑒也，其言有云：（今據《加爾各答評論》五九號轉錄米爾克洪之《阿薩辛史》。）

納霞堡有伊瑪目曰莫瓦法克，呼羅珊之聖哲也。得人尊崇，受天眷顧，壽逾八十五。皆以為從之窮經考古，必致榮福。吾父乃遣余與法科博士阿布德‧烏斯‧沙瑪德自突斯往納霞堡

是信與雅必不得兼，寧喪其信，不失其雅。失其雅，則爲之奴矣。
玄思猶是，況詩情乎？是以吾人常讀詩之譯，識其辭，而不能辨其味。蓋其譯者，不顧其扞，強求信而實傷雅也。此在玄思，或爲辭之滯耳；在詩情，則並喪辭與情也。故詩之譯，信爲最下矣。彼費氏結樓之迻譯《魯拜集》也，得譯之道，具辭之雅。故能不爲奧瑪珈音之奴，而翻爲其主也。余頗怪今之迻譯費氏者，必反其道而行之，甘爲之奴，何耶？
奴譯者，盡意於楮墨之內，步趨原作，矜矜其信。然則吾人一旦能讀原作，所譯即成已陳之芻狗。主譯者，著意恒在楮墨之外，曲通彼情，有不能必信焉。蓋彼之詩情，寫諸此之文辭，其情扞者其格。惟不欲其齟齬，忖度彼心，考量吾文，屬筆之際，遑顧其信哉！竟忘亦似亦趣，差得不似而似，然亦在讀者之會心也。爲之既久，乃悟此亦江西派點鐵成金之法。惟彼所點化者古人之典實，此所點化者異域之文辭耳。孰謂既知古人之典實，遂可廢彼之詩派？然則能讀原作之文辭，亦終不廢此之迻譯。
《魯拜集》之譯亦夥矣，大抵皆奴譯耳。惟七言絕句體譯本，庶能爲主譯之想。蓋既肖魯拜之體，又備吾國詩體之風致。惜哉！自西風之東漸，世人竟欲爲非類之奴，數典忘祖，於吾國舊體久不能嫻。其體之乏，求其合度者，十無一焉。余不才，以爲其實可符主譯之名者，前則黃克孫氏，後則眭謙氏耳。康德云，有天才，有賞鑒。黃譯與眭譯，各得一偏，均見美質。後之爲譯者誠不易焉。而吾譯何爲哉？余別有意在。蓋今之爲譯者，竟尚奴譯。文辭既爲非類奴，情與思亦必爲之奴矣。此余所深憂焉。故不揣固陋，黽勉爲之，甘附二賢之羽翼，未懼衆人之嗤點也。
乙未六月廿四，時當立秋日，自序於我瞻室。

波斯短歌行

譯 序

譯事之難，曰信曰雅可矣，何必曰達？蓋不能達，譯何爲哉！而有信與雅，達又豈待言？夫《金剛經》之譯也，達摩笈多之不能達，烏有其信？鳩摩羅什之足乎雅，必有其達。故曰：譯事之難，曰信曰雅可矣。其難，則信與雅有不得兼也。玄奘之譯《大般若經》第九會中《能斷金剛分》，固宜後出轉精，而事乃有不然者。曰其信，實無其倫；曰其雅，則殊不若鳩師，其流通之廣亦遜焉。豈奘師中土之產，反不及鳩師異域之材耶？信與雅有不得兼也。

且夫文辭，非孤生者也，必與乎其族類之情與思也。欲爲譯事，情與思扞，勢所然也。奘師之譯是也。蓋其思必欲符乎天竺，其辭又欲曉之中土，無所避其格，終無能爲其雅矣。不强必信，曲通其扞，文辭之格得以稍緩，格稍緩則進於雅矣。鳩師之譯是也。蓋不斤斤於貌合，常戚戚於神離，躊躇之際，有以緩其格，文辭之不期而雅者至矣。故譯之道，方其情與思扞，必使彼以從我，以緩文辭之格。不然，直學彼之文辭可矣，何譯爲？

波斯短歌行

菲兹杰拉德《鲁拜集》译本五版汇刊

其四十二行：隐指马穆德王征印度而役其黑种降民。

其四十六四行：幻灯今犹用之印度也，内置一柱筒，绘诸色人其上，巧使平稳，兼使风生，环其内之烛火旋焉。

其五十四行：原文有一句甚诡，辞之断续颇类吾国《木鸽记》，言伊每从中断处重操也。

其五十四三行：二辞即昴宿与木星也。

其六十六二行：斋月每令回教徒众疲弱躁厉，将终，新月彼为分年之度也，之初睹，久跂足待，而今为一欢呼矣。窖中庸夫结束之声亦可闻矣。奥玛别有佳什言此月，曰：「闷时已过可为欢，直待新光贳酒餐。老月不堪成禁断，羸容惨色送将阑。欢令，阴鬱之斋月已死，新月将来偿吾。为光阴、斋戒之困，老月已作羸弱，佝偻，苍白之相，奄奄于天际。」

二六

其十三四行：彼處，玫瑰最盛地也。

其十七二行：波斯波利斯城，有傑姆西王御座之名。依《王書》說，是城即此王興築。

其二十四行：一行星為一千年也。

其三十二行：土星，第七重天之君也。

其三十四行：吾汝、獨、一之與全也。

其三十八四行：吾以為商隊在元日即春分日後夜行，蓋穆罕默德之命也。

其四十二行：或自嘲其算學也。

其四十三二行：七十二宗何指，回教久歧其說。

波斯波利斯城，有傑姆西王御座之名。傳同神古，其王之最稱者，即傑姆西王也。依《王書》說，是城即此王興築。彼以柱支殿堂，兼為飾焉，柱有蓮礎與牛首，數猶倍之，而今太半為地震兵燹所毀。無問誰作此者，必一湮滅舊朝或為無央數神工之遺跡也。其殿堂、房室、回廊，皆鐫文字，若楔形之狀。亦刻像焉，有半人形類尼姆魯德者，甚偉而挾翼；有祭司與兵士成列者，中疑無女子焉；有王者，或踞座，或蓮華。有法拉瓦什者，存在之徵，並其飛翼圓球，此於亞述、埃及亦常有之，蹈其頂焉。與夫飛渠蓄池，及官室之諸附著。又有兩側飛梯攀露臺而上，交互岩側，直凌慈山。舊日之祆教君主盡葬於此，俯瞰美爾達什平原。

波斯人，亦如他國人，喜於國中遺址留其姓氏，偶亦題一二詩句。賓寧言，自前揭遊歷紀撮述，於波斯波利斯得若是者如干，一處為哈菲茲之佳句，另一顯出無聞之詩客，然哀情頗合。而吾人覺其辭句與緩節似曾見之，竟於加爾各答寫本之奧瑪《魯拜集》五百章中檢得。老奧瑪此詩曾為彼一鄉黨引述，譯出嫌其節稍促耳。詩云：「廢宮遺柱上凌空，日角龍顏想像中。惟有斑鳩偏稱意，自來自去叫春風。廢殿荒蕪，惟遺柱高矗，上指蒼穹。而當日殿門之端，固曾畫君王容顏也。我來惟見斑鳩孤飛，其聲咕咕然，哀呼不止。」似波斯人操英倫之斑鳩調而言巴列維語，亦確同波斯語之「何處」也。

巴拉姆，有野驢之號，為其獵驢之名也。薩珊朝帝君，亦有七城，而每城異彩，城居一妃，妃為說一傳奇。此據阿米爾‧霍斯陸所作之波斯名詩也。東國小說家云七城象七重天，若波希米亞王，霍斯陸之詩故名《八重天》也，既凌彼七重，遂使環之旋行。今尚遺廢址三，鄉人以為名勝。亦有廢沼，巴拉姆王逐驢時陷焉，一若雷文斯伍德之主家。

注　釋

其一二行：大漠中，擲石於杯，「上馬」之示也。

其二行：所謂「幻曙」者，真曙前約一小時，天際頃刻之光芒也。此天象在東國人皆能詳。波斯人謂晨為灰色時，為昏昧時，「亦狼亦羊時」，「彼是相持時」。

其四一行：必知此新歲之始為春分。蓋舊有之太陽曆久為陋劣之太陰曆所替，彼計日起自穆罕默德之改邑。以春分為元日佳節，傑姆西王之命也。奧瑪每言彼王，且嘗與其曆之修訂。

近有遊波斯者言：「春色忽來，頃時漸滿，殊動人也。冰雪方解，已見雜花生樹，新芽破土矣。元日之雪點綴山際，明滅谷間，園樹萌蘗，郊青處處。『冰雪淺作冠，夏榮繁作飾。』斯觀一何諼……」譯注：此出莎士比亞《仲夏夜夢》第二齣，蓋謂冬神毳氅，著淺冰冠，而綴夏榮以為花環，譃飾其上也。群植新生者中，吾猶識數種，而頻年未睹矣。有薊二種；野春菊，頗類馬頭蘭；紅白之首蓿，闊葉之酸模，藍矢車菊。而沿水岸，遍蒲公英，黃華采采。」夜鶯未聞，玫瑰未放，然畫眉與啄木鳥固皆能喚北鄙之春矣。

其四四行：見《出埃及記》四章六節。彼處言，摩西方出其手云云，而波斯人固未言痲瘋如雪，惟言色白耳，殆類吾地春日之山楂花耶？彼又云，耶穌愈病之力存乎其息中。

其五一行：伊蘭園，夏達德王之所建也，今湮於大食國沙磧中。傑姆西王之七環杯，以象七重天海、七耀星宿諸事，神杯也。

其六二行：巴列維語，古波斯雅言也。哈菲茲亦言夜鶯之巴列維語，未與吾人之語偕易。

其九三行：魯斯塔姆，波斯之赫拉克勒斯也，扎爾其父，《王書》盛言其績。哈蒂姆，以豪爽疏財聞名東國。

其十二四行：是鼓，官外所擊者也。

其七十五

賓客藉草而坐，散如星羅，汝行其間，銀足閃閃。值汝事此歡役，請至我據之一席，爲覆其杯。

菲茲杰拉德《魯拜集》譯本五版匯刊

其六十九

誠爲吾之中聖也，盡誤人間聲望。吾有榮乎？杯雖淺而足沒。吾用名乎？歌一曲其可易。

其七十

吾固常生悔，固常言誓，而其時吾固未夢夢耶？他日春來，玫瑰盈手，薄懺紛如矣。

其七十一

酒，無信者也，奪吾榮名之服者也。然吾猶不解，彼賣酒者所得何物，其價能及彼所賣者之半耶？

其七十二

青春將偕玫瑰而逝，華年之香稿亦將掩。枝頭百囀之夜鶯，自去自來，孰知何處？

其七十三

吁，予美！吾汝若得與彼同心，執萬物不仁之設計，毋乃將先毀之，而後從心更鑄之耶？

其七十四

吾所歡之月更無虧時，而遙天之月又升矣。猶是園也，彼將幾度升，幾回照，以尋吾一人，終爲徒然！

其六十三

無人應此，既安，一瓬器曰：「眾皆笑我扭曲若倚，安知彼時陶匠手偶戰耶？」

其六十四

一曰：「人言彼乖戾酒保，以地獄之煙灰汙面，將勞吾輩筋骨。咄！彼誠善者，所爲無不善也。」

其六十五

其一深自歎曰：「棄置既久，我乾欲裂矣。倘得以舊漿注我，我其漸復。」

其六十六

陶器一一言時，一人早瞥見眾所殷矚之新月。彼遂傾敲相抵，若互致言：「吾兄，吾弟，倘聞擔酒者肩上作響乎！」

其六十七

呀，吾生其萎，請以葡萄之酒洗我身，藤上之葉殮我體，葬諸佳園之側。

其六十八

雖吾埋骨成灰，猶以酒香爲網羅，施之空中。而過往之正信士，恒於不覺間爲之縛也。

其五十七

汝置惑誘於吾遊宕之途,豈非先以命定之惡憭我,及入彀中,乃以罪我耶?

其五十八

汝以污泥造人,以蛇置樂園中,以衆罪黷人面,汝能恕人,亦能爲人恕!

其五十九 下八首爲《甕雅》

再聽之。齋月將逝之夕,好月初懸,吾獨立老陶坊中,諸陶成族,行列而環焉。

其六十

頗怪彼泥坯中,有能言者,有不能者。忽一褊急者呼曰:「請言:孰是陶工?孰是陶器?」

其六十一

又一言:「殊非徒作也!擇諸凡常土泥,巧塑吾形,乃復蹴吾凡常土泥間。」

其六十二

其次言:「雖狡童不壞其歡飲之杯盞,彼既樂作器成,即逢盛怒,必不相毀!」

其五十一

無稍留之指,執筆而書,書畢即去之。汝雖極虔竭智,莫能使返而銷其半行也,傾汝之淚,亦莫能泯其一字也。

其五十二

彼覆盌,人呼之為天。下覆我輩,匍匐生死於其間。毋舉手乞其援,彼自徒旋,一若吾汝。

其五十三

太初之土摶為終末之人,耘此種也,將求終末之穫。既書於開闢之朝,必誦於終計之晨。

其五十四

吾語汝:初發終極處,彼即擲昴宿與木星,過畢宿火色之肩,墜吾塵與魂之定命中。

其五十五

葡萄之藤蔓已生深根,吾生倘附其上,任彼道人譏誚耳。吾以此賤質為管籥,得啟其戶,而彼自在戶外嚻嚻。

其五十六

吾知之,或以真光燃愛,或以怒火毀身。雖然,使吾得於酒肆中稍窺見之,即勝失路於廟宇中也。

其四十五

任誇智術者辯,吾獨與天地之不和處。踞喧囂之一隅,與戲謔者還相戲謔。

其四十六

出入上下不止,胥幻燈之戲耳。燈中之燭火則日,環之往來者則如詭影之我輩也。

其四十七

若汝飲之酒、汝吻之唇誠與萬物同歸乎無,試思方汝有時,汝有亦但將爲無耳,汝何喪?

其四十八

值川上玫瑰盡開,與老珈音共飲此瑩如紅玉之美酒。一旦天使持黑酒邀汝,亦須徑飲而毋戰栗。

其四十九

此晝夜之枰也,運命遣人若棋子,推移爭劫既了,一一擲歸筥中。

其五十

毬無得曰然曰否,於左於右,但憑擊者耳。墮汝於地,亦自由彼。彼知一切也。彼知之!彼知之!

其三十九

不知爲若此若彼之所守與所斥,而陷此無窮之求者何多日也?葡萄之實纍纍,盡足爲歡,豈不勝彼無實抑苦實者?

其四十

朋汝知乎?時日已久,吾嘗於室中再開婚宴。彼智老而無嗣,吾既休之矣,今以葡萄之女爲配

其四十一

是非,可以尺墨繩也;上下,雖無之,吾亦可定也。

其四十二

前時,客舍之門戶猶敞,有若神者,自暮色間熠熠而來,肩負一罍,使吾嘗之,則葡萄美酒也。

其四十三

蒲桃之酒,道譬至真,直能杜彼七十二宗之囂口。其若仙耶?一彈指頃,人生之鉛水轉而成金矣。

其四十四

馬穆德赫赫若全勝之主,持其降魔之劍,異教黑奴盡懷憂懼,頃時死散矣。

其三十四

吾唇轉對此陶盌,試問生之奧旨。唇唇方接,杯自呢喃:「生則飲耳!一朝死,不復返生矣。」

其三十五

彼器,方喁喁應吾者,必曾有生,必曾為歡。吾今所接之唇,一何冷淡,其授受之吻亦多矣!

其三十六

予嘗於黃昏至市上,見一陶匠甚急陶土,陶土以上世中斬之語喃喃相乞:「敢請吾兄,為吾緩,為吾緩。」

其三十七

吁,滿注此杯!反復云「時自吾足下逝矣」,何益耶?但得今日之歡,何有於未生之明日,已死之昨日也!

其三十八

荒漠片刻之駐,命泉霎時之飲。而星斗已沒,商隊直赴虛無之晨。吁,速飲哉!

其二十八 與彼同播智慧之種，復躬身培植，而所獲止此：吾來如水，吾去如風。

其二十九 入此宇宙，不知其因，不知其所來，如水漫漫而流焉；又復出之，亦不知其所去，如風漫漫，沿廣漠而吹焉。

其三十 從何而來耶？由此何去耶？何無問而匆匆耶？呀，杯復一杯，爲澆此不慎之念。

其三十一 吾自地之中，升至天之第七門，遂踞土星之座上矣。天行之惑盡解，而吾生死與命之惑徒在焉。

其三十二 有戶也，莫能得其鍵；有簾也，莫能見其內。或有片語及吾汝，倏而之間，吾汝若不復有矣。

其三十三 吾乃呼彼運行之天，問曰：「運命以何燈燭，昭示冥行中匍匐之嬰孩？」天曰：「瞽知也。」

其二十二

新葩又飾夏日,而吾輩爲歡之宅,舊主安在?吾人亦終將卧地之下,且不知吾身又將爲誰卧也。

其二十三

吁!及吾尚未入土,所餘者直須揮盡。不然,塵土相重,置身其下,無酒無歌,亦無歌人,至於終古。

其二十四

有人也,綢繆於今日;有人也,矚目於明朝。叫拜樓之報呼者自暗塔呼曰:「愚人!斯處也,彼處也,胥無汝償。」

其二十五

究天人之聖哲,寧不鴻博?摒之一若愚妄術士輩。其言遭唾棄,其口爲土掩!

其二十六

吁,來共老珈音,辯付彼多方者。此生飛逝,惟此爲信。惟此一事爲信也,餘皆是誑。不見花開一度,終付飄零。

其二十七

吾少日每懷渴慕,訪於聖賢,聞其宏論,反復辯説。然所從出者,正入時之門也。

其十七

人言昔傑姆西王高宴之宮，今惟付猛獅巨蜥矣。野驢直踐巴拉姆王塚上，聲回顧頂，彼善獵者兀自酣眠。

其十八

吾計玫瑰無紅逾凱撒墓上者，爲其染英雄之血也。今園中一一風信子，皆恐自當日美人頭上墜焉。不知此芳草出誰唇中也。

其十九

芳草怡人，嫩如翠羽，遍覆河畔。相與枕藉其上，爲惜之也，切須輕緩。蓋河水彎環，其狀若唇，政不知此芳草出誰唇中也。

其二十

來！予美。滿注此杯，以銷去日之恨與來日之憂於今日。明日耶？明日之吾，恐已在昨日之七千年中矣。

其二十一

若輩皆爲吾人所慕、時運醞釀所出，最稱佳美。而方飲一二巡，遽相隨泉下長眠矣。

菲茲傑拉德《魯拜集》譯本五版匯刊

其十一
巨枝下，詩一卷，酒一壺，乾餕一片，汝傍我而歌，雖在荒野，直爲天堂！

其十二
或慕權勢甘人，或以天堂可企。吁，執現錢，棄其餘，不聞鼓聲雖壯，尚自逍遙？

其十三
視彼玫瑰環吾人怒放。彼云：我來此世間嫣然而放，少頃錦囊之絲穗將解，其中珍寶遍園中矣。

其十四
俗世之願，固人所常置心，亦豈無榮耀時？而終爲死灰。譬彼龍沙之雪，明滅一時，倏然而逝。

其十五
或勤耘佳穀，或靡之如雨隨風去，而同不得似金沙，彼一朝沉埋，尚能復爲人發。

其十六
汝未思耶？天地，敝壞之逆旅耳，日夜爲其門戶。處其間，雖君王代代，一俟時至，必挾其聲勢而行矣。

其六

大衛之歌唇鎖矣。而夜鶯之天囀，聽如巴列維語「酒，酒，酒，殷紅酒」之聲，顧向玫瑰頻呼，遂令花頰如暈。

其七

來，滿注汝杯！昨日之非如寒衣，請擲諸春陽間。時之疾也如鳥，逝路無多，而今已振其翅矣。

其八

日見千花之開，必知有千花飄墜於泥土。茲初夏之月，亦誠攜玫瑰來者也，不又將彼傑姆西、凱柯巴諸王去耶？

其九

且隨我老珈音，而忘彼凱柯巴王與凱霍斯魯！魯斯圖姆之欲為，哈蒂姆之呼宴，無預汝。

其十

隨吾逐牧草而行，有路蜿蜒如帶，界窮壤與耕田。當其處也，安知輿臺與君王之別？而轉憐馬穆德高踞金座上。

菲茲杰拉德《魯拜集》譯本五版匯刊

其一

醒乎！晨投石於夜天之碗，迫星斗盡飛散也。觀乎！東君之獵也，拋金光之長索，弋蘇丹之高塔。

其二

曙色之左手方見天際，夢中已聞客舍有高語曰：「醒乎！兒輩徑須滿此杯，及杯中生生之酒尚未晞也。」

其三

雄雞方啼，客舍外已聞人呼：「速來啟關！我輩惟頃刻之留耳，一旦行，不復返矣。」

其四

新歲之來，吾人亙古之欲恒為之動，惟玄思之魂退藏於寂。彼寂處也，枝綴白華，色如摩西之手；而耶穌之息，出乎其地中。

其五

伊蘭園之玫瑰與園俱敗，傑姆西王之七環杯再無人知。而野藤之上，仍生舊日葡萄，色如紅瑪瑙。春水之畔，尋常人園無數，其中花常競發也。

斥。既敗偽信，雖無能得真信，亦無能正之，然猶有則守。盧克萊修得伊壁鳩魯之學，視宇宙為運數所成之機械，雖循法度，而無制之者，如機械之戲劇，自身亦在戲劇中，並相環者，一若其壯詞所賦之羅馬歌臺，較伊壁鳩魯尤嚴苛。獨坐凝視，觀宇宙之運行，如機械之戲劇，自身亦在戲劇中，並相環者，一若其壯詞所賦之羅馬歌臺，俱為帷幕慘色之映而黯然，彼帷懸諸天日與觀劇者間。奧瑪並此繁瑣之統系亦無所望之定命也。乃付其深學富才於萬有之遍壞，此遍壞但於一瞥之際有所現耳，且出之以苦澀、滑稽之談笑。嗣委其覺知於花酒之間，但為移其思以得調適乎命志存滅之際也。此不過蘇丹大行途中暫息之穹廬耳。譯案：初版遺之，二版列其六九、七十。

詩云：君若去為屍解仙，御風直上自泠然。多慚客養千金軀，長在齊州九點煙。倘神得棄軀，擺落牽掛，淩虛而遊，猶輾轉土骸之間，彼寧無愧耶？大行途上一穹廬，冥侍迎王暫駐輿。王去自將收拾起，明朝過客尚堪居。

此不過蘇丹大行途中暫息之穹廬耳。彼黑天之從，一俟蘇丹行，即卷而藏之，以為後來者備。

厥述今之所譯。魯拜之名，奪回文之一音，增英言之搖曳。本一子立之短章，章四句，皆律句，時有變化，而格度略同。四句或皆入韻，然第三句多不入韻，若今所擬者是也。此略似希臘阿爾凱奧斯之體，不入韻處逆挽其韻，令其稍止，復墜於末句也。東國之詩卷，胥依入韻字母次序，《魯拜集》亦是也。故墓與樂竟成詭列，為其首字母之同也。今所選者，適成一田園詩集。「醇酒婦人」本東國詩人屢愛言之者，雖未知果出其誠否，而今所刪餘者於比率則殊少矣。然此終爲悲懷詩也。悲之甚者，無過於名矜逸樂，而實則令彼老廬帳工能傷不能怒也。蓋徒然欲步出定命，往瞥明朝，然復墮今日，又將無盡遲明朝也。彼惟能於今日立足，而今日又轉瞬從足下逝矣。

辭句頗異，蓋初稿也。

故其所言俗世之娛必非妄托神道，酒也實出葡萄之漿，酒肆也實有其處，行觴者也實爲血肉之軀，玫瑰也實花，凡此皆其今世所欲來生所期。

且其算學之才，每制逸思，遂成別體，無多贅詞，殊非波斯及東國之詩也。如言希臘之文猶童子饒舌，則波斯之文無乃又成一童子耶？不曉幾何學之希臘人無得入柏拉圖哲學之宮，而無異思奇彩之波斯人亦無得競於波斯詩域，蓋其視馳想繁言爲決定之力也。波斯詩人精算學者惟奧瑪，能持異族異教敗波斯族魂前之古風毅性者亦惟奧瑪。頗類其先輩大家菲爾多西，略無玄思，雖一字爲新來之教所被猶不屑也。然彼疑世者，非奧瑪無神者比也，或疑其潛附往古蘇魯支之衹教，蓋彼所歌列王皆信奉焉。

無問何故，前已言奧瑪之詩向未馳聲國中，亦眇傳海外。其詩集稿本，支離不全，通行《東方散佚抄本集》中未錄。雖在東國猶稱罕覯，況傳乎西海耶？然西人每能盡得東國之兵械與技巧也。其副本，印度學舍無有也，巴黎之國家圖書館亦無有也。吾知英倫存一寫本，在牛津鮑蠹樓，標識號烏斯利一四零，西元一千四百六十年寫於設拉子，凡魯拜一百五十八章。加爾各答之亞細亞社會圖書館藏一本，吾得錄副焉，存五百一十六章，亦非完本，然重見與妄擬者已充斥其間。而馮·海默爾言其有副本約存二百章施普倫格著錄之魯克諾寫本又倍其數。牛津與加爾各答寫本之抄手，其寫此也，似均出所迫。卷首皆有四行詩一章，先毋問其真贗，實自原字母之排序中別出。加爾各答寫本爲懺辭，蓋誠奧瑪之愚，其愚也適足罵之。〔評論者附言曰：「寫此文竟，吾等又遇一極罕版本之副本，一千八百三十六年加爾各答刊行。凡四行詩四百三十八章，附錄中尚有五十四章不見諸他寫本中。」〕

評論者譯前引奧瑪生平詳目，且以文述其詩若干，於文末以盧克萊修譬奧瑪，蓋二人不但氣稟與天才相近，即所遭亦相近也。

皆敏於見，勇於行，學深才富，求是慕義。國有偽信，愚人竭誠，俱能以正相

其軼事尚有一可述者，宜綴篇末。見之其詩集之序文，文出何人手、出何世，均莫能詳。海德有書名《波斯古教》，附錄之四百九十九頁，有其波斯原文。戴波盧之《文庫》，海音目下亦有之。「回敎哲人，約當一世紀末二世紀初，專力精修，住於神聖之香境。」珈音之與彼也，但同爲哲人耳，外皆無所類。

古之編年史有言，智之王者奧瑪於海吉拉曆五百一十七年，西元一千一百二十三年，卒於納霞堡，學邁往古，範垂當世。撒馬爾罕之長者尼札米，嘗從其學，有言：「吾每與吾師奧瑪珈音語於園中，一日，謂我：吾墓所在，當有北風颳玫瑰於其上。我固訝其言，然知非謾語也。戴波盧以此文辭氣近率，與《可蘭經》之言抵悟，蓋經言：「無人能知其將死何地。」奧瑪之軼事使吾憶及另一事，此庫克而非霍克沃思之《再航記》第一章三七四頁所述者，蓋吾居倫敦所隸之敎區也。彼衆乞吾數言之，俾彼亦能言，其言也哀。「方辭烏列特亞，奧瑞奧惟欲吾我。知不可必，遂問吾葬所。雖所問甚詭，吾仍徑告之曰斯特普尼，蓋吾居倫敦所隸之敎區也。彼衆乞吾數言之，俾彼亦能言，頃時百人齊呼：「斯特普尼墓間無圖特。」吾後知福斯特亦在水濱遭此問，彼所答異，然尤當也。彼云：「無長處海上者能言其將葬何地也。」」數年後，吾重過納霞堡，吊其葬處，正鄰一園，園中橫枝逾牆，結實纍纍，而傾其朶墓上，墓石爲盡覆焉。

吾不憚剽奪之嫌繁錄《加爾各答評論》之文如右。

雖王甚致恩寵，而奧瑪於逸樂之坦然根於思、形諸言，多爲時人側目。皆云諸蘇菲於奧瑪懼恨交并，蓋彼輩之踐行，常爲奧瑪所嘲；彼輩之信仰，若去其爲奧瑪不屑之玄秘與虛飾，又實無以過之也。彼國詩客多取資奧瑪，雖哈菲茲亦猶是也，蓋自菲爾多西外，哈菲茲實波斯最可矚目者也。然盡轉而爲玄秘之用，俾其詩於己於衆實有所便。蓋彼衆輕於疑信，敏於形神，愉於二者之冥合，遂藉詩句爲羽翼，恣遊乎天國凡塵，今世來生，不執一端。惟奧瑪知命而疑天，重生而輕死，雖云過，想思盡出乎誠。故寧於今世極其所有，用所遇諸物娛六欲而撫一心，不徒擾擾於將來之憂也。然吾人亦見其於俗世之求實不逾度。於感官之娛也，得滑稽乖張之趣，用以尙心智。雖其於心智也，亦頗有足樂者。然心智不足指其津

波斯亦思馬因教魁首。亦思馬因教人皆狂信，陰蓄已久，得哈桑行其凶強之志，遂成極惡。西元之一千零九十年，哈桑竟取魯德巴省之阿剌模忒堡，在里海之南，亂山之間，遂傳其號曰「山中丈人」。其大行畏怖，幾遍回教之地。今歐人語中行刺一詞，疑其凶念之孑遺也。其字源或出哈石失，蓋大麻葉所制之煙食也，印度謂之bhang，服之能致人迷幻，陰鬱顛倒，失志走險。被行刺之害者固多，其同學故交，尼查木·烏爾·莫爾克竟其一也。阿特嘗使尼查木·烏爾·莫爾克用其友奧瑪語（《魯拜集》其二八）：

「尼查木·烏爾·莫爾克之垂死也，號曰：天乎！吾從風之手中逝矣！」

奧瑪珈音亦往見相君請其所有，然非名位也。曰：「君所能惠莫若處我於一隅，為君佳運所蔭，廣播學問之澤，吾兼為君之福壽祈。」相君告吾輩曰，既知奧瑪之卻名位實出其誠，乃不復勸，即敕納霞堡公庫，年予之一千二百金。

奧瑪珈音遂居納霞堡，亦卒於是。

珈音者，蓋其賦詩之別號也，考其義，厥為制廬帳者，傳其嘗事此業，殆在尼查木·烏爾·莫爾克渥恩厚予使能自立之前歟？波斯詩客例以所業為名，若阿特嘗為方劑師、阿薩為榨油匠也。亦若吾英倫之史密斯（鐵匠）、阿切爾（射手）、米勒（磨工）、弗萊徹（箭工）等，不過呼先世之業為姓氏耳。奧瑪嘗有奧句隱括其名，曰：「珈音以智織穹廬，何事忽投憂患火？命剪其絲今世哀，望虛其報來生左。」珈音既作知之帳廬，而終為憂患之爐火所燔。運命之

奧瑪珈音：波斯之天學詩客

奧瑪珈音者，呼羅珊省之納霞堡城人也。生當十一世紀之後半，卒在十二世紀之前二十五年。生平甚略，獨與當時國中二顯人頗相糾葛。其一名尼查木‧烏爾‧莫爾克，嘗述三人事。莫爾克歷相韃靼人脫幹鄰勒‧伯克子阿爾普‧阿爾斯蘭、孫馬立克‧沙。初，馬赫穆德大帝之後繼裒能，脫幹鄰勒‧伯克遂有波斯，是為塞爾柱朝，終致歐人十字軍之役。莫爾克之書曰《遺書》，蓋遺後之為政者為鑒也，其言有云：[今據《加爾各答評論》五九號轉錄米爾克洪之《阿薩辛史》。]

納霞堡有伊瑪目曰莫瓦法克，呼羅珊之聖哲也。得人尊崇，受天眷顧，壽逾八十五。皆以為從之窮經考古，必致榮福。吾父乃遺余與法科博士阿布德‧烏斯‧沙瑪德自突斯往納霞堡，期從明師，沉潛於學。師於我特加垂青，而吾為弟子亦盡忠愛，親侍講席，四載於茲矣。我初至此，即見年相仿者二人，哈基姆‧奧瑪‧珈音與厄運之本‧薩巴赫，皆新來從學者。二人皆捷才異稟，遂為至好。伊瑪目講席每罷，二人常共我遊處，溫故時習。奧瑪固納霞堡人也，哈桑‧本‧薩巴赫父為阿里，屬行而務實，然所遵信多近異端。一日，哈桑語吾與珈音曰：「皆以為從伊瑪目莫瓦法克學者必致淑命。雖三人俱致，或有所疑，必有一人致焉。如將相約，當有何誓？」吾與珈音曰：「從君所願。」彼曰：「善，請為此誓：淑命天降，必與共之，毋得專！」吾與珈音曰：「必如是。」誓遂定。日居月諸，吾自呼羅珊往河中，且遊伽茲尼與喀布爾。既返，被命入宮，旋相阿爾普‧阿爾斯蘭王。

越數年，二同學循之至，因昔日之誓請共淑命。相君踐誓，無少吝。哈桑求一官，王因相君之請予之。然不饜於遞遷，遂與東國之亂謀，擬代恩相之位。謀既不成，失王寵，竟遭斥。屢經困躓顛沛，終為

不敢題糕字」之慎,「古文之體忌小說、忌語錄、忌詩話、忌時文、忌尺牘」之迂,良有以也。然近代以來,新學漸盛,古文之約束,亦頗貽人惑。乃有數輩人物,徑用新辭,倡言寫口,黃公度其尤也。行之既肆,知有必不能若此者,始幡然有悟。故公度晚年定詩草,刪之太半矣。雖前人之鑒不遠,而後人之學益肆,昧於斟酌去取者固多,俗體流傳,聖學播蕩,深可哀也。

余以古文之體迻譯此集,實逢此斟酌去取之際,然不敢不慎也。躊躇再三,得數法焉。有彼是相當之辭,固其上者;必無有之,亦當使彼順乎此之句法,不相齟齬,中者也;句法猶不能順,則必求之辭氣之肖,其下也。辭氣尚不能肖,毋事此可矣。故知吾國文體,程式雖峻急,亦非不能隨順也。要須忖度,實忌顢頇。然余不學,心有餘而力已殆,勉乎其難哉!果可自負者,寧失之迂,未失之肆,知者其憫而恕之耶?

己亥六月十二,我瞻室序。

醽醁雅

譯 序

《醽醁雅》者，錢公默存譯《魯拜集》之名也。公嘗譯其十一曰：「坐樹蔭下，得少麵包，酒一器、詩一卷，有美一人如卿者聊樂我員，雖曠野乎，可作樂土觀！」嗣改曰：「坐樹蔭下，得少麵包，酒一甌，詩一卷，有美一人如卿者為侶，雖曠野乎，可作天堂觀！」皆余所謂筆譯。彥和之言曰：「今之常言，有文有筆。以為無韻者筆也，有韻者文也。」余以無韻之散行迻譯是集，先以《魯拜筆譯》名，終不及錢公譯名之淵雅，敢冒僭竊，公然改用。

此譯何為而作也？余既以七字絕句譯之法，聊為述之。吾國詩古文，與吾國學合，崇乎性，蔑乎情，故久為程式，難與俗諧。蓋俗生乎情，利之趨也。去俗逾遠，於性逾幾，庶乎康德所云德性之徵。所以「劉郎

三

爾雅